PYRES

PYRES

Derek Nikitas

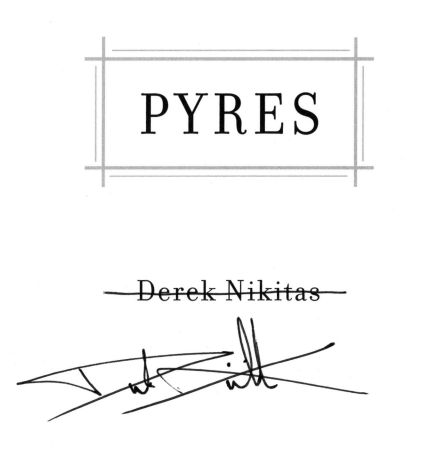

St. Martin's Minotaur

New York

This is a work of fiction. All of the characters, organizations, and events portrayed in this novel are either products of the author's imagination or are used fictitiously.

www.minotaurbooks.com

Library of Congress Cataloging-in-Publication Data

Nikitas, Derek.
    Pyres / Derek Nikitas.—1st ed.
       p. cm.
    ISBN-13: 978-0-312-36397-0
    ISBN-10: 0-312-36397-4
    1. College teachers—Crimes against—Fiction. I. Title.

PS3614.I54P97 0227
813'.6—dc22

                  2007021726

First Edition: October 2007

10 9 8 7 6 5 4 3 2 1

In memory of my grandfather,
William Henry Pepin, Jr.

ACKNOWLEDGMENTS

Thanks to my uncle, Emre Arican, of the Rochester Police Department, for his patient ear and his precise scrutiny. If there are any inaccuracies, they exist because I fumbled his perfect passes.

Thanks also to my writing and literature teachers at SUNY Brockport, UNC-Wilmington, and Georgia State University—Clyde Edgerton, Bob Reiss, Todd Berliner, Mike Wentworth, Stanley Colbert, Anne Panning, Paul Persia, and Josh Russell. And thanks to those teachers who got me started: John Baynes and Kathleen Cadle. Most of all I thank my mentor, Wendy Brenner; I cannot express how grateful I am for the knowledge she's provided and the dedication and encouragement she's shown.

Thanks to Jeff Gerecke and Michael Homler for giving me this shot and then showing me where to aim it. Thanks also to those who have championed my short stories: Janet Hutchings, Lauren Kuczala, Karen Ackerson, and Alfredo de Palchi. And a special thanks to Joyce Carol Oates and Raymond Smith for their deeply humbling support.

Thanks to friends, students, and colleagues who, like the saint in this novel, have helped focus my vision: Craig Renfroe, Bob Gatewood, Andrew MacDuffie, Beau Bishop, Sandra Holinbaugh, Jim Georger,

Ralph Black, Ryan Doody, Danielle Montagne, Dave Graupman, and all my partners-in-crime at Killer Year. Thanks to Eric Vrooman in particular for his insight and his proverbial red pen.

And the deepest, profoundest thanks will always be for my love, my Caroline.

PYRES

one

DEATH OF BALDR

O nce upon a time is hell. Lucia would learn to wish that her life could unfold more than just once upon a time. Maybe then the story of her family might improve each time it was told. Maybe then she could cut away the dark spots, just like her dad used to do when he read her those Swedish fairy tales, hunched on a kid-sized stool near her bed. He often tilted his fables away from the brutal bits, bypassed whatever would cause nightmares. Only the bright stuff, kiddo.

"You missed the part where the goblin stole the baby," Luc would say. She'd be tucked under her comforter in her Care Bears p.j.s, six years old, wearing mittens and her Yankees cap just for the heck of it. Downstairs Mom watched *Dynasty* and pretended she was studying for a bio test. Back then Mom had only two semesters left to snag that college diploma that she'd been postponing for the sake of mothering her only daughter.

"I forgot the goblin part, that is true," Dad said. He scratched his blond moustache and flashed a smirk that meant some slips happened on purpose. The sky blue binding on the book he held was thick as a dictionary. On the cover was a painting of a bearded gnome—*tomte*, in Swedish—no bigger than a cat and saddled to a deer's antlers. The *tomte* gripped those antlers with two thick mittens, throwing out his stubby legs. He wore a pointed felt cap and a leather tote strapped from his shoulder to his opposite hip. In the background the fir trees held aloft snow tufts on their upturned branches. *Tomten* are the creatures that deliver your *Jul Mas* presents if you've been a good girl.

And Dad showed her the pictures inside the book: a *tomte* crouched on a pillow and whispering into a sleeping child's ear, the child's loose hair twined around his legs and his little yarn-laced boots. That picture was for the story about a princess who finds a *tomte* caught in a rabbit trap in her garden. Afterward she keeps him in a burlap sack tied to her bedpost, and he doesn't mind the tight quarters. There's an evil queen with precious gems lodged in her eye sockets, a talking bear, an ice fairy who tells the future while a cold blue heart beats inside her chest. Even years later Luc remembered those stories.

Her father was Swedish, born and raised near Stockholm. Before Luc was born, even before Dad met Mom, he moved from Sweden to New York to go to school for his literature doctorate, and he'd only been back to Scandinavia a few times for research and visits with his distant half siblings from his father's first marriage. Dad's own parents died long ago. Luc had never visited Sweden herself, so she didn't know any better than what Dad would have her believe, though he always promised they'd go in the summer of '97 when she graduated from high school.

But for now Luc was fifteen and scrawny, five feet tall in her purple Doc Martens. Scraping her boot soles over sidewalks and down school hallways, clomping like a puppy on its adult feet. Luc's moon face teetered on her thin stalk of a neck, and her big wet eyes always looked shocked though they hardly ever were. Black-dyed hair, black pleated skirt, black fingernails. Black that stained bathroom towels and armrests and pillow cushions and incited Mom's hollered threats.

Blair Crowley-Moberg was her mother's name. Mom was only thirty-five, ten years younger than her professor husband. Sure she was still attractive, but she was frumpy more often than not with her wood brown hair and her orthopedic sneakers. Last time Luc saw her mother looking halfway glam was when Mom went as Madonna to the English faculty

Halloween party, with the blond wig and the cone bra. "I feel totally retarded," Mom had kept saying until she drank enough amaretto sours to
cheer herself up. Luc went as Gregor the human dung beetle from
Kafka's "Metamorphosis" even though she'd never read it. At the party
Mom snuck Luc enough sips of amaretto to give Luc blurred sight even
with her glasses on.

But that was more than a month ago, long before the bucktoothed
jack-o'-lanterns rotted greenish on the front porch until Dad finally
threw them out. Thanksgiving '93 had passed with a roasted chicken
because nobody in the family liked turkey, and then it was back to
school. Now it was the first Saturday in a December that had started
warmer and wetter than usual, but with the same perpetual upstate
winter gray. Nine days until Luc's sixteenth birthday, until she could
test for her driver's permit.

And if she'd had that permit just nine days earlier—

Look: if only decisions weren't just once upon a time, then with a
second chance Luc never would've begged her parents—Mom first—to
drive her from where they lived in the Village of Hammersport to the
Ontario Ridge Mall twenty minutes east toward Rochester. But there's
no pulling back from that decision. Time rushed Luc only forward. Living backward, fixing what's already been broken—it's like crawling back
into the womb: it's impossible.

How it happened was Luc found her mother in the backyard raking
up the dead leaves they'd neglected until now, piling them beside the
vinyl pool that had been covered since September. Mom wore sweatpants and an insulated flannel shirt, her shoulders getting damp from a
falling drizzle. Her hair was beaded with moisture and her lips shuddered from the chill.

"I can't take you right now. I have to finish this," Mom said.

Luc squinted at the dark churning clouds. "It's raining."

"That's why I need to finish."

"Well—later?" Raindrops piddled against Luc's glasses.

"I doubt it," Mom said, like such decisions were out of her grasp.
"What do you need to go to the mall for anyways?"

Luc shrugged and laced her fingers together over the top of her head. She stood near the walkout basement door and the concrete steps leading up to the driveway. The Mobergs' patch of village property was landscaped lower than the yards around it, surrounded on three sides by stone walls like an excavation site. Back there everything loomed above the yard—their house with its finished basement and ground floor and attic, the trees shivering off the last of their dead leaves, Dad's boat draped with a tarp for winter, the neighbors' driveways. Next door, right that moment, Quinn Cutler was up there working in his mother's garage. Luc couldn't see him but she heard his tools clank and crank against his motorcycle as he tightened it up like a huge metal fist.

"Is there another rake?" Luc said. "I could help?"

"That's a first," said Mom. She hunched down and ripped away the wet leaves clogging the rake. For months Mom had been blurting smug quips like the two of them were still tangled in some argument that Luc had forgotten about. "Anyway, you don't need to be spending any more money. You still owe me for those towels you ruined."

"I was just asking," Luc said.

And then, five feet above them, just at the crest of their stone wall, Quinn Cutler appeared on his mother's driveway in jeans and an Overkill concert T-shirt, wiping his hands on a greasy rag. His denim knees were stained with smudges of dark oil. He was part Native American—with tanned skin and sharp cheekbones, silky brown hair parted down the center that draped past his shoulders. Hard little muscles with veins thick as drinking straws running through his arms. He was a senior at the high school, older than most because he'd been kept back one or two years. Luc held her breath while Quinn nodded down at them. He muttered, "What's up?"

"Hey," Luc said. Her face felt warm now, even in this wet December noon.

Mom gripped the rake handle with both hands and scowled up at their neighbor. The tendons in her neck twitched, almost like she could sense how Luc's blood heated up whenever Quinn made an appearance. Luc had seen him twice at school just yesterday, passed him walking between classes, but the thrill was the same every time—a pulse of ecstasy flashing out from her unconscious mind.

Back inside the basement, Luc detoured into her dark bedroom. The stereo glowed its liquid green readout, and pale daylight leaked red through the curtains. She swiped her jacket off her bed—a denim jacket safety-pinned with a dozen rock band patches, decorated with strips of duct tape and blotches of black and silver fabric paint. It was her self-styled uniform, along with the boots and the skirt and the black-and-white striped leotards.

Lucia Moberg: named after Saint Lucy only because of her birthday falling on Sankta Lucia, December thirteenth, the night in Sweden when little girls marched around singing carols in white dresses and flaming-candle tiaras. The saint of light and eyesight. Luc had seen icons of Saint Lucia that showed her carrying a bowl of bloody human eyeballs. Pretty freaking cool, especially since Lucia Moberg herself was badly myopic and wore glasses with thick black hipster frames, almost flaunting her impairment. Without her glasses the world was a greasy color smear.

Lucia's closest friends Gina and Kit called her Luc, pronounced like the boy's name Luke—never like *luck*, which was lame, or like *loose*, which made her sound like a slut. She'd throw a sucker punch at the gut of anyone who called her Luck or Loose, or worst of all, Lu-Lu.

Up the stairs, shoving her arms through her jacket sleeves, gunning through the kitchen and the hallway. She grabbed the wrought-iron rails of the spiral staircase leading up to her father's attic study, swung herself onto the bottom step, and craned her head backward, gazing up the twisted center of the stairs to the light above.

"Dad!" she called. "You up there?"

"Present," he said—his lame-ass college professor joke, just like how he raised his hand at the dinner table when he wanted to speak, even if nobody else was talking. They might've gotten all the way through dinner most nights without speaking if not for Dad.

"What are you doing?"

"Grading a relentless stack of freshman essays."

"Can you take me to the mall? Mom won't. All you need to do is drop me off."

"And then drive all the way back to pick you up."

"So—you can hang out at the bookstore."

"Ah, touché," Dad said with his creaky Norse lilt, and in a few minutes he was driving her through rain in an aging Volvo station wagon, wipers pushing away the drench that kept beating down. Maybe if she'd known what would happen she could've shoved open the passenger door and tossed her body to the road's pebbly shoulder and captured the pain for herself. She could've stopped what she'd started. But she didn't know, and there's the guilt that will not subside.

At the Barnes and Noble Luc split from her father and headed for the other end of the mall. Twenty minutes later, in Wonderland Music and Video, she dawdled. She tapped her fingers over the CD stacks, eyeing the employees, studying the two-dozen other customers in the store. One clerk chatted on the phone while he scanned purchases at the checkout line. Another one restocked the video aisle—a lardy woman who gasped and wheezed just because she was standing upright. Her waddle bunched above a rubber neck brace that kept her head locked in forward. Five minutes back, a third Wonderland clerk had ducked into the break room with a half liter of Pepsi and a brown-bagged lunch. So this was the best layout Luc could hope for. Now or never.

She needed two CDs for Gina and Kit—the fraternal twin sisters who lived two blocks away from her house, her best friends since forever. But nothing for Luc. She never, ever stole for herself, trusting that karma would keep her safe if she worked without a reward.

Luc plucked out a random CD that was locked inside a white plastic security case, just like all the others. Something like the Lamest Hits of Tom Petty. She pretended to read the back cover while she aimed her eyeshot toward the lardy shelf-stocker punching a label gun against video cases. Luc grabbed for the Smiths' *Louder than Bombs* and thumbed the plastic lock with her fingers, jammed it quick and hard, and snapped it loose.

Even a toddler could beat those stupid locks, but step two was to peel the raised rectangular sticker off the back, the one with the secret computer chip trapped inside it. Usually a piece of shrink-wrap tore along with it, but nobody would notice if Luc moved fast enough. This particular sticky white rectangle came free, no problem.

Then came the amateur magic where Luc crouched down like she'd dropped something and meanwhile slid the CD into the inside breast pocket of her jacket. The pocket was wide and deep enough for her prize, almost custom-made for it.

The Smiths disc was meant for Gina, older than her sister Kit by something like twenty minutes. The younger twin Kit wanted a techno sampler—any techno sampler, it didn't matter—because she was obsessed with raves even though she'd never really been to one. So Luc figured she'd pick Kit an ambient mix. The cover was a dizzying color pattern that turned 3-D if you stared at it long enough. Thumb, jam, crack—the security lock popped like a twig in a campfire, loud enough that Luc flinched her hand away too fast and made a spectacle.

Sure enough, Lardy Clerk lurched herself into motion and limped off toward the front counter. Fast, too—like she had a mission, like maybe she'd caught that fumble in Luc's not-so-sleight-of-hand. Luc watched as Lardy grunted out one frantic full-body twist in Luc's direction, enough to confirm Luc's fear.

So Luc made for the exit, half a store's length away. She cruised but she didn't run, swerved around a lady hogging the aisle with her kid's stroller. Luc's hardened criminal act had flushed away. Now she was just a girl terrified of getting nabbed and vowing never to shoplift again if she could just clear this one last mistake.

"Hey—hey, you! Where you going?" Lardy's voice was squeezed off by her tight rubber choker, but it rang loud enough to perk half the heads in the store.

But Luc still didn't run. She couldn't let herself panic like that. Her path through the security gate was clear—until somebody grabbed at her. All she saw was an arm wrapped in a Buffalo Bills vinyl jacket. Just some asshole who thought groping a hundred-pound kid is what makes a hero. She ducked that hand and it missed her.

Luc tossed herself out into the human river streaming through the mall. She wove between the calendar kiosk racks and hurried along the inside edge of the opposite lane, squeezing herself between a jewelry stand and the slow-moving flow of Saturday shoppers headed toward the food court. Ten competing music sources hummed against the honeycomb skylights. She circled around the fountain spitting whitewater ten feet up. She passed a cottonpuff snowscape where automaton elves were busying their stiff limbs in a toy shop manger. Their hand-painted faces panned on mechanical necks, tracking her like hidden cameras. She trucked past the Mrs. Smith's cookie stand, down toward Barnes and Noble, where she prayed she'd find her dad browsing.

Lord—if they snatched her now and locked her in some empty room and paged Dad over the intercom, she'd never forgive herself for causing that shame. Tenured English Professor Learns Sad, Ugly Truth About Hoodlum Daughter—news at eleven.

Luc power walked something fierce. And she was huffing too, heaving stale mall air into her lungs. Nothing nondescript about black-dyed hair, decorated denim jacket, striped leotards. Up ahead, a security cop leaned against the Sprint cell phone kiosk chatting up the clerk. When Luc passed, he reached for a voice crackling some urgent news over his walkie-talkie, unclipped it from his belt. He weighed about two-fifty, gut pressing against his blue uniform shirt. He looked easy to outrun if it came to that.

Never again, God, never.

She reached Barnes and Noble just when the first sweat dab wet her bangs. This end of the mall was almost deserted, and the open space made Luc feel more vulnerable. She risked her first look back and saw no one recognizable in her tracks. There at the bookstore entrance she paced for a minute, hands on her hips, catching her breath and composure.

Luc found her dad where she expected, seated on a stool in the coffee shop and sipping a latte from a tall paper cup, wearing his blue rain parka, which looked wet even though it wasn't. He slouched over a hardcover book laid open on the table. Six-and-a-half feet tall. His golden hair sprouted in nine directions, disheveled from having been trapped inside his toque.

"Hey, I thought we were meeting in the food court," Dad said. He checked the watch he kept in his pants pocket because one of the straps had broken months ago. "A half hour from now." His face glowed ruddy from the warmth of his latte, which had also left foam on his mustache.

Luc stood behind the low iron railing that partitioned the coffee shop from the bookstore, afraid her dad would catch the scent of her panic if she stepped any closer. "I started feeling like crap," she said, "like nauseous. Can we go? I feel like I'm going to puke."

"You look feverish. Are you hot? Would you like an herbal tea?"

Luc watched the mall entrance. "Can we just go?"

"Sure, but—come over here for just a minute. I'd like to show you this." He lifted the book spine, but not high enough that she could see the pages from where she stood. Luc peeled off her jacket and balled it against her chest while she moved around the gate. At least then security would miss her if they were looking for a kid with rock band names painted on her coat. Dad talked while she came around: "This is a brand-new translation of the *Prose Edda*. They had an Icelandic painter do these full-color plates."

What he showed Luc was a painting of a Viking longship bright with yellow and orange flames as it drifted out to sea. Luc snatched her father's toque from the table and stuffed it over her obvious black hair.

"I thought you were hot," Dad said. "I've just been reading about the death of Baldr—you remember that story? I told it when you were younger. There're some subtleties of language here that I haven't found in any other version. This is fantastic."

"Are you going to buy it?" Luc said. Her knees twitched.

"Ah, alas, they're charging seventy-five dollars. Maybe I'll ask the *tomten* to bring it to me for Christmas. Do you like this cologne? It was a sample." Dad exposed his wrist for Luc to sniff, waving it under her nose.

"I'll hurl if I smell it, Dad."

Luc waited in the entrance foyer while Dad moseyed back to reshelve his hardback *Prose Edda* where he'd found it. Compact earthquakes rumbled in her chest and trembled down her limbs, only partly caused by the cold, wet air that hit her when customers pushed open the doors. Outside, people trudged through the rain, heads bowed under umbrellas and hoods. Cars stopped and waited at the crosswalk out front, then rolled with a hiss over the wet ground, steam rising off their warm headlights.

"Are we ready?" Dad asked. They stepped out into the chill and the rain, and Luc nudged her head against her father's ribs. There in the crook of his arm she felt invincible, even as the rain chilled her clenched face, even as the car marked MALL SECURITY rolled to a stop beside them. She held her breath. The rain and the thumping wipers hid the driver from her view, and she waltzed with her father over the crosswalk.

Dad had parked the Volvo at the far end of their aisle—the closest spot he could find on a Saturday three weeks before Christmas—so by the time they reached the car and Dad fished out his keys, Luc's leotards clung damp and heavy against her legs. She climbed into the backseat and sprawled herself there, shivering even more violently from her relief. When Dad climbed into the driver's seat, Luc pulled the stolen CD from her jacket and slipped it underneath the passenger seat. Her prize seemed worthless now. Gina could come dig it out of the car if she wanted it so bad.

Dad sparked the engine and the wipers kicked to life. He sipped his latte through a plastic lid while Journey crooned "Open Arms" from the back speakers. Luc hunkered down, planted her wet boots against the opposite door.

"Hey, Luc, sit up," Dad said. "You need to have your seatbelt fastened."

"I don't feel good."

"I know, but I'd rather you were safe—"

A shadow washed across the back window and stopped beside the driver's door. It came too fast for Luc to register the shape as human, until a gloved hand rapped on her father's window. The jacket was a brown zip-up darkened by rainwater. His head, his face, loomed too far above the curve of the car roof for Luc to see. She gasped. Mall security, she was sure. Already her mind crowded with apologies.

Dad pressed the automatic window control and the glass hummed downward. Luc propped herself on her shoulders, lifted her head. This new posture only further blocked her sightline, but it was better that she didn't see the frown this guy was probably feeding her father, prepping Dad for some shit news about his spoiled only child.

The visitor wrapped his fingers over the lip of the half-open window like he meant to push it down faster. Then he said, "What's up, doc?" Smarmy—somebody who thinks busting teens for shoplifting is a laugh riot.

"Excuse me?" Dad said.

Then the guy shoved his other hand into the opening and pointed one thick finger squarely at Dad's face. In that blank second, Luc thought her dad was being accused, and then all her assumptions were fizzling away.

"Give me your fucking wallet!" the guy grunted. His edict rattled through his teeth.

"*Vad i helvete?*" Dad said, and his right hand grabbed at the gearshift. The paper cup went airborne and splashed brown muck against the dashboard and the windshield. Luc's brain caught up to her eyes: this man wasn't pointing his finger. He was aiming a gun with a dull sliver barrel and slanted groove marks near the muzzle. It was trained inches from her father's head.

The Volvo jerked into reverse, shoved Luc's tensed body against the front seats, crammed her down onto the floorboards. Even while she tumbled she didn't look away from the gun that smacked the window frame and fired a shot and then vanished from sight. Her ears went deaf, stunned by the gun blast. Moist breeze flicked across her face.

Then came a collision and the whole earth jostled. Glass shards sailed. The back window, the whole panorama of it, collapsed in a million crystal bits that poured onto the seat where Luc had just been reclining. Rain splashed through this new wide maw like a cloud had burst overhead. She would understand only later that their car had heaved across the parking aisle and slammed its rear against an empty Neon parked there.

For a moment Luc's shocked eardrums heard nothing but Steve Perry on the speakers, crooning about hoping you'll see what your love means to him. Through the white-fogged windshield Luc saw a glob of darkness—the man with the gun, still poised in the parking space they'd just escaped, pivoting his outstretched arm, aiming his gun where the car now idled.

"Are you all right?" Dad asked.

"No," Luc said, though she felt no pain.

Now the Volvo's windshield warped sugary white and crackled a million fibrous trails but did not break. Dad lurched backward into his seat and there were thick warm droplets of dark red rain wetting Luc's upraised hand and spackling the back window. And puffs of yellow foam coughing backward from Dad's headrest. And his head reeling like it was flushed with booze.

"Dad?" Lucia said. One of her arms lay trapped and throbbing between her body and the floor, but she flailed her free hand, now realizing what had doused it. Her father's two hands dropped down between his open knees. This limp gesture hunched him forward and laid his ruined skull against the steering wheel.

A DOG YAPPED FROM the back of an Olds parked two cars down from the Neon that had been smashed by the victim's Volvo. A toy breed, Chihuahua maybe, perched in the back windshield, but the poor mutt barked mute over the sirens and radios and traffic and the rain that was still pounding like hard pressure from a showerhead. It had rained nonstop for the last two hours, at least—the span of time since Greta Hurd had answered the page from Public Safety that had begun another fresh murder case.

She stood in a damp trench coat and mulled among the techs and brass crowded around the Volvo. She was older than many of them, and the only woman on scene in business attire. Hair cropped sensibly just south of her ears and streaked with white strands overtaking the pale blond. No makeup covered the creases in her forehead and the years of worry puffing below her eyelids. She stood barely sheltered under her black umbrella while rain fell slantwise and soaked her pants and her socks below the waterproof coat. Soggy clothes made her sore legs ache worse, made her want to sit down someplace and rip off her block-heeled shoes. The fever that pulsed under her skin didn't help either, but at least it kept her warm.

A mall parking lot had to rank on the list of the worst-possible crime scenes, but so far the department had managed to contain the chaos. The techs had cordoned off an inner perimeter of a couple hundred feet across, and the outer was another hundred past that. The toughest snag was the fleet of parked cars inside the circle, all belonging to holiday shoppers who'd soon be waiting on the sidelines, fuming because they couldn't leave, couldn't get home on a Saturday night. And with the crime scene eating a full quarter of the lot spaces, several cops were needed just to run traffic, diverting the vehicles loaded with customers, media, and rubberneckers. Parking was a nightmare: squad cars and ambulances endlessly shifting, reversing, clustering, clearing out space for more incoming cars.

Lucky, at least, that the Volvo itself sat far enough away from the nearest mall entrance to allow full-circle access by the investigators and technicians. All four Volvo doors stood wide open and water dripped from the door frames. The windshield was nothing but a pane of milky crazed glass so that you couldn't see inside unless you crouched in one of the open doorways. Cameras flashed like weak lightning when the techs took shots of the interior. The vehicle was empty of occupants now because the teenaged witness, the daughter, was headed to Gene-see Community Hospital in an ambulance. The victim was in another ambulance idling nearby. Rabid EMTs first on the scene had polluted evidence when they dragged out the deceased and staged their resuscitation tricks. Some medics will dig up a buried corpse and defibrillate it if you let them, even though any pair of eyes could see the blood on the seats and the organic material still wet on the back window. No question the victim was gone the minute the bullet hit him: a cranial impact with a hollow-point bullet.

The bullet had already been recovered for ballistics from where it was embedded in the driver's-side headrest. Nasty little hollow-point slug built to be gratuitous, deforming itself on impact into a dime-sized mushroom. Extracted from the front passenger-side door was a second, identical bullet, but only one spent casing had been recovered from the parking lot pavement. Greta guessed that rainwater rivulets had ferried the other casing down into a nearby storm drain.

No, there were no medical heroics to be witnessed here. And if revival was possible, Greta needed some herself, though more than anything she needed the coffee she'd left in her partner's unmarked Taurus—needed it for the caffeine and to wash down a couple of aspirin from the pill bottle in her pocket. The rain was winding down some now, and a slightly brighter sky lurked on the horizon behind the McDonald's across the street. Greta headed up toward the end of the aisle to where the car was parked. It was jet black and slick from the moisture, conspicuous police antenna stuck to the roof.

Her partner, Moe Arslan, was in the driver's seat writing notes into a spiral pad the size of a credit card. He wrote left-handed, his wrist cocked sharply so that his hand was almost upside down. And still his script was illegible. Moe was just a few seasons into the investigation gig, but he'd been shrewd as a veteran on the day he took the job. Before his promotion he'd spotlighted himself by busting a major theft ring via his meticulous cross-referencing of burglary reports and pawnshop records that no other officer would touch. The icing: he'd arrested the ringleader after conning the perp into driving himself down to Public Safety. Dumbass thought he was showing up to offer witness testimony in some unrelated crime, but instead he gets a pair of metal bracelets and a cell.

Moe was short for Muhammad. He was ten years younger than Greta, a Turkish-born Muslim who'd been in the United States since he was a kid. Stored a Qur'an in his desk at work, skipped lunches on fasting days, but otherwise kept his spiritual business to himself. Coolheaded, too: she'd seen him hold poise while goading perps called him towel head, sand nigger. He wore a thick mustache with his black wavy hair, a look that brought to mind a certain Iraqi dictator, and Greta guessed he cultivated the resemblance just to rile up the urban Neanderthals. Moe lifted weights three hours every morning and looked like he could KO a bull with his fists. Carried himself around like a bruiser when the situation called, but Greta knew better. Most of Moe's cop work happened in his head.

Greta eased herself down into the driver's seat and took a gulp of coffee. Moe reached over and turned down the heater without her even needing to complain. He was getting to know her moods too well, anticipating them too readily. Greta snuffed her gratitude because she was pissed at herself for being so transparent. Pissed at Moe for coddling, like he was babying a cat for getting its claws removed.

"Any ID on the victim yet?" Moe said.

"We have his license from his wallet," Greta said. "His name was Oscar Moberg, forty-five years old, an address listed over in Hammersport."

"We're assuming the girl is his daughter?" Moe said.

"That's what she told the first officer on the scene," Greta said. "She was in shock, but no apparent life-threatening injuries. Said her name was Lucia Moberg, same address."

Moe stopped writing and asked, "Who's doing the death notify?"

Greta sighed and said, "I just love those kinds of house calls."

"I'll take care of it," Moe said. He tapped the pen on his lower lip and scowled at the rain misting on the windshield. "But first I wanted to tell you: so far we only have a statement from one half-blind elderly gentleman who says he heard gunshots and saw somebody running from the scene. Problem is the guy's taking a nap in his car with his bifocals off. All he saw was a blur. Couldn't even ID a race."

"This huge parking lot—Saturday in holiday season—and only one witness?"

"Nobody was loitering, because of the downpour. I have lots of people hearing it—at least a dozen separate accounts saying there were definitely two shots a few seconds apart. We have that, but we're still looking for eyewitnesses. We'll examine the lot security cameras, though a quick look tells me they got nothing. Too far-off and it wasn't the right angle."

"There's a Chihuahua over there who saw everything. What I need is to talk to the girl, Lucia, especially if it looks like she might be all we have for information."

Voices crackled on the police radio under the dash—city and administrative channels. Greta wasn't tuned into the talk, but she knew the bulk of it concerned this crime scene.

"It's a shame, you know," Moe said. "This girl has to witness her own father—"

Greta drank the last of her coffee and thought about her parents' house in Buffalo when she was sixteen, just about the same age as this girl. It was always there in her mind, lingering, that moment when she sprang down the basement steps on her way to grab a bottle of pop from the icebox her dad kept in his carpentry workshop. Blade on his table saw spinning, slicing nothing. Her father gasping on his knees in the sawdust, crouched like an ape. She'd grabbed his cold hands and tried to lift him up but he was too heavy. She'd anchored her feet on the workbench but he kept slumping, clutching his chest. He tried to say something. That table saw blade screeching, and the arteries of her father's heart clogged shut forever.

IN A ROOM at the Genesee Community Hospital, Luc watched the dark empty screen on the TV mounted high in the corner. In that reflection she saw herself wearing a thin gown instead of her clothes. She saw the brace with the Velcro straps snug on her right arm—the wrist that the nurses said was sprained in the accident—and the bandage on her forehead covering a gash picked clean of glass shards. The radiator blowing by the window that overlooked the rain-soaked parking lot five floors down. The empty, neatly made bed beside her. Luc saw, sitting cross-legged in a plastic hospital chair next to her bed, a policewoman named Investigator Hurd. She'd already asked Luc to call her Greta.

"Is he dead? My dad?" Luc asked.

"I haven't heard anything yet. I'm sorry." Greta Hurd had draped her damp trench coat over the back of her chair. Underneath she wore a white blouse, navy blue slacks. She looked more like a banker than a cop, except she had a gun holstered on her belt alongside a Rochester Police Department badge.

"He shot him in the head," said Luc.

Greta cleared her throat, uncrossed her legs, and crossed them again. She said, "I've got an excellent team down at the mall right now. They're checking into everything."

"I know he's dead," said Luc. The paramedics had rushed her away, heaved her onto a stretcher, and strapped her down even though she could walk. She'd been breathing like her lungs had collapsed, seeing through a fizzling white haze, hearing like she was underwater. All that red glass. Those chunks of headrest foam infesting her hair.

Greta told her, "This is horribly difficult, I know. You don't want to talk to anybody right now, especially some stranger like me. I want you to know we're working on getting ahold of your mother. My partner, Investigator Arslan, is over at your house right now, all right? But most importantly we need to catch that person who shot at your father, you understand? We need to talk before you start forgetting because forgetting happens faster than you think. Happens to all of us." Greta rested her hands on Luc's hospital blanket. Bony, ringless fingers with those tan splotches that meant she was likely more than three times Luc's age. You could tell how pretty she must've been years ago.

"I couldn't see," Luc said, "but I heard him tell my dad to give him his wallet."

Greta nodded. She watched Luc with her eyes flicking in their sockets, almost like she could read news printed on Luc's face. There was no pen, no notepad in the policewoman's hands. Maybe she was turning Luc's voice into words and typing them onto her memory. "Did he? Give the man his wallet?" Greta said.

"No—I don't think. He—got—he shot the gun before my dad even had a chance—just right away without any warning. He didn't even wait."

"Did the man say anything else to your dad?"

"No—well, he said, 'What's up, doc?' when my dad unrolled the window."

"Like Bugs Bunny says?"

"Yeah, like he was just joking around."

"Did your dad say anything?" Greta asked.

"He asked me if I was okay."

"After your dad hit the other car?"

"Yeah, but the man shot him first. That's—he was still alive when he asked me." Luc considered the stupidity of what she'd just said. She closed her eyes and forced the images back. They came jumbled together, reversed—first the blood and then Dad talking like nothing was wrong. Like they'd coasted safely through the danger.

"You didn't see his face—the man with the gun?"

"I was lying down in the backseat. I couldn't see. He had leather gloves."

"You didn't see any of his skin, his color?"

"No," Luc said. Every few seconds a strange current passed over her vision, as if she were watching Greta Hurd through aquarium glass. And Luc's voice—how could Greta understand when all the words leaked like syrup from her mouth? It might've been the shock, but it was probably more about those pills the nurse had brought in the plastic cup. Outside, five floors down, ambulance sirens wailed, getting closer and louder. Luc wondered how many times in one day that sound hailed the ruin of somebody's life. She dropped her eyes, fiddled with the Velcro on her brace. Only now did Luc wonder what those pills had been for.

"You look worried about saying something," Greta said. She pulled her chair closer, ready to catch the secret pushing out of Luc's chest. She tried to smile before she said, "I lost my dad when I was your age. He died of a heart attack one day just out of the blue, and I was the one who found him dying. There wasn't anything I could do."

"You know my dad is dead," Luc said.

Greta stood up from her chair like she'd decided to leave, but instead she moved toward the window. Her shoes clapped over the linoleum floor. The heat from the vent rippled across her blouse as she put her hands down on the windowsill.

"I stole a CD," Luc admitted. "I stole a CD from Wonderland in the mall. They almost caught me—the managers, and this customer tried to grab me. There was a security guard on a walkie-talkie, but I kept running until I got to Barnes and Noble. Then outside I saw a security car and I thought they were going to tell my dad. I thought the guy who came to our car was—but he just knocked on the window and shot him. I thought it was a security guard at first." Luc's chin and throat clamped, urging her to burst out crying, but she wouldn't let it happen.

"Why'd you think that?" Greta was still examining the gray, beaten city buildings cluttering up the skyline. "Did he look like a security guard?"

"I thought the gun—but no—he was wearing a brown zip-up jacket."

"And he asked your dad for his wallet, right?"

"I thought he wanted ID, like a cop—police."

Now Greta reached for Luc's left hand. She cupped it in both her palms, offering up the warmth she'd borrowed from the radiator. The gentle strength in her grip stilled Luc's first instinct to pull away. "Lucia," Greta said. "Nobody'd do this to punish you for stealing. Your dad—it doesn't have anything to do with what you did, understand?"

"Then why did it happen?"

"I don't know yet," Greta said. She let Luc's hand slip out of hers. Luc raised that hand to her eyelid and scrubbed out saltwater she couldn't quite admit was pooling. Nothing of her existence felt authentic, not since she'd stolen that CD. Her father's limp bloody hands slipping down into his lap—it was some hallucination. No real experience should be so suddenly frenzied and vicious, so quickly permanent. There were cosmic laws—weren't there?—that said disaster must arrive with notice, like in a morning dream announcing that today her father would die and that Luc's grief should begin while he was still alive and able to console her.

Instead, his murder hit so fast that it was only memory by the time Luc could grasp it. And all memory was false because memory could be reversed and denied and erased and prevented. Otherwise, what were these cops like Greta Hurd except cruel ghosts haunting behind fate, mocking you with their own uselessness? Here was this stranger sitting at Luc's bedside, where her father should've been. But unlike him, Greta couldn't pluck the rotten fruit from Luc's sight. She couldn't change a thing.

An hour later Luc waited in the hospital lobby thoughtlessly folding Investigator Greta Hurd's contact card in halves. Then she smoothed it out flat again, salvaged it—the only thing she had left to grasp. She'd begged the doctor to discharge her from that overheated hospital room, and he agreed, as long as she promised to wait in the lobby for her mother. Nurses had washed her clothes and returned them, and Luc put everything back on except her leotards. Those she stuffed in her jacket pocket because there were spots of pale red on the fabric that she didn't want to see or think about.

The news on the lobby TV had said nothing yet about her father. Even when the news came they'd offer nothing to explain what happened or why. Stupid shallow pity for ten small seconds so nobody could see the horrible facts: that Oscar Moberg got shot in the face, there was blood, his daughter saw and there are stains on her clothes, the man who shot him gave him no chance to fight back.

The sliding Emergency doors came open and Mom appeared, hunched and blinking at the harsh indoor lights. She was still wearing sweatpants with her winter jacket, holding her purse like it was trash she had to throw away. She didn't see Luc until Luc stood up.

"Mom?" Luc said. Her mother was like a distant relative approaching down the terminal at the airport. Months had passed—seemingly— since their afternoon squabble in the backyard. Luc wanted to vow all sorts of childish promises to her mother, but she knew that even now, almost alone together, they wouldn't manage to be so close as that.

Mom stopped in the main hallway and stared as if she was unsure that this girl looming halfway across the room was actually her daughter.

Her jaw shivered when she said, "Did you get hurt? What happened to you?"

"Just my wrist." Luc raised her arm to exhibit the plastic and Velcro brace.

"Oh, God," Mom said. She came forward and dropped her purse on a side table full of magazines, then propped both her hands under Luc's injured forearm. Delicate, like the arm was formed of thin porcelain. "Is it broken?"

"It's just sprained a little. It's fine, Mom."

"And your head?" She dabbed Luc's bandage with two careful fingers. Her eyebrows cramped together across a worried cleft in her forehead. She said, "You saw it happen. How can you be fine? I could've lost both of you."

"I didn't see important things, but Mom, I'm okay. I'm going to survive. That's all I'm saying." Luc broke away from Blair's stroking hands. It was like her mother was blind and couldn't tell her own child without touch. Over at the admissions desk the receptionist was on the phone with her back turned to them, unconcerned.

"What do we do? I can't think," Mom said.

"Just calm down right now. Please." Luc took the purse and her mother's elbow and led her back toward the exit. Luc wished again that she had her permit so she could drive the Saturn home, but Mom would have to do it instead. In the car the radio was set on scan so it played three seconds of every station, and both of them seemed fine with letting it run like that.

The rain had stopped, and the red lights mirrored on the wet roads like puddles of toxic waste. Mom drove past the plazas and parking lots into the browning farmlands west of Rochester. Even with her glasses, Luc's eyes strained at night. Her vision sharpened the passing headlights into long yellow spears.

"I remember all of a sudden that I loved him," Mom said. "Isn't that awful that I can feel it so clearly and now he's dead? It was so many years ago since I felt so much—but maybe you remember how it was back then."

"I'm sorry I made him take me to the mall," Luc said.

"He was my teacher. I told you before, didn't I? My professor in a stupid folklore class that I just took for liberal arts—and somebody told me he was—his accent—he was a passionate speaker, but I didn't think it mattered so much. Who falls in love with their teacher? That's what people wanted to know from me. When they found out—my parents—they thought he was, you know, despicable. They wanted the college to fire him. Did I ever tell you this story, Lucia? But nobody could tell us we weren't in love. What happens to that feeling? Where does it go?"

Luc wanted to cry again if only because the convulsions and the tears helped shut down her head. Crying made her forget how his warm blood had misted on her hand like spray paint from an aerosol can. But she knew that her mind would never wipe away that sensation, and the worst was fearing this flood of grief would never dry away.

Mom flicked on her high beams as they hit a dark stretch of road overarched by tree limbs. Road signs warned them to reduce speed ahead and welcomed them to the VILLAGE OF HAMMERSPORT, POPULA-TION: JUST RIGHT! Luc couldn't tolerate the certainty of that exclamation point, knowing what it did not know—that Hammersport was now one citizen short of paradise.

Within a minute they were on their street and parking alongside the curb. Luc's wrist fired up with pain as she squeezed the handrail on the door. She watched a cat skitter across the road in the spotlight of a street lamp.

In the mudroom Luc unlaced her boots and kicked them into a corner. Mom closed the door, and neither one of them turned on the light. The den was still dimly evident from the bleak blue glow coming from the kitchen. Luc tried to ignore the coffee table where Dad had left a half-drunk glass of chocolate milk and a plate of sandwich crumbs. On the mantel over the TV were his Swedish folk-art figurines, pastel Dala horses and chickens arranged in a procession. He'd hand-painted them all with rosemaling.

Mom eased down into the recliner, but Luc remained standing. She didn't want to be near the table where Dad had left his dirty breakfast dishes. He should've known if he came home alive that Mom would've nagged him about it. If he just turned the wheel fast or ducked away from the bullet, if he'd just given that monster his wallet without any of his worthless Norse heroics—but he panicked instead and failed, and now Luc found herself simmering with anger even toward her father. She hated herself for that feeling.

"I screwed it up, Mom," Luc said. "We weren't supposed to be out in that parking lot when we were. I rushed him out there. It's my fault."

"You know what he told me?" Mom said. "Years ago after he bought that boat—that stupid boat and started his summer chartering business. He said he wanted to be cremated and have his ashes spread across the lake. He wants to be taken out and dumped in Lake Ontario. Do you believe it?"

"Like Baldr," Luc said. A warm rush burst in her chest and her knees almost buckled from it.

"I don't understand what you're saying," Mom said.

"Baldr—a Norse god. His boat was his funeral pyre."

"But I can't do it, Lucia," Mom said. "I can't get onto that boat with his ashes." She cowered on the recliner, hugging her knees to her chest. Outside, a truck dragged its grumbling muffler down the street. Its headlight beams flashed through the curtains and doused her face with a shine that she grimaced against.

"I can do it," Luc said.

A DAY EARLIER, Tanya Yasbeck had rolled a borrowed Cadillac Deville into the Ontario Community Bank parking lot and twisted the wheel sharp toward a spot between two parked cars. The monster car screeched, muffler belched, and Tanya had to stomp the brake with both feet to stop. On her left was a leafy green, shiny new sedan, and Tanya knocked its passenger-side rearview mirror off with a noise like lightbulbs popping. She winced and tried to reverse but she wasn't good with backward. Now the broken mirror was just sitting on her hood inside its dented casing like some ornament. There were five thousand dollars in cash in Tanya's purse on the seat next to her and she'd come to deposit it for her boyfriend, Mason Renault.

Two old ladies standing close on a sidewalk saw her accident and were gawking at her now. The heater inside the Caddy was broken so it stayed on constant, pumping hot dry air into Tanya's face. She cranked down the window for cool air and to think what next. Crumpled the purse against her chest because somebody might break a window and steal it. Shit like that had happened to her before. Not with five thousand bucks, but still. She'd never had a savings account and didn't know how to start one, but Mason said she could figure it out. Mason gave her trust she thought she might not deserve to have.

The bank was in front of a supermarket on Route 104 just over the Wayne County line. Frozen custard shack attached to the bank, closed for the season. Tanya and Mason rented a trailer two miles up from here—and here was mostly this road with some trailer parks, bars, some lumberyards and diners. Otherwise it was thick forest mostly, which Tanya loved because she'd grown up in a dumpy part of Cleveland with hardly any trees until she turned fourteen and left her dad and wicked stepmom. Escaping into the woods, just like a fairy tale.

"Hey," somebody said. Standing at her window was a guy with gray, gel-slicked hair and a gold necklace on his hairy chest where his shirt was unbuttoned. No jacket, even though it was only forty out. Checkbook in his hand because he'd just been in the bank. Tanya tried to smile.

"Did you do this to my car?" he asked. They both looked at the shattered mirror sitting on the Caddy's hood. Her loaner car was scrap metal—fifteen years old at least—but this guy's car looked brand-new except for the shredded metal where the mirror should be.

Tanya said, "I'm not used to this car. It's not really mine." She turned off the ignition because the heat was blasting so strong she could hardly hear. She was starting to breathe shallow—panic because already she was getting too much attention and she hadn't even gotten into the bank yet. Mason would curse if he was here to see this. He'd be stomping his hands on the dashboard probably.

"Well, I'm sure as hell gonna need your insurance card," the guy said.

There was no insurance. Tanya pushed her driver's door open and put her legs out one at a time, then propped her arms on the door frame to lift herself up. She was almost sweating, even in this cold. Breathing like she'd just run around a track. Under her ski jacket she was wearing one of Mason's T-shirts and a pair of jeans with a stretchy front that she got at the Goodwill. The guy looked down at her belly and his cramped face went limp right off.

"Look," he said. "I wouldn't make a big deal out of this except I'm leasing the car so it ain't mine to wreck. If you just give me your insurance information—do you have insurance?"

Tanya said, "My boyfriend—he does, but I don't know what it is."

The guy cocked his head to one side, trying to crack his neck, keep his cool. Nobody wants to yell at a girl nine-months pregnant, nobody right off the street. Some people loitering around the bank entrance watched them now. Cars and huge cargo trucks zoomed past on the highway ten feet away.

The guy took a pen out of his pocket and turned his checkbook over to the back cover to write on. He said, "Why don't you just give me your name and number and I'll call later to get the information. Do you have your license on you?" He looked at her purse pressed against her chest. There was nothing in it but that wad of money, tissues, some lipstick and chapstick, a compact, a few condoms she'd had since before she got pregnant. She'd never had a license in her life. Her asshole stepbrother taught her some driving before he joined the Marines, then over the years some of her boyfriends taught her more.

"I don't have it with me," she said. The baby was kicking its feet up against her lungs, making her gasp for breath. Her head was scrambled. Needed time and quiet to think what she could do here. She didn't have any money except the five thousand and that wasn't hers to spend. But maybe if she only gave him a couple hundred, maybe Mason would forgive her when she explained the story.

Or else—she could offer the guy a favor. He was old and leathery, shady enough to take her offer maybe, but she hadn't done anything like that since before she knew about the baby, not with anybody except

Mason and on rare occasions a couple of the dudes he ran with. Plus there was no place private to go around here.

"Just give me your name and number then," the guy said.

"Debbie Howard," Tanya said, then she rattled off a fake phone number that started with the local three digits. Mason had taught her how to do that without hesitating. She loved being able to remember his lessons when she was alone. He was a genius about how people worked, how to get along in public.

"How do I know if that's your real info?" the guy said.

"Huh?" Tanya said.

He picked his front teeth. "Never mind," he said, and then he took his mirror off her hood, opened his passenger door, and threw the mirror there on the seat. Tanya waited until he drove off to head into the bank. The line inside was long and she needed a drink from the watercooler. She filled up one of those cone cups they give you and drank it down. Thought about ditching everything so she wouldn't have to tell Mason what happened, how clumsy she'd been. Last thing she wanted was to piss him off, even if she liked when he acted tough because it was so much different than her chickenshit dad who never did anything to protect her, did nothing but sit around smoking his dope all day, coughing in the den with his sports games on TV.

Mason didn't touch dope or any harder drugs. That was one thing that made her love him almost right off. That, and how he messed up her dealer/addict ex-boyfriend back in Cincinnati, where she lived for a while. Even Tanya was on the needle back then, a real mess, but Mason took care of that problem too. Locked her in a motel room until she was done freaking and puking and totally clean. She'd be dead probably if not for him.

She got in the line and waited to talk to a teller. She wondered: if she ran right now, how far away would five thousand bucks get her? Maybe clear across to California where she could live near the beach and get on state assistance. She could have her baby girl in Hollywood, and her girl could grow up to become a star like Winona Ryder or somebody.

Mason kept saying it was going to be a boy, but Tanya didn't think so.

She'd never tell him what she thought because he'd throw a major tantrum. Maybe she could've gotten one of those X-ray tests at the doctor's to find out, but she'd stopped going to the checkups back in the first trimester.

Tanya pinched her nose bridge until it hurt, until she stopped thinking crazy thoughts about running off to California on a Greyhound bus with this money Mason gave her to deposit. People in the bank line were looking at her funny. She was happy enough with Mason, and she didn't want to think what would happen if she ran off and he found her again. Plus she loved him more than anybody else except her dead mom.

She was always thinking about her mom during tough patches like this. Debbie Yasbeck, the Ohio State Region Five Women's Bowling Champion. Tanya siphoned courage off her first childhood memories: sitting in the bucket seats at the bowling alley munching French fries and watching Mom bowl. Mom with a smoky red crystal ball propped up against her chest, cotton headband on her brow, magnificent white cleavage hoisted up, cigarette fuming in her mouth while she psyched up for the shot. Every throw, the ball would skirt the edge ready to gutter until her mother's magic curved it back at the last second to nail a strike that sent all the pins crashing. Tanya loved that clatter sound. And the perfect X's running down the scorecard like the tallied boy-kills of some Amazon priestess.

Now it was Saturday night in the trailer kitchen and Tanya was boiling noodles until they went soft, then mixing in cheese powder and butter. She cut open a tuna can, drained it, forked it into the macaroni. Last were canned peas and then she scooped the dinner into two bowls. Midnight already and she wanted to have dinner set for exactly when Mason got home. Tonight he was getting his rocker patch, joining up official with the club where his friends were members. One of the hugest deals ever in his life.

Tanya slouched so as not to smack her head on the trailer ceiling. They'd only been crashing there a couple months so far, she and Mason. Kitchen in the front, then a spot for the couch and where a TV might go. In the back, the bed and bath were blocked from everything else by a thin red curtain. The trailer was just a Twinkie-shaped tube that tilted a little when you walked across it. Ugly, so she'd bought some crap to spruce it up: a garden gnome on top of the fridge, and propped next to the couch a big painting of a lake with some mountains behind it. It was on the floor because you couldn't nail it to a metal wall.

Nothing for the baby yet, like a crib or a high chair, because Mason kept talking like they'd be someplace better by the time the baby came. He was thinking about a double-wide the next county over, one he saw in the newspaper, but Tanya knew better than to expect anything to happen, especially with the kid due just about any day. Mason didn't want to own any more stuff than you could pack in five minutes if you had to bolt.

A car rumbled into the park entrance ten trailers down. Tanya hoped it'd be just Mason tonight, but she'd have to be nuts to think he'd come back alone on a special night like tonight. She put the two bowls down on the table—just a wooden slab that folded up against the wall. Fetched two cans of Sprite and slapped them next to the bowls. A couple spoons. The baby was awake, shouldering her bladder so she needed to piss every five minutes. She pulled back the curtain and flicked the outside light on so she could see better.

The yard was dead brown because they drove on it so much. Mason was pulling the Caddy up, still on loan from Buck Hanson, the guy who was in charge of the club and who was like a second dad to Mason. Mason's real dad got killed when Mason was fourteen, drunk-drove his Indian motorcycle off a bridge like some kind of old ballad hero. Dead parents were one trait Tan and Mason could connect on—except Mason's mother was still alive, living with his big sister in Detroit, in a house where he wasn't welcome anymore because he sort of flipped out for a couple years after his dad died.

Three men got out of the car on the lawn and Tanya knew which one was Mason by his slouch. His buddy Blisters she didn't recognize until he walked under the porch light. He saluted Tan by grabbing his crotch, and Mason punched him in the arm for it. Tanya laughed, but she covered it with her fist so Mason wouldn't see.

Blisters's real name was Mitch, Tanya knew. Early twenties and handsome, not gorgeous like Mason but hotter than most of those guys Mason ran with. He had a nose that looked broken from punches, and he always wore a red bandanna on his head. Mason said it was because he was going bald. Tanya had loaned her mouth to Blisters twice before, but only because Mason was pushing for club membership and he said it'd help win them over if Tanya kept them amused when they visited. Maybe now she wouldn't have to do those dirty favors for the other club people anymore.

They bashed their boots up the porch steps—Mason, Blisters, and the last guy, who Tanya didn't know too well. Mason came inside first, grinning like a retard, and Tanya knew why. She hugged his ribs and kissed his neck just under the goatee. He stank of beer and nicotine, but also that cologne page from the *GQ* he'd rubbed on himself at the grocery store. She let him lift her up with his hug, and the baby was pressed there snug and safe between them.

Mason said, "Hey, pretty momma," with that bogus country twang. He used Vitalis tonic to lift his hair in front like Elvis Presley or some other fifties greaser. He'd called her momma ever since she told him about the baby. That was five months back, and to celebrate he'd danced on the lawn and howled so dogs a mile off called back. He'd said right then it would be a boy, said he was going to show his son the world, how to hunt, how not to take shit from nobody. No chance the baby was another dude's because Tan had been saving her kootch only for Mason Renault since the day he drove her out of Cincinnati in her junkie ex-boyfriend's stolen van.

"Come on, let's see it," she said, clapping her hands together. The lightbulbs in the trailer were all bare, so they threw hard shadows and made her eyes hazy. But Mason turned and showed her the back of his leather jacket, where his buddies had sewn a picture of a human skull wearing a coal miner's hat with a mounted flashlight. The picture was for the name of his club—Skeleton Crew—and it meant he'd won a lifetime pass. Tanya ran her fingers over the waxy stitched threads around the patch. It also meant they were now bound to other folks who'd always keep them from sinking, people who'd drown themselves to save Mason and Tanya and the baby if it ever came to that.

"When's the tattoo coming?" Tanya asked him.

Mason shrugged. "Don't rush it," he said.

"Your old man's a pussy," Blisters said. "He fears the needle."

"I'll tattoo your ass," Mason said.

"Too late, Brick. My ass has a naked bitch wrapped in barbed wire," Blisters said. They called Mason Brick because his first name made them think of bricklaying, and also because of another jacket he liked to wear that was made out of a reddish leather almost brick in color.

Blisters and the other guy were still waiting outside on the landing. They were showing respect for once, and Tanya loved this new setup so much that she wished the other guys were gone so she could show Mason how raunchy his skull patch was making her feel. Instead, she turned him back around and kissed the fading black eye he'd gotten from a bar fight the weekend before. He wasn't a steroid case like some of the others, leanest of them all really, but he knew fighting moves from the Marines and the karate his dad had taught him. Still, Tanya didn't want her man rumbling because she hated to see his face fucked up, that ugliness that violence did.

"I made this dinner for us," Tanya said. She showed him the tuna noodles and the Sprite on the table. "But I didn't know these other guys were coming."

"No sweat," Mason said. "Just open another box. Takes ten minutes."

Mason gave room for his buddies to step inside the trailer. He sat down and popped open his Sprite can, took a deep gulp. Blisters came in and said, "I love mac and cheese, but don't put none of that tuna shit in mine. I don't eat no chick's tuna. Not even yours, Tan."

They all got a laugh, even the other guy, who hardly ever talked, the guy they called Ox. Tan didn't like looking at him. He had wild coiled hair bursting out, and his whole skin looked stained with oil. He scared her, especially when they were sitting quiet alone in a room together. His face always seemed like he was thinking about blood and pain. And he stank like armpits and stale gasoline, and thank God Mason never once made her party with that werewolf man.

She poured more water from the tap into the pan and rinsed it out so Blisters wouldn't get any of that tuna taste. Mostly she liked having the guys around even if she pretended to be miffed. Made her feel protected, these brutes who'd rip to shreds anyone who tried to hurt her or the baby. Only problem: she needed to savor this time because they'd leave as soon as dinner was over and take Mason with them. Already Mason was half-done with his noodles, leaning his face over the bowl and spooning it in. They'd go out to drink and riot and Tanya understood. Right under their bed was that Smith & Wesson automatic handgun that Mason had given her, loaded and ready to fire if anybody came around to fuck with her.

"How was church?" she asked them. Church was what they called the meetings they had in Buck Hanson's basement in Winslow, the next town over toward Rochester. Tanya'd been there a few times, cooked bulk spaghetti meals with Buck's old lady, Brenda. Lots of good Italian food and it almost was like real church because Buck was a mail-order minister who could legally marry Mason and Tanya if they ever wanted. They'd talked about it some, but decided not until they were more permanent someplace.

"Buck gave a stirring speech on his boy Mason," Blisters said. You could tell he was stoned from the pink in his eyes and the slur in his talk. "Made me shed a tear, I think. We belted out a song or two, took turns cracking his head with a bat. Everybody took turns pissing in Brick's hair a little. Then to round off the evening Brenda did a striptease. Typical church shit."

"You're a sick son of a bitch," Mason said, laughing with his mouth full.

Tanya cringed thinking of lumpy Brenda Hanson gyrating in her supersize panties, even though she knew Blisters was just bullshitting that it happened. Tanya wanted to laugh again, but instead a fast cramp made her catch her breath and slap her hand on her belly.

"You all right, Tan?" Mason asked.

"Just one of those cramps," she said.

"She ain't gonna have the baby tonight, is she?" Blisters said.

"It's not time yet. Don't be an asshole," Mason said.

"How should I know? I never had a fucking baby."

"It's normal," said Mason. "They call it Braxton-Hicks. False labor."

"Listen to the gyno doctor," Blisters said.

"He's reading all about it," Tanya said, feeling better now. She pointed to a couple library books sitting on the side table over by the couch. Books on pregnancy and birth, stuff Mason skimmed almost every night. He wanted all the information he could get. Wanted his kid to have the kind of father he had—full of energy, knowledge, security. Tanya got dizzy thinking about her happiness right now. And Mason finally getting the prize he'd been hunting so long—that Skeleton Crew patch on his back.

LUC DIDN'T LEAVE HOME again until the next night at dusk, when the Sunday evening church bells clanged downtown. She went on foot, followed by her friends Gina and Kit, fraternal twins who would've looked identical if not for Gina's head shaved down to her pale white scalp. As they walked, Gina's wallet chain chinked a steady rhythm against her thigh. Kit followed last, sucking on her lip piercing, tuned into the techno beat that pulsed from her headphones. The intermittent rains had dumped mud across the village sidewalks, but one cloudless day dried the mud back to soil. Luc kicked it into dust with her boots.

The girls passed under a set of railroad trestles and entered the State University of New York at Hammersport campus limits, where before them were spread vast parking lots and brick buildings doused with floodlights. Blue safety phone lamps glowing at intervals into the distance. Brocton Hall, the oldest building on campus, stood with its clock tower lit as a beacon. Home of the English department where Oscar Moberg taught and held office for almost twenty years.

"I think it's this way," Luc said, and she broke from the blacktop walkway, cutting across the lawn. In these last few minutes her stomach had gone queasy in honor of the assembly ahead. She noticed the flag fluttering at half-mast from its pole, but she barely caught its significance.

Gina said, "What do you want us to do?"

"Nothing," said Luc. "I just want to see it."

Gina hissed at the cold, hugged her own arms. She wore a ragged wool sweater with her thumbs jabbed through holes in the cuffs. But even clothes couldn't offer much warmth since she'd attacked her own head with scissors and a Bic razor. It was a ploy to avoid resembling Kit, whose hair was bleached platinum like Gina's last hairdo.

Luc led them alongside Brocton, that edifice of brick and concrete. She scanned the dark pane-glass windows, forgetting which was her father's office. She and the twins crossed a promenade with a raised median of wood chips and young leafless trees. Around them other pedestrians walked in silent pairs and groups, heading toward the campus quad.

Already the open courtyard was packed with figures huddled in a loose circle. Some stood apart from the others, and still more sat on benches or building steps. The crowd was gathered inside a warm light halo formed by flame points that sparkled inside the human sphere and wound in orbits around it. Luc's weak night eyes flared these candle flames into star beams.

Beside Luc two solemn college girls lit candlewicks from someone else's fire, and Luc grew woozy at the tenderness she felt toward these people and this light. A hundred candles with paper hilts to catch the hot wax. There was an elderly man circulating with a boxful of these candles, and he plucked one out and passed it into Luc's hands. She thanked him just the same as these other people who had formed this vigil in memory of Professor Oscar Moberg.

The old man passed two more candles to the twins standing behind Luc. She'd almost forgotten them—Gina passing for a lanky boy if you glanced too fast and Kit with her platinum hair glimmering. They were maybe her only friends, or at least they were the only ones who'd offered up their company tonight. Even Mom hadn't willed herself out of bed long enough to make an appearance. "I can't face those people," Mom had said. "They're going to want to console me, and I can't listen to their talk right now. It makes me sick listening to that condescending—"

Those people were her husband's students and academic colleagues, people she'd rejected years ago when she quit college, deciding college was juvenile, a fairyland for people who couldn't handle workaday truths. Mom was certain that the scholar-snobs pitied Oscar for marrying a townie like her, and she faced them only during departmental Halloween parties, when she could hide behind her costumes and her mixed drinks.

Luc's candle was unlit until Gina sparked up her lighter and passed the flame onto its wick. With her braced right arm, Luc cupped her flame against the wind. Everywhere hands sheltered tiny shivering fires, hands that caught the warm light and contained it. Faces beamed with heat like the coils on a stovetop, and mirrored in their moist eyes were a thousand orbs of gathered light. It was as if these living bodies kindled from inside and cast their furnace glow just beneath the surfaces of their bare skin.

Luc headed into the tightening huddle of her father's mourners. At first she saw only jacket backs and bowed heads, but these people stepped aside as if a murmur had sung her arrival. The assembly had circled itself around a tea candle display that was decorating the courtyard bricks. Yellow light blips swam in aluminum cups of liquid wax. There were flowers wrapped in green tissue paper, strewn like they'd been tossed to a matador. And there were tiny messages on slips of paper folded down to bookmark size, urged to dance by the wind. Luc wanted to hoard them up and read them all, save them in a scrapbook forever. But already one slip had caught fire and was passing its gray ashes away.

THE ELECTRIC MURAL on the wall was an animated waterfall flowing through an Asian forest scene, a hypnotic blue beacon in the darkened Thai restaurant. Paper lanterns strung above the tables shed only a faint light down onto the three diners: Greta Hurd, her daughter Sandy, and Sandy's fiancé Max. This was Greta's first dinner with Max Thornton, the young man who would become her son-in-law in exactly one week. He was a Rochester Philharmonic violin player and high school music teacher raised in the manicured suburbs east of Rochester. A world away from where Greta herself lived: a sketchy downtown apartment complex that offered discounted rent to cops and was inconveniently located near many of the crime scenes she'd investigated. She'd never even been to a Thai restaurant before, and the nonsense words on the menu meant jack to her. One of the dishes was called Evil Jungle Prince.

Sandy said, "What are you going to order, Mom?"

"I don't know yet," Greta said.

The word *Mom* sounded strained whenever Sandy used it on Greta. Sandy had been calling another woman Mom for thirteen years, and through the worst five of those years Sandy and Greta had been as distant as strangers. Even when they were together, Greta could only bear to throw quick glances at her daughter. In a sense Sandy was as recognizable as a reflection, but Greta hadn't truly studied her daughter's face long enough to make it familiar again, not since Sandy was a kid.

"I recommend the Pad Thai," said Max as he leaned back in his chair with his healthy paunch kneading against the table, creasing a necktie decorated with icons of musical notes and saxophones. He was plump and in his midthirties, arguably too old and homely for Sandy, if Greta could ever trust her own assessments of other people's love.

"Yeah," Sandy said. "You'll like the Pad Thai." She nuzzled her head into Max's shoulder as he planted three fast kisses on the top of her head like he had some compulsive tick. They'd met just over a year ago, around the time Sandy had entered the Eastman School of Music as a doctoral candidate in musicology. She'd started visiting Max's evangelical born-again church, and then some sort of rebirth had taken place for her. Apparently, the fact that Sandy and Max were living together caused a hubbub in their church, but they'd escaped hypothetical exile by pledging a sexless engagement. Greta had absorbed this information without judgment, truly, because years ago she'd forfeited her right to hold any opinions regarding Sandy's life.

"How long have you been with the police?" Max asked Greta.

"Going on twenty years next spring," she said.

"Then it was after Sandy was born?"

"Yeah, she was five. When she went into kindergarten, I started the academy."

"You've probably heard about that professor who got shot in his car?"

"Yeah, you could say that," Greta said.

"Actually, she's working that case," Sandy offered.

"Seriously? So do you know who did it?" Max swallowed the rest of his red wine.

Greta said, "That's what I'm trying to figure out."

"You're asking her about confidential stuff, babe," Sandra said.

"It's all right," Greta lied, and then covered her mouth with her teacup. Nothing wrong with Max being curious, but sitting here was agonizing for her, more than almost any cop work. Not so much the dinner itself because Greta was forty-eight years old and for God's sake she knew well enough how to conduct a conversation, how to look sufficiently cheerful. But she dragged herself through it with a constant, desperate wish that her heart would finally just break itself open and gush. Just this once was all she asked of herself, yet she couldn't shake the notion that she was out on display like some broken artifact—Sandy's "other mom," her biological mother, not the paralegal socialite stepmother named Corrine who'd raised Sandra since she was a preteen. Greta assumed that Max had already been briefed about the family history: how at age ten Sandy had picked her dad as primary custodian at the divorce hearing, and how Greta hadn't contested her daughter's choice.

"Don't get me wrong," Max said. "Lord knows I understand what you're doing and I think you must be so unbelievably strong to handle all that you deal with on a daily basis. It's a sacrifice you made—you know—for women."

"What women?" Greta said.

"Mom," said Sandy. "He's paying you a compliment."

"I know," Greta said. "Thank you." She was drinking more tea than wine. No tolerance for booze anymore, so just a few sips might cloud her brain into shutdown. A foggy head was not an option because she needed to stay clear for later, for all those Oscar Moberg case reports she'd be reading through—the technicians' findings, the meager witness statements, the preliminary autopsy report. Random shootings generally offered a forty-eight-hour investigative window, and this one was already half-shut with nothing blowing through—a stark indication that it would likely be chucked into the unsolved files with that hopeless library of other cold randoms. But still this case was itching at her even now, the way some cases did until they closed up tight or sputtered out over time. That itch was what reminded her she had any senses at all.

Sandy said, "So are you ordering the Pad Thai?"

"I guess so," Greta said. "Excuse me for a second." She pushed back her chair and laid her cloth napkin on the table. They probably expected that she'd head toward the bathroom, but instead Greta pushed through the front door and into the parking lot. She didn't look back at her dinner party, didn't offer a reassuring nod that she'd be returning soon. If either of them were sharp enough, they'd notice she hadn't taken her jacket off the coatrack beside the door.

Greta found her Buick and unlocked it and sat down in the driver's seat with her feet still planted on the pavement. The cold night had laid frost across her windshield. She huddled there and shivered while she dug a pack of Marlboros out of the glove compartment, her Bic lighter tucked between the packaging and the cellophane. She lit one and smoked. It was not until the airborne tobacco hit her lungs that she realized how urgently she'd needed that fix. It burned the black anger from her head, and the relief made her want to cry.

She fixed on the Moberg case and especially the daughter, Lucia. Greta had rushed from the crime scene to the hospital because she hadn't wanted to wait for the girl's memory of the event to lapse, as memory was prone to do in the face of such trauma. She'd forced the girl to remember, a brand of torture that always kindled Greta's sense of guilt, so then she'd tried to alleviate that guilt by telling a sob story about her own dad's heart attack. Greta had shared grief and held the girl's hand like she was some kind of counselor. In retrospect, Greta couldn't understand why she'd been so candid, and the total illogic of it terrified her. Any cop who offers morsels of herself to strangers—even kids—is begging to have her self stolen away.

She imagined the end of Oscar Moberg's life unfolding as he sat in a driver's seat, just as she was now. In this displaced dream she looked toward the restaurant parking lot, briefly certain she'd find a faceless gunman stalking toward her in a brown leather jacket, snarling "What's up, doc?" Stickups relied on the paralysis of surprise—don't think, just hand over your wallet and have a nice day—but somehow Professor Moberg had managed what victims rarely do in the shock of the gunpoint moment: he'd tried to escape. Moberg's choice to flee was equal parts admirable and stupid. Admirable because nobody, probably not even the perpetrator, could've known whether the robbery would lead to murder or carjacking or kidnapping. Stupid in that his choice had gotten him killed. Although it probably shouldn't have—not when a perp misses his first shot and must fire again through a windshield from several feet off. But this afternoon's prelim autopsy reports had laid out the results like they were stereo system specs—"primary tissue trauma due to recovered 200 grain lead projectile consistent with a .45 caliber 240 grain hollow-point bullet, along with secondary tissue damage due to temporary cavity created by supersonic projectile." Ballistics had concurred from a recovered shell casing that the weapon was an autoloading Colt .45 handgun. This shooter was either an expert marksman or a lucky sonofabitch so juiced and dizzied by his own magic bull's-eye that he fled the scene without the cash he so coveted.

Tonight in this neon-lit parking lot, nobody appeared with a .45 caliber handgun to confront Greta with a fatal choice. Instead, it was Sandy hugging her navy peacoat over her shoulders and trying not to look surprised that Greta was still on the premises. Sandy walked toward the Buick and nudged her sneaker into her mother's shoe. "Hey," she said, "I thought you quit smoking."

"I did. Only when I really need it. When I'm stressed out."

"Are we really all that stressful?" Sandy complained.

"I'm not very good at this kind of stuff," Greta said.

"Max thought you left, but I knew better. I came out to tell you to relax."

"What for?"

"I don't know. I guess some of us enjoy making other people happy."

"I'm coming back," Greta said. She dropped her cigarette on the pavement and crushed it with a stomp. No need to say anything more. Greta would return to the dinner table and order her Pad Thai—at least make one more attempt to tinker inside her own life and work to get it running smoothly for once, instead of prowling around crime scenes picking through the fresh debris of other people's lives.

Greta tried to meet eyes with her daughter, but she noticed instead a darkened video store at the far end of the plaza. Streetlights hit the storefront window, where crude imitations of characters had been latex-painted on the glass: Cinderella, some blond elf with a sword, and Bugs Bunny munching on a carrot. In Greta's mind the faceless killer muttered again that phrase he'd stolen from a cartoon rabbit. But this time he snarled the last word, *doc,* giving it emphasis and meaning—capitalizing it. *Doc*—as in *Doctor.*

"Damn," Greta breathed out for a full three seconds.

"What's the matter?" said Sandy.

"Nothing. Probably nothing." It was a fleeting insight, already fading to a hum deep in her bones, but it couldn't be ignored—this sudden notion that the gunman knew his victim was a Ph.D., that there'd been nothing random about the target.

LUC'S RADIO ALARM told her it was past three in the morning, but still she tossed and twisted, awake in her bed, kicking the sheets untucked from the mattress as her jostling flung cassette tapes and socks off the bed. At first she had been squeezing a tiny candle in her fist, a memento from the vigil, but it was cold and waxy now. She gave up and slapped it on the nightstand beside her folded glasses. Luc fidgeted because if she kept motionless long enough, the grief started seeping through again like a gash that wouldn't clot.

The stereo shed a dim greenish light across the room, enough to etch the shape of a dresser, a desk, and the drywall almost obscured behind her rock band posters. The dehumidifier snapped awake and sucked air and died every few minutes. There was faint scratching coming from within the basement walls—probably a mole or a mouse burrowing through the insulation for warmth. Most nights she'd slam a fist against the wall to hush the rodent, but tonight its company gave her a hint of assurance.

Luc noticed a lump of blended color down on the carpet near the molding, rendered green from the stereo glow. She thought it was maybe a sock, or a cassette, or a hairbrush that had taken a dive off her dresser, but this shape wobbled, even slinked an inch along the carpet while Luc squinted at it. She heard that scraping sound again, and it was synched with the faint movement of that lump that Luc now decided was that mouse or mole finally braving the world outside its nest.

Luc grabbed for her glasses, and her sudden reach sent the rodent darting off toward her bedroom door. She pulled open the glasses' frames, slipped them onto her face, and blinked at the instant focus. She was already sitting up when her bare toes tested the cold cement floor of her basement bedroom.

What Luc saw instead of a mouse didn't register with her brain. It was like a mouse, but without a tail, and it was scurrying upright on its hind legs. But she could've seen wrong—must have. This thing, it slipped through her bedroom door faster than Luc could develop its image in her mind, so she accepted none of what her eyes reported. She gasped and then cringed at her own girlish nerves, then rushed out of her room into the dark of the finished basement. She tugged the dangling twine that snapped alive a bare hanging bulb. She looked past the staircase and caught sight of the creature as it dived through the dust ruffle under the spare sofa.

"Hey, wait," she blurted. Stupid—talking to it.

Here the basement was plywood walled and carpeted with throw rugs that were arranged like a patchwork. A plot of it used to serve as Luc's playroom and Mom's sewing area, but now in that corner their old den furniture sat propped around an old turn-dial TV: a love seat, a card table, the couch where that creature was now hiding. Nearby stood the washing machine and dryer.

Down on her knees she lifted the ruffles around the sofa and pressed one ear against the floor. Nothing under there but pitch dark, and no surge of willpower could get her to reach her bare hand into it. But she listened. And when the dehumidifier shuddered to a stop again, Luc heard from underneath that couch tiny, wheezing whiffs of breath, like the sound of a balloon spitting out helium in minute bursts.

Luc recoiled and scuttled backward against a foundation beam, gasping. Every follicle in her skin prickled and under her arm brace her sprained wrist throbbed. Her brain kept posting images of what she'd seen in her bedroom, what had fled out here under the couch, and she was losing her bout with denial.

"Holy holy holy crap," Luc muttered.

Upstairs the floorboards creaked. Luc assumed her mother was up there, prowling through the house at three in the morning, awakened by something. Luc slapped a hand over her mouth because she guessed she'd been screaming without knowing she was screaming. She couldn't remember, couldn't discern what was true.

What she'd seen was a dream figment born from her grief, she decided. Too much time spent dredging up childhood tales and Luc had gotten herself lost in a wonderland. But then, as she renounced it, her figment appeared again, bursting through the sofa ruffles like a racehorse from the gate. It rushed across the rugs, chugging its bare pink arms. Most of what Luc saw was the color of rawhide—a creature draped in dried animal skins. The exposed face and arms and feet were ruddy like scalded flesh. Long tangled strands of hair danced around its coverings—dark hair grayed by cobwebs and dust. It skittered like a rodent but it was faintly human. Hands instead of paws, lidded eyes, a distinct nose jutting out over its wild gray beard, but it was small enough to cage in Luc's cupped hands if she dared catch it.

The creature stumbled on the edge of a rug or maybe over its overgrown beard, and it somersaulted with loose limbs flailing. After an indistinct grunt it was up again, making for the washer and dryer. This time it squeezed into the inch of space between the two appliances.

Luc lost sight of the creature in the long shadows formed by that single low-wattage lightbulb. She waited. She listened to her mother's progress across the floor upstairs. And Luc would've stayed there pressed against that beam, silently freaking until Mom came down and found her—she would've sat rejecting this conscious dream until it fled—but instead she saw a white sliver of paper on the floor under the dryer, the edge of something hidden.

On hands and knees she approached. Her spine buzzed a silent alarm as she reached for whatever was under there. It felt like paper, so she pressed down and she slid the paper out, curling it up against her thumb. A wrinkled white envelope with blue watermark on the inside to keep it opaque. Nothing written on the front, and on the back the unsealed flap gaped open. The envelope was plump with cash, a stack much larger than any she'd ever before held in her hands.

Luc stood and backed away from the dryer and whatever else was lurking there. She shimmied the money into her hand and passed her thumb across the curled edges. It was all one-hundred-dollar bills, and a rush estimate counted fifty of them. Five thousand dollars. Luc tried to swallow, but her dry throat retched instead. She waited for this mirage to fade and convinced herself that the money was a dream, just like everything else she'd seen tonight. The creature was gone and Luc could reject it, but the money stayed, and the money was palpable.

The lull lasted only seconds before another noise snapped Luc's bone joints into lock—the thunderclap of a heavy weight dumping onto the floor upstairs, noise blasting through the basement ceiling beams. Luc jolted and the money leaped from her grip. The bulk of it slapped down at her feet, but a few bills had broken loose and fluttered off course. Luc snatched one from midair. She scooped the rest off the concrete and the throw rugs around her, then she hurried the money back into the envelope and thumbed it into place. The envelope she shoved back under the dryer and tapped once with her finger so the stark white corners were concealed. All that cash, Luc wished it away. She wanted to replay the evening without it, but too late for that. She was already bounding up the stairs toward this abrupt new crisis.

Luc found her mother lying naked on the bathroom floor. She was slumped against the tub with her bare breasts flattened against the rim and her arms dropped limp inside the empty tub. Her raw knees shivered on the bath mat. A small night-light leaked dim yellow from the socket beside the door and bathed her mother in a sickly aura. Mom strained to lift her head. She squinted at Luc through the hair coils dangling over her face. "Oh, I woke you up," she said.

"I was already," said Luc, wincing at the acidy puke stench that hit her nostrils then. The toilet lid was open to exhibit dark congealed splashes of vomit inside the bowl. Luc pressed a hand over her mouth and nose. She pushed the door half-closed in order to reach the towel rack on its back side, then peeled away Mom's towel from the rightmost hook. Dad's hook was empty. And there were only two toothbrushes propped inside the cup beside the sink, hers and Mom's. Dad's can of Gillette shaving cream was gone, but its rust ring was still stained onto the counter. An orange prescription pill bottle was overturned in the sink basin and had spilled six white pills around the drain. The moisture had bloated the pills into grainy mush.

Mom's sobbing resounded through the empty tub like the moans of a child trapped inside a well. Luc draped the towel over her mother's shoulder and thigh. She tried not to scrutinize this naked body, but it was a curious prototype of her own body, and she hadn't seen it this exposed since forever. Mom's hips had been sculpted into sleek rounded dunes by a two-year membership in an all-women's gym, and pale bikini lines swept across skin that had been darkened over the autumn months by visits to Island Tan. Sad that Mom always snuffed this beauty with loose and mannish clothes and with that morose slump of all retail workers, but sadder that she should allow this ugly indignity—surrendering herself to grief.

"I got sick all of a sudden," Mom said. She dragged her arms out of the tub and braced her knobby spine against the rim. She said, "Grab me a tissue there please," as she hugged the towel up under her armpits.

Luc lowered the toilet seat shut while she plucked a tissue from the box on the shelf behind it. The box was just beside Dad's dozen stacked *New Yorker* magazines, which Mom had missed in her frenzied effort to remove the boldest reminders of Oscar Moberg's daily existence. Mom hadn't touched the more timeless artifacts like portraits, the Swedish folk art, the shelves of mythology books in his attic office. These things could persist beyond his life, unlike the routine trinkets that seemed to claim that they were still in use. Luc understood why her mother had dumped a half-empty carton of V-8 juice and a bottle of Morley's discount vodka down the kitchen drain, though Luc could never have done such things herself. It was that willingness to stifle these reminders, maybe, that had veered Mom so fast into this breakdown.

"I had this feeling—I just wanted to take a bath," Mom said. She rubbed the tissue across her lips and nostrils, snorting back fluids. "It's disgusting—throwing up like that. Just to have a bath, but then my stomach—ugh."

"At three in the morning?" Luc said as she flushed the toilet. The pill bottle in the sink caught her attention again. This time she noticed the damp ink on the label had bled from the wetness, but the patient's name—*Blair Crowley-Moberg*—was still legible. Dated just one day ago and filled out for thirty pills. A few of the spilled ones were melting there in the sink and a dozen more were still in the bottle. The rest were missing.

"What are these?" Luc said. "Valium? How many did you eat?"

"It doesn't matter, Lu-Lu. I threw them up." Mom struggled to stand up, but she fell sitting onto the tub rim and slumped her head and her forearms onto her knees. She clenched and unclenched both her hands, staring at them like she'd just learned how they worked.

"Mom—what are you doing? What happened?"

"I just wanted to sleep. I took some pills ten minutes ago, but it was nothing. I'm sorry, you know, because taking them was a bad idea and I knew right off, so that's why I puked. Not even enough time to digest, right? Just a stupid mistake."

"We should go to the hospital," Luc said.

"No hospital, because it's out of my system now. You can see there in the toilet, the pills. I just need to sleep right now is all. I'll be fine—just—please—just help me up."

Luc didn't move to help as she watched her mother raise herself upright on wobbly legs. Luc wanted to slap the woman across the top of her skull and knock her back into awareness. Her mother, who was indulging that same hysteria that Luc resisted, who wasn't qualified to fall apart because she hadn't even witnessed his death like Luc had.

Backing out into the hallway, Luc glanced at the floor-level molding along the wall, almost expecting to catch signs of a sudden small movement there. She wasn't yet ready to erase the dream of the little bearded man, even if she was now convinced that her sleepwalking mind had conjured it. Mother and daughter—two totally different manifestations of collapse, and Luc couldn't decide which was the more hopeless condition.

"What I need is a glass of ice water," Mom said.

"I'll get it for you. Just walk." Luc ushered her mother down the hall by pressing one tentative hand below Mom's shoulder. They walked into the master bedroom, where Dad's clothes lay folded inside cardboard boxes on the floor and on his side of the waterbed. He was dust now, Luc knew. The Webster Funeral Home had burned his body down to ash, even before his first vigil candle was lit. She had refused to think about his literal body until now, now that it was gone forever, and she clenched her fingernails into her fists to assure herself that she hadn't also vanished.

"Here we are," Mom said. She sat down on the foot of her waterbed, and the waves rippled under the blankets. The boxes of Oscar's clothes bobbed like they were the flotsam of a shipwreck. "Hand me my bathrobe, will you? Ugh, my throat."

Luc lifted the discarded robe off the floor. "Just lay down. I'll get the water."

"What if I can't handle this?"

"You said you threw up, and you're okay—"

"Not the pills. It's worse than that," Mom said. "Look at me. What's wrong with us? I'm supposed to be helping you, Lucia. Why can't I even manage? And I want to know what happens when you realize we're not going to be fine. That's the truth."

"I already realized," Luc said.

Minutes later Luc was kneeling on the basement floor again with her fingers digging into the space under the dryer. She wanted to be sure because never in her life had a dream been so vivid. She could still feel the weight of that fantasy money in her hand, and she could smell its musty scent. If dreams were this real then she might be sleeping even now without knowing. She shouldered the dryer door and tilted the front end off the floor. Then she slapped at the dust underneath, just to be certain there was nothing.

But the envelope was still there, still thick with hundred-dollar bills. She took it while she eased the dryer back down to the floor. The dryer's rusty underside spread orange grime across her knuckles. The money stack fanned out across the seal, and Luc gripped it until every corner of her mind admitted its reality.

This couldn't be Dad's money, stashed away for some plan that had died with him. He wouldn't have picked the dryer for a hideout—never even did the laundry, and rarely came down to the basement. He'd probably hide a cash wad in his office, maybe up there inside that hardback copy of *Bleak House* that wasn't really a book because it had a hidden safe embedded in the fake pages. Luc had discovered that false book years ago, but she'd always found it empty.

Maybe these were Mom's cashed paychecks. It made sense because Dad was always saying she didn't need that seven-bucks-an-hour slave labor working front-end management at the local Shop-Mor. But Mom had her own account at the credit union. She had no good reason to squirrel away such cash, and anyway Mom would've had to keep every dime she'd made for months in order to reach five grand. The envelope seemed too fresh for that kind of savings plan.

Luc tucked the money back into the envelope and slid it back underneath the dryer, this time within reach of her seeking fingers, just in case she needed to accept once again that it was there. Believing in the cash wasn't so hard. Much worse was admitting to herself that she'd found it because she was chasing down an imaginary man no bigger than an apple. So it must've been a mouse, or some dirt particle floating in her eye. Otherwise her mind was drawing mirages, and she refused to lose trust in her own five senses.

THE LIVING ROOM TV played an infomercial about a heavy-duty stain remover, but Luc turned it off before the salesman reached his blood demonstration. She'd stayed awake in the recliner overnight to be closer to Mom, who was in the bedroom snoring through her deep drugged sleep. Luc worried about how much of those sedatives had seeped into her mother's veins, so she'd kept watch all night, spying into the bedroom every half hour to check Mom's rough but steady breath.

Again at dawn Luc crossed the hallway toward the master bedroom and eased the door open a few inches. Mom was awake, seated on the edge of the bed with two orange ibuprofen pills in her palm. She tipped the pills into her mouth and gulped down the last of the water in the glass Luc had left on the nightstand for her. Mom was already dressed in her Shop-Mor outfit: black slacks and black sneakers, a baby blue button-down shirt, and a red vendor's vest with a matching red tie. The pin on her vest said, BLAIR MOBERG, ASSISTANT MANAGER, TEN YEARS AT YOUR SERVICE!

"I didn't hear you get up," Luc said. "You're going to work?"

"I have a burning headache, but I need to get out of here. I know if I don't start moving I'm going to feel sick for—forever."

Dad's homemade lighting fixture was glaring down at them—a system of cupped bulbs attached to interlocking metal beams and cables that spanned the walls like a border. He'd wanted to outfit the living room and kitchen with his light fixtures, but Mom complained that they looked too sterile, like they belonged in an art museum or a doctor's office. Now Luc expected that her mother would soon dismantle the whole apparatus and pack it away. Oscar Moberg was gone and Luc wanted to mourn him but instead she hated him for his failure, for leaving his life gaping wide open like this. And when she swallowed that hate her throat shuddered and her eyes moistened and she loved him again.

Later that morning, after Mom had left for work, the doorbell rang. Luc was still in her sweatpants and tanktop drinking coffee from a plastic travel mug. She opened the door and the brisk air splashed over her bare arms and feet. It was Quinn Cutler from next door, standing on her porch and clutching in both his hands a lidded white casserole dish wrapped in a kitchen towel. Steam roiled up from the lid. Quinn flexed his sharp jaw muscles. He wore a dark suede jacket, and most of his hair was tied back into a ponytail. He was nineteen, old enough to shave, but his face was smooth and hairless as a child's. People said it was because of Iroquois blood.

Luc was instantly conscious of her ratty hair and the hole in her sweatpants and her coffee breath and the way her A-cup bra was visible through her tanktop—the wrinkly pink knuckles of fabric that her measly boobs couldn't fill. She crossed her arms over her chest and concentrated on how theoretically lame Quinn looked holding ceramic cookware. And that towel with roosters and picket fences printed on it.

"Hey, you're Lucia, right?"

"Hey. Luc, yeah. What's—what are you doing here?"

"I got this thing," Quinn said, tipping the glass lid so that steam gushed out in one white cough. "My mom made it—next door—like ham and instant potatoes with cheese or whatever. She wanted me to bring it over in case your mom didn't feel like cooking right now. Because of your dad. I figured I'd swing by before I went back to school 'cause I'm home a few minutes for my morning break." He nodded in the direction of his house, over where he kept his Ford Thunderbird in the garage with his motorcycle.

He'd only been riding the bike for a few months from what Luc could tell, and rumor was he didn't even have his license for it yet. That car, though—he'd been driving it to school for almost two years now. Mornings when Luc walked to school, she'd hear his muffler chugging up the street behind her and she'd wonder: what if he pulled up to the curb and offered her a ride? She'd probably freak out and bolt away, but not without regretting it later.

He said, squinting into the house behind Luc, "So maybe your mom, she'll want to take it if she's around anywhere?"

"She went to work a few minutes ago, but I can—"

"Cool. No problem. Luc, then. Like Luke Skywalker?"

"Sort of. It's just short for Lucia."

"This is hot, though, this dish."

The coffee sloshed inside her travel mug. She said, "Oh, jeez, I'm sorry," and pushed open the screen door. "Here, come in, sorry," she said, while Quinn slouched inside her house, brushing his jacket sleeve against her arm as she held the door for him. He stood there in her foyer in his big scuffed electrician's boots with the laces untied and the tongues lolling out. Kit and Gina would never believe it.

In the kitchen, he set the casserole on the counter, then flapped his overcooked hands and hissed through his teeth. His hands were scrubbed clean of the motor grease that was usually stained into the creases of his knuckles and in his cuticles, even back when he was sixteen roaming around the neighborhood all summer with his friends, shirtless and drinking liquor from a picnic thermos. He used to smoke his mom's cigarettes, ride the bumper on the back of the neighborhood ice cream truck for laughs, swipe Bomb Pops from the cooler in the truck bed without the driver even knowing. Back then thrash metal rushed from his boom box and filled the quiet spaces between all their houses. Pets skittered from him as if they knew the rumor that he'd once fried a cat with jumper cables and a car battery. But Luc knew it was a bullshit story made up by the kids who envied his freedom and nerve.

"You're a senior now, right?" Luc said.

"Yeah. I'm supposed to be graduated, but they held me back in third and eighth. That's your grade, right? Eight?"

"Tenth," Luc said, baring her teeth a bit too much.

"Shit, sorry. I don't see you around school much."

"I'm there—mostly," Luc said. Twice every day he'd pass her in the hallway. She'd watch him in the mirror stuck to the inside of her locker door, and her heartbeat would sputter.

Quinn said, "This morning during homeroom this dude's car started on fire in the parking lot. Spontaneous combustion, right? He wasn't in it but his car is toast. My ma, you know, she wanted to come over here herself to give her condolences, but she didn't figure it was time yet."

"Right," Luc said. Their two mothers had been knotted in a feud ever since Quinn had developed a habit of vandalizing neighborhood cars—something like four years ago. Blair had found her old Toyota's driver's side window busted in, broken most likely by the red bocce ball that was still lying there on the passenger seat. No hard evidence that Quinn was the culprit, but everybody knew, and Mom bitched his mother's ear off about it. Later Mom even griped with Dad after he suggested maybe she should just chill out. For days afterward, Mom slept with an aluminum baseball bat under her side of the bed, eager for a chance to use it upside Quinn's skull. Through the living room windows she'd watch Quinn parade down the street with his friends and his loose-armed strut. She'd say, "Who the hell does that scrawny shit think he is?"

Took forever for her to cool off about it, and only in the last year or so had Mom finally settled into a quiet smolder. She kept her mouth shut about Quinn these days—never much mentioned him at all. Still, Luc guessed her mom wouldn't go striking up any welcome tunes for Quinn Cutler with his ham and cheese offering. She sure as hell wouldn't care to know that her own daughter often ached, madly, with the imagined crush of his body.

But Luc didn't care to consider what her mother might think. Only a few hours ago the woman was lying naked and helpless like a newborn, and Luc had practically nursed her with glasses of water. Their roles, mother and daughter, didn't make sense anymore. That woman who was her mother, who was always scolding, nagging, and disapproving over trivial shit, always irritated—maybe she didn't exist anymore. Maybe she died alongside her husband. The possibility weighed Luc with more loneliness than ever.

"You skipping school today?" Quinn said.

"I don't have to go back right yet."

"That's cool. It's cool they're not making you. They could be assholes about it, right?"

"Yeah," Luc said.

He watched her with his eyelids dipping sleepily over his pupils, his jaw muscles still pulsing like he was chewing on some faint idea. Luc let their eyes stay latched for longer than she should have been able to manage. It was like a lift off the ground, that stretch of time. Her temperature climbed at least a full degree.

"I'm gonna get going," Quinn said. "I got a mandatory study hall in ten minutes."

"Right," said Luc, laughing at God only knew what. It was a weak and nervous laugh that Quinn answered with an equally awkward grimace. Luc recognized his pity—pity like what you feel watching TV news and seeing those orphans wandering naked and dusty through the rubble of a bombed-out village.

MASON PARKED THE CADILLAC at the far end of the parking lot where there were no other cars nearby. The spot seemed to Tanya like it was at least a mile off from the store entrance, and here the weather was getting cold enough for snow—wind pushing carts into car bumpers, wrapping sales flyers around radio antennas like little sports pennants. Tanya was in the passenger seat drinking a grape soda she'd bought from the gas station back when they started their trip an hour ago. She sat wishing she'd brought along her jacket, but it had felt so hot earlier. Now she was freezing. Couldn't get her body temp straight anymore.

Mason cranked back his driver's seat and lit up a cigarette. He smashed the empty soft pack in his hand, then he rolled down the window some to tap away tobacco ash. Tanya wished he wouldn't smoke around her because it could go through her lungs and down the tube and get the baby addicted before it was even born. Sure Tan smoked sometimes herself, but she'd heard that secondhand smoke was the worse killer.

"You ready for this?" Mason said.

"I guess so."

He turned the classical radio station down. Tan liked him to play or-chestra stuff in the car so the baby could hear it and grow extra net-works in its brain. She'd read all about that in the pregnancy magazines the doctors sent in the mail, back when she used to get mail.

"Go over it with me," he said.

"Why'd you park so far away? It's cold out."

Mason put his face in his hand to prove she was getting on his nerves. Without looking at her he said, "Because I don't want anyone around here to see me. They got security cameras pointed at the parking lot, you know. It don't matter if they see you because you ain't got any pri-ors. Nobody has your picture."

Tanya had spent three years on the street, starting when she was fif-teen. Her junkie boyfriend at the time made her sell meth and junk, and sometimes she helped him raid houses for cash and jewelry and guns. After a while the asshole even pushed her into turning tricks. She spent three years running like a rabid dog, out of her mind and drooling, but in all that time not once did she get collared. The other junkies and whores called her Cherry because she never got popped by the cops. She thanked God and Mason that she wasn't in that shit anymore because her luck would've run stale for sure by now. Here she was nineteen years old, clean, almost a mother, and still no rap sheet.

"Go over it with me, Tan," he said again. Out in the parking lot was a worker kid loading shopping carts together. He came close enough that Mason got antsy and popped down both sun visors to put shadows on their faces. Mason said, "Are you gonna be nice in there?"

"No. I'm gonna be a threat menace. I'm gonna say: no fucking around."

"Growl," Mason said.

Tanya grit her teeth and growled, but doing it made her laugh. Ma-son blinked at her, then he tossed his cigarette out the window and scowled until Tanya dropped the dumb grin off her face. He said, "This ain't funny, Tan. You need to be angry for real. You ain't angry enough yet."

"I haven't gone inside there yet—" Tanya said.

"Pretend somebody stole your baby and you want it back."

Tanya pressed a hand against her belly. "Mason, that ain't funny."

"I didn't say it was. It pissed you off, though, didn't it? So use it that way, like you're an actor or something. Go in there and use it. You remember what to say?"

Tanya nodded. She shivered fiercely now, but she didn't want Mason to see her nerves going haywire. She said, "Let me borrow your jacket, honey. It's cold out."

"Nobody's supposed to be wearing my jacket but me," he said, but he was already pulling it down off his shoulders, struggling to get it off in the cramped space of the car.

"Nobody'll find out if I wear it for five minutes," she said. By nobody she meant Buck Hanson and his posse, the family that Mason had finally joined, all of them miles away from here. Tanya figured you need to break some rules in any family, and one of the major rules with Mason's crew was never to let your old lady wear your jacket.

"Why don't you get me a carton while you're in there?" Mason said.

"Sure," Tanya said. She hoisted herself up from the car seat and out into the open. Pushed her arms through the leather jacket with the spanking-new skull rocker stitched on the back. The jacket was too small to zip over her belly, so she let the lapels flap open in the wind and hugged herself as she walked down the aisle toward the store.

Frozen air lashed at her face, but she wore that jacket like it was Prince Charming's perfect-fit glass slipper, just like in that Cinderella Disney flick she saw on TV back when her mom wasn't dead from the cancer in her breasts. She remembered that movie and thought about how almost the same exact shit that Cinderella went through wound up also happening to her: a new stepmom who screamed and drank, called her a whore and a retard. Pervert stepbrother who made her take off her pants and lie stomach down on the coffee table when she was twelve years old. So much blood, sopped up with paper towels, but the wicked stepbrother said he'd slit her throat if she called the doctor. Tanya hoped someday she'd get the guts to tell Mason about that molester bastard.

She knew Mason would for certain track him down and fuck him up good.

THAT AFTERNOON LUC TOOK a walk so that the stinging breeze could cool her thinking down to a simmer. She left home and headed west one block past the student apartment houses that were crammed too closely to the road. Along her route the curbside tree trunks were thick around as car tires, their roots groping up between the sidewalk slabs. The neighbors' plastic trash bins lay overturned and emptied after the early morning pickup. She'd known these obstacles her whole life, though they seemed more determined than ever to make her stumble.

Monday afternoon traffic was sparse on this village side road, but now a black Ford sedan passed from behind Luc, traveling at a crawl. Then twenty feet ahead its break lights lit just before a swift K-turn brought it back to her side of the road. Luc stiffened at the sight of this sudden maneuver, dragged the Walkman earphones off her head. She slowed her pace and then stopped as the car veered toward her curb and glided to a full halt. The driver was male, with a thick black mustache and a pair of sunglasses, a hard face trained in Luc's direction, yet locked behind a sheet of glass like a snake in a terrarium.

Luc panicked. It was only one block back to her house and the front door lock and the deadbolt and the long sharp cutting knives in the kitchen drawer if she had to. But she warned herself not to start up with this fear that could be the first twinge of some lifelong posttraumatic nutcase problem. When the passenger door opened, Luc steadied herself with one hand against a nearby tree and buried her fingertips in the deep grooves of the bark. She checked the ground for rocks, branches— anything that might work as a weapon.

The person who appeared from the passenger side was also wearing sunglasses that covered half her face. Her hair was tied back into a bun, and a scarf hung loosely across the front of her trench coat. She slipped off her sunglasses, folded them, lost them in a large coat pocket. Luc recognized her, but Luc's heart kept pounding.

"Lucia—I'm Greta Hurd. We spoke in the hospital, you remember?"

"I remember," Luc said.

The automatic driver's window slipped down and the mustache guy raised one open hand as a reluctant greeting. He was olive skinned, maybe a Middle Easterner. His chronic scowl kept Luc feeling nervy—feeling like this guy probably kept some master list of all Luc's petty thefts that she once thought she'd never have to answer for.

Greta said, "This is my partner, Investigator Arslan. We've both been up to your house just now. I wanted to see if I could catch you or your mother, but no one was home. Then I recognized you walking and—well, I apologize if we startled you."

"You didn't—" Luc said, but she didn't see the use in denying it. "My mom went to work this morning. She works up at the Shop-Mor on Route 31."

Greta had already shut her passenger door and moved around the back of the car. She stepped through the exhaust fumes puffing from the muffler. Standing in the roadside grass, she said, "Maybe I'll head up there to talk to her."

"Do you—" Luc ventured. "Have you found out anything?"

"There's no significant news yet, but it's early still," Greta said. She leaned against the side of the car, folded her arms. "We'll figure this out for you, all right? You and your mother."

"She's a wreck," Luc said. "Like last night she took all these sleeping pills and I worried all night long. I don't even know why she went to work this morning. Tomorrow at noon we're supposed to spread my dad's ashes at the Piper Marina, and I wonder if she'll even be able to handle it." Luc was only partly conscious of how easily this woman could draw out her secrets. With Greta, Luc wanted to talk—and she was relieved, released, when she did talk. "I'm scared for her, you know? She's too weak to handle any of this, and I don't know how to help."

Greta's partner sat silent with his arm on the windowsill, sipping coffee, like he was a taxi driver waiting for a fare to knock on his window. Down the street a laundry van backed out of a driveway, and when Greta looked toward it the trance between them faded. Now Luc felt and heard her own music thrumming faintly from the earphones resting on her collarbones, and she turned the dial on her Walkman down.

Greta said, "Do you need a ride where you're going? It's pretty cold out."

"That's all right, thanks. It's just a couple blocks and I like to walk."

BACK IN THE CAR and headed down the road, Greta watched Luc in the rearview mirror: a lonely girl moping down the sidewalk in her flimsy unbuttoned overcoat, hanging her head, watching her own boots scrape across the concrete. Knock-kneed in her baggy pants. With both hands shoved in her overcoat pockets, Luc raised her arms and spread her jacket lapels like wings at her hips, like she might've taken flight if her despair wasn't keeping her grounded.

Moe said, "Not for nothing, but that kid needs one of those Sally Jesse teen makeovers. I'm not keen on these every-day-is-Halloween types. They creep me out."

"Moe, her father was just murdered three days ago."

He turned the car onto the main road, and Greta's mirror view of Luc was swept away.

Moe said, "So I take it those are her mourning vestments?"

"When are you going to start pretending you have a heart?" she asked.

"Soon as I retire. What happened to the ice queen I knew and tolerated?"

"Believe me: you don't want to hear my explanation," Greta said, wondering if she could even articulate the energy responsible for her melting moods anyhow. Moe was a creature of logical analysis, deft at charting patterns and motives but a plodder at human empathy. Secretly, Greta regretted that Moe had chosen to deliver the death notify to Blair Moberg because now his elliptical account of the woman's reaction was the only first impression Greta had available. She didn't want Moe getting offended, so she'd loaded this morning up with other local casework to dilute her main objective—talking to Blair again.

They had already gone over to the SUNY Hammersport campus to interview some of Oscar Moberg's colleagues. In the campus quad they'd seen a wooden cross with flowers in cellophane strewn around its base and a poster hanging from the crossbeam that said, WE'LL MISS YOU, DR. MOBERG. Greta couldn't look at it long. These murder victims who entered her work, who took her life hostage time and again—she never knew them, never met them. She always arrived when they were already gone. To her they were nonentities, except for those rare, fleeting times when she caught some trace of that lost life still lingering like cologne on laundered clothes. Those moments showed her what it must be like to grieve the violent death of someone you love. Usually made her think of her own father dying in the sawdust on the basement floor.

They'd searched two hours in Moberg's college office and found only innocuous student papers and faculty memos. Moe noticed he'd been a tough grader, so he jotted down the names of students who'd gotten failing marks in his grade book over the last three years. Greta had interviewed the colleagues who'd known him the longest, some of whom had been out fishing with him. Asked them the ugly questions: Was he a gambler? Recreational drug user? Did he ever visit prostitutes that they knew of? She got the resounding denials she'd expected. The departmental chair, an old friend of Oscar's, told Greta, "These questions disgust me."

"Me too," Greta had said.

Now, a few hours later, they parked in the fire lane outside the Hammersport Shop-Mor and headed inside, where the air was humid like someplace tropical. Ten checkout lines open and at least three customers cued at each. The cashiers were middle-aged and dumpy, every last one of them, and they were all cast in a vapor of sickly green light coming down from the ceiling. ABBA sang "Dancing Queen" through the intercom and it echoed in eerie, sad waves across the vast sales floor.

Midway down the aisle of checkout counters they found the manager's cubbyhole office, and Greta glanced in at the drywall cell—saw spiral-bound manuals and fast food containers spread atop monitors that fizzled grainy security footage. The only manager present was a scarecrow of a man wearing an untucked dress shirt over his jeans and a tie that dangled all the way down to his crotch. He rolled his office chair back and stood up taller than the door frame. He said, "May I help you?" with the distress of those who recognize cops by experience.

"We're looking for Blair Moberg," Moe said as he showed off his badge.

"I'm afraid she's gone home sick for the day, Officers," said Lloyd Lauderschmidt, Store Manager—according to his nametag. He had tinted glasses and a bald crown that was sharp as a mountain peak. "She wasn't feeling well this morning to begin with, and after a small altercation we decided she'd be better off taking a personal day. That was almost an hour ago, I think." He checked his watch and nodded at it.

"You had a fight with her?" Greta said.

"Oh, not me," Lloyd explained. "Just a spat with a customer, I think. I'm not certain of the circumstances, but as I say it was minor—and common, since managers have to deal with complaints, you know. She's been understandably on edge because, well, I assume you know that her husband passed away just recently and frankly I don't even know why she came in today. She needed more personal time."

Lloyd the store manager migrated to a nearby display case while he talked, and he started tidying a shelf of Pringles cans and Combos—the retail veteran's version of fidgeting. Greta had already had enough of this greenish light and wet radiating heat and the gasoline stench of Lloyd's aftershave. She decided to slip outside for a cigarette and leave Moe there to ask the rest of the questions. On her way out, the glass doors whisked open for her like a sign of surrender.

LUC PASSED THE FIRST minute of midnight in the half bath at Gina and Kit's house. She was sleepless and drunk off the bitter shots of Jack Daniels that Gina had swiped from her mom's liquor cabinet. There'd been some cramping in her gut, and now on the toilet Luc knew why. Red blotching her white cotton underpants. Her period arriving like clockwork, but with everything else Luc had completely forgotten that it was imminent.

The whiskey swam in her head. Noises pierced more loudly—the tub dripping, the buzz of the vanity lights, even the spindle as she rolled toilet paper around her fingers. She cursed at the blood she produced. Blood soaking fabric, blood on her skin. The memory of her father's limp hands dropping into his lap as he died.

"Kit," Luc said.

The twins' family room was just outside the bathroom door. Out there the girls were sprawled on the couch watching TV with the volume low. The open bottle of Jack was on the glass coffee table, one-quarter emptier than when they started. That and a bag of Ruffles potato chips with a tub of sour cream and onion dip.

"Kit!" Luc said more loudly.

"Hey, you all right in there?" Kit whispered through the door frame. She rattled the knob but didn't twist it. "You need something, Luc?"

"Do either of you have a pad I can borrow?" she said. "I forgot."

"Borrow?" Kit said. "I don't want it back."

"Keep, stupid," Luc said, and they both laughed like they were tired of laughing. A rumble shook the house, but it was only Kit jogging upstairs.

"Still alive in there, bitch?" Gina said.

"Yeah," Luc said. She smiled at the insult because it meant Gina hadn't changed on her, hadn't morphed into some coddler just because Luc saw her dad get killed. Luc needed her friends to stay the same. The whiskey buzz made her believe she could hide here forever with the twins and the TV and endless bags of chips, just lazing on the couch through everything, even the apocalypse itself. Never need to go back to Mom and her sniveling, her mental collapses.

When Kit knocked on the door again, Luc cracked it open and grabbed the maxi pad that appeared there. Luc came out five minutes later, but Kit had already gone off to bed. Gina was still there on the couch in her army camouflage tanktop and track pants, dragging on a cigarette and tapping it into the ashtray balanced on her knee. Her eyes were puffy from lack of sleep, and she didn't seem concerned that homeroom roll call was less than seven hours away. Across the room MTV was playing a grunge video with screaming people covered in mud.

"Hey—at least you're not pregnant," Gina said.

"It'd need to be an immaculate conception."

"You mean to tell me Quinn didn't take you right there on your kitchen counter?"

"Shut up," Luc said. She swatted at Gina's legs to make room for herself on the couch. Almost knocked over the ashtray doing it. "I told you—he just brought over a casserole. He thought I was in eighth grade."

"That's hilarious," Gina said.

"Screw you," said Luc.

"Not in your condition, thank you very much."

"You lezzie."

"You gonna talk to me or what?" Gina said, mashing out the cigarette she'd finished, one of a dozen she'd taken from her mother's purse. She set the ashtray on the coffee table and folded her legs underneath herself, getting serious. She hadn't shaved her head in a few days, so dark bristles were sprouting all over her skull.

"I'm losing my ability to give a shit," Luc said. "About everybody, but especially my ma. She's turning herself into a child. I feel like I don't really know anyone and never did. I feel totally lost. What do you do when you keep trying to make sense of things but nothing helps? What do you do when you're trying and trying to change things but you can't change anything? I mean, right now she's at home alone—and I feel neglectful, like I'm her babysitter, because she's this self-destructive wreck. For all I know she's swallowing a bunch of pills again, and tonight I'm not there to fix it. I couldn't save my dad, so how am I supposed to save her? She doesn't even know where I am."

"You want to call her?" Gina said.

"No," Luc said.

Smoke haze lingered around Gina's face. Guitar chords pounded at low volume on the TV, and even now Luc found herself dozing, eyelids coming down like an eclipse. A sticky, empty shot glass was hovering in the air beside her elbow. No—it was resting on the glass-top table, but down below that invisible glass was a man the size of a human hand. He stood on the carpet, dressed in rat hides and leaning against an iron table leg. His pink little hands clutched a ridged potato chip, and he was munching it. He used his dirty beard to wipe the grease away. But no again—there was no such thing as what she saw. Luc strained her eyelids open and with her full, wide sight she saw that her *tomte* had vanished.

TANYA SAT NAKED on the edge of her bed. It was barely dawn and mist was seeping through the woods behind the trailer. There was a chill odor that meant snow was on its way. Before the baby, she'd never have gotten up before noon, but now every morning its womb squirm woke her at seven sharp like an alarm. And Mason crowding her, tossing and groaning in his boozy sleep, kicking her awake in the dinky twin-sized bed they shared. He snored behind her now with one bare leg stretched over the covers, his naked ass pink like a peach.

A full-length mirror that was leaned against the wall let her see herself sitting stoop shouldered, red kneed, with bleached hair in tangles and fresh pimples on her face. Her breasts were swollen and sagging with heavy milk already flowing. She spread her hands on her belly where the skin stretched tight and where a thin strip had turned dark from her navel to her kootch. No fuzz down there because Mason always made her shave it, even now when her stomach bulge made the razor-work even tougher.

Last night Mason had come home drunk and he'd stood between Tan and the empty spot where she'd been pretending a wide-screen television was set. He called her Momma and begged for a taste of her milk, so Tan had unbuttoned her flannel pajama shirt and scooped one boob out of her bra cup and let him kneel between her legs and suck the tender nipple until it gave him a few clear drops. It was almost sweet how he pouted for that teat from her. Weird, but not rough and perverted like other men before him—no more belts, no hands on her throat or stuff from the kitchen stuck up inside her.

Afterward, they'd rushed to the bed and Tanya sat on Mason's prick with the lights on and he watched how they did it in this same mirror while the whole trailer shook. He only laid her now when he was drunk. Sober, he worried the baby might get poked, even though the guide-books told him there was no way. Stinking like beer and vodka, he was still gentle, and the liquor made him last so long that they both burst to-gether. He'd licked the tears off her cheeks. And if she lay awake in the dark a half hour later feeling like she wanted to slit crosses into her wrists—well, she knew that feeling was only because of her mother hor-mones flying wild. Nothing to get ashamed over.

But this morning she watched her naked mirror self, a hairless go-rilla. Her baby kicked so hard she could see her belly bulge where a knee or a foot pushed it from the inside. She felt around between her legs and then looked at her fingers to make sure there was no blood there from screwing, nothing to worry about. Then she put her face in her hands and cried without any noise.

After a spell she stood up and shivered from the cold as she lifted the full-length mirror and turned the reflective side against the wall. A space heater on the floor near the bed kept the room above freezing, but it smelled like a gas leak and gave her headaches and even then the rest of the trailer was still like a refrigerator. They had to keep the taps drip-ping water so the pipes wouldn't ice.

Tanya knelt down and patted her right hand under the bed until she found the S&W handgun. Slid it out and gripped it in her palm until her hand stopped jittering. It was a small, safe gun that Mason had picked for her—bluish steel with a black-checked grip and the safety on, ham-mer down. There were rough scratches in the metal where the serial number was supposed to be. She flicked off the safety like Mason taught her, like her asshole stepbrother taught her before that—both of them Marines, though Mason got out early because of his stomach ulcers.

She leaned over the bed and came close enough to Mason to feel his stale breath on her cheek. Sandpaper stubble on his face needed shaving, but Tanya wasn't going to say it to him. She held her breath, aimed the gun barrel an inch from his forehead. She bent her finger over the trigger, knowing that if she wanted to fire she'd need to pull hard the first time so the hammer could go all the way back. Double-action, Mason had told her, another safety feature. Now he just snored, and Tanya was careful not to touch his head with the gun. Her nipples still stung from his love bites.

For a long time there'd been these dim patches growing inside her head—images and ideas that were too dark for her to recognize most of the time. She'd darkened them on purpose so she wouldn't have to think much about them. Thoughts of her dead mother, of her rapist stepbrother, her junkie pimp ex-boyfriend. But sometimes they came back in a jolt of hard light like a camera flash, burning inside her head. It made her sick and dizzy. It laid the taste of metal on her tongue. Right now she was thinking of that five thousand dollars in the bank under her name and how that money could get her a bus ticket all the way to California, a plane ticket even.

Tanya grit her teeth until her jawbone cracked. Then she flicked the S&W safety back on and dropped the gun back under the bed where it'd been. She kissed with her pursed lips that spot on Mason's forehead where she'd aimed the gun. She pushed her fingers through his hair and Mason winced but didn't wake up. She let him keep on sleeping.

GRETA RAN. She bashed her sneakers against the rubber tread spooling out fast enough to tear off the soles. Clocking the half-hour mark, three miles on the readout. Running nowhere in the living room of her townhouse in sweatpants and a sports bra, watching CNN on mute while an ancient metal box fan propped on her coffee table cranked air gusts at her face. Endorphins pulsed toward every outpost in her body to quash that creaky pain in her spine and her knees better than any aspirin. Better than those estrogen tabs in the orange pill bottle.

Her lungs heaved. Her heart punched inside her ribs. Her body was morphing itself from a woman into the sexless ghost she'd been impersonating for so long now. She was invincible, and she wanted to capture this feeling and wield it, uncork it whenever the impulse spoke.

She needed the strength because she'd seen hundreds of ugly deaths, the very first one nineteen years ago: a teenaged runaway dumped in a tenement stairwell with her throat slit. You can tally the ways that the gore and the stench emblazon your brain, but what had struck Greta most was how the girl slept with eyes softly shut and her arm crooked like a pillow to prop her head. How that greasy sheet of blood was aged black and speckled with flies and grit. It was the violence of contrast—the sudden disparity of napping child and ugly soured blood—a signal that all existence was a fever dream, a failed and fucked-up sketch rendered in black ink against a black cosmos.

The dead she had seen were all nameless at first, but into that void of identity rushed thoughts of loved ones, mostly her daughter Sandra, especially that first time. This is how you are destroyed: dragging your own children into your mental picture of the crime scene, powerless to stop yourself. The fear that death defeats love is the worst possible injustice. But worse still, you realize, because nothing contradicts that fear, nothing proves it false or qualifies it. Nothing real. Instead, those corpses just keep calling your name at night, aiming you onward toward their empty reckoning.

At forty minutes she slowed her stride and gulped down water from a plastic bottle. She listened to the voice of her latest dead—that college professor Oscar Moberg murdered in his car. His call was now too loud to ignore. It was chanting like a blood rush on her eardrum.

She hopped off the treadmill and toweled her face dry on the way to the bathroom, twisted on the steaming shower water, stripped off her drenched clothes, checked for signs of blood—but there was nothing, just as she expected. Three days overdue already—she was headed for another dry spell.

Greta knew that Blair Moberg would be at the Piper Marina in a few hours to take part in her husband's memorial ceremony. And Greta had decided: she'd be there on the dock with Moe Arslan. She'd be there when Blair and her daughter stepped off the boat, ready there with questions. There'd be no more stalling, and no more appeasement. She'd tuck away compassion, just as she'd always done in cases like this.

IN THE MORNING there was a weightless snow dust in the air. Luc walked home from the twins' house through the hovering flakes, and she noticed when she reached her driveway that her father's Grady-White boat was gone. She guessed his fishing club buddies had already come to retrieve it. They'd latched the boat to a pickup truck and transferred it to the Piper Marina ten miles north on Lake Ontario, where the plan was that they'd dock it and get it prepped for the noon ceremony—everything arranged the way Oscar Moberg had suggested when he was half-kidding in a morbid state. *Svårmod*, he called that mood, the Swedish word for that cozy gloom that hits you like semiconscious dreams on a winter night.

Luc unlocked the front door with a key hidden under an old coffee can full of birdseed. She stepped into the living room and saw that her father's wooden scattering urn was set atop the coffee table. It was shaped like a box of cards but twice as big, engraved with a border of Viking runes. Her father's burned remains were packed inside.

Seeing the urn magnified her desperation. She wanted her father returned—here, alive, in this home that he owned with all his furniture, the objects he earned still here even though he was gone. Her scant two hours of sleep had brought her father back to life in dreams, and for a few sweet seconds after waking she believed it—before the truth flooded up and drowned her denial.

The hum of a hairdryer in the bathroom told Luc her mother was home, but the hairdryer shut down while Luc was in the kitchen pouring orange juice. She'd guzzled the juice and loaded the glass in the dishwasher by the time her mother appeared from the hallway, pressing hairspray into her bangs with one hand over her eyes to protect them from the chemicals. She wore a black dress and a black wool shawl that hung down to her knees. Her high heels clicked on the kitchen linoleum until she was startled at the sight of Luc. She took a step back and said, "Jesus!"

"Nope. Just me," Luc said.

"Where have you been? I didn't sleep I was so sick with worrying." She stammered, gestured in several directions for no apparent reason. "How could I know whether you took off on your own or if something happened—"

"You file a missing persons report?" Luc said. "Did you come looking for me?"

"Lucia, please don't be hostile. Not today. I knew you had to be at the twins' house because that's the only place you'd go. After the other night I—"

"Could've called to check. If you cared so much. Just don't even bother with the bullshit, Ma. Forget it." Luc held her breath, swallowed the rage back into her gut. Instead of exploding, she grabbed Quinn Cutler's casserole dish from the counter and spooned the cheesy slop into the wastebasket under the kitchen counter. It'd been left out overnight. It was spoiled.

"The neighbor lady made this casserole," Luc said, scraping it out in thick, dramatic globs. "And her son Quinn brought it over. Quinn Cutler was right here in your kitchen, and I let him in here. No joke." But then Luc realized she was talking to an empty kitchen. Her mother had already wandered into the living room without another word.

Luc shut herself up, suddenly unsure what she'd hoped to gain with this chiding—some maternal outburst, some eruption from a dormant fire. Anything but the lazy surrender that her mother was performing now. A show of defeat from the woman who'd once stood in the front yard bitching out the local cops for going lenient on Quinn with a noise-ordinance warning.

By the time Luc and her mother got to her Mom's Saturn, the weak film of snow had already melted off the earth. They drove northward through metallic skies full of phone wire, grassy fields with bare trees that looked like raw nervous cords, farmhouses lost in the slanted shadows of their barns. Something baroque trickled on NPR, and Luc bit at the insides of her cheeks to keep from screaming.

The parking lot at the Piper Marina was a vast stretch of old pale pavement spanning a half mile along the lakefront. Mom parked alongside the few cars huddled around a shack that looked like it had been sided with rickety driftwood. A hand-carved sign over the awning said, THE LANDING, though Luc didn't need a sign. She'd known its name practically her whole life. It was a seafood place, closed for the season since Labor Day.

A flight of wooden steps leading behind the restaurant also gave access to a back deck and an attached, elevated pier that jutted out over the water. In the summer amateurs crowded the pier with lawn chairs and dangled their fishing lines thirty feet down into the gentle waves, but now the only life up there was the seagulls scavenging the pier planks for food. Years ago, the farthest few yards of the pier had collapsed. The wooden guardrails had been restored, but some of the old pilings still jutted from the water out beyond the new limit, splintered at their heads like broken bones.

This marina was Oscar Moberg's sacred refuge, and there was his boat already in the water, already moored alone at the dock. For a while this had been Luc's refuge, too—up until she turned thirteen and abandoned her lake for some teenaged fairyland of black clouds and rock songs. Now was the first time she'd been back in those two years, and she hoped she could muster enough fight to claim it as hers again.

Luc jumped out before the car was in park. She scrambled ahead of her mother and stomped her boots onto the wood-planked dock as if enacting a war march. Two men stood farther down beside her father's boat, charter fishermen named Dale and Reggie, old friends of Oscar's. Dale leaned against the bollard that the boat was roped to. He was a lean sailor with gray hair curling out from under his Yankees cap. Reggie was a chubby black guy wrapped in waterproof rubber, flannel, and wool. He busied himself hoisting a cooler over the boat gunwale, down onto the fiberglass deck liner. Glass bottles and ice clattered inside the cooler. Molson Canadian, Luc guessed, same as ever.

The dense waters were frostbite blue and they chopped against the boat and slapped under the dock with a hollow, tuneless beat. Mom stopped two feet above the dock on the edge of the parking lot. Her face was wrenched, eyes slammed shut, and her grief emitted no sound.

"Are you coming?" Luc asked her, but she already knew the answer. She should've realized from the beginning that her mother would never agree to take part in this water burial. Mom hated the lake, and she despised those fishermen that her husband went slumming with almost as much as she despised his academic comrades on the other end of the scale.

"I told you I couldn't," Mom said. "I promised I'd come this far, but, please, I can't go out there. I'll just stay here—right here and I'll watch. The water—I can't get on that boat."

"Fine," Luc said. She turned toward Dad's boat, which had the word *Ringhorn* printed in fading crimson on the hull. She guessed her mother didn't know or had long forgotten the significance: that the *Ringhorn* was the Norse god Baldr's mammoth longship, the greatest ship of the ancient world. It was the ship that became a funeral pyre for that nearly invincible god after he was shot to death by an arrow poisoned with mistletoe—a grossly benign death, a cosmic joke. He'd been the most beloved among the Aesir, the gods of Asgard, and he was a willing plaything for their drunken parlor games. They'd slash him with axes and bludgeon him with clubs just to honor his impervious flesh. But the jealous god Loki knew Baldr's bane and tempted blind Hod to fire his arrow and incite the epidemic sorrow that would not end until the doom of all gods called Ragnarok.

Because December was well past boating season, all the marina launches were barricaded with locked gates, so Dale and Reggie had probably spent the morning unloading the Grady-White from an abandoned state boat launch a few miles down shore. Now Reggie was untying the rope from the bollard while Dale climbed into the boat and unpacked the orange life jackets from the cuddy cabin. As Dale worked he bit on his cigarette and coughed the smoke back up. Reggie held the urn for Luc while she climbed down onto the deck and secured her life jacket. He grinned solemnly as Luc loosened straps that were several years too tight and ran her fingers over her own name scrawled there in Magic Marker by an uncertain hand.

Without fanfare the twenty-two-foot *Ringhorn* chunked into gear and puttered away from the dock with Dale seated at the helm in the captain's pedestal chair. The bow cut through water thick as slush. Reggie sat on a cushioned fish box and flipped open the cooler, plucked out two Molson bottles. At the stern the outboard motor tossed back whitewater that melted into the blue expanse streaming backward toward shore, toward Luc's mother standing like a mannequin on the pavement above the dock.

They hadn't gone far before Dale piloted the boat back around toward shore and shut down the motor. The quiet was sudden enough to convince Luc she'd gone deaf, but then came the sound of water licking against the hull. The lake was empty of all vessels but theirs—an expanse of frigid blue churning up its billion jagged crests. Behind them was the long horizon, beyond which Canada waited like some unconfirmed legend. Ahead, the diminished shoreline of slate beaches and naked trees and The Landing with its rickety pier reaching out, falling short.

Dale and Reggie uncapped their beers. Dale's foamed over and he cursed at it, held it out over the water while it bubbled up spittle. He was standing in the cockpit, shadowed by the hardtop just overhead.

Luc shifted aside the urn's slide top to reveal the speckled gray ash inside. The weight of her mistakes crushed down on her hard enough to sink the boat and everyone aboard. Once upon a time was not enough. She ached to live through that day her father was killed once again so she could deflect his death away. She wanted to find him standing on that shore, alive, ready to help her fix what she had ruined so badly. But these were fantasies no truer than those *tomten* scurrying through her basement and stealing potato chip crumbs.

She raised the urn past the gunwale and over the dark waters. Dad's dust swirled—not falling, but carried on the wind, drifting like smoke and then vanishing. She shook the urn and only the thickest clouds of ash struck the water—tiny gray islands wetting and drowning.

"To Oscar," Reggie was saying.

"To Oscar," Dale repeated, and they tipped the heads of their bottles together.

Soon Dale twisted the key and the engine snarled back to life. Luc watched through the misty droplets settling on her glasses: Reggie flashing his awkward grin and Dale squinting at the oncoming shore, teeth bared and both hands on the helm like some geezer in his Cadillac. The land approached, marked by a few parked cars including Mom's Saturn and now another car just pulling in. Two joggers trotted along a shoreline trail headed toward the marina.

There was no sign of her mother anymore, but two more people were stepping from the black car that had just arrived and was now idling. A driver and a passenger rising up from their open doors in unison, both of them dressed darkly like fellow mourners. As the distance shrunk Luc saw that they were the police investigators, Greta Hurd and Muhammad Arslan.

Luc stood upright as they headed into the docks. The boat slowed and lowered its keel back down into the lake as the motor calmed to a grumble. Dale steered the starboard edge of the boat against the rubber bumpers installed along the dock and the boat lurched with the minor impact. Luc did not stumble. Reggie tossed the rope toward the bollard, but the loop dropped flat onto the dock.

Greta was crouched there on the dock with the bottom hem of her trench coat skimming the wooden boards. She took the empty rope in her hands and fastened it over the bollard. Her partner stood at the head of the concrete steps exactly where Luc's mother had promised to stay until the boat docked again.

"We thought your mother was with you," Greta said. She was there above Luc with hands offered outward, ready to lift her out of this chaos. "We need to talk to her, Luc."

"Mom was here," Luc said, "in the parking lot when we left on the boat."

Greta tapped the silver badge clipped to her belt so that Dale and Reggie could see. She said, "Rochester Police Department. Let's turn this boat off, can we?" Like churchgoers the fishermen quietly took their seats. They'd already set down their beer bottles, empty and conspicuous. Dale turned the key as instructed and the motor shuddered and died out.

"She's up there," Luc said, and she pointed skyward, aiming over Greta's shoulder toward the sun smearing its dull light through unbroken clouds. Just beneath that looming sun the elevated pier teetered on weatherworn legs that looked poised to run, and the spiny shadow it cast on the water was riddled with slices of light—gaps that had split over time in the planks. Beyond the pier's stunted limit, those tall splintered pilings jutted from the water like grave markers.

Luc was pointing because she had suddenly spotted her mother on that pier wandering out toward its farthest reach, far enough now that even the strongest arm couldn't pitch a rock to hit her. Luc wanted to scream out, but her lungs refused the air that would propel that scream. She knew in her gut that Mom wouldn't stop when she reached that guardrail barrier.

Luc announced, "She's going to jump off the end."

Investigator Arslan's immediate response to that prediction was to dart across the parking lot, crunching the concrete with his stride. He bounded up the restaurant's deck stairs while Greta sprinted behind him with her trench coat fluttering, and Luc ran last on scrawny legs that couldn't keep pace. Even the two joggers she had seen from the boat were there alongside Luc somehow, huffing with their sweat and their arms pumping.

Luc rushed with the urn still in her grip. Preserved inside it were the last pinches of her father's dust that she hadn't spread over the lake— one last handful to keep for herself. She skirted the edge of a rocky bank and above her the pier pilings shot thirty feet upright. Greta's partner had mounted onto that pier from the stairs, racing down its length toward Mom. Whatever he bellowed Luc couldn't hear over her own panting breaths. Greta scaled the steps behind Arslan, hunched now from her fatigue. The pier rumbled with their heavy footfalls.

Up through the open slats Luc watched her mother climb the wooden guardrail and swing one leg out over the precipice. She couldn't see her mother's face, couldn't gauge the intentions written there. But Luc knew, she knew even before Mom leaped, taut and deliberate at first. Her mother jumped into the empty air above the lake with her arms and legs extended like a skydiver's. But then her body struck the edge of a lone splintered piling and was snapped out of its graceful descent. She dropped limp and broken.

Luc stopped short. There was no reason to keep running. She knew her mother must have been unconscious by then because her body fell as dead weight, dropping backward and facing the pale sun above. Her loose arms curled toward that sun as if reaching for it, and the icewater took her with barely a splash.

two

CHILD OF LIGHT

Luc was eight when her mother sewed from scratch a white Luci-adagen dress with a crimson sash, long ago when Mom was happy and didn't always seem to want to flee the life she'd made with Oscar Moberg and their only daughter. Luciadagen, December thirteenth, was Luc's birthday and also the Feast of Saint Lucy, Sankta Lucia, in Sweden. Each morning on four consecutive birthdays they honored a tradition: Mom woke Luc just before dawn, both of them groggy and squinting at the bedroom light as they pulled the homemade dress over Luc's body and crowned her head with a wooden tiara hot glued with fake mistletoe leaves and ribbons. Then the white candles the size of jumbo crayons, shimmied into the four tiara holes and lit with a box of matches Mom kept in the huge plushy pocket on her bathrobe.

For each of those four consecutive years mother and daughter stole into the kitchen, keeping quiet so not to wake Oscar, who was lying in his bed by now only pretending to sleep. Careful, so not to drip candle wax into Lucia's silky blond hair. On the counter waited a tin breakfast tray printed with a mural of festive *tomten* dancing around a Christmas fire. Placed on that tray: a steaming mug of hazelnut coffee and a plate of egg-glazed buns curled into a shape called a Judge's Wig, with red saffron slivers baked into the dough. Luc carried the tray down the hallway in both hands, cautious about the coffee but always spilling a few drops that soaked into the green napkin folded there.

A one-girl procession down the hallway toward the master bedroom, and Mom following behind with the video camera held against her eye. Luc walked one step at a time like a flower girl at a wedding. The tiara candles fired light through the hall—four yellow arches clashing and melting together on the ceiling, four shadows of Luc tapering on the floor like compass arrows. In Swedish, together, mother and daughter sang the Sankta Lucia hymn that Oscar had taught them, the words that meant:

> Forgotten by the sun,
> All earth wears winter's gloom.
> Darkness surrounds us all,
> Shadows fill every room.
> Comes she with candles bright—
> Who is this child of light?
> Sankta Lucia, Sankta Lucia.

And in the bedroom Oscar raised his head, fully awake but feigning a daze, rubbing his knuckles into his eyes for effect. He gawked at Lucia as she arrived washed with light like an apparition he couldn't believe.

Four consecutive years and then it ended—because the dress no longer fit, because Mom wouldn't sew another one, because she'd forgotten to wake Luc on the morning of her thirteenth birthday, because Luc was a teenager now and eager to end these child games. Because fights started breaking out too easily. Hours, days of bickering when before there was none. Bullshit about house chores and Luc's grades and Oscar's *passive condescension*. Dad's patience was thick, but even he could slam doors hard enough to make the whole house rumble. Once he'd punched a dent in the living room wall, but then he patched it himself within an hour. Luc still remembered that punctured Sheetrock and her fear that even her sturdy shelter might soon cave in.

GRETA AND MOE WERE working four open murder cases at once, a mother lode for this time of year, even in a department with seven patrol divisions and over six hundred sworn personnel, fifty of them investigators. There was the Jane Doe from that empty lot in the Fourth Ward two days back. The corpse had to be in her seventies, found curled up in a pile of brush without any shoes or socks, but there were no visible signs of trauma. The medical examiner said it looked like natural causes but his official report was pending.

And there was the drug shooting out at the Harriet Tubman Estates. A black kid named Elroy Taft was found dead in the parking lot with a bullet in his chest and ten bags of crack in his pockets. One anonymous 911 call and Elroy was still breathing when cops responded, but he was dead by the time the ambulance pulled up. Moe Arslan had cased the neighborhood with officers and got squat for info from the paranoid faces peering through chain-locked doorways, saying, "Didn't see nothing. Didn't hear nothing, neither." Everyone lying to survive.

And one week prior was that domestic out on Park Avenue where two gays got into a kitchen knife fight. One dead from a throat slash, the other listed as satisfactory at Genesee. Greta and Moe had logged four hours at that crime scene picking through the strewn groceries, the battered pots and pans. Seemed like the boys had started off pitching eggs at each other, then graduated to knives. At the scene a paring knife was embedded in the wall just over a cheap print of that van Gogh French café painting. The victim himself was sitting upright in a kitchen chair, head nodded forward like he was taking a nap, blood soaking his T-shirt in the shape of a bib.

But the one that tortured Greta worst was this Oscar Moberg case, not just because of her noontime disaster at the Piper Marina, and not just because the local media were hounding her, loading up her voicemail with messages. A crime writer for the *Democrat and Chronicle* had accosted her at the front doors of Public Safety that morning, scrounging for quotes—and all this morbid interest even before Blair Moberg goes and tosses herself off the pier, instantly doubling the feature story appeal.

Only a few hours had passed since the marina, and already Greta was back at Public Safety again, chasing down the possibilities. She and her partner Moe were sequestered in a conference room watching black-and-white Shop-Mor security surveillance images play out on the television. Bowed wide-angle shots of the superstore aisles, customers bending and swelling as they pushed their carts toward the camera. Everything snuffed in dead quiet, surreal, as the digital clock on the edge of the frame tallied up time.

Greta and Moe were scrutinizing these security tapes they'd collected from Lloyd Lauderschmidt, the store manager at the Hammersport Shop-Mor. The footage was from the previous morning when Blair had clocked out sick after an argument with a customer, according to Lloyd's original statement.

Greta was hunched over the conference table, squinting at the television and sipping from her takeout coffee cup. When she pressed buttons on the remote the lazy shoppers skittered and bounced down the aisle like Keystone Kops. Moe sat across from her, shining a penlight onto his notebook and jotting notes there.

"Here it is," Greta said. She played the tape at regular speed, and they watched the moment when Blair Moberg first enters the on-camera drama. She wears her Shop-Mor uniform and sidesteps down the aisle as she straightens detergent boxes on the shelf. She crouches down to tidy something on the lowest shelf, and just then someone else steps into the shot. A puff of bleached hair, a dark leather jacket. The new actress onstage shoves Blair Moberg in the shoulder, almost knocks her onto the floor, but Blair rights herself and stands upright. The woman lingers in the bottom edge of the frame. Sometimes she leans entirely out of it, but mostly her head and one arm are visible. She's jabbing her finger toward Blair. Surely she's blabbering a wealth of information, but all of it is completely lost to this soundless recording.

"Can you see what Blair is saying back?" Greta asked her partner. The image was washed-out and bluish, the type that would fizzle apart if you tried to magnify it.

"She's mostly just responding—yes-and-no answers," Moe said.

"So we agree that this argument appears unprovoked by Blair?"

Moe said, "And therefore it appears suspect, yes."

Greta pressed STOP on the remote because she knew there would be nothing more. Not on this tape. They'd already seen the mystery woman's arrival and departure on the tape that monitored the store's front entrance. They'd watched it ten times or more and gathered nothing beyond the immediate evidence that this woman was in late-term pregnancy, or pretending to be.

"I'm not sure we're going to get anything more from this," Greta said. "She's too far out of the frame. If the angle was on her mouth, we could maybe get a lip-reader."

"The patch on her jacket was visible a few times when she leaned forward," Moe said. "It could be a rock band symbol—or a gang rocker, which is illegal to wear in public." He shined his penlight onto his notepad as if to illustrate. There on a page of its own he'd sketched a cartoonish rendition of a human skull wearing a miner's hardhat, headlight and all. On the table between them was a still-frame Xerox of the mystery woman entering the Shop-Mor with the back of her leather jacket exposed. Printed, painted, or pinned to her jacket—they couldn't quite tell—was that same skeletal miner's head that Moe had rendered his sketch from.

Greta: "But if it's an unknown group—maybe something new, underground."

Moe: "We'll send it around, see if anybody has seen it before. And we'll have Major Crimes run intelligence reports in case it has popped up before. Narcotics, too."

"This might be something," Greta said. Could've been the coffee, maybe the estrogen pills kicking in, but a new jolt of energy had roused her from a stupor. She'd thought the case was headed nowhere after Blair Moberg's dive off the pier, but now—now this footage might feed them something edible. Still, Greta had learned early in her career that murder cases weren't like autopsies. They didn't lie down dead for your scalpel to pick at. They squirmed and kicked and screamed right up until you had them buried in the hole.

AN ORANGE SUN was trapped low in the scrawny trees behind the Hansons' place when Mason and Tanya showed up for a special Tuesday afternoon church meeting. Buck and his old lady Brenda had their own actual house in an old cul-de-sac where mostly grannies lived and where the trees in the yards were taller than the houses. Buck's place was two floors but level two was stunted—two bedrooms with ceilings sloped by the roof. The driveway was gravel and steep, loaded already with cars aimed toward the garage.

Buck himself was headed down the driveway while Mason parked the car on the street by the mailbox. Buck was past fifty, with a thick white beard that came down almost to his belly—a belly like a grain sack stretching out his blue tanktop. He was holding a beer slipped inside a cozy, and he tipped off his baseball cap to greet them, showing a stretch of hairless scalp. In the back his hair went on forever, tied in knuckled knots like a second spine. He was tinted red and jolly, nose the shape and look of a lemon. Tough to see him and believe he was bloodthirsty, but Tanya knew. She smiled at him and waved anyhow. Despite the truth, she liked her visits here, the only real home she'd visited in years without breaking in through a window.

On the dying brown lawn Buck hugged her and snuck a bearded kiss on her ear. He said, "How's the little momma holding up? How about Brick Jr.?"

"He's already kicking ass in there," Mason said. "Shadowboxing."

They went into the house through the garage, where the door opened onto a kitchen that smelled like sausage and pasta sauce. Shining wood floors in the kitchen and farther on some carpets so nice that Tan could've slept on them if she had to. Over by the sliding back door were a table and a hutch that Buck had built, china plates stacked behind the glass.

The sliding door showed off the backyard deck and the hot tub. The Hansons' dog, Furnace, sat back there watching them, still as stone except for a twitch in one tall cropped ear when he saw the new guests arrive. His breath steamed on the door glass, where his snout and paw prints were streaked. He was a two-year-old Doberman that never barked, though you could hear his low angry growling whenever you got close.

Brenda Hanson was fixing a spaghetti dinner in a huge silver pot, same as ever. Buck's old lady had to be over forty, 250 on the scale, mostly butt and thighs that made her teeter in her high heels like a rhino walking upright on wineglasses. She blew Tan a kiss and said, "Hey, there, no baby yet?" Tanya touched her inflated gut and sighed.

Brenda and Buck were married almost twenty years but kept two separate bedrooms. And Tanya knew this only because she saw the proof herself once when she went upstairs to use the toilet. Brenda's room was down the hall from Buck's and it was loaded up with stuff that she hoarded for her weekend garage sales—dolls, baseball caps, kitchen gadgets, men's shirts, and towels, lots of it still in sealed packages. She was always asking Tan and Mason if they had any stuff they wanted to sell off, forgetting they had almost nothing.

From the fridge Buck fetched Mason a beer and Tanya a Diet Coke, then they went on into the living room where the leather couch and matching chairs sat around a couple thousand bucks in stereo and big-screen TV shit, a record turntable, laserdisc player. That psycho guy Ox was sitting in an armchair with his wild hair pulled back almost nice for church. When they came into the room Ox didn't look away from the TV, which was showing close-up porn in a bigger scale than life—all pink skin and hair and juice like some abstract art you couldn't figure out. Ox smirked at the movie and grumbled something to himself that Tanya didn't even try to hear. She took a swig of her Diet Coke to keep the bile down. Didn't look again at the TV because she'd seen too much ugly fucking already in her life.

Most of the other Crew folks weren't around yet, but the one named Paula was there, sitting cross-legged on the floor and leaning against the couch with a Game Boy gripped in both her hands, thumbs punching and eyes bugging out. She pressed the "pause" button and looked up and nodded and said, "Hey, motherfuckers," and went back to her playing. They had nicknamed Paula Dread because her hair was dreadlocked in thick brown tufts like cattails from a swamp. The sides of her skull were shaved and tattooed with tribal-looking swirls. They also called her Dread because she was a bitter cruel bitch, hardly of legal drinking age but already ruined. To prove it she had a deep pink scar curling across her throat like a big psycho smile. Story went: she had her throat sliced by some rapist bastard and still didn't die, ten years old when it happened.

Dread was nobody's old lady. Instead, she was the only bitch allowed to wear the Crew patch—plus she was a wide-open dyke with scabs on her knees who challenged men twice her size to drinking and drugging contests that landed them in clinics to get their stomachs pumped. Tanya almost liked Dread, but then again she stank like rotted meat and flaunted her furry legs and armpits. She invited your hate with a chapped-lip smile.

To get away from the porn Tanya left Mason and Buck and the others, went back into the Hansons' kitchen, where Brenda was lifting the top off a steaming Crock-Pot and stirring up the meatball and Italian sausage sauce with a wooden spoon. Out back Furnace growled, and behind him the setting sun cast the lawn in gold and laid the trees' naked shadows long across the ground. Brenda tasted her own sauce and gave it a thumbs-up while Tanya drew herself a seat at the breakfast table. She sat down with her legs stretched out, moaning from the relief.

"It's almost done," Brenda said.

"Still a few weeks away," Tanya said.

"I meant the spaghetti, but all right. You having a boy or a girl?"

"Mason thinks it's a boy."

"But he don't got the kid in his stomach, does he?" said Brenda.

"I don't know what the hell it is, except uncomfortable."

"Hey, you're lucky to have it come this far. Did I ever tell you I was pregnant once?" Brenda patted the sweat off her face with a dish towel and took another seat at the breakfast table. She'd hushed down far enough so that what she said would be covered by that porno music and the grunting and the blips from Dread's Game Boy. Only Tanya and the baby could hear her. "It was about fifteen years back. I told Buck four months into it hoping he'd do the proud papa dance like your Mason did. Instead, he tells me to get rid of it, gives me the money right away, and drives me over on the back of his bike to where they do those procedures. He said there was no way he was bringing a kid into his twisted world. The point is I did it—and no regrets anymore. Buck was right thinking we'd be shit parents."

Tanya put her hand over Brenda's swollen fingers. So much flesh in the woman's face that she looked sad even when she wasn't. They didn't say anything while Tanya thought about what Brenda was telling her.

"I'm gonna be a good mom," Tanya protested.

"I don't doubt it," Brenda said.

"And Mason's all psyched about it."

"Which one, though?" Brenda asked her. "Brick or the baby?"

"What do you mean?" Tanya said, but now other voices were rising up the driveway and bouncing through the garage. She recognized Mitch Wendt's parade of pomp and noise.

"Which would you pick if you had to, Brick or the baby?" Brenda said.

Tanya looked to Furnace like he'd answer for her. He blinked his onyx eyes.

The garage door came open and Mitch sauntered in with his new girlfriend under his arm and a six of beer in his hand. Five really, because one beer was gone and he was gripping the pack by its empty loop. The girlfriend looked about twelve, with crimped hair bigger than her head and a cigarette tucked into the corner of her mouth.

"No smoking in the house, Blisters," Brenda told Mitch.

"Oh, sorry," the girlfriend said, and she ducked under his arm back out the door to finish her smoke. Mitch smacked her ass on the way out. Tanya felt cold, and she saw through the sliding glass that Furnace's hide was shivering, too. There was no forgetting that this place was just a mirage of normal life—because Brenda snorted more coke per day than she took sugar in her morning coffee, because in a secret room blasted out of a basement corner was a meth lab big enough to make tweakers out of a whole city middle school, because the second time Tanya had come to this house, more than a year ago, Buck Hanson paid Mason fifty bucks for Tanya to blow him in that hot tub out on the deck, and she'd done it for ten minutes crying and gagging and wishing he'd hurry up and finish, and Brenda Hanson had watched.

LUC WASHED HER HANDS at one of three sinks in a Genesee Community Hospital restroom, and as she rinsed away the soap she realized this was the same sink she'd used three days before, back when she believed that the worst hell of her life was past. Clear now that her father's death had sent out ripples like poison waves from an atomic bomb.

The girl in the restroom mirror looking back was not Lucia Moberg, not Luc, not the girl she recognized with the black eye shadow and lipstick, the white-powdered face. Instead: these pale lips and swollen eyes that were bigger, more alert, raw pink around the lids. At the twins' house overnight she'd hacked down her black-dyed hair with a pair of scissors because she was eager to be rid of it. Now her cropped hair was feathering upward around her ears and her natural blond had sprouted at the roots as if she were beginning to molt.

She headed back to the room where they were keeping her mother, still unconscious seven hours after her head had struck a pier piling. The nurses with their voices hushed had called it an accident because they believed such a word might help Luc to stop feeling that she'd been forced into the center of a storm circling and bearing down on her from all directions. *The Fall,* they called it, as if her mother's botched suicide had taken on the scope of an entire season.

Because the nurses believed it would help, they had also contacted Luc's maternal grandmother Norma Crowley at her home three hours away in Binghamton. And she'd arrived already, now hovering at Mom's bedside like she'd been there from the start. But Norma hadn't talked to

the Mobergs in months. This was all news for her, even the widely pub-
licized murder of her son-in-law that she'd somehow missed or subcon-
sciously ignored. Yet she'd rushed to the rescue, encamped herself in
the hospital room sipping bottomless cups of coffee. The woman lived
off coffee, apparently, and so she was mildly humpbacked, brittle, not
more than a hundred pounds. Luc guessed she was in her midsixties,
but frankly she had no idea.

The only equipment monitoring Blair Moberg's battered sleep was
the electrodes stuck to her chest to track her heart rate. The IV bag was
dripping its clear liquid food down through plastic tubing into a needle
embedded in her wrist. The doctor had explained that there was slight
hemorrhaging and swelling and no one could predict what damage had
been done. A specialist had exhibited his backlit CAT scans and pointed
out the dark smudges of bruising, the contusions on the temporal lobes,
her temples—the left side where she'd struck the broken pier piling and
the right side where her brain had ricocheted against the opposite side
of her skull. *Contra coup,* they'd called that ricochet effect.

Luc winced when they mentioned the impact. She couldn't ever forget the soundless jolt of her mother's head against wood, and that instant certainty that her mother had been killed or would soon drown or
freeze to death in that frigid water. But then the *Ringhorn* had pulled
her body out so fast—even faster than Greta Hurd or her partner could
scramble back down the pier steps. Dale had sparked that boat back to
life and Reggie unmoored it, more agile than you'd expect for his heft.
They swung toward the pier and by a teamed effort pulled Mom onto
the boat and laid her out on the deck covered in blankets they'd found
in the cabin. A steady heartbeat, no bleeding gash on her skull, she
coughed up water and then breathed on her own.

Mom's doctor was named Mahoney. He was a gray-haired Canadian
no taller than Luc who spoke with a trancelike calm. He'd advised them
to talk directly to her because familiar voices might bring her out faster.
For a while Norma tried: she recounted stories about long-dead aunts
and summer camping trips, but she ran out of worthwhile memories after an hour or so. Luc couldn't muster anything, and she couldn't bear

sitting in that plastic chair beside the bed watching the IV drip, watching the minute twitches in her mother's fingers, watching nothing. Mom had broken one leg in the fall, and now it was wrapped in a cast that Luc couldn't bring herself to touch. Mom was alive, but over the hours she'd become a kind of object to Luc, an immobile weight to which Luc could attach only the faintest emotions. Her mother, but not her mother. Luc lived among strangers now, and every second inside that room she fretted over how she should be feeling.

Norma Crowley leaned over the bed, adjusted the sheets, combed her hair, dabbed away the moisture on Blair's lips with a tissue from her purse. When her chores were done, she went to the cafeteria for more coffee and came back to watch the annual run of *The Grinch Who Stole Christmas* on the TV set mounted in the corner. Luc knew that Norma was letting herself believe Blair had fallen from the pier by accident. When Luc would listen, Norma blamed herself for failing to show up and rescue everyone sooner, as if she had any more power than Luc to alter what happened.

"You know she broke this same leg when she was little," Norma said. She stroked the smooth plaster cast and watched the TV with her mouth gaping open. "She was a tomboy like you, always being crazy with her bicycle."

"I'm not really a tomboy," Luc said.

"Well, not much anymore. You're growing up."

It was the change in Mom's breath that alerted them first. Her long, sleepy inhalations that had become white noise in the room—now suddenly quickening, faltering, and loud enough to turn Norma's attention from the TV set. Mom's IV arm twitched as it had done before, but this time more forcefully, pulling the tubing taut. Norma gulped down the last of her coffee and put the empty cup on the bedside tray.

"Should we call a nurse?" Luc said.

"Tilt the bed up farther," Norma instructed. "Give her some leverage."

Luc pressed the button and the top third of the bed hummed another fifteen degrees upward. Her mother gave a startled grunt from deep in her throat. Her eyes darted under her closed lids like she was battling a nightmare in REM sleep.

Norma stood halfway up and hunched over the bed rail. She put a hand on her daughter's shoulder. "Blair? Blair, can you hear me? It's your mother."

Mom mouthed something that came out as gibberish. Her IV hand swiped across her stomach and anchored there. Then her other hand also pressed into the thin gown covering her navel. Her fingers searched and her back arched away from the mattress and she moaned deep and guttural. She sucked in a deep, deliberate breath before her eyes broke open. Those eyes looked first at Luc, then at the TV set, where the Grinch's scrawny dog hung by a rope from the edge of a snowy cliff.

"Did you see that?" Norma asked. She was already thumbing the nurse call button on the wall above the bed. "Did you see her open her eyes?"

"Yes," Luc said. She felt scraped out, like an empty melon rind.

"Blair? Blair?" Norma insisted. She kept jostling her daughter's shoulder.

"Maybe you shouldn't—" Luc started, but her words were too weak for Norma to hear. Mom again prodded blindly at her stomach, and Luc found herself parroting the gesture against her own body.

"Mm—" Mom complained.

"Blair? Can you hear me?" said Norma.

Her eyes were open again, blinking lazily.

"Ma?" she said more clearly. "Wha—?"

"You're in a hospital, honey," said Norma. "You're just waking up. There's a nurse coming. Honey, calm down. You're in a hospital. You see?"

Mom's fingers worked furiously on her belly, like she meant to dig through her skin and yank out her organs. Her breath shuddered. Her body jerked. "Where—my baby?"

Luc's throat tightened and her hands wrenched the metal bed rail as her apathy shrunk like ice in hot soup. Someone arrived in the doorway, a nurse saying, "Oh, goodness—she's awake," and then disappearing again.

"My baby," Mom said with both hands bunching up her gown. She winced, and Luc wondered which of her injuries had sent its pain signal first. The IV was still attached to her swinging arm, and the metal stand rolled forward on its wheels and knocked against the armrest on Luc's chair. The stand teetered, and Luc grabbed for her mother's arm to stop her. Luc could feel the forearm muscles hard and hot as firewood. Her wild eyes turned on Luc again—drilled into her, petrified.

"Let go!" Mom screamed.

Luc released her grip. She said, "Mom."

"No—" she said. "Oscar? Oscar?"

And the nurses in their aqua uniforms enveloped the bed, asking, "Can you tell us your name? Do you know what day it is?"

"Blair," she said. "My husband. What happened? My leg—"

"Your leg has been broken, Blair. Could you tell me what year it is?"

"What year?"

"Can you tell me the year? It's to see if you—"

"Nine—nineteen seventy-seven," Blair said. "What did you do with my baby?"

HOURS OF SHOP-MOR security tapes and Greta found herself starved and claustrophobic, so she stepped out to order drive-through burgers and fries for herself, a roast beef sandwich for Moe. Coming back, she parked in the Civic Center garage and on foot crossed the courtyard paved with the same drab concrete as the Public Safety Building ahead, the cold gray Hall of Justice on the right, the L-shaped jail wing hugging one corner of the lot. Public Safety was a huge concrete box with windows, topped by a 911 transmitter that resembled a crappy miniature Eiffel Tower. She smoked a cigarette by the entrance before going back inside.

On the ground floor she passed the glass panes that overlooked the building's daycare center. Nobody around at this hour, but in the daytime there were some thirty kids, partitioned by age and overseen by child-development students from the downtown Metro Center. The daycare area was a gymnasium floored with rubber multicolored puzzle pieces where babies sat in circles sucking on chew toys and toddlers finger-painted at stunted plastic picnic tables. But tonight the room was dark and abandoned, and Greta missed those kids because watching them helped brush the dirt of death out of her mind. Sometimes she wished she could pick one out of the litter and start her parenting from scratch, maybe see if she didn't fail the mother job the second time.

Her cubicle was on the fourth floor in an open space with all the other Special Crimes investigators, desks separated by rickety portable partitions. Her desk and filing cabinet were sparsely decorated: an engagement portrait of Sandy and Max and a large plastic jar of Bavarian pretzels. She set her fast food bags on the desk and fished Moe's roast beef out of a spilled pile of French fries. He was already coming toward her desk before she could deliver it to him.

Moe said, "Two things. I just called over to the hospital for a status check. The Moberg woman is conscious and talking, as of an hour ago. They're telling me they suspect possible amnesia. Do you buy that?"

Greta handed him his sandwich. She said, "I don't know yet. I'm probably going down there after I finish up here. What's the other thing?"

"The guys in Narc recognized the skeleton miner symbol because they saw it recently on a fence they collared—a small-timer. When they asked him about it he claimed it was a heavy metal band called"—Moe consulted his notepad—"Skullcracker. He was quite obviously being untruthful with them."

"So what are we dealing with? A gang hit?" Greta asked.

"What I know is his name's Mitchell Wendt, the guy they collared. He's been in custody for possession a few times, disorderlies, assault. If there's a gang involved, the Narc guys aren't building any conspiracy charges, so there's no intel on such a gang as of yet. Certainly nothing like contract murder. He's not in custody at the moment but he has outstanding warrants. Major Crimes already put him on the wanted board for us."

"Going public with footage of the skull jacket woman won't get us anywhere."

"Not unless we want to scare them way underground," Moe concurred.

"So we wait," Greta said, spitting out the final word. She hated the inevitable stillness that followed these revelations because it made her feel like she was holding a live grenade that nobody would let her hurl. She chewed on her hamburger and tried to forget about it, picking out the limp bitter pickles that she hated.

After dinner and paperwork Greta took the short drive over to the hospital and began the long lobby wait for Blair Moberg's doctor. When he finally arrived he was wearing a stark white lab coat that clashed against the dark hair on the backs of his hands and his face. He held against his chest a manila file thick with papers. "Fred Mahoney," he said twice to introduce himself. The ID badge on his lapel said the same.

"I need to see her as soon as I can," Greta said.

"You understand she's deeply disoriented and recovering. She can't be stressed."

"We're doing a murder investigation," Greta reminded him.

"All I'm asking is that you take it easy," he said. "She's not going to be very lucid because she's recovering from a head injury and she's on heavy painkillers and sedatives. Don't push her to remember, because all that's going to do is confuse her."

On the way up Mahoney explained that Blair Moberg appeared to be suffering some variety of amnesia, but the certainty of brain damage hadn't yet been determined. Scans showed contusions on the temporal lobes of her cerebrum, in keeping with the injury she sustained when she struck her head during her fall, taking into account any possible damage caused by the anoxia and the minor hypothermia she suffered from her near drowning. Memory could return in a day or two, maybe weeks or much longer.

They were alone in the elevator when Mahoney said, "There is an outside possibility of a nonorganic, psychological cause. It's called dissociative amnesia—the result of some emotional trauma. The fact of her husband's death, and her earlier suicide attempt—they're the sort of events that commonly precipitate dissociative amnesia. With that type, recovery is usually fairly spontaneous and can be helped along by hypnosis and similar therapies, but the length of the condition is an unknown factor. Still, I have to stress that we don't know the basis of this amnesia just yet, and we might never know. What we can say is it's retrograde. She's forgotten such a large chunk of the past that she thinks it's nineteen seventy-seven."

"Nineteen-seventy-seven," Greta said as she shook her incredulous head.

They exited the elevator and made their way past the nurse's desk. On the way Mahoney admitted to Greta that such a long time span—fifteen years—was nearly undocumented and further suggested that brain injury was most likely, since cases of psychological amnesia often exhibit much shorter temporal blackouts. A few hours, maybe a day—whatever's enough to block out a precipitating stressful or traumatic event.

"So we can't rule out a psychological motive?" Greta said.

"Not totally, no," the doctor said.

"Or even outright fabrication?" asked Greta.

The doctor winced and said, "Highly unlikely, considering the real evidence of damage and the degree of it. I'd have to say she's not faking, but I can't be one hundred percent."

Blair was alone in her room, cocooned by the thin curtain drawn between her bed and the empty bed beside her. The TV was on but muted—showing a news broadcast of President Clinton speaking at some black-tie function. Mahoney entered first and slipped aside the curtain. He greeted Blair in a hushed, reverent tone, then he consulted the nurse's report clipped to the foot of the bed. Blair was propped upright with a lunch tray elevated over her lap. She was chopping a thawed hunk of Salisbury steak with a plastic fork, frowning at it.

"How are you feeling?" Mahoney said.

Blair didn't answer. She was entranced by Clinton on the TV, dropping her mouth open to receive a forkful of beef that she'd stalled halfway up from the plate. Other than the clunky cast on her leg there were no visible injuries. But Blair seemed ill, dazed, only half-aware of the doctor's presence, and she hadn't noticed Greta at all.

"Blair?" Mahoney said. "How are you feeling?"

This time she set her eyes on him and blinked in slow motion. "My head," she told him, circling her open palm over her forehead. Her left cornea was flushed with a deep red blotch of capillaries.

"Are you in pain?" the doctor asked.

"It's just—it's. Tight. And woozy. I can't think."

"I don't know if TV is exactly a good idea," he told her.

"I wanted—see it," Blair said. She scooped the remote off the night-stand and presented it to Mahoney, to Greta. She said, "This thing," and then she let it drop onto the sheets beside her.

"The remote?" said Mahoney.

"Right. And look." Blair lifted a disposable plastic water cup from her lunch tray and showed it to them. It was covered by an aluminum seal with overhang tabs for easy peel-away. "See this?" she said.

"Yes, I've seen those," said Dr. Mahoney.

Blair nodded and turned toward the window overlooking the Rochester cityscape. A light dusting of snow had begun to drop from the flat gray heavens.

"Blair? Blair, I have someone here to see you," said Mahoney.

Greta stepped toward the bed. "My name is Greta Hurd. I'm a homicide investigator."

Blair nodded again at the window. The tendons in her neck were taut as guitar strings. Her bloodshot eye swam with moisture that broke free and streaked along the edge of her nose. She said, "My husband is dead. They told me that. The nurses when I asked, said he was. Somebody." She winced, and cupped her skull in her hand, shuddering. It was agonizing to watch, but Greta moved closer and slowly crouched into the chair beside the bed.

Greta said, "I'm sorry I upset you, Blair. I'm just trying to help."

"I don't remember you," Blair said.

"We've never met before."

"Did you see her?" Blair said. "Lucia?"

Mahoney cut in: "Blair, we weren't sure if you were ready to see Lucia again just yet."

"She's fifteen—fifteen years. Almost sixteen they said. I saw her in my dream. When I woke up and I didn't have the baby. My mother, and Lucia was on this side."

"That wasn't a dream, Blair," Mahoney said.

"Everything keeps changing." Somehow her eyes looked both alert and languid, edging on sleep. She seemed to be ratcheting through levels of consciousness and unable to find a lock. She said, "Where is my mother?"

"She's here in the hospital," said Mahoney. "Would you like to see her?"

"My father? I don't want to see them. Both. I just want to see Lucia."

"How long have you been married, Blair?" Greta asked.

She knuckled a tear from her eye. "I don't know. Two months. But they're saying more. Maybe fifteen years. The time is—on the TV. I don't know what anything is."

"What was the last thing you remember before you woke up?"

"I was coming here—but not this hospital," Blair said. "Oscar drove. I was—having my baby? In the hospital, in the bed, waiting, and I woke up here."

"What day was it? Do you remember?"

"No," Blair said. Then she nodded. "Yes. St. Lucy's Day. Oscar told me. December thirteen. We named her Lucia if she was born—we decided. If she was a girl. Luke for a boy."

Greta struggled to remember 1977 and instead produced a haze of impressions layered over by almost sixteen years of solid memories. She recalled Jimmy Carter and the Incredible Hulk, but she couldn't dredge a scrap of her own life except to realize it was the year before her separation, the year before she'd moved into the same meager apartment where she still held a lease today. Cold dull nights as a patrol cop in the cab of her cruiser, all those domestic calls—squalid, angry families worse off than hers had ever been. The year she'd finally permitted her job to split open her chest and consume her heart.

"Do you know what happened to your husband, Blair?" Greta asked her.

mind. Instead, she panicked and combed the house like a guard dog sniffing for danger signs. Caught the stench of stale coffee down the hallway, heard Letterman on TV. Gramma Norma was in the breakfast nook hunched over the table with two fingers hooked through the handle of her coffee mug. On the table was a Ziploc baggie full of tissues and a cordless phone that had rung five times since they'd come back from the hospital, each time Norma's husband John calling from their house in Binghamton and begging for directions on how to work the dishwasher or the dryer or the stovetop range. *Grandpa* John, Luc supposed.

"Did you hear something?" Luc asked.

"Hear what?" Norma said. "The phone? Maybe it was the TV."

"No. I thought I heard something. I don't know."

"I'm sure she'll be fine, Lucia," said Norma. "She was just a little dis-oriented at first, that's all. You watch—by tomorrow she'll be all settled again, after she calms down. She's just so lucky it wasn't worse. To think she could've fallen like that. I can't figure it—"

"She doesn't want to remember," said Luc.

"Remember what, honey?"

"Fifteen years—my whole life," she said. "The length of her mar-riage. How am I supposed to look her in the face?"

"I don't understand what you're saying," Norma complained.

"There's a lot you don't know. She tried to kill herself two days ago, for starters. And she didn't think of me, what might happen to me. Leaving me alone, with nobody, and how much that would . . ." She opened her mouth, shook her head to dislodge some final declaration, but nothing came.

"Luc, she—she didn't mean to do that," Norma said.

"Quit fooling yourself. She didn't fall. She jumped."

"Your mother wouldn't do anything like that," said Norma. "She should've called me after what happened to your father. I would've come earlier, right away."

"Why?" Luc demanded. "So you could bitch at her again for marry-ing Dad? Maybe you could gloat about my dad getting killed? You should open your eyes a little."

Luc stormed back downstairs toward her room. She couldn't calm her heart that rattled like a film tripping off its reel. No guns in the house to protect her, but in her pocket Luc carried the leather-sheathed hunting knife her father had kept under his bed for so many years. His security in case anyone ever broke in, but Dad had never expected that those people, whoever they were, would be waiting to ambush him out in the open world away from the safety of his home.

In the basement she clicked on every possible light switch and pulled the strings on every possible bulb. She crouched down beside the dryer and lifted the machine off balance. Gobs of dust underneath, stray coins, but no money envelope lying where Luc had seen it only two nights before. She closed her eyes tight, but the truth was still the same when she opened them. She snarled into her cold grimy hands speckled with flecks of rust.

Then she got up to check the back basement door and it was locked. Took the key off the nail and disengaged the deadbolt, cracked the door open. The backyard was dark and quiet except for the leaves shifting in the wind. The pool was humped like a barrow, a black silhouette.

She stepped outside and felt the chill pucker her skin, the ground moisture seeping into her socks. The Mobergs' yard was five feet lower than the surrounding yards, fortified by stone walls like a mass grave still unfilled. To the left, five feet up, was Quinn and his mom's driveway and detached garage, the garage door open with light spilling out. A long formless shadow shifting in that light.

Luc approached the stone wall and planted her hands on the cold pavement above. She hoisted herself up. For leverage, she hooked her toes against an outcropped stone in the rock wall, but it broke away and she skinned an elbow, hissed, scraped her knuckles. The ache in her braced right arm refused to fade away. Clumsily she stood, and her own shadow drew itself down the length of Quinn's driveway toward his parked gray Thunderbird pocked with rust spots.

Quinn was in his garage tending his motorcycle, wiping his hands on a greasy rag. The motorcycle was propped on its kickstand over an outstretched blanket that was loaded with tools and shining silver parts—gaskets, plugs, cylinders, whatever—that he'd amputated from the bike. He surveyed his work like a surgeon only halfway through his procedure.

Luc was almost inside the garage before Quinn spotted her.

"Shit," he said. He backstepped, kicked a monkey wrench with his heel.

"Sorry," Luc said. "I saw a light on. Didn't mean to scare you."

Quinn eyed her hands looming beside her hips. Her left hand was gripping the knife.

"Oh, oh shit," Luc said. She transferred the knife from one hand to the other, then dug into her pocket for the sheath, covered it up, saying, "I'm sorry. I was sneaking around because I thought I heard something in my house—in my yard—I don't know—but it was probably just me going crazy. I was scared, so I had this knife. I just saw your light on and I thought—"

Quinn nodded. He let his shoulders sag a little.

"I didn't come over to murder you," Luc said. "Honest."

Quinn finally spoke. He said, "That's good news."

"I feel like such a freak."

"Well, you're wandering around in the dark with a knife. That's pretty freaky."

"I know," Luc said. "I'm sorry. Really. I just wanted to come say hi."

"Hi, then." Quinn dropped the rag on the seat of his bicycle and hunkered down over a six-pack of Honey Brown sitting on the cement garage floor. Three of them were empties, but Quinn took a full one and uncapped it. "Want a beer?" he said.

"No thanks," Luc said. "Man, I'm really sorry."

"Forget it. The beer was making me groggy, but you woke me right up, no question. I was just tinkering with my bike, even though there's nothing wrong with it. I just get curious, you know? Tighten things up, some modifications. See if I can get it to run more badass."

"It's like two o'clock in the morning. Kind of weird to be doing it now."

"Can't sleep," Quinn said. He took a long swig while Luc thought of the time she'd seen him in his front yard growling along with heavy metal music on his boom box, holding a rubber bicycle handle instead of a microphone. That was an almost-bygone Quinn, the one who used to yell "Panties!" at girls who walked down the sidewalk past his house. Back then Luc and the twins thought he was probably mildly retarded, but over the years something had changed her thinking. Something inside of her or inside Quinn, she couldn't tell which.

"Mind if I ask you something?" he said as he rubbed the back of his neck.

She felt drunk, like gravity was letting go of her. She managed to say, "Sure."

"I heard about your ma today. I'm sorry for all this stuff you're going through."

"Thanks," Luc said. "Is that a question?"

"Naw. I mean, her and me had problems, you know, but what happened to her—"

"She did it herself," Luc said. "It didn't happen to her."

"She did that jump herself, on purpose? If I'm not getting into your business."

"No, it's fine," Luc said. "She tried to kill herself already, the day before, by taking all these pills. But she puked them up. Now she's in the hospital and her head's all messed up. She banged it pretty bad, she almost drowned—but the doctors have been doing their tests, their CAT scans and whatever. She was unconscious for hours before she came out of it."

"I'm just sorry I was such a royal asshole to her," Quinn said.

"Past tense?" said Luc.

"Yeah—everybody's got to grow up, I guess."

It had been at least a year since Mom had even mentioned Quinn's name. She'd still scowl whenever she noticed him around, but not with that former venom. Luc understood now that the change was because Quinn had grown more subdued, more sober, like he'd survived some crisis. Luc didn't know what had changed him. Maybe it was his father splitting, but that happened long before she even knew him, before his teenaged wasteland years. Maybe it was that friend of his who the year before got drunk and drowned trying to swim across the Erie Canal in the middle of the night.

Luc said, "Something's messed up with my mom, though. It's crazy. She didn't recognize me and she thinks it's nineteen seventy-seven. Dead serious."

"Holy shit," Quinn said. He took a seat in a fold-out lawnchair. In a few more seconds his throat had cocked down the rest of his beer. Even in this weather Quinn was wearing a tanktop that bared the compact muscles on his shoulders and his hairless arms.

"I'm totally lost, you know?" Luc said.

"Yeah." Quinn watched his boots kick a scattering of oil-soaked kitty litter on the ground.

Luc had shocked him into silence, so she eased off. Instead of loading him with more of her baggage, she fetched another folded lawnchair from against the garage wall. She opened the chair facing him, but not too close. "You gonna graduate this year?" she said

"Yeah. I better, or my ma will moan and groan for a week. She's already been moping about this bike because my dad bought it. It's supposed to make up for his living in California and never seeing me. But I'm fine with that. He's an asshole and I get a sweet ride out of his guilty conscience. Luc, are you serious about what—"

She raised her voice to cut him off: "Do you have your license for it yet?"

"Why?" he said. He took ten more seconds to ask the inevitable: "You want a ride?"

"No." She stretched out the nerves tightening in her limbs. "Seriously?"

"Serious," Quinn said. "I just need to throw some parts back on."

Ten minutes later her bones hummed in harmony with the engine that rumbled in the crook of her bent and tightened legs. No helmets or pads to keep her safe, no shoes even, nothing to stop her from sailing off the back of the motorcycle down onto the village street. Nothing except her arms pinned around Quinn's torso and her mouth pressed into the warm musty bend of his shoulder blade. All her petty fears were gone when that bike tore down a dark road through the center of town and bulleted past the locked cars and the late-night traffic signals blinking cautious yellow. There could be no caution when Quinn's muscles pulsed beneath her fingers and his hair fluttered against her face like ravens' wings.

The frost sharpened the night air, but Luc couldn't tell her own shiver from the engine's deep hot purr. Street lamps strobed overhead, and the bike's motor roar bashed against the storefront windows. Every darkened side street could've hidden a village cop, but none did. So Quinn revved toward the Erie Canal lift bridge, and together they mounted over the last hump of pavement, lifted through a weightless gasping clutching instant of empty space before the tires seized the metal bridge grating and soared with a tender buzz over the black water below.

TANYA HUNG SOME wet jeans and T-shirts on a clothesline strung between the edge of the trailer and a leafless tree. Winter cold was chill enough to make the clothes freeze before they dried, but Tanya was chancing it anyway. The rest of the clothes were in the trailer hanging from everything she could think to hang them from. She'd hand-washed a load in the kitchen sink using a bottle of Tide and a soup ladle to agitate. The ground out here was still all mud and mushy leaves, which she had slogged through in her bare feet to cool her swollen heels. The baby lay still in her belly. She got anxious when it didn't move because most of all she didn't want anything dead inside her.

Down the road came Mason in the Deville nailing the tires over the trailer park speed bumps so hard that the suspension strained like trampoline springs. He cranked the car onto the uneven yard and slid a few feet over the wet grass before stopping. Tanya knew there was trouble when Mason lunged out of the car and slapped the door shut with the engine still running, keys dinging in the ignition.

He stomped toward her with his face hollow and snarling. Tanya tossed a pair of jeans over the line, keeping up her chores like nothing was wrong—but it was her last move before Mason grabbed a knot of her hair and wound it into his fist and yanked so her neck got wrenched down low and her face was bent upward just under his. Mason's nostrils were flaring.

"What did you do?" he asked her. But he didn't wait for her to think before he led her like a bridled horse toward the trailer porch. She stepped blindly through the mud slicks and the hard sharp twigs. "Ow, ow," she said. She gave him no help up the steps so they both stumbled onto their knees. His pulling made the hair on her head almost tear off like a scalping.

Inside the trailer Mason dropped her down on the couch with her filthy feet scrambling on the floor, but she sat upright fast. He fumed over her and asked again, "What did you do?"

Tanya watched his fists. She knew better than to guess an answer.

He said, "What did you tell that bitch? That teacher's wife?" He was manic, full of movement but standing still, the leather in his jacket and boots all creaking like ship masts. "Whatever you told her you fucked it up bad."

"She didn't give over the other part of the money?"

"She's fucking dead, Tanya." He turned and punched the trailer wall and the noise blasted through the metal like cannon fire. He shook the pain off his fingers. Their clean-washed clothes were hanging from chair backs and armrests all over the place, dripping onto the floor. The whole trailer smelled like fabric softener. He told her, "I just found out the bitch killed herself. Jumped off a pier into Lake Ontario."

Tanya couldn't remember where he'd been driving from, or if he'd even told her his plans when he left. She sat hunched with her arms hugged around the baby in her womb. Her feet spread brown tracks onto the floor and Mason paced his boots through it, grinding wet dirt into the linoleum cracks. She tried to think about that other, uncollected lump of five thousand bucks that they'd suddenly lost, but such an amount of cash didn't make sense to her. A bonfire made of five dollar bills. The money never seemed real anyhow—just a wish to blabber on about, now gone. She said, "What are you gonna do?"

"I don't know. I don't know what you said to her."

"What you told me to."

"Whatever you did it made her off herself."

"Did it?" she said, snide like she meant it to sound.

Mason backhanded her face. She screamed and flopped her head down onto the armrest where a waterlogged sweatshirt was laid out. Felt as if he'd knocked her jaw loose from her skull, with a grinding pain like hot sand between the joint and socket. He grabbed a tuft of her bangs and pulled her head backward until her neck was strained. Pointed a stiff finger at her face and said, "You want to screw up some more? I been reading those books and I know my boy could live fine if he came out right now. I'll cut you open to get him and leave you dead. I don't need your stupid ass. I could get a knife right now and slice you open and pull him out. Leave you here to bleed, you hear?"

A thunderstorm raged inside her head. His voice came at her like it was a faraway storm rolling in, but still she heard it clear enough. She nodded, wiped the dampness pooling under her nostrils.

Mason let her loose. He went to the fridge and ducked his head inside, came out with a can of Bud that he popped open and drank deep, anchoring himself by one hand against the trailer roof. A hail had started outside and it pinged and rolled on that rounded roof like buckshot. In seconds it got loud enough to rise over the noise of Tanya's sobbing.

"What are you blubbering about?" Mason said.

"The cops are gonna find us," Tanya said. They were almost yelling in order to hear each other over the hail fall.

"No way," Mason said. "Nobody's finding us."

Tanya swallowed dry nothing in her throat before she said it: "Mason? You need to tell me. You killed that professor, that woman's husband?"

"I don't need to tell you nothing, Tan, you got that?"

She sniffed. Dug a hand into her pocket and found a balled-up tissue. When she dabbed her nose the tissue came back speckled with blood. Mason had already said enough to prove that he'd done what

Tanya guessed a long time back. He'd done that murder that was supposed to win him a wad of cash and some clout with the Skeleton Crew. She guessed shooting that professor was what tipped him over from a prospect to a member, not because anybody in that gang personally knew that college teacher to want him dead for any reason, but because killing was just what they did to stiffen their hearts against the ugly world they hated. She didn't want to think how much murder they had tallied up among them and notched on their ragged belts.

Mason slapped his empty beer can on the table. He said, "Don't start getting that self-righteous smirk on your puss now, babe. You been part of this whole operation from the start. What about that junkie pimp I took care of? You forget him?"

"You beat him up. You stole his van, that's all."

"Come off it, Tan. Are you that deluded?" Mason went for another beer in the fridge and started drinking it on the way back toward her. She tensed, and the trailer tilted and creaked when he moved. He sat down on the couch next to her. They both looked at the empty wall opposite as if there were a TV set there showing the news of what had happened back when they met. He said, "You know damn well that rotten motherfucker is nothing but a set of broken bones stewing in a Cincinnati landfill."

Only one strange memory of her ex slipped into Tanya's thoughts just then: the two of them huddled under a naked lightbulb in an apartment stairwell, clothes wet from a freak rain, sharing one Burger King Whopper and a bag of fries, neither one eating the pickles. His face was dark brown, his hair in a flat-topped fade, his jaws were pumping as he chewed. Gold bracelets on his needle-pocked arms. She said, "I didn't know any of that."

"Let me tell you: I slit his throat with his own blade, then I stuck it in his eye all the way to the hilt. Afterward he drained out into the bathtub till his nigger face was almost white as yours. And you damn well know I needed to do that so he wouldn't slave you no more. I fucking liberated you, Tanya, just like I'm trying now. You think I'm new at this? The Crew wouldn't join up with some rookie punk."

Tanya nodded. She took Mason's beer from his hand and had a sip to wet her throat.

"Don't pour booze into my baby," Mason said.

"Sorry," Tan said. "I forgot. I just needed a quick sip."

Mason grabbed his beer back. "You need to be more fucking grateful."

"I'm sorry."

"You bet your ass you are."

"What are we gonna do now?" she asked.

"That's for me to figure out, soon as I find out more news."

"But you said she was dead. What else—"

"Forget what I said," he told her. "I was pissed off. You know what happens when I get pissed—I don't know what I'm saying. Right now all I know is she tried to off herself, so I'm waiting to hear if she got away with it or what. Either way we need to think about getting out of here, soon as we can. You could start loading all these clothes all over the place into suitcases."

"They're all wet," she said. "I was just washing them."

He reached into his pocket and scooped out a handful of coins, jiggled them in his palm, then tossed them on the couch cushion next to her. At least half the silver money fell into the crease or rolled onto the floor. Mason said, "Take them to a fucking laundromat, then."

THE MONROE COUNTY Medical Assistance van pulled into Luc's driveway with its headlights shining harsh white. It was December ninth, four days to Luc's birthday, and winter had finally killed the last warm southerly gusts. Snowfall still melted, but grass and leaves were matted heavy with ice, the black trees naked against the sky. Frost clouded across the window like cataracts on the eye. Downstairs the furnace clattered and pushed its breath through the vents.

Mom was in that van, a homecoming two days after she'd broken her stupor. Two days of observations and tests and reports, but still Luc wasn't ready to welcome her mother home. Luc hadn't visited the hospital since those first frantic and confused moments of consciousness when Mom had screamed for her nonexistent baby. After that, Luc had anticipated weeks of in-patient care and rehabilitation, but according to Gramma Norma, Mom was desperate to leave the hospital and Dr. Mahoney had pronounced her out of danger. He wanted her back three times a week for testing and study—his own human guinea pig—but she was free to enter a world that had passed fifteen years beyond the limit of her memory.

The van driver cranked open the sliding door while an orderly jumped out of the passenger seat and jogged around the front of the vehicle to help. They both wore winter jackets with the hoods pulled over their heads. They slouched with their hands in their pockets, bopping to some unheard beat as the automatic elevator platform unfolded.

Only a cast-wrapped foot was visible at first, but then the rest of the leg glided out from inside the van and onto the platform. There was Blair Crowley-Moberg propped in a wheelchair with her elbows jutting out as she pushed, her head nodding lazily to the right. There was Luc's mother the same as always but also rendered ugly and foreign by this humiliating process of wheeling her own chair out. Gramma Norma had arrived in her Oldsmobile and was pulling alongside the curb. She'd been following behind the van like the only car in some pathetic funeral procession.

The orderly pushed the wheelchair up the pathway toward the porch. A heavy gray blanket was draped over Mom's body, the kind people used to staunch small fires. Her brow was ridged with pain or disbelief, and her mouth sagged open. Luc wanted to scream through the window: *Close your mouth! You look like a retard! Is that what you are now?* Instead, Luc would have to greet her mother like a stranger, a distant relative from some faraway state: *Hello, I'm your daughter, Lucia,* recited deliberately, as if to a child.

Outside, the orderly had turned the wheelchair around to get it up the porch steps while Norma trotted up behind him to complain about something that Luc couldn't hear. With each upward step, the back of Blair's head jostled like a cotton-stuffed doll's.

When the indignity was over Norma thanked the orderlies and they were gone. There Mom sat: wet eyes peering at Luc, slumped in her seat. Norma pushed the chair into the kitchen and pressed her hand against Mom's shoulder like she expected her daughter to suddenly pitch forward or jump upright. But Blair's movements were all slow-motion. She blinked drowsily. Her face was like ill-fitted clay. A smile formed, but it was mangled and frightening. She lifted one shuddering hand and grunted, and Luc was struck certain that her mother's brain had rotted like an apple dropped in the dirt.

But then she said, "Lucia," clear and sharp. Luc felt herself being named a second time. Her mother looked more alive with every second that passed—especially as she dislodged herself from Norma's hand and pushed the wheels across the floor toward Luc.

"I remember you," Mom said. "From the day when I—when I woke up again. You were there. I know your face. It's my face. Oscar's."

"My face—" Luc repeated.

"You're fifteen. It's nineteen—ninety—three," Mom said. She touched her own eyebrows to ponder each impossible fact. "Hard to believe."

"You don't remember anything?" Luc said. "This house, even?"

"It feels like here is right," Mom said. "That towel—"

Luc was holding a raggedy dish towel that she'd taken to dry dishwater off her hands. It was nothing, just a shred of white linen that had been around Luc's whole life, common as the silverware. White with purple fringes and grape bunches repeated in patterns that were all faded now. Luc passed the towel into her mother's eager hands and said, "You remember that towel?"

"I bought it. Last year—but now it's so old."

"We'll find lots of thing you'll remember," Norma said.

"Is this the truth? Are you my daughter? If you are—you're beautiful," Mom said, and it sounded like the last dose of truth left in their lives. Her eyes were so desperate, the left one so raw and red. This woman, somehow, was not the same woman who'd taken those pills, who'd dived off a pier, who'd twice tried to leave her only child an orphan. Luc watched her mother clutching and kneading that damp sixteen-year-old towel in her hands, and in that passing instant, at least, Luc could accept what she saw.

That afternoon Luc got on her knees in front of the TV and crammed tape after tape into a VCR that was too slow for her frantic ejecting and rewinding and playing. Home videos of Luciadagens past: Mom's steady lens trailing Luc down the hall with her plate of coffee and saffron buns. The bulging candle auras on Luc's tiara overtaking most of her head. Here's Oscar sitting up in bed, wild blond mane and bushy blond chest. Eight-year-old Luc belting out the last verse of "Sankta Lucia" with searing treble. Oscar beaming at his wife through the camera, sipping his coffee.

Now the Mobergs' backyard, five years earlier. Here's Oscar cannon-balling into their pool while howling like a Norse berserker. Here are three scrawny little girls whisking belly-first across a Slip 'N Slide laid out on the grass in the foreground. Two of the girls are identical twins, and even their pink one-piece swimsuits match, their hair tied up in braids. Ten-year-old Luc charges toward the camera dripping wet and, apparently, wrestles it away from her mother. There's scuffling, giggling into the microphone, shoddy camerawork now that Luc's in charge.

Mom jogs out from behind the camera, waving back to her daughter. Pink-frosted lips and big hair. She's wearing a sheer sundress over her swimsuit, but still she flings herself down onto the yellow rubber mat and careens across its length as the sprinkler douses her. Everybody's laughing, even Gina and Kit, even when Blair plows them both down onto the grass like they are pins in a game of human bowling. Even Oscar, who springs up from the pool water headfirst, a mythic sea beast surfacing.

A few seconds of static fizzle, then fragments of Puerta Vallarta three years before. An adobe resort rearing up amid the coastline, the jungle mountains, and the dusty village streets full of dogs and chickens. A man pushing a shaved ice and melon cart. Sunburned Luc in her bikini wading into the sandy ocean water. Racks of Mexican dresses rolled onto the sidewalks and tourists haggling to lower their price. Mom lounging in a wicker chair underneath a coconut tree while a native woman weaves small beads into her hair. A little chubbier back then, slick with sweat, Mom takes swigs of bottled water. She crosses her eyes at the camera and sticks out her tongue. The sun tweaks everything two shades brighter. Every day the temperature roasts the air at over a hundred until the purple evening thunderstorms slice out across the coastline like a jackknife unfolding.

And now her mother watched those tapes from where she sat in her clunky wheelchair, pale and breathing shallow, noisy breaths. Mom touched her fingers to her tightened mouth. She was horrified, as if somebody were screening footage of violent death and she couldn't withstand the sight of it anymore.

On the tape Luc and Oscar wade into the Pacific bay waters that are almost stagnant and brownish with sand, but undaunted they scoop and splash it at each other with their cupped hands. Oscar's handfuls are much bigger than Luc's. She squeals and contorts when the water hits her.

"Oh, God," Mom said in the present world.

Luc hit "pause." Freeze-frame on the back of Oscar's head and his sunburned shoulders.

"What's the matter?" Luc said, more like a complaint than a question.

"I was—here?"

"Watch more. Maybe you'll remember," Luc told her. A jump cut to Oscar and Luc hiking toward the Maria grotto at the top of a long stone staircase. They're turning and waving down to Mom and the camera, but Mom suddenly screeches when she spots a fist-sized tarantula shuffling across a nearby step. The picture breaks into meaningless swish-pans of color.

"I can't. He's—look at Oscar," Mom said now. She was almost hyperventilating, squirming in her chair and gripping the armrests with her hands. "Look at him. Why do you keep saying he's dead? Why do you want to say that?"

Luc stood up too fast. She felt nauseous, full of some bile that she needed to purge before it poisoned her. She said, "I don't want to, but it's the truth."

Mom pulled her wheels backward, but they rolled only a foot before the couch jammed them into a stopped position. "Who are you?" she said with a show of wide-eyed horror like some silent film actress.

Luc said, "I'm your daughter, Blair. Your *daughter.*"

"Lucia. I know. But I'm in—this—dream—and my head—"

"You did it to yourself, remember? You jumped. Because you're weak? Huh?" Luc jammed her finger at the TV screen to show her, as if all the answers and memories and truths were caught in that single paused jittering frame. She loomed over her mother like a tyrant.

"What did I—do—?" Mom asked, terrified.

Luc sat on the couch and pulled a throw pillow to her chest. She was spent, pissed, and quite pleased with her own capacity for cruelty. Only gradually did she begin to realize that the gestures and tones of her outburst were familiar because she'd learned them all from her mother.

After her meltdown Luc was relieved that she'd already plotted an escape: two late-afternoon hours at the Starlight Cinema watching *A Nightmare Before Christmas* for the third time with Gina, Kit, and, because Luc had been gutsy enough to call him after school let out, her neighbor Quinn Cutler. In the dim vintage theater she sat between Gina and Quinn sneaking sips of vodka from a communal flask. She hadn't seen this movie since her father's murder, and all the whimsy about death and monsters didn't amuse her anymore. Just stop-motion lumps of clay and their sickening game at being human.

Quinn drove them home in his rust-pocked Thunderbird. Luc sat shotgun with her boots on the floor nudging aside dog-eared copies of *Easyriders* magazine. Every cover featured a boob-job case with an aerosol hairdo.

"Sorry about the mess," Quinn said. He cranked the ignition and the car shuddered. Sounded like the muffler was rattling against the underside of the car. The heat coming from the vent smelled like maple syrup and cigarettes.

In the rearview mirror she saw the twins both smirking like they had to piss and couldn't hold it. Kit listened to her Walkman and Gina kept kneeing Luc's seat on purpose. Quinn parked up the street from their house because they didn't want their mom asking questions about who was driving them around town. On her way out of the car, Gina whispered in Luc's ear, "Keep your pants on, kiddo." Luc punched her in the spine and Gina made a wild show of pain, dancing on the sidewalk with her arms bent around backward, clawing for the imaginary wound.

"What was that about?" Quinn said, twisting them through a breakneck U-turn. "I hate to say it but she looks like a Nazi with that cueball head."

"She's just lame," said Luc. "Seriously." She watched his hands: one rested at twelve o'-clock on the steering wheel, the other slapped along to the music beat on the seat between them. She'd wanted to touch his free hand, but now he used it to click the engine off. They were parked in Luc's driveway instead of his.

She studied the sharp cheekbones on his face and thought about touching them. Right there in his car, getting her hands underneath his jacket and into his shirt so she could feel the hard muscles under his skin. She even imagined unbuckling his belt and touching him down there without shame, without anyone else finding out, but it seemed way beyond what she had the nerve to attempt. So Luc surprised even herself when she closed her eyes tight and let her lips catch his for a second, but then she drew away and shoved herself hard against the passenger door.

Quinn was still turned toward her with his elbow on the steering wheel. His jaw muscles flexed, but he wasn't showing any certain cues that could help her read him.

"Man, I'm really sorry," Luc said. "I wasn't thinking."

"You caught me by surprise is all," he said. "I thought it was an accident."

"I didn't even know I was going to." She pushed open the door and dropped one boot on the pavement.

"So what you're saying is you regret it?" said Quinn.

"I don't know. I got to go."

"Hold up," Quinn said. He took the back of her neck in his grip. The shock of his touch made her gasp, and her head moved where he guided it. He brought his mouth against hers and pressed his other hand into her cheek. Luc felt herself flooded by an ocean of relief filling sweet and clear inside her head.

"I don't think my mother's going to get better," Luc said.

"What makes you say that?"

"She's not my mother anymore. It's not like being sick. It's not temporary."

"Here's an idea," Quinn said, smirking a little. "Bring me in there to meet her, you know? Meet her again. Right now. I bet I'll bring her memory right back—'cause how could she ever forget how much she hates my punk ass?"

Luc glanced up at the house where she dreaded returning by herself. "Yeah," she sighed.

"Sorry. I'm just messing around. It's only stupid talk."

"No, I want you to come inside for a minute," she said.

"I was only joking about seeing your ma."

"I know, but—just—just come in. Come on."

Quinn stalled a minute while he tied his hair back with a rubber band, as if a ponytail somehow made all the difference. Then he followed Luc up the driveway, dragging his boots on the blacktop. Inside, Luc found her mother in the living room watching television. Mom swiveled around and grinned at her full toothed, a freakish smile that didn't falter when Quinn stepped into the room behind Luc.

"You came back," Mom said. She pointed a limp finger toward the hallway and let her grin slacken a bit when she said, "Nap. My mother is taking a nap down there."

"Mom, this is my"—Luc hesitated—"my boyfriend, Quinn."

Quinn shoved his hands into his back pockets. He didn't seem resolved to stepping out from the mudroom.

"I don't know if—" Mom stuttered. "We ever—met. I'm sorry. I have trouble—"

"No problem," said Quinn.

"I thought you should meet him again," Luc told her. "Start off fresh."

"Yes. That's nice. Start off fresh," Mom said.

Quinn cleared his throat and said, "So you really don't remember me? I admit you didn't like me much when I was a kid, but I was a hell-raiser, so you had reason. I'm much better now."

Mom said, "Sorry. There was—an accident. I can't remember."

"I heard about that accident," said Quinn. "But it's cool. I mean, don't worry about remembering me because I'm nobody you need to re-member. You know—we could probably get along pretty good now, I think. Start off fresh like Luc said."

"Yes," Mom answered. She watched her own hand swipe over the surface of her leg cast while she repeated, "Yes," like she didn't know if she believed that word or knew what it meant anymore. A sudden grav-ity had descended upon them, and it was so oppressive that Luc could hardly breathe the heavy air.

To break it she quipped, "Guess your big plan didn't work, Quinn."

THE MIDGET THEY called Runt sat on the couch next to Tanya's open suitcase. His lumpy head was too big for his stunted body, and the greasy brown hair on top of it was side parted like he was a dwarf Hitler impersonator, except he had a goatee thicker than Mason's that he twirled down into two satanic needle points. Fingernails long and pointed sharp. Had a voice deeper than most men three times his build, and it made Tanya cringe every time she heard it.

He was sitting drinking whiskey on the rocks from a cocktail glass and his legs didn't touch the floor. Tanya noticed that he kept looking into the suitcase where her leopard-print panties were lying on top of the other clothes, so when she came back out of the bedroom with an armload of Mason's T-shirts she stuffed them inside there and closed the lid.

The whole trailer rumbled like an aftershock while Mason and Tanya packed up their belongings, even the silverware and the ketchup from the fridge. There were trash bags on the floor full of kitchen stuff, and all the clothes were in that giant battered suitcase with the paisley design that Tanya'd had as long as she could remember. It was her mom's old suitcase, and it had fled with Tanya when she ran away from her wicked stepmother and again when Mason freed her from the junkie ex. All her life kept getting loaded into its belly.

In the kitchen area Tanya tried to fetch her ceramic garden gnome off the top of the fridge too high for her reach. She said to Mason, "Get that for me, will you?"

"What for?" Mason said.

"I like it. I want to bring it with us."

"All right, already," Mason said. He slapped it off the fridge top and Tanya had to catch it in two hands so it wouldn't break on the floor. Even then she almost dropped it. She felt herself trembling, nerve wracked, like a sixth sense deep inside her head knew that there were wraiths out there in those woods behind the trailer, and they were slicing through the trees toward her, and she had to hurry or else she'd be torn apart by their teeth and the baby stolen screaming right out of her womb.

Runt had showed up about half an hour ago and stationed himself on the couch. Now he was thumbing through one of the pregnancy books Mason had left on the side table, studying a drawing of a curled-up fetus that looked almost like him without hair. Almost every night Tanya had painful dreams that the baby would come out shaped like Runt or even worse: something twisted inside out with its lungs exposed and teeth in its stomach and eyes where there shouldn't be eyes. She was getting barely any sleep from thinking about it.

Runt was in the club, an honorary member if nothing else. He was an old friend of Buck Hanson and owned a partnership in one of Hanson's downtown businesses. Apparently it was the midget's job tonight to help Mason and Tanya abandon their trailer and then escort them over to their new hideaway. Even Mason didn't know where this place was located: a cabin Buck owned way out in the woods somewhere down near the Finger Lakes, more than an hour away. Tanya was eager enough to leave that cramped trailer and the threat of snooping cops, but she guessed that they didn't have a choice left anyhow. No reason to think so except the way Runt eyeballed them and kept that vintage snub-nosed .38 revolver tucked against his ankle inside his boot. Stupid notions, she told herself, because Mason wasn't a piss-on prospect anymore. He was certified Crew with clout just as golden as anybody's.

Runt said, "Don't bother with the appliances. There ain't electricity."

Tanya put down the electric can opener she'd just unplugged. She looked at Mason and he shrugged and took a swig from his beer can. He was already pretty drunk, and the beer made his face droop ugly and his eyelids swell. Every time Tanya studied his face it was a vertigo of hurt and lust that made her swoon.

"No lights?" Tanya asked.

"Good old mother sun," Runt said. "There's plenty of kerosene lamps and candles if you need. You don't got to worry about the cold because Buck's got loads of firewood in there and a stove to keep you toasty. It's just like camping, right?"

"But how long?" Tanya wondered.

Mason said, "I told you we don't know yet."

"But the baby's gonna be due. Is there a hospital?"

"We got that covered," Mason told her. He squeezed his empty beer can and tossed it in the sink, where it'd probably stay for weeks until the park manager came snooping to collect rent from his two missing tenants.

Tanya wanted to puke, so she eased herself down into a wooden chair at the breakfast table and covered her eyes with her hand. The baby was awake and on spin cycle. On the table next to her the ceramic gnome was wearing a tall red hat and a beard that swirled like vanilla frosting down his chest, a smile so big and rosy red that he looked insane. Garden shovel in one hand and a lantern raised in the other— painted yellow to help you imagine light.

She said, "What are we gonna do?"

Mason pushed a warm hand through her hair, rubbed her scalp with his fingertips. His touch flashed through her body and calmed her nausea some, but she didn't want that midget squatting like a toad on her couch gawking at their love. Mason said, "You know I been reading those midwife books, so now I got the whole thing mapped out. There's some supplies I got to get—some clean towels and washcloths, some alcohol to keep things clean."

"No way—" Tanya said. Mason squeezed a lock of her hair and started to pull.

"People been doing it that way since forever," Runt added.

"And the best part is our boy will have a clean slate, too," Mason said. "No birth records with the state, no Social Security. He's gonna be nobody's number."

"What are you gonna name him?" Runt asked.

Mason said, "Don't know yet. We got some time to think about it."

"It could be a girl," Tanya muttered. She didn't know why she'd said it, but she was pissed and also suddenly terrified. She couldn't see herself pushing out that baby in the cold wilderness with nothing but candlelight and natural pain.

"Then we'll just toss her in the river like them Chinks do," Mason said.

Runt's laugh was gigantic and startling. He slapped the baby book against his puny knee and let his face turn reddish because of how amused he was.

"I'm only fucking with you, babe," Mason said. "Plus it'll be a boy anyway. You watch. I'm positive about it. Nothing's gonna go wrong, and if it does then we'll just get in the car and drive. There's got to be someplace, right? We'll even score you some of those drugs they give you to help with the pain."

"There's a county hospital not too far off," Runt said.

Tanya said, "I don't really get why we have to do this."

"You really want to discuss this now?" Mason asked. "The bottom line is if we stick around here the cops will grab us sooner or later."

"Do they know who we are?" Tanya asked.

"How should I know?" Mason said.

"Hey, Brick," Runt said. "What about that bitch? You heard anything more about her?"

"They're saying she's got amnesia."

"What the fuck's amnesia? She a vegetable or something now?"

"What it is, is bullshit," Mason explained. "I'll tell you what's going on is this bitch is trying to scam me out of my five thousand bucks, so she's got this wild fairy tale about knocking her head up so bad that she loses her mind. I ain't falling for some ridiculous insanity plea. This bitch is fucking us over and I ain't letting her. Soon as we get situated up at this cabin I'm gonna be moving this situation along. I've had enough."

"You need to talk it over with Buck," Runt reminded him.

"Me and Buck already discussed it. He's with me on this."

"Fine, then. I'm gonna get the car warmed up," Runt said, his method of warning Mason to get moving. He grabbed his kid-sized leather jacket off the couch armrest and shoved his stubby arms through the sleeves. He scowled, Hitler hairdo and forked beard warning you that his hate was as big as that of any full-grown man. He fished a cigarette pack from his jacket pocket and headed out the door.

Tanya felt a headache flaring in her sinuses, same as always when she heard too much she couldn't understand. All this angry talk drew her into what she didn't want to know about. She carried the gnome over to her suitcase and shoved it inside, zipped it up tight. In her womb the baby kicked to get out, but more than ever she wanted to keep it stored inside her—because birth was always the start of pain and vice.

Mason came up behind her and kneaded his thumbs into her tight shoulder muscles.

"Please don't hurt nobody else," she said.

Mason said, "Nobody deserves nothing except what they earn. You think it's cake to shoot somebody in the face? It hurts, Tan, I'm telling you. You get nightmares, so I want to be paid for that. What you need to do is clot your bleeding heart, you hear?"

"Yeah," Tanya said.

THURSDAY NIGHT GRETA and Moe got the call that their wanted man, Mitchell Wendt, had been spotted downtown by a patrol officer. At ten P.M. they drove out toward the meeting point, coming off of the

Inner Loop and waiting in line through three city stoplights. Even with an arctic front settling in, the sidewalks were loaded with pedestrians, mostly teens loitering around the nightclubs and fast food joints, tattoo parlors, a sex shop, consignment shops full of hippie and old-timer clothes. Moe pulled into the 7-11 parking lot they were looking for. The patrol car was idling in the building's shadow, and across the street was the Submarine Bar and Grill, brick faced and wedged between two storefronts that were closed for the night.

Moe pulled up alongside the cruiser, driver to driver, and unrolled his window. The woman cop in the driver's seat was Officer Farris: dark hair pulled taut into a ponytail, pale lips on a slit of a mouth. She looked more like a librarian than a cop, but lots of people had scoffed the same about Greta during her early stint on the force. In the passenger seat was a tubby male officer whose name hadn't surfaced in the radio call. He leaned forward and passed the arriving investigators a limp wave.

"How long's he been in there?" Greta asked Officer Farris.

"Twenty minutes. We spotted him driving his Mustang into the parking lot behind the bar, verified his license plate number. We've been kind of casing the place because we know he hangs out here. I'm the one who collared him last time for possession."

Greta glanced down at the mugshot copy she had in her hands. Mitchell Wendt was twenty-two, but he had at least thirty years of wear on his face. A smashed-up nose and a caveman brow, decorative nick-marks in his eyebrows to complement the fancy thin sideburns that sliced along his jawline. But much of that could've changed by now.

"We have units in the back alley?" Greta said.

"Done," Farris said.

"I think I should take the lead," Moe said.

Greta said, "Better not. A lady is less likely to upset the hive."

Moe said, barely kidding, "You're stepping all over my machismo."

Greta said, "You still get to stand around and look tough."

On foot the investigators crossed the damp and grimy street, watching the bar and grill through their own clouding breath. A few bar patrons loitered outside and gulped beer from pint glasses, but Greta stalked past them like an alpha female prowling untamed jungle, knowing that they knew she and Moe were cops because their profession was like a scent wafting from them.

Inside there were no windows, just garage junk nailed to the walls: fifties campaign posters, rusted car parts, high school football jerseys, and of course the dead mounted fish for the ocean theme. Dim and bluish lights hung down by anchor chains over the tables to give the idea that you were underwater and to keep everything dark except the food on the table and the faces of the people eating it. The Eagles were playing over the loudspeaker. The crowd was maybe a few dozen, most of them just working stiffs who'd heard news about the Sub's killer smoked barbecue—like one family in the corner booth with a kid in a high chair and another in a booster seat, airheaded suburbanites with no clue that three people had been stabbed in this place over the last five years, one of them fatally.

Greta spotted Wendt seated in a booth with a wide rack of ribs on a plate in front of him. Same pug nose, same pencil-drawn sideburns and eyebrow ticks, but his hair was covered over with a red bandanna. He was wearing a black jacket with an eagle patch above the breast. A woman sat with him across the booth, and he shouted at her over the music while he jammed a ravaged rib bone against his plate to punctuate whatever point he was making. "Fuck that," was all Greta could hear before she moved close enough to shut him up. He chewed lazily, snorted down some phlegm.

Behind Greta, Moe hung back in the entrance foyer with a couple late-shift construction guys waiting on some takeout. He leaned against a wall and let the lapel of his suit coat ease open far enough to show off his badge and gun. No reason to pretend he was anything but police.

"Who're you?" Wendt asked when Greta arrived. "You from the escort service?"

His date didn't laugh at his quip. She wore her own bandanna as a headband, but it was nearly lost in the jungle of her primped black hair. She had bocce-ball tits hiked almost up to her chin. Her earrings were made of feathers and beads and she wore fringed leather gauntlets on her arms. Looked like a teen in a Halloween costume.

"Rochester Police Department," Greta said. She showed him the badge clipped to her belt. "Mitchell Wendt, correct?"

Wendt scoffed at her. Likely he had a gun or a knife tucked into his belt or one of his boots. On the table next to him was a half helmet made of bright chrome, biker fetish gear, odd paraphernalia for a guy whose evening ride was a Mustang. The helmet was reflecting back a walleyed image of Wendt, Greta, and the girlfriend. Maybe he had something under that helmet, or even the girl might be packing some form of weaponry. Greta watched their hands. The girl reached into her breast pocket, but all she produced was a pack of cigarettes. She went on pouting her baby fat cheeks because a lady cop had ruined her dinner.

The static of conversation in the bar was markedly quieter now that Greta had found her target, but Glenn Frey was still on the speakers telling everyone to *take it easy.* Even with her back to the bar Greta knew the thugs were lined up sipping their Buds and watching the dinner theater over at the Wendt booth. She'd have to play her role proper or else there'd likely be a pandemonium of bikers and cops, hours of arrests and five days of paperwork to follow.

Greta said, "I'd like to talk to you outside if you're willing."

Wendt said, "I ain't going nowhere."

Greta said, "This isn't about you."

Wendt dropped his rib bone and used a cloth napkin to wipe the sauce off his fingers. He showed her the gap where a canine tooth should've been, and said, "Why don't you come back with ten more pigs besides you and Ali Baba and see if you can get me out of here."

The girlfriend lit a cigarette, and when she slid herself out of the booth she forced Greta to take a courtesy sidestep she didn't want to take. The girl wobbled like a drunkard on her stiletto-heeled boots. "Pardon me," she mocked, "I need to use the cat box."

Greta was polite: she waited until the girlfriend was far enough gone to resume. She said, "Mitch, do you really want me to have to bust this place open tonight? Ruin the evening for all your buddies and screw up the tips for all these waitresses? Think of the owner, how pissed he'll be at you for disrupting his business. He'd probably never let you in here again, and just because you had to be a hard-ass to some friendly cops with some questions that aren't even about you."

Wendt said, "You got no reason to be here harassing me." He was tamer now, picking at his tooth gap with a long pinkie nail. He leaned forward and spoke into his plate a message that was for Greta's ears only: "You got to pull this shit in front of my old lady and these other dudes? What do you expect me to do, pull down my jeans and let you spank my ass right here so everybody can watch?"

Greta glanced at Moe, who was still playing bouncer at the exit door. She crouched down and said to Wendt, "No, sir, I don't. If you like, we can do this outside where you don't have an audience. I'll be across the street in the 7-11 parking lot for the next ten minutes, if you're interested—but I should also mention that we've got some officers casing exits, watching your Mustang, and generally ensuring my continued well-being. Just think on it is all I'm asking."

The investigators waited for Mitchell Wendt back in their unmarked Taurus, which Moe had parked in a slot beside Officer Farris's cruiser, facing the Submarine Bar and Grill. Greta warmed her hands in the dashboard heat because her swollen knuckles cramped on her whenever the temp dipped below thirty.

"Did you notice the file says Wendt's nickname is Blisters?" Moe asked.

"Isn't that one of Santa's reindeer?" said Greta.

Wendt was alone when he exited the restaurant at ten minutes on the mark. Lit himself a cigarette and smoked it on his journey out to the sidewalk and down to the intersection and the crosswalk. He flicked the cigarette and it hit the pavement sparking orange before it bounced and dived into a sewer grate.

Moe and Greta popped their doors open in unison. In the next car over, Officer Farris and her partner started to follow suit, but then Greta stayed them with an open palm. The officers eased back into their seats, though Farris still left her door cracked open an inch.

"Thanks for helping us out," Greta told Wendt. They were on the sidewalk, the three of them meeting like old friends under the street-lights.

"I ain't helping shit," Wendt said. He was wearing sunglasses now, as if he worried that the cops could peer down into his soul if he let them see his eyes. "I just don't want you kicking around my joint, ruining people's nights, you know?"

"I'm sure they appreciate that," Moe said.

Wendt was antsy, hands in his jeans pockets. They let him take a few more steps off the sidewalk until they were all standing behind the un-marked in the darkest quadrant of the 7-11 parking lot. It was tougher now for any curious folks across the street to see what transpired.

Moe pointed at the back of the unmarked, where the tailpipe was gusting white smoke. He said, "You don't mind, Mitch, do you? Just for everybody's safety?"

Wendt snorted at him but stepped over to the car and put his hands on the trunk without incident, spread his legs wide. Moe asked him about sharp objects in his pockets and Wendt said no, so then Moe searched the jacket and the pants legs, reached into the boots, but they all knew whatever Wendt usually carried he'd stashed somewhere else in preparation for this palaver. They allowed him to relish that small triumph.

"All right," Moe said. "Thanks for that."

"Whatever gets you off, Jafar," Wendt said. He turned and leaned his ass on the car, folded his arms over his chest, struck a chill pose that was meant to salvage lost honor. He spit next to a pavement crack, dot-ting his own exclamation point.

"We'd like to clarify something you said a while back while in previ-ous police custody," Greta explained. "About a patch you had on the back of your jacket at the time of your arrest."

"Skullcrusher," said Wendt. "A band. Hardcore shit, man. I bet you'd like it."

"What is it—like, punk rock?" Greta ventured.

"Naw. Punk rock's for faggots," Wendt said. He sneered at Moe as if there'd been an insult implied, despite Moe's having at least twenty more pounds of muscle on him. Wendt was still a kid in his head, locked forever on disgruntled sixteen, but Greta knew better than to confuse him for some fresh and frightened street pup. He told her, "Skullcrusher is hardcore, beat-you-bloody kind of shit. Heavy metal, you know?"

"The thing is," Greta said, "we've got it down as Skullcracker."

"Skullcracker," Moe repeated. "That's what you told them last time."

Wendt said, "You got it down wrong, then. It's Skullcrusher, not cracker. You scalping front-row tickets for a concert or something? Cause last I checked scalping is illegal."

Moe said, "Instead of what you're telling us, we were thinking that Skullcrusher or cracker or whatever it is might be the name of a local club, too. Have you ever heard of such a club? Because these guys we just took in, earlier today, they were wearing a patch just like yours on their jackets, and they told us it was club colors. As I'm sure you know, wearing club patches is also illegal."

"If there's a club called Skullcrusher, I never heard of it."

"Wasn't it Skullcracker?" Moe asked, faking his doubt. "Didn't he say 'cracker'?"

By now Wendt was shifting on his feet and watching through the 7-11 storefront window to where the cashier inside was leaning on the cash counter reading a magazine, oblivious to the proceedings outside. Wendt's lies were blatant and unrepentant, like he was daring them to call him out. So Greta hitched two fingers in the air as a sign for Farris and her partner to jump out of their patrol car and finish him off. The two beat cops came crashing the party in seconds. Farris was almost six lanky feet of blue bitch in action, one hand planted on the pepper spray clipped to her utility belt.

Greta told Wendt, "Well, I appreciate your clearing up these issues for us, Mr. Wendt." She was lathering up the mockery. "And we sincerely appreciate your taking the time to talk to us tonight, and we appreciate your being straight with us."

"What the fu—" Wendt started, but Farris had already pounced, barking orders at Wendt and dancing him through the whole routine in one fluid run. She had him swiveled back around with his gut against the car trunk, hands behind his back. Her handcuffs glimmered once in the beam of a passing headlight before she whacked them shut around his wrists. Her partner lurked behind her, scooting empty-handed like a tight end on the gridiron with nobody to tackle.

When it was finished Moe took his last shot: "You've been so helpful, Mr. Wendt. I wish there was somehow we could help you with these outstanding warrants. I'm sure these two fine officers will settle up with you."

AT NINE THAT NIGHT Norma and Luc wheeled Mom into the master bedroom. They helped her out of her clothes and into her robe while she struggled onto the bed with the two of them holding each of her arms. Luc folded the sheets over her mother's body and concealed that ugly cast. Mom smiled, and her face was a beaming source of light. If anyone else had regarded Luc with such intensity, the unbroken gaze would've shriveled every nerve in her body. But it seemed proper, like the first minutes after birth when you're cradled in your mother's arms, a milestone that now neither one of them could recall.

Back in the kitchen, Luc scraped dinner leftovers into the garbage and rinsed off the plates before she put them into the dishwasher. Gramma Norma came out from the bedroom and poured herself another cup of coffee from the lukewarm glass pot on the counter. She sipped it black. Norma looked oldest at night—frizzled dry hair and the way her upper lip creased when she sipped. Her swollen knuckles seemed even more engorged.

"She went right to sleep," Norma said. She turned the power dial on the portable TV sitting on the counter edge, then she sat down at the table. She kept the volume low and gave it little of her attention.

"Are we supposed to keep an eye on her?" Luc said.

"I think so. The doctor didn't say. I'll be up, anyhow, so you don't have to worry. We have an appointment tomorrow morning with the financial adviser about the insurance policy."

"What, like Dad's life insurance? How's she supposed to do that?"

"I don't think she needs to do much. It's all arranged."

Luc plugged the sink drain and started the hot water, then she squeezed in a few drops of dish soap and wetted the sponge she'd use to scrub the skillet and the pans. She toweled off her hands and stepped between her grandmother and the TV. She said, "Why is Mom mad at you? She hardly talks to you."

"She's a little confused."

Luc mashed her hands into that same towel with the grape patterns that Mom had recognized earlier, and she waited patiently for her grandmother to realize that she was not going to drop this line of questioning.

Norma said, "You know, we had a few fights many years ago. Mostly your grandfather was upset by what—that everything was going too fast with your mother and Oscar. Your father, I mean. You have to understand we didn't know anything about it almost until they decided to get married, and your mother was still so young. And you—"

"You hated my dad?" said Luc.

"No, certainly not. I was devastated when you told me what—"

"I mean back then. You and Grandpa. Is that why he's not here?"

"Your grandfather isn't feeling well enough to travel," Norma said. "You need to understand this is fifteen years ago we're talking about. Your mother was only twenty—just a child as far as we were concerned, and we thought that everything with Oscar was happening so fast. That's all. We've learned different over the years, of course. We all know that she was very happy with him."

Luc grunted at her. Norma knew almost nothing about Blair and Oscar's marriage except those curt formalities people mutter over the phone to each other once or twice a year. If she was half-right it was only by accident.

"Your grandfather has always been a stubborn man, so much so that it affects his health. But he's not angry at your mother. He cares very much about her, and that's why he has such strong opinions. He thought she was very vulnerable because she was still recovering, and he didn't think—"

"Recovering from what?"

"From the boy," Norma said. "Humphrey Reid."

"Who's Humphrey Reid?" Luc asked. This strange name, this sneak attack. She took a seat at the table before the shock could strike her off-kilter. Luc was sure she'd never heard this name Humphrey Reid before, but still it nipped at her like a memory she'd let run astray. This is what it meant to be a stranger in your own head.

Norma said, "Oh, honey, I'm sorry. I thought your mother would've said. Humphrey was a boy she knew in high school. A troubled boy. He'd been arrested a few times before she got to know him, I think. He lived just down the street from us and he was—not a boyfriend of your mother's, but he liked her very much. We also knew that he—he was immature, and unbalanced. You understand they didn't have the kind of help they have today for people like him. The drugs that can help those kinds of people. I think he tried to date her, your mother, but we knew he wouldn't be right for her, not with his problems. She was a very good student who was already accepted at college, and that's probably what made her attractive to him. When your grandfather found out about that boy, he made his opinion known as usual, but I don't think your mother was much interested anyway. Even at her age she realized there was something wrong."

Norma spoke through four fingers pressed against her mouth, and the loose flesh underneath her chin wobbled when she talked. Luc was disgusted, but the woman kept talking: "What happened was he took his own life. Awful, and worse, this was just a few months before your mother graduated. You don't know how difficult it was for her, not knowing why he'd—hang himself like he did. Your mother didn't date anybody after that. Not until your father, but this was when she was a sophomore in college. We thought—we thought there was a reason she felt she needed to date someone—so much more mature."

"What, like, getting back at you for Humphrey?"

"Not that," said Norma. "She told us she couldn't trust people her own age because they were so—so unstable.

"Maybe she was right. Maybe she has a good reason to be mad at you."

"But it was so long ago now. I hardly remember."

"She remembers," Luc said. Over these last two days there'd been lulls like this—when futile talk was finished, when her mind buckled after raking again and again through those same eternal calamities in the Volvo, off the pier—a past fixed like permanent etchings on her retinas. In these silences Luc imagined herself condemned to nights of lifting her invalid mother into bed, and over time Gramma Norma would burrow into their home like a termite because nobody else was left to care. Luc saw a future working cash registers and flunking high school—and it would have to be like this because you can't just go unscathed. If only she were three years older and had graduated from high school she could drive off toward her own life, but there was no fudging such numbers. Even the gods couldn't win their passage out of the underworld.

THEY REACHED THE CABIN after dark with only an oil lamp to guide them. Tanya smelled the endless pines and the wind that carried off the lake down at the base of the mountainside, but she saw nothing. The midget Runt had told them the cabin was an old horse barn with the stables now converted into sleeping dorms and a bathroom, so that night she slept in one of those dorms together with Mason in a bed covered by thick blankets to ward off December. She lay with her eyes wide in a darkness thicker than she'd ever known.

In the morning, light came, but along with it was fog that pushed up against the cabin windows. Nothing but dull white, as if Runt had led their nomad family into a nowhere zone beyond all human sight. But Mason trekked outside and came back intact with an armload of chopped wood that he used to light the den stove. Tanya yawned on the couch, wrapped in a blanket and bearing out the cramps that rippled across her stomach. She felt both saved and doomed as the cabin filled with smoky warmth.

There were two deer heads, mounted on rafter beams because the wood-panel pressboard walls weren't sturdy enough. And half the walls were missing, showing off the stud gaps stuffed with pink puffy insulation that looked like raw muscle when the skin's torn off. An old pee-wee hockey stick was hanging on the wall above the hallway arch. Its blade was wrapped in gray tape and the shaft had the name *Bucky* burned into it. Beside it was a framed picture of ten-year-old Buck Hanson snarling in his padded ice rink getup. The story went that Buck Hanson used to be some regional kid hockey star before the Nam draft snagged him.

And after breakfast the mist faded enough that Tanya could see the gray outlines of pine trees looking like huge spears rising out of the ground. She went outside still wrapped in her blanket, out onto the frosted white grass. From there she saw the whole cabin for the first time: gray wood siding, glimmering windows, concrete slab for a porch, dark stovepipe jutting from the roof and kicking out white smoke. Still hazy in the morning fog, the cabin looked to Tanya like some enchantment, a place of magic rearing out of the deepest woods. She was thinking in fairy tales again: Hansel and Gretel banished from their home by another wicked stepmother, forced to wander until they found that magic house made of pure candy. Maybe she and Mason were those lost, hounded children—but for now they were safe in these woods.

GRETA DEALT WITH Mitchell Wendt again first thing Friday morning. Her cubicle on the fourth floor of the Public Safety Building was just down the hall from the interview room where Narcotics had kept Wendt all night. The narcs tamed him with snacks and cigarettes and auto body chit-chat, and in turn he'd dropped them some useless gossip about inner city drug deals. Nothing they didn't know already. The narcs had been planted to schmooze with him, make him feel special, but most of all to drain him down for his morning round with Greta.

Outside the interview room Greta slid her police issue Beretta 92F in a locker slot. The narc who briefed her said that Wendt had turned ornery from his sleep deprivation. He'd started talking lawyers and Fifth Amendment rights, so they'd backed off of him a little. On three cups of sludgy coffee, Greta entered with the best vigor she could muster from scant sleep and an ever-strengthening headache throb. It had to be the flu for real this time because her thermometer was topping a hundred and her breakfast bagel had sunk heavy and sour in her stomach. Nothing she could do now but sign the interview form and unlock the door.

Inside was a cinderblock cell painted lime green, the color of calm. A plastic table like the kind you find at McDonald's with the chairs hovering on metal rails, fixed so they couldn't be used as projectiles. Nothing else in there but Wendt. The chairs were darker green, three of them, and Greta took the one closest to her interviewee, the chair that implied she was his pal. Wendt was sitting with his back to the entrance. His left hand was cuffed to his seat rail, and he had a cigarette in his right. His eyes were red and heavy. The paper coffee cup on the table Greta knew was secretly decaf.

"How are you this morning, Mr. Wendt?" Greta said.

He groaned and rubbed an eye with his thumb tip. "Just peachy," he said. She noticed now that his coffee was all but finished and that his cup was now being employed as an ashtray.

For twenty minutes she sweetened him with small talk, making friends. The narcs had killed the greasemonkey angle, so Greta had to delve into the mental fact-files she'd scrounged about his childhood in Scranton and his current gig assembling copiers at the Xerox plant. She briefly broached the girlfriend subject since Greta and the girl had already been acquainted. She knitted the pieces of his life together, building a warm sweater for him to wear. He talked like he was taking a short-answer test, but he kept chatting as long as she kept feeding him smokes. Greta smoked a few herself, letting herself believe she did it for the sake of feigned camaraderie.

Then finally she worked her business into the mix: "Mitch, there's these two guys we picked up. They're telling us some stories, and we don't know whether they're bullshitting us or not. They're telling us about this club with the skull-head rocker wearing the miner's hat. They both had it on the backs of their jackets."

"What guys are these?" he asked.

"I promised them I wouldn't say," Greta told him, "and I don't screw around. You need to understand that about me. If I say I'll do something for somebody, I keep my word. I hope you can respect that, and I think you can. The problem is, I don't think these guys are being straight with me, so I'm coming to you, hoping you'll shed some light."

"I don't got any light to shed."

"Well, you're saying the patch is for a rock band."

Wendt glared at her for a long minute, scratched the overnight scruff on his cheek. Finally he leaned forward and said, "Lawyer."

"That's fine, Mitch. That's fine," she said, and then she did nothing. She sat with her arms folded over her chest, pretending to fixate on the emergency sprinkler head on the ceiling. Something in her stomach told her she'd better wrap up the session soon or else Mitch Wendt would be wearing her breakfast.

Luckily, Wendt only wasted thirty seconds of silence before he voluntarily waived his rights once again. He asked, "What'd these two assholes you're talking about—what'd they do, anyway?"

"Breaking and entering. A convenience store."

"You drag me in here for some lousy B and E? What do you really want?"

"The name of the club, Mitch." Her stomach cramped and her throat tightened. She channeled all her thoughts into keeping the nausea tame.

"Why?" Wendt asked.

"Because sooner or later you'll want to make a name for yourself, for your club. Because that's how the game is played. I mean—if you started an outlaw club, you'd want people to know about it, wouldn't you? You'd want to be able to attract the best guys for the club and scare off the losers and fuck with the other clubs. That's what it's all about, right? Even the cops—you'd want us to know you're legitimate. You party like most guys, but nothing serious. You'd want us to respect you. I'm saying: what good's a club if nobody knows about it? How are we supposed to meet if I don't know your name? You know what I'm saying?"

"There's no two guys," Wendt proclaimed.

Greta said, "Look, that's beside the point. If we don't really have two guys in custody, then we don't really have anybody in trouble. Right? All we have is curiosity."

"Why's this so fucking important to you?"

"Because you made it important. You put it on your jacket."

"You came to me, remember? I didn't invite you to ask me shit."

"In a way you did. You dangled the bait, and I bit. You got me. I'm curious as hell, and I'm willing to help get some charges dropped if I can satisfy this curiosity."

"I ain't a fucking snitch."

"There's no snitching here," said Greta. "Besides, to say you're not a snitch is to admit there's a club, right? All I'm asking you to do is to legitimize yourself, to step into the ring, just like you planned on doing all along."

Wendt wiped his mouth with the back of his hand. He sat upright, fully awake now, and every twitch of his body warned Greta he was about to spill something honest. He asked, "You like Stephen King? You ever read any of his books?"

"Not that I can remember. They're too long for me. Short attention span."

Wendt said, "There's this one book he wrote and on the cover of it is that wind-up monkey toy with the cymbals, you know? *Skeleton Crew*, it's called. That's the title of his book." He tossed the butt of his cigarette into his paper cup, and it fizzled in the swamp of ashy coffee at the bottom. Then he pushed a hand through his hair and laid his weary skull against the wall behind him.

LUC WOKE AT NINE, already two hours late for school, though nobody would be bothering her to go. She grabbed for her glasses and pushed them on her face, and then she smiled for a second. She'd been dreaming she was on Quinn's motorcycle again with the smell of his skin and the quick perilous blur of the night. It was a drug to think of him, a mainline shot of some dizzying mood serum, to remind herself again and again that he had kissed her and that his kiss had proved she was significant, she was desired.

Her father's sprinkling urn was there on her nightstand. She had no memory of putting it there, but she wasn't surprised to see it. Noticing it made her feel like she was tucked inside a velvet womb. She cast away every thought of this new life without him, loaded all that waste into her unconscious. And then she watched the urn shift one inch across the nightstand, heard the scrape of wood against wood until it bumped against her alarm clock and stopped.

Upstairs Gramma Norma was napping in the guest room and Mom was lying in the living room recliner half-asleep. In her lap she cradled one of Oscar's *dalahasten*—those hand-carved horses the size of kittens, splashed with blue rosemaling designs. She petted its crest and its flank, and the wooden horse came alive. It leaped out of Mom's hands and trotted down one armrest and across her knees. It tossed its painted mane, and Mom caught it again, kissed it on the muzzle. Mom was far away in her mind, deep enough maybe to dredge some relics of what she'd forgotten, but still her face flickered like a candle, soft and orange bright.

There was one new message on the answering machine, and it was from Quinn. He said, "Hey, Luc. I'm calling on a payphone at school. Skipping history class, I don't know why—for the hell of it. Let's get together after school, all right? Hang out or something. Man, I wish I could get the hell out of here right now. Fucking hall monitors, though. Here they come to get me. Later."

In the bathroom Luc peeled off her arm brace, careful not to move those tender joints that wanted so badly to twitch, wanted to hurt. It'd been only six days since her injury, not even a fraction of the time she'd been ordered to wear it, but today she decided on her own counsel that the pain was gone and she could be freed from that cramped rubber for good. She dropped it into the wastebasket under the sink. In the bathroom mirror she saw someone who did not look like herself—that terrible expression loaded with all its hard knowledge that felt like it was stolen from somebody else, some war refugee or cancer survivor, someone stronger than Lucia Moberg could've ever hoped to be. But here she was, still alive. She touched her fingers to those pale lips to see if they'd fade out like a mirage. They did not.

She took a shower hot enough to scald her flesh pink. She wondered if maybe some dreams were mighty enough to alter you forever. It seemed impossible, but these recent days were twisting back over one another like dreams. Like dreams, these days echoed and then were muted. And these days were renovating her so utterly that she couldn't recognize her own memories anymore. Those memories had become like dreams.

OVERNIGHT, CLOUDS HAD drawn low over the empty fields and the suburban tracts that edged the highway. By ten in the morning the fog still washed out the horizon as Greta rode shotgun in the Taurus, wincing at her relentless aches. At first Moe was using high beams but the light reflected hard against the fog wall. He turned the beams down and followed red taillights, crawling ten miles under the posted speed.

Greta had already lost her breakfast in a public toilet five minutes after she'd finished questioning Wendt. Before leaving the station she'd crushed two dissolvable flu tablets into her bottled water and then she'd drunk it, but the aching radiated from her cheeks, her armpits, her eyelids, and it made her think back to Blair Moberg propped in that hospital bed punch-drunk and dazzled. For Blair the reward was fifteen years of fuckups suddenly flushed away. A weaker woman than Greta might have envied Blair's blind resurrection. Someone else, someone more desperate, might have started thinking that redemption only kissed you with a blow to the head.

They arrived at the Moberg house at eleven, and when they rang the doorbell Luc answered squinting at them like she'd just woken up. She was wearing sweatpants and a green SUNY Hammersport sweatshirt.

Greta said, "Lucia, can we come in for a minute?"

"Did you find something out?" the girl said. Her bleariness evaporated on sight.

"We should sit down and talk, I think," Greta told her.

Inside, Blair rested in the recliner with the footrest up, still in her bathrobe and holding some kind of wooden horse with rustic spirals painted on it. She was changing the channel on the TV every few seconds and didn't seem much bothered about the two plainclothes cops who'd wandered into her house. Somebody'd been sleeping on the couch, but Luc scrambled to remove the scattered blankets and pillows so Greta and Moe could sit.

The grandma came in from the kitchen affecting a smile that looked painful to uphold. She offered the investigators coffee and they both declined, so she lingered in the archway with her own coffee mug, scratching at the marks that a pillowcase had left on her cheek.

"Do you remember me, Blair?" Greta asked as she sat.

"At the hospital," Blair said. She clicked the remote power and the TV went dark.

Luc sat down on the recliner's armrest and laid a hand on her mother's shoulder. They might've looked like they were posing for a family portrait if not for the sleep clothes, the disheveled hair, and the bulky cast on Blair's leg. The strain of their togetherness would've been evident even to a total stranger. The girl, especially, paled like she had overdosed on a brand of denial that would eventually poison her, render her dumb and baffled like her mother.

"We have some news and some questions," Greta told them. She opened a manila folder and removed a single print sheet, a six-pack of brutish white mugs all in their twenties, all of them passing for Mitch Wendt look-alikes except number four, the man himself, scowling in the booking shot they'd taken the night before. She set the photo array down on the coffee table.

Greta said, "Do either of you recognize anybody in these pictures?"

"Who are they?" Luc said.

Blair furrowed her brow and said, "They're the same."

"They look similar but they're not the same. Do you recognize anybody?"

Lucia shook her head and Blair, after noting her daughter's reaction, said, "No."

Greta dug back into the folder, took out two glossy photographs, and laid them side-by-side next to the Wendt and Company lineup. These were both stills from the Shop-Mor surveillance tapes—one a freeze-frame shot of the bleach-haired woman who'd argued with Blair, and the other the cartoonish skull patch on the back of the woman's jacket. The skull was blurred from too much zooming, so Greta also laid out an artist's sketch of the gang rocker.

In fact, it had been Moe who'd drawn the sketch, and he leaned forward now to explain. He pointed to the appropriate sheets as he said, "This woman was videotaped by a surveillance camera in Shop-Mor Tuesday. This is a frame from the video, in which she is seen arguing with y"—he faltered now, likely deciding whether to address mother or daughter—"your mother. We don't know who she is yet, but we're confident that she's associated with one of the men depicted in this series of photographs."

"Which man?" Luc asked.

Greta said, "I'm sorry, Lucia, but unless you can identify him, we can't point him out. If any of this ever went to court they'd accuse us of prejudicing the witness, planting ideas."

"But, if he's the one who—" Luc started.

Greta interrupted: "We have no reason to suspect that this man was involved with your father's murder. At any rate he's already in police custody and not going anywhere. We're more interested in the woman. They both wear this patch, which we've come to understand is a rocker, an insignia, for an outlaw gang possibly called the Skeleton Crew."

"Outlaw?" the grandma chimed in from the corner. "Isn't that Old West talk?"

"Fringe groups," Moe said. "Reactionary militia types, motorcycle gangs, hate groups."

"Have you ever heard of the Skeleton Crew?" Greta asked. She tried to cough the scratching out of her throat but it wouldn't give. A long morning of talk had scraped her voice down to its tattered threads.

"No," said Luc. "This is crazy. Hate groups? My dad was Swedish."

Moe picked up the two photographs—the skull patch and the Shop-Mor woman. He pressed them toward Blair Moberg so she could get a clearer look at them. He said, "Look, we know you spoke to this woman the day before your accident. Is she memorable to you at all?"

Blair took the picture and ran her hand over the glossy surface. She said, "I can't remember. I'm sorry. It's like flashes of black—a black hole where everything goes."

"Why don't you keep these pictures in case they jog your memory?" Moe said.

"These people—did they? Kill Oscar?" Blair said.

"We don't know," Moe told her. "I'm asking do you know anyone who wears this kind of insignia that Mr. Moberg might have associated with? Anyone you can think of?"

"He didn't know anyone like that," Luc said. "At least, I didn't. Maybe there was somebody down at the marina, but that's all I can think."

Blair asked, "That woman—I knew these things?"

Moe gathered his paperwork together and tapped it against the coffee table sharply enough to draw everyone's attention. He sneered and said, "To be blunt, Mrs. Moberg, we think you knew an awful lot. Your remembering could settle this whole business for everybody."

Blair answered like a child who'd just been scolded. "I'm trying," she said.

"We appreciate that," said Moe. His sarcasm was blatant enough for the deaf.

"Luc," Greta said. "What about that money you found, in the basement you said?"

"I looked again right after I talked to you and it was gone. Totally gone."

"Five thousand dollars, right?" Greta said. "That's a lot of money."

The grandma added, "You found that much money? Here?"

"I asked Mom about it but there's no point. She doesn't know."

Greta said, "You saw it Sunday night, and it was gone by, when?"

"By Tuesday night after I got back from the hospital. That's when I checked."

"Why did you check?"

"Just to see."

Greta let herself consider the possibility that Luc, a petty thief by

her own account, had taken the money. Greta could even sympathize—
the urge for control, for security. Unsecured money could make you
panic just by the thought of it, and panic could blur your head. It was
how Greta felt now, burning up from her illness and the oppression of
this house. She was afraid she'd combust if she didn't leave soon. She
managed to ask, "So the money was there before her accident but not
after, right?"

"Yeah," Luc said. "I spent the night at my friends' house Monday, so
I don't know, I wasn't here to see what happened."

"Has anybody else been in the house besides you, your mother, and
your grandmother?"

Luc said, "Dale and Reggie, the two guys from the marina. They
were here to get my dad's boat. My neighbor, Quinn—but he's—"

"Her boyfriend," Blair blurted proudly. "I met him."

"Your boyfriend?" Greta asked.

A slight ruddiness spotted the girl's cheeks. She said, "Sort of. He's
been in here twice but only for a couple minutes both times. And I was
with him the whole time. I mean he was never out of my sight and he
wouldn't know where the money was anyway."

"What about these two fishermen?" Moe asked.

"They saved my mother's life," Luc insisted.

"Luc, we're just trying to explore every angle," Greta told her. "Would
you mind showing me the spot where you saw the money?"

The basement was at least cooler, but walking downstairs made
Greta queasy once again. Without the strength to help, she let the girl
drag the dryer aside by herself. On the bare concrete floor underneath,
there were globs of dust, water stains, a few stray pennies, but no cash
envelope.

"I keep wondering whether it was ever there at all," Luc said. "I think
I'm going crazy."

"I can see where the dust is unsettled," Greta noted. "Something
must have been there."

"What's happening to me?" Luc said. Her voice wavered, losing its
poise. From upstairs came hushed voices, Moe and Blair and the

grandma talking like they were guests at a funeral. Greta stepped toward the girl, not wanting to touch her, not wanting to infect her with this illness, but certain that an embrace was the only reply left to offer. The girl was all bones, but she softened in the heat of Greta's fever. Her crying turned convulsive and wet as Greta held fast and let the girl melt.

AN HOUR BEFORE dusk Grandma Norma drove off toward the slot machines at the Indian casino the next county over. She'd be gone until after midnight, and it was implicit that Luc should babysit her mother. They'd ordered pizza with a dozen wings that were now just dry slivers of bone soaking in greasy hot sauce in a Styrofoam box. They listened to the radio and Mom grinned at the alien music broadcast from some era she'd never visited.

But then Quinn Cutler pulled his Thunderbird into his driveway, and Luc watched through the blinds of her dining room window, watched as Quinn got out of his car and inspected a busted headlight, bashed it a few times with the meaty side of his fist. Nothing happened, so he cut the engine and headed for the back entrance to his house.

In the living room Mom watched nightly news that must have seemed just as alien as the music had been. On her lap she'd spread out the pictures that the investigators had left, and she was studying them, pressing her fingers into her temples like she was a psychic channeling a telepathic signal. She shook loose from her trance when Luc leaned down beside her.

"I tried," Mom said. "Right now I have to pee."

Luc helped her mother up, their arms slung together. Mom hobbled on one good leg while she used Luc's body for leverage. There was a sour, bodily odor, and Luc realized that even a bath would be a miracle of physics with that cast on her leg. Maybe when they finally sawed the plaster off, maybe then a more familiar life could return. In the bathroom she helped Mom raise her bathrobe and eased her down onto the seat while both of them grunted from the strain. Then Luc waited on the edge of the tub, where not long ago she'd found her mother almost dead from too many pills. It was a memory that she still carried, and a memory her mother had guiltlessly shed.

"Thank you," Mom said. She nudged Luc's chin upward with her thumb. Luc tried to smile back, but the shame of the moment kept her sober. She was saved by the telephone.

"Just a sec," Luc said. She left Mom alone in the bathroom while she went for the cordless, and even though it was Quinn she fretted through those minutes her mother sat helpless on the toilet. As if, unattended, Mom would fall in the bowl or tumble to the floor while trying to lift herself.

"I want to see you. Serious," Quinn said. "You need to come over here, though."

"I got my mom to take care of," said Luc. "I don't think I can leave her."

"Just for a minute. I want to tell you about something. In person, I mean."

"All right," said Luc. She listened for her mother down the hall and heard toilet paper unspooling and then the flush, the sounds of a woman taking care of herself. Luc hung up the phone and hurried back to the bathroom where her mother was already standing upright with one arm braced against the wall. Luc helped by tying Blair's robe belt back into a knot around her waist. Luc told her, "I'm just going to go over to Quinn's for a minute. You'll be okay, right?"

"Handsome," Blair said. "That boy."

"Quinn? You think Quinn's handsome?"

"You do," Blair said.

"He's my boyfriend. Never in a million years could I guess, Ma."

"A boy—he looks like—a boy. I knew him. Humphrey."

The name struck Luc like an instant migraine. "Humphrey Reid?" she said.

"Poor Humphrey," Blair said. "Sad boy."

BY FRIDAY NIGHT the flu bug had anchored deep into Greta's stomach and sent tendrils through her body. She drove home after dark and decided she'd better eat, so she peeled open a batch of frozen Salisbury steaks. She saw two messages on the answering machine that she didn't bother checking, but the phone rang again while she was preheating the oven. Even before she answered she knew it would be her daughter, Sandy. She answered anyway.

"You sound awful," her daughter said.

Greta told her, "I caught a wicked virus or something."

"I missed you at my bachelorette party tonight."

"I know. I was going to call you this morning," Greta stammered, unconvincing even to herself. "Did you leave something on my answering machine? I just got in so I didn't get a chance to listen to it yet."

"Yeah, I did," Sandy said. "See—I could've sworn you said you'd be able to make it. Remember I asked if it wouldn't be too awkward for you with some of the other guests? And you said no? First I thought you might've forgotten, but then today I got your wedding gifts in the mail with a shipping date from a few days ago, so it seems more like you weren't planning to come to my party or my wedding." Her words were rushed and recited—like she wanted to ensure she wouldn't forget to say anything, like she was maybe still a little drunk from the evening's revelry. And her voice was strained, so awful to hear that Greta almost wished she could break the phone connection.

Instead, Greta balked badly: "Did you like the towels?"

"I did, Mom, but—you know, I want this to work out. We keep trying to reach out to each other, but nothing seems to be happening right. I don't even actually have your RSVP for the wedding yet, so I still don't even know for sure if you're coming and it's two days away."

The wedding invitation was still on Greta's fridge, tucked under a magnet on the freezer door waiting for her to tick the box that said she'd attend. Every day, like a morning ritual, that little RSVP card sought to terrify her. She said, "Of course I'll be there, Sandy. I just haven't had a chance—I'm sorry I forgot to mail the card. Look, I'm sorry I didn't come to the party tonight but, I don't know, I thought I'd probably make people uncomfortable, being there."

"Like yourself? What's going to be any different at the wedding?"

"Nothing will be, but I'm going to be there anyway, all right? You can put me down on the guest list for certain. I just need to work through these issues—that's all. That's my job—I understand—believe me. I want this to work, too."

After the phone call Greta couldn't think about food anymore, so she rewrapped the steak patties in cellophane and put them back in the freezer. Self-diagnosis was simple enough: the problem was that Greta's old guilt was still burning fast, and it consumed all the willpower she needed to accept Sandy's forgiveness, which of course sparked new debilitating guilt all over again. What Greta couldn't yet manage was the grueling treatment program. In her ugliest thoughts she wanted to be free of this monumental reconstruction project she'd undertaken with her daughter, but Greta knew it was wrong, hopelessly wrong, to wish against her own salvation.

WHEN LUC KNOCKED on Quinn's front door his mother answered wearing a chevron-patterned poncho, her coal black hair tied in a braid that coiled over her shoulder like a pet. "I'm Lydia," she said, and when she shook Luc's hand her palm was moist from the condensation on a cocktail glass full of ice and clear booze that smelled like rubbing alcohol. Luc couldn't remember ever meeting Quinn's mother in person, though she'd seen her a thousand times at a distance. Living twenty feet apart for Luc's whole life, and still they were complete strangers.

"Is Quinn around?" Luc asked.

"Upstairs," the woman said—giddy, like she'd been waiting years for a visit from the neighbor kid. She led Luc to the bottom of the plush-carpeted staircase. "He's the first room on the left." The ice chimed in the glass she held. Around them the house was dark and crowded with more furniture than any two-person family could ever need. Deep-cushioned couches that were probably bought secondhand back when Quinn was born.

While Luc climbed the stairs she straightened the black skirt she'd put on to match her Nine Inch Nails T-shirt and her fishnet stockings.

She hadn't dressed for the part she used to play since the day after her father's death, and now she almost felt like that girl again, a kid with no bigger problem than her own self-esteem.

She followed the thumping music and found Quinn on his bed leaning against the headboard, dressed in jeans and a flannel shirt. The only lights in his room were black lights that made the white clothes on the floor glow neon purple. On his wall was a poster of Cindy Crawford in her bikini with beach sand peppering her ass.

"Come on in," he said. "Hey, close the door." He kicked a swivel chair away from his desk for her to sit on. The chair and desk were crammed into a narrow alley between bed and wall. Desktop littered with soda cans and biker mags. He flicked on a desk lamp to give them more light, but it was a weak glow that kept the corners in shadows. The room was a windowless alcove with a sloped ceiling. There were glow-in-the-dark stars glued to the ceiling, and from the corner of her eye it looked like the wide dome of heaven was spread out above them.

"I got your message this morning," Luc said. "You all right?"

"I don't know. This is fucked-up." He chewed on the inside of his cheek and watched a cordless telephone sitting on his bed like he was expecting it to ring. Nearby sat a crate full of vinyl records, and above that a shelf holding tons of CDs, most of them still sealed in their long boxes: Cannibal Corpse, Megadeth, Ministry, Motorhead, Napalm Death, Saigon Kick, all in alphabetical order.

"What's the matter?" Luc said. "Where'd you go after school?"

He hugged himself and tapped his fingers against his collarbone, ticking off the heavy seconds like a metronome. "I had some crap I had to take care of," he said.

"Look, if you're trying to break up with me—"

"No," he said. He shifted himself toward her, dropped his feet onto the floor, splayed his legs open so that Luc's knees almost touched his inner thighs. He said, "That isn't it. The problem is that I'm crazy and I want you to know that. I mean I'm messed up in the head." To illustrate he formed his hand into a gun and pressed the index barrel against his temple, clicked his thumb hammer.

"Join the club," Luc said. She clamped her teeth so they wouldn't chatter. She dug her knees into his mattress. "But you're creeping me out, man."

He pressed his hands onto her legs just above the knees and drifted them over her fishnets, his fingertips slipping through the open spaces in the netting. Luc closed her eyes and they were kissing again— mouths open and searching, teeth knocking together. They laughed against each other's lips and breathed hard gusts. His hands slid underneath the hem of her skirt, circling in patterns that kept widening, seeking around her thighs. She took those wandering hands, one in each of hers, and guided them gently back down her legs.

"Hold on a second," she said. She didn't want to cry, not now. She felt again that motorcycle speed and her mother's drop from the pier and the backward jolt of her father's Volvo. She laid her forehead on his shoulder and thought of Mom alone back at home watching the clock, addle brained, slipping unconscious. Luc kept thinking her mother would forget more of who she was if Luc didn't watch out for her. She could drop those last fragile relics of her memory and her daughter wouldn't be there to catch them.

"I don't want to stop," Quinn said. With both hands he raised Luc's head off his shoulder and slipped the glasses off her face, folded them, and set them on his desk. His face was a blur, so Luc moved closer until they were almost nose to nose before he came back into focus.

Luc said, "I'm practically blind."

She allowed herself to be lifted off the chair. In her delirium she was weightless. Mom would be fine, just for this minute. She was a grown woman after all. The stars on the ceiling were burning giants, closer than they'd ever been. They were together on the bed and Quinn's hands were tracing the knuckles of her spine. She was high on her hormones, and his groin pressed against hers. Nothing between them but clothes. His hands were on her ribs, on her breasts. His thumb flicked across her nipple and it was like shocks of green light sparking in her nerves. Never before had anyone touched—but there was nothing wrong or strange. Her skin stopped shivering and invited more.

Her own hands smoothed over the warm flesh on his knotted abdomen, seeking now across his arms toward his shoulders. She was throbbing, full of blood and expectation. Skirt hiked up around her hips and Quinn's knee wedged between her thighs, pressing, bone and flesh and denim against her silky black underpants.

"Your mom," Luc whispered.

"She won't hear us," Quinn said. They rolled onto the bed and something jutted hard against her ribs. When she grabbed for it she found that she held the cordless telephone. It rang in her hand. She thought she'd accidentally pressed a button, but then it rang again.

"Don't answer," Quinn said. He took the phone from her, and it disappeared. It rang muffled a third time, like he'd somehow buried it under the floorboards. Luc was awake now from her stupor, suddenly aware of his weight and her awful moaning and his thigh shoved between her knees.

Quinn whispered, "Man, if your mother could see us now . . ."

"What?" Luc croaked.

In the dim light Quinn's eye sockets darkened into black holes and his face glowed moonlike. He sat up and his head thumped against the sloped ceiling. "Shit," he grunted, and they laughed together. Quinn's laugh issued from the wavering sphere that Luc understood to be his face. Every time the phone rang, it hounded Luc like an unanswered question. She could feel the stiffness in his jeans, pressing into her stomach like the end of a broom handle. He was smothering her again, wet mouth on her neck.

"I can't with the phone ringing," she said. Maybe it was her mom calling. Impossible.

"My mother will get it," he said.

But the phone kept ringing, and this time she thought it might be her father calling. The ceiling pressed down on them and the plastic stars were all falling, burning through her flesh. There were fists knocking on the walls, heavy fists that could break through if only they had substance, if only they weren't just brittle bones and ether. Her father's hands, risen from the ash inside the sprinkling urn. But there was no savior tonight for her, not even the tiny men skittering across the floor. The beating she heard was her heart in spasms.

"I can't do this," Quinn told her, but Luc had already unhooked herself from whatever line had dragged them into this configuration. He talked but she wasn't hearing anymore.

"I have to pee," Luc whispered. "The bathroom. I have to pee."

"Seriously? Right now?" he said, huffing into her ear canal.

She reached for her glasses and with her groping knocked a stack of magazines and empty cans onto the floor before she finally had the cold metal frames in her hands. The lenses were smeared with her fingerprints by the time she got them on her face. She stood and brushed her skirt back down over her hips. "Please," she said.

"It's across the hall, but I want to tell you—"

"Just give me a second," Luc said. She was already out the door, sliding along the wood-paneled wall that spanned down the hallway. There was the bathroom as he promised, the sink and toilet waiting in the dark. She found the light switch, flicked it on. Dried toothpaste in the washbasin, coiled hair strands on the counter, lumps of old soap on the tub rim, one screened window too small to fit through. Luc had meant to go inside the bathroom, to chill a minute, but instead she pushed the interior lock button and shut the door from the hallway. The light came through underneath the door, casting the illusion that she'd locked herself in there. It seemed now a better plan to vanish completely than to simply hide where she could be found.

She sneaked down the stairs and into the foyer. In the living room Quinn's mother was sprawled on the couch watching TV. Luc twisted the doorknob in both hands and pulled open a view of the street lamps and the frozen black ground. She ran, stumbling down onto one knee in her own front yard, one steadying hand crushing frozen grass. She scrambled upright and raced through black and sharp empty branches darting for her face.

Her legs carried her back up her own porch steps through the front door that was already inched open. Hands on the warm doorknob, boots on the foyer floor. She slapped for the switch on the wall and tripped it.

"Lu—" Mom said. Her mother was on the floor beside the couch, both hands pressed into the carpet, legs sprawled behind her. The cast on her leg was split wide open, snapped threads and powdery chalk. Like an infant she raised her weak head and squinted at the light. Red and black colored welts blooming on her face. So many gashes raw and puckered. One eye wouldn't open. The backs of her hands bloodied. So much maiming for an ordinary tumble.

Luc's fear ignited like match-lit gasoline. She screamed and leaped backward with her shoulder blades arching like some dream of bearing wings, but her scream was snuffed by a wet suffocating hand slapped over her mouth from behind, crushing her nostrils shut. A hand from behind the door, yanking Luc's head backward. Another arm slung around her waist and tightened, fingers digging between her ribs. A jacket made of dark red leather, and the earthy smell of a man's dirty hand.

Luc thrust herself backward against this other body grappling hers. She threw her legs upward and kicked her boot soles double-barrel against the foyer wall, hard enough to crack the Sheetrock and propel her backward with her captor. He hit the open door, crashed a glass pane out of its porthole. He coughed out one astonished breath. Now Luc's feet had nothing to punch. His fingers stabbed. Luc's lungs spasmed for the air that his crushing palm withheld.

She went limp from the pain. Harsh white conquered her vision and her balance reeled. She was barely conscious when he tossed her forward. She saw her own descent, but her hands wouldn't work to save her. Her face punched against the carpeted floor and the fibers dragged a burn across her cheek. Glasses still on her face but bent at the earpiece. Mom on her stomach five feet off with one eye mashed shut and the other thrown wide. Mom had no voice, so with that one good eye she screamed.

Luc dragged herself toward her mother. She gulped oxygen and braced for the kick or stab or shot that she expected. When nothing happened, she looked at the intruder. He was twenty or maybe older, pompadour hair and long sideburns and a goatee that was just a tuft under his lip. A spanking red-leather jacket ribbed at the elbows and zipped all the way up to his chin. A handgun with a square silver barrel aimed toward her. She squinted, and waited for darkness. What she saw in her head was her father's blood, and that same gun barrel shoved through his driver's window.

Luc raised herself up on hands and knees, marked like a sprint runner set for the starting gun. She'd fly if she had to. She'd burst out that kitchen window ten feet away and sail down into her backyard. Crash through the glass because otherwise she'd die. She knew that, like she knew that Quinn wouldn't save her. He'd be dozing on his bed, nursing a hard-on, waiting for that bathroom door to open.

The intruder said, "You know where the money is? Huh, bitch?"

"I don't know," Luc said. The money was just a dream. Five thousand bucks under the dryer. She wanted to tell him it was just a dream. But the pain in her ribs, the burn in her cheek, the taste of that man's flesh on her tongue—not a dream. All of it true as daylight or nothing was.

"Bullshit! Wake her up! She knows where it is and so do you. Don't you? I'll kill you both to prove it. Get me my demon wings."

"It was under the dryer but then it was gone," Luc said. She was kneeling now, facing away from him. She might as well have been blindfolded, awaiting an execution that might've arrived if Mom hadn't groaned and rolled onto her back.

Mom blinked one eyed and said, "Oscar. Where?"

"Tell me!" The intruder aimed the gun back and forth between the two of them. It would fire, Luc thought, if only out of pent-up force, but she refused to witness such ruin again.

"She had an accident! She can't remember!" Luc screamed. "The money was gone when I checked, and you can see yourself! You can go look if you want but it's not there!"

Mom lurched toward the intruder and grabbed his ankle with both of her hands. For a second Luc believed something like a miracle would happen, but he kicked his leg out of her grasp and stomped on her fingers. Mom drew back her damaged hands, too weak to cry out.

"I'm gonna shoot your kid in the face, Blair," he said. "I'm gonna kill her dead if you don't cough up that money. None of this amnesia bullshit. You got that?"

"She doesn't remember," Luc pleaded.

"One . . ." He turned the weapon toward Luc and set the cold gun-metal against her ear. He said, "Two, bitch. Money. Now. You're gonna make me say three?"

Luc's mind clamored for one last concrete thought, but nothing came. The gun pulled back. The intruder heaved his arm toward Luc's head. There was hot, crushing pain and then black silence. But not death, not yet. She was drifting in a gray pool of static. It lightened, and Luc could feel the carpet against her face again. Her mother screamed. Luc wanted to scream but she couldn't feel where her mouth was. Another blow full of bright flashbulbs smashed her in the skull. It was an instant short circuit.

three

DAUGHTER OF HEL

A summer noon in lazy bliss, tuned to the hum of the trolling motor. The *Ringhorn* was swayed by placid waves, and Luc was on deck, seated on a fish box cushion, sunscreen lathered on her face, two Sprites gurgling in her belly. A fishing rod bent off of each aft corner from the tension of the downrigger. Luc was eight or nine, almost nodding asleep while she waited for a trout to tug her line and release the catch. At the helm Dad lounged in his swim trunks with his shoulders freckled brown and his nose skin peeling from a sunburn. His chest was bursting with hair translucent blond. Underneath Luc, the fish box was empty. The water glittered with shards of sunlight, horizon hazed like a dream. They were out on the lake beyond sight of the shoreline and it was like floating over a depthless ocean.

Her father nudged her in the knee with his sandal. "Did you see that?"

Luc flinched awake. "What?" she said.

"Over there." He pointed out beyond the reach of their two fishing lines, but Luc saw nothing except the dancing crests out there. He said, "It's the Midgard Serpent."

"Cut it out, Dad."

"I have a good feeling we'll catch it this time. Today is our day."

"Maybe we'll catch the Loch Ness monster, too."

Dad said, "You laugh, Flicka. But remember: the return of the Midgard Serpent heralds the coming of Ragnarok, the Doom of the Gods. The end of the world is nothing to joke about." He was affecting his story-teller voice—booming announcements like he was a corny Shakespeare actor.

An instant yank on Luc's line and the downrigger released. She gasped and jumped up to throttle the rod with both hands. She flexed her body against it, raring to fight, hoping she had a weighty lake trout with a frown and tan spots mottling its greenish scales. More than twenty pounds would beat her record—but while she was dreaming the line went slack again. She reeled a few inches and felt no more resistance. The sweat on her nose made her glasses slip downward, but she pushed them back up with her shoulder.

"See? The serpent is taunting you, Lucia."

"Knock it off, Dad. You'll give me a complex."

He cleared his throat and leaned toward her, smirking like he always smirked when a story possessed him. He said, "It will begin with three great winters full of darkness, three seasons without sunlight or warmth." He swooped his hands overhead to mimic the catastrophes. "There will come hailing ice storms and arctic winds. Fear and anger will wound the hearts of men and gods alike, and they will wage violent battles with one another full of swords and clubs and arrows and blood."

"Are you finished?" Luc groaned.

"That's just the beginning," Dad said. He was cranking up the down-rigger cable.

"You never told me this part when I was little," Luc said.

"I didn't want to scare you for no reason, but now—with the serpent in our midst—I have no choice—"

Something bashed against the hull and caused the boat to lurch and toss. Luc's heels lifted off the deck, but she slammed them back down. A sleek hollow noise dragged along the hull, a noise like the boat was skimming against the length of a rubber hose wide as a sewer pipe. Luc tried to catch sight of it, but she couldn't see anything beneath the sunlight reflecting on the surface of the water. She said, "What the heck was that?"

Dad chuckled as he kneaded the back of her neck with his hand. "Now you're coming around, *nej?* Next the earth will rumble with earthquakes so powerful that mountains will collapse in great avalanches, and even the hardiest trees will be ripped from the ground by their roots. Even worse, the tremors will break the great wolf Fenris free from his bonds and awaken the Midgard Serpent from its ancient sleep. It will rise up and slither its way toward shore."

He pointed over the lake again, far out toward the north horizon, where another vessel had now appeared. It was just a dark blotch at such a distance, but still Luc could see it was more massive than any of the boats she'd ever spotted out on the lake. Tall masts without sails speared into the cloudless blue sky, and Dad explained: "And what you see out there is the ghost ship *Naglfar.* It has been constructed over centuries out of the stolen fingernails and toenails of dead men. An evil frost giant named Hyrm commands that ship. It carries the troops out of Hel—which is spelled with just one "l" in the old Nordic tongue. Those undead soldiers are coming to bring defeat to the gods."

"But there aren't any gods, Dad," Luc pleaded. "It's just stories."

This time, off the starboard side, the lake surface broke and revealed a dark span of the serpent's tubular body, crusted with black scales and algae. Again the boat tossed and now even her father's line released the downrigger ball. He grabbed the rod and grunted while he struggled, but in seconds it jerked from his grip and slapped against the lake water and disappeared below. He hissed and shook the pain from his hands, chuckled, wide eyed, like he'd just been bested by a practical joke. He leaned over the gunwale for a better look, oblivious to the danger.

"Dad—what are you doing?" Luc asked. She was frantically reeling in her line, but something caught hold and bowed the rod low and stiff like an archery bow. She watched the thin line straighten rigid as it pulled away from her.

"Hold on, Lucia! Don't let it go!" her father commanded in a voice full of fire and life. He bellowed over the sound of a phantom rumble that boiled out of the depths like the first tremors of an earthquake: "It ends in chaos! The evil god Surt will ride out of the fire region called Muspell with his demon legions, and with his flaming sword he will set fire to the earth. Nothing will be spared."

"Ragnarok," Luc said. Her arms ached from the struggle, her skin reddened between her hipbone and the fishing rod, but she held fast to the cushioned rubber handle. Strange pressure built in her lungs and filled her throat until it almost choked her. She let it loose and heard that it was a laugh, loud and fearless as her father's. Twenty feet out something huge was churning up swells of whitewater—dull black fish scales on its back and maybe an eye the color of egg yolk but a hundred times that size. She anchored her shoes against the gunwale and held her straining rod. Kept reeling and yanking upward while her palms burned and cramped. That rod would snap to splinters before she'd let herself release it.

GRETA HAD CRASHED bedridden by eight-thirty Friday with nothing for dinner but a medicine cup of Nyquil. Her sleep was infected with hallucinations: Luc Moberg starved to the bones, Greta spoon-feeding oatmeal into her mouth. Then Luc was a bald baby whimpering in a high chair. Greta woke sweating in a silent apartment with the digital clock reading midnight. She'd kicked the sheets away and her pillow was on the floor. Her throat felt like it'd been scraped with a wire brush.

In the bathroom she poured tap water into a Dixie cup, drank it down, saw her mirror face looking sallow in the orange-tinted nightlight. Face like the living dead and only one day until Sandy's wedding. She held back the bitterness as best she could because all this divorce and remarriage and animosity—it all trailed back to her mistakes. She'd sliced open those permanent wounds and now it was her job to nurse them, not Sandy's.

The phone rang on her third cup of water. She caught it just after the second ring, thinking it'd be Sandy again. But it was her partner

Moe Arslan, and he told her, "Listen, I'm sorry to call you at home, Greta, but there's been a—we think Luc Moberg's been kidnapped. Earlier tonight a break-in occurred at the girl's house. The mother's been badly assaulted. She's currently at Lakeshore Hospital in Hammersport."

"I'm getting dressed," Greta told her partner before she hung up on him.

She eased down on the edge of her bed because her sick muscles had crumpled. Again came a vision of that baby from her dream, but she couldn't tell if the specter was her figment of Luc or her memory of Sandy. It was the same baby somehow, and Moe had announced that Greta's whole life was hijacked—her murder case, the wedding, everything. It was ugly logic from a fevered mind, but it still hurt like hell.

THE THROB IN LUC'S skull base was sending sharper flares over her head, down her spine, deep into her ears. She was lying prone in pitch dark and growing aware that this terrible pain had lifted her from a dream. She thrashed against her stiff bedding and thrust her feet into an unyielding wall. She sought rightward with her hands and squeezed a blockade of cushioned foam that felt like the stuff inside of snow boots. A memory flashed: years ago sitting on porch steps while her father yanked her snow boots off, how they'd laughed because the foam sock still hugged stubbornly to her foot.

She couldn't remember what had happened. She thought she was dead and already crammed inside a coffin, but what about this constant rumble in her bones, and the way she was jostled every few seconds as if they'd buried her in a ground prone to earthquakes? Ten seconds of perception was all she needed to know she was still alive, trapped in the trunk of a moving car.

Cars passed in wavelike wisps, a white noise broken by the sudden blast of a semi truck. The muffler sputtered underneath, wafting up dirty fumes that Luc feared would asphyxiate her long before the car ever stopped. She didn't want to fade unconscious into death like a sickly animal euthanized, but she coughed up fumes that inflamed her headache and made her woozy and confused. The liquid pulses of her heartbeat spilled across her eardrums.

Luc tried to touch her head wound but her wrists were twined together with tight plastic snap-cuffs. Another pair also bound her legs, slicing at her ankles through her fishnet stockings. She groped around the trunk and touched dead leaves, damp foam tufts, an empty plastic bottle of motor oil. She reached for the cold metal hatch and shoved but it wouldn't budge. Grasped the latch device but her frosted fingers found no way to open it. Bashed her fists against the hood hatch and screamed until her throat was shredded.

She fought back panic by tugging wires until they broke loose from their connections. She thought maybe she'd disabled a taillight that could now catch a traffic cop's attention, but her hope vanished when the smooth pavement glide cut into crunching and trembling gravel. They were driving away from whatever main road they'd been on, leaving behind all the miracle patrol cars waiting in vain at their roadside speed traps. The tires spit pebbles against the undercarriage. Luc's head wound fired with fresh pain. The sighs of passing cars were long gone now.

EN ROUTE TO HAMMERSPORT, Greta stopped once at a highway gas station for Evian, two ephedrine pills, and a soft pack of Marlboros. Her bone marrow buzzed by the time she turned onto the Mobergs' street and saw that local cops had kept the circus discreet: just two cruisers parked on the road and no sirens flashing. A manageable audience of gawkers loitered on the sidewalks, their attention focused on the lights blaring from every room in the Moberg home. Greta parked curbside and got out.

She flashed her badge at the townie cop guarding the Moberg porch, then spotted boot scuffs on the wall, blood on the carpet. Probably the full force of the Hammersport PD was in attendance at this party, but Greta skirted small talk as she moved into the kitchen and saw, bagged on the breakfast table, Luc's black-framed glasses busted on one side.

Seeing them wrenched her stomach just as viciously as if she'd caught sight of a severed limb. She had to brace herself on the table edge. When the Hammersport chief of police materialized, he seemed ghost-like, casting his messages from someplace outside her perception. He spoke of the emergency call that had been placed by the neighbor kid, Blair Moberg unconscious and beaten on the living room floor, Blair Moberg waking in the ambulance to rant about a single assailant who'd simply rung the doorbell to gain entry, her daughter Luc rushing home from the neighbors' to be ambushed by the same assailant.

Greta shut herself inside the Mobergs' bathroom and ran cold water to splash on her face, hoping it would make her feel less stale and used and static brained. The woman in the mirror could've played a corpse in a Halloween hayride. All night she hadn't been able to shift her perspective right—vision blurred like she was trapped inside a camera zoomed too close to its subject. And now she'd let this happen. Greta wiped her face on a damp hand towel and warned herself to remain intact.

She left the Mobergs' and tracked across the yard to the neighbors' house. Inside stank of mold and dog urine, though there was no animal in sight. Easy to tag the family as pack rats, especially in the kitchen, where the counters were loaded up to the overhead cupboards with beer crates, junk mail, empty paper towel rolls, twine balls, potting soil bags, empty Tupperware, sugared cereal boxes, bundled plastic utensils and paper plates, mason jars full of coins and buttons and rubber bands and something pickled.

Moe Arslan flashed Greta his red groggy eyes. He was sitting with the hostess and her son at a Formica-top table. His notebook was open, current page filled with notes, but the pen lay dormant on the table now. Moe stood up and made the introductions, pulled out a vacant chair so Greta could sit.

The woman, Lydia Cutler, babbled an incoherent greeting, and her son Quinn said nothing, barely glanced at Greta. They were both smoking, flicking ashes into a glass ashtray already loaded with butts. They were obviously of Native American descent, and the mother was wearing a hempen poncho for the final touch. She was bleary and possibly drunk, zoning like she'd been hypnotized. Quinn was holding back tremors, riled enough to burst forth snarling if the command was given. Seeing him, Greta remembered that Luc had called this kid her boyfriend. She supposed that his pain was on par with her own.

"The police chief gave me sketchy details," Greta said. "Where's the gramma?"

"Blair Moberg told the Hammersport guys that she was out gambling," Moe said. "She must be on an all-nighter because we haven't tracked her down yet."

"We're sure she wasn't at the scene?"

"Fairly certain," Moe said. He flipped back one page in his notes and skimmed them. "Quinn here tells me Lucia Moberg left this house at approximately seven-fifteen. About twenty minutes later, concerned about her, he visited the Moberg home and discovered Mrs. Moberg had been assaulted and that Lucia Moberg had been abducted."

"I called the cops right away—after I checked on her—Mrs. Moberg," Quinn said. He was drumming his knuckles against his own tensed forehead, staring at the tabletop.

"How long was Lucia at your house?" Greta asked Quinn.

"I'd say about ten minutes—not much more than that."

"Somebody was watching the house for an opportunity," Moe theorized.

"Why only ten minutes?" Greta said. "She's your girlfriend, isn't she?"

"I didn't even know she'd left at first. She said she was going to the bathroom."

"And it took you twenty minutes to realize she didn't?" Greta pushed.

"Because she tricked me. I mean, she turned on the bathroom light and shut the door and even locked it. I thought she was in there the whole time until I knocked and nobody answered."

"How did you know she wasn't just not answering you?" Greta said.

"I kept knocking. I kept saying things at the door—until my mom told me."

The woman fidgeted with her lighter in one hand and fanned herself with a *TV Guide* in the other. She said, "Right, I saw her leave out the front door, but I didn't think nothing of it till he started yelling after a while."

"Yelling?" Greta asked Quinn.

"I was worried about her, and I'm still pretty freaking worried about her, even more."

"Greta—" Moe said, pointing at his notebook, trying to wrangle her back to the page he'd started her on. But Greta wouldn't let herself be nudged, gently or otherwise.

"Why were you worrying? Why did you yell? What happened?" Greta said.

Quinn kept his gaze on the tabletop, as if some better answer than the truth was carved there for him to read. "I think she got spooked, I don't know. We were messing around."

"And you pushed her too far, is that it?" Greta asked. The cottony stupor inside her head was burning off fast, and now she realized how far she'd strayed from the pertinent facts.

"No," Quinn said, stabbing his spent cigarette into the trayful of stale yellowed stumps. "No—I let up right away, and I just let her do what she wanted. But I was worried she was still mad and that's why she wasn't coming out of the bathroom."

The mother was getting antsy, digging at the scabs on her forearms. She said, "Quinn, he didn't do nothing wrong here. You know, he's the one that went over to that house and found her bleeding, the neighbor lady. She might be much worse off if he wasn't there to call 911 for her."

Moe said, "We understand that, Ms. Cutler. We appreciate what Quinn did here."

Greta's jaw shuddered. She yearned to machine-gun all three of them with her ugliest words, but she settled for: "He didn't keep Lucia from getting taken, did he?"

TANYA WAS ALONE in the cabin kitchen, wrapped and shivering in a ragged blanket that she'd found folded on a cot in one of the sleeping

stalls. It was way past dark and the only light came from some oil lamps—
one of them set on the kitchen table with its glass chimney charred
brown. The heat breathing from the wood-burning stove was too far-off
and weak to warm her. She hated this quiet, sitting around waiting for
Mason, knowing she was the only human person around for miles probably. For all she knew, Mason could be dead in a car crash or snagged by
cops. The world could end and she'd never hear the message. She'd go
on living and after weeks she'd finally give birth by herself like some
grunting mammal in the wild.

She'd already wasted the last hour snooping through the kitchen.
She'd lifted an oil lantern by the handle and shined it on three open
shelves to better see the stock of canned vegetables and pastas, paper
plates, tea boxes, rice bags, rat traps, unopened cereal boxes, generic
batteries, mosquito candles and matchboxes, stained coffee mugs, liter-
sized propane replacements for the portable gas range they cooked on.
She'd already boiled water for tea and drunk it from a mug with an im-
print of a Doberman that was just like Buck's dog Furnace. She'd even
swept dirt off the kitchen linoleum floor, which was blistered and curled
at the edges and cracked when you walked so it sounded like you were
crunching roaches. She'd torn down and chucked five glue-tape flytraps
because they were all dotted with empty dead blackfly husks.

There were some measly windows, typical height but not even wide
enough to fit your head through, all of them covered by plastic sheets
stapled up. The one over the sink was the only wide one, and that's
where Tanya put her garden gnome so he could look outside from the
sill while she washed the dishes. And it was through that same window
that Tanya finally saw the Deville's headlights flash through the trees up
the road. She blew a kiss to God or whatever for showing her some
mercy for once, then she hurried outside, still snug in her blanket, onto
a porch that was really just a concrete slab with cinderblock steps leading down.

When the Caddy turned into the yard, it slumped down a few inches
through the fresh snow that had been falling onto this mountainside all
afternoon. The car slowed fast and the tires groaned and spun. Mason

reversed it, then gunned forward again and plodded another couple feet before it screeched and sank back down into the snow. From maybe fifty feet off, Tanya heard Mason yell, "Motherfucker!" She was glad to hear his voice.

She rushed out into shin-deep snow that buried her tennis shoes. Closer to the car, she smelled burned rubber and exhaust fumes. She called out, "Mason, you're stuck!"

Mason pushed open the driver's door and told her he knew damn well he was stuck, and just then the engine stalled on him. The door alarm was pinging nonstop, so he got out and slammed the door shut. He said, "It ain't this kind of weather anyplace else but here."

"I was worried about you," Tanya said, but he was already stomping toward the back of the car, futzing with the keys in his hands. She said, "What're you doing?"

Mason said, "Why don't you get back inside, Tan. It's freezing."

"Did you get the rest of the money?" she asked.

"Things got fucked up," he told her.

SOMEONE WAS TAPPING the key around the trunk hatch, poking for the keyhole. Luc squeezed her eyes closed. She heard their muttering voices and she slammed her mouth shut to keep from breathing, as if holding her own breath would somehow make those voices and that key tapping vanish. But the trunk hatch lifted. When the arctic air pushed inside, her eyes shocked open and she saw the two blurred faces leering down at her, a man and woman stretched like reflections in funhouse mirrors. Luc only saw like this with her naked eyes, so she knew that her glasses were gone. Falling snow pellets peppered her upraised hands and settled on her face and eyelids and everywhere.

"What did you do? What happened?" the blond woman asked.

"Just get out of my way for a second," he said, the man who'd been inside Luc's house.

"That girl—she's the daughter, isn't she? What are you doing with her?"

The man grabbed Luc's two bound hands and twisted her jacket sleeves in his fists. He lifted her like a twist-tied bag of trash, dragging her torso across the lip of the trunk, spilling her onto the snowy ground. The impact punched her ribs from behind. Another pain blast in her skull, another spasm of hard, hacking coughs dry as gunpowder.

"Where's her mother?" begged the woman.

He said, "I left her."

"Is she—"

"No."

Luc tried to find footing but her hog-tied ankles kicked only loose snow. The man squatted down and lifted her up two-handed, cradled her—one arm under the crook of her knees and the other behind her back. Luc might've struggled free, maybe slammed her clasped fists against his face, but she knew he carried a gun and she didn't want to wind up shot through the head for trying something stupid. Another memory flash: New Year's Day, age seven, minutes after midnight Dad had carried her just like this to her room while she pretended to sleep against his chest, listening to his heartbeat thump like an endless count-down: ten, nine, eight, seven . . .

In fact, all memories seemed suddenly open to her now, crowding into her mind and calling out at random. The day on her father's boat when she'd caught a twenty-pound trout he'd helped her reel. Drinking her first warm beer with Gina and Kit on the high school dugouts after dark. Candlelight Christmas dinner with Mom and Dad and three roasted Cornish hens on glazed red and green ceramic plates. Still in a stroller being pushed through the mall past a fountain bursting airborne water, pennies and dimes gleaming in its shallow pool. And just last summer: Dad with a sledgehammer lumbering across the backyard toward a sagging, empty shed, then Dad heaving the sledgehammer two-handed and smashing it down. How wood had splintered and spiraled and how the rotting shed had collapsed.

BLAIR MOBERG WAS in the emergency ward at Lakeshore Hospital—a tiled hallway lined with cots and curtains, fluorescent tube lights in the ceiling. All the beds were empty with the curtains pulled back, except for the one occupied bed halfway down the corridor. Greta and Moe followed a nurse toward it and there they found Blair lying awake without IV bags or monitors or anything to show her life was threatened. She wore a baggy hospital gown and was fitted with a new leg cast. Her face: two raw gashes shut with stitches, one on her forehead and the other across her right cheek, snagged on her mouth like a harelip. Right eye cast in blue from bruises, left eye socket stuffed up with a round bandage and cross-taped—no telling what damage lurked under there. She was sliced and trampled like the scalpel work of a drunk plastic surgeon.

"Blair Moberg," Moe said.

The right eye darted toward him, wide and alert. "Where's Lucia?" Blair said.

"We're doing what we can to find her," Moe told her. "We're devoting every second to finding her, Blair, and we've already made some progress. But first and foremost we need to identify the man who assaulted you."

The attending nurse dabbed salve on Blair's wounds, and the contact made her flinch like it was a hornet stinging her. She moaned and clamped her good eye shut and jerked her head away from the nurse's treatment. Blair's mouth hung in a heavy scowl when she said, "He pushed his gun on her head, that man."

"Did he shoot her?" Greta demanded, loud enough that her voice resounded in the ward.

"I don't—no—he hit her."

"Did this guy say anything to you?"

Blair said, "'Where's the money?' He kept saying it. He said, 'Where's my money,' and he was hitting me over and over." She was red faced and tearful, stiffening her grip on the bed rails.

"Did he find his money, Blair?"

"Wha—"

"Did he maybe tell you why he thought the money was his to take?"

Moe said, "Greta, watch it—"

"He kept saying, 'Where's my money?'" Blair repeated.

Greta slapped the metal footboard with both hands and the impact knocked the patient chart onto the floor. "You said that already, Blair. I'm asking for what makes some kind of rational sense. Must be nice to forget all that stuff, huh Blair? Pretty convenient? You want to take a wild guess why you might owe this bastard money?"

"Greta, lay off. She's not Mirandized, and it wouldn't help anyway. Not now."

The rage had rendered Greta weightless and drifting, drugged into a frenzy.

Blair Moberg was hyperventilating. "Oscar?" she cried. "Stop saying he's dead."

"You can't deny what you can't remember," Greta said. She stormed through the hall and out the main entrance. By the door she fired up a cigarette and took long deep drags while the arctic front blasted her face numb. She remembered thinking when she was a kid that her soul was this white orb glowing in the pit of her stomach, swaying in there like a clock pendulum timed to the beat of her heart. She'd thought it was there to weigh her down, to keep her from drifting off into infinite cold space. She hadn't thought about her soul much since then, but now she felt that pendulum swinging again. Every minute it swayed was another minute some nameless fucker had custody of a teenaged girl who didn't belong to him, who he could rape or torture or kill or whatever the hell he pleased.

The automatic doors parted and Moe came out slouching with his hands in his pockets. He stood beside her a few quiet seconds before he said, "That pointless grilling did nothing for our case, so I hope it had some ulterior personal benefit to you."

"You bet your ass," Greta said.

"At this point we should do something a little more productive," Moe suggested, "like releasing pictures of the pregnant woman to the media, see if anyone recognizes her."

"And show our last low card to these Skeleton Crew assholes?"

"Unless you have a better—"

"No, Muhammad, I don't," Greta said. "Let's just get it over with."

TANYA TRAILED BEHIND Mason while he lugged the dazed girl across the yard to the property edge. He grunted and panted from the strain, stumbled once and righted himself. A hundred questions bothered Tanya's thoughts but she voiced none of them, scared to mess with Mason's focus. It was too dark to see, but she remembered what was out here: a derelict pickup truck, and hitched to it was a trailer with plain aluminum siding, a trailer hardly bigger than an overturned elevator car.

Every new start to her life with Mason got wrecked by sudden shocks like this, even though Mason himself was immune to the fear that seemed like the most natural reaction. Except this time—because this time Tanya caught a whiff of his panic. She sensed blame buzzing around their heads, hunting for a place to land.

"Take the keys out of my pocket," he said. "Unlock that door."

Tanya obeyed, though her hands shuddered and Mason swore at her twice while she knelt in the snow and tested keys and tried to work the trailer bolt lock in the dark. When it snapped open she breathed again and slid it out and pulled back the latch.

"Lift it up," he demanded. He jostled the girl's limp weight in his arms.

The door was lengthwise metal slats that curled upward on tracks and rattled angrily. Inside was cold enough to be a meat locker, lined with a slatted metal floor. Mason stepped up and laid the girl inside. She gasped awake and thrashed like a fresh-caught fish you'd been tricked into thinking was dead. Tanya flinched, slapped her hand over her mouth.

Mason told her, "Give me that blanket." He tore the blanket off Tanya's shoulders and tossed it over the panicked girl like a net. Then he wrenched the door downward and slammed it and threw the latch. Inside the girl was still flailing, bashing the door slats, shrieking a feline racket that was muffled by the trailer walls.

"Put that lock back on there," Mason said, and headed up through the snow toward the cabin.

MOMENTUM AND FRIGHTFUL ideas had kept Greta trucking all night long. She'd seen dozens of kidnappings in her time, but most were secretly runaway kids who'd boomerang home within a month unless they had stellar motives for keeping themselves gone. The rest were largely family deals, snatchings by noncustodial parents, situations that were volatile and ambiguous but rarely deadly. There'd been a handful of true stranger abductions—the flyers, the pleas, news reports, searches, desperate parents—anguish enough to set a cop's spirit into concrete. Because without fail these cases had ended with corpses or bones or permanent mystery, every last one. This was the fact that spurred Greta onward, though she dared not voice it.

Mitch Wendt sat in her presence, fuming from his green plastic chair. He wrenched the handcuffs that kept him clamped to a metal beam underneath the interview table, a futile show to prove he was pissed about being dragged out of the city jail three hours before dawn for talk and doughnuts with Greta. He told her, "Yesterday you said you'd get me out—but here we are again. I think it's pretty shitty when people break promises." He had some leftover doughnut powder on his lips.

"I didn't promise anything," Greta said, "and new developments have now forced us to detain you." They were sharing another interview room, but this time she wasn't using the buddy seat beside him. She was on her feet and leaning against the back wall because if she came any closer she'd likely indulge her desire to slash those handcuffs at his bull-dog face over and over until the metal claw gouged him down to nothing but his hard white skull.

"What developments?" he asked.

Greta showed the Xeroxed still of the preggo blonde at Shop-Mor. "Know her?"

Wendt hardly glanced at it before he said, "No."

"Why don't you look at it carefully? You don't know her or the man she works with? He wears a red leather jacket, Elvis-style hairdo, carries a Colt .45?"

"Nope," he said.

"Whoever he is—he kidnapped a little girl last night. Maybe murdered her."

Greta noted a twitch in Wendt's scowl. If only to avoid eye contact, he pulled the Xerox toward him with his free hand and gave it more attention. Licked his powdered lips, scratched the back of his head. He asked her, "How's this my problem?"

"That's funny, Mitch," Greta deadpanned. Arms folded tight on her chest, face drawn—she didn't blink. She made fists and let her fingernails cut into her palms when she said, "It's your problem because these people are part of the Skeleton Crew, or closely associated, and even though you were locked up in jail last night when it happened you can still be implicated in a conspiracy charge. That's how it's your fucking problem."

Mitch laughed an ugly grunt. He grabbed the picture and made a convincing show of studying it. "I'll tell you straight, man, this chick ain't in the Crew. I never seen her before."

"A little girl, Mitch," Greta said. "Think about that."

"I'm thinking," he said. "And I'm feeling like shit about it, like anybody else would. But I'm telling you I don't know this bitch or whoever she rides with. Serious." This time his denial was more exasperated than smug, as if he'd convinced even himself that he was a stand-up citizen. Greta stared him down and he shrugged in response.

She worked on him for another hour with pleasantries, trick questions, offerings, setups, subtle intimidations, and a feast of outright lies. The insurmountable hurdle was that Wendt had enjoyed a passable night's sleep, while Greta was running on fumes that made her head scream like an engine dry of oil. She wouldn't get him talking even if she offered him a free pass out of the inferno when he croaked. So another prospect itched at her: why not just let Mitchell Wendt walk away and then put somebody on his tail to see where his journey of freedom would take him? He'd almost certainly make contact with other members, maybe even the kidnapper or the pregnant woman. In Greta's wildest dreams he'd lead them straight to Luc Moberg herself.

She left Wendt in the interview room and went roaming for Moe, found him snoozing at his cubicle. She nudged his foot and he said, "Just resting my eyes a minute."

"He isn't talking," Greta reported. She wanted badly to punch something and howl her throat ragged and then sleep for ten hours straight—in that order. "I mean—he's talking but it's just nonsense. He's playing the best pals game right back at me and he's giving nothing. Every second I'm in there, Moe, I want to rip his throat out. I never wanted to kill anybody more than I want to kill him right now."

"I'll work on him awhile," Moe said. He covered a yawn with his fist while he told her, "Maybe the male dynamic will—"

"Come on, Moe, don't give me that shit," she said through her teeth. "Let's cut him loose and put a tail order on him."

"All right, fine—if my follow-up interview doesn't produce. I can go in fresh."

"Fuck off, Moe," Greta spat.

"Calm down, Greta."

"Don't tell me what to do, you chauvinist asshole."

"Greta—" Moe pleaded, like he was placating a child.

In a sensible corner of her mind, Greta knew she was surrendering to panic, but the rage gushed through her like dope, like lust, and she was blazing with the ugly pleasure of it. She told Moe, "Grill him, then. Good fucking luck," and then she stormed out, swiping her jacket from where it hung on her partition wall. She shared the elevator with a madwoman who was panting and burning and gnashing her teeth—but Greta was alone and the walls were mirrored.

TANYA WONDERED HOW little it would take to lose whatever made her human. She shivered under four blankets, sleeping only in short fits.

She couldn't for a second stop musing about the girl locked in that trailer with just one thin blanket for cover. In a skewed way that kid was even more like Hansel and Gretel than Tanya was herself—half-orphaned, lost in the woods, trapped in a cage. But thinking about it that way made Tanya into the witch, and she didn't want that role. She wasn't scheming this kid's death, wasn't black hearted like that girl's mother, who wouldn't pay owed money and who'd forced Mason to get desperate. It was the mother's fault. She was the wicked witch who'd tossed the girl out into the wood to care for herself.

And maybe in another twisted way the kid was better off here where Tanya could try to keep her safe. Because Mason wouldn't have brought her back here and paraded her in front of Tanya's face like a rescued stray if he'd just meant to—it didn't matter what. Whatever filth he stirred up he'd never once brought it home with him, and Tanya wouldn't let him start that now.

INSIDE THE TRAILER Luc saw only dark and heard nothing but wind, couldn't discern consciousness from shallow sleep. She struggled with the blanket her captors had thrown her—hands bound together as a single limb with ten useless digits. She tented the blanket over her body and breathed down inside it to collect the warmth of her breath. The blanket smelled like stale urine. Luc thought she would freeze finger by finger, limb by limb, hardening like petrified wood.

The floor was ribbed metal flaked with rust and road salt. Her head skimmed the ceiling when she stood, and the walls were not much wider than her outstretched body. When she tugged the snap-cuffs they seemed to tighten and already they'd dug through her skin into raw flesh. She tried to bite through them but they were too thick, and there was no sharp corner she could find that might work as a knife edge. Just once in her dream of lost time, Luc raised her bound legs and jammed a boot into the gap between her two wrists, pushing until the bands hurt like they were scraping bare bone. Still the cuffs didn't snap, and the pain made Luc want to vomit.

She gazed at the dark and kicked the trailer walls. Too sick with pain for hunger, but thirst made her organs feel shriveled dry. Her throat felt loaded with hot sawdust. Lying on the floor, she noticed a spark of orange. She blinked to dispel the mirage but it lingered more intense now and drifted closer to her weak naked eyes. It focused at an elbow's distance: a tiny hand held an acorn by the cap stem, and the acorn's pulp had been hollowed out like it was a jack-o'-lantern, a single candle flame flickering inside it. The light shone on a minuscule face with a beard full of dirt and dust and cobweb silk. The creature had bare feet with sharp unkempt nails like a rat's. He wore a leathery poncho stitched together with what looked like black strands of human hair.

"How did you get here?" Luc whispered. She was far too gone to be alarmed.

The creature stepped close enough that Luc's breath sent ripples through its beard and long knotted hair. No red cap or shiny boots, none of the flashy color and drunken joy that Luc remembered from the *tomten* in her father's storybooks and those murals on the Christmas trays and tapestries. The *tomte* raised its acorn lantern over its head, and Luc caught the orange warmth radiating from that single flame as it soaked deep into her skin and woke some sense back into her cold-numbed face. Heat wafted down through the crevices of her blanket and against her body, and Luc folded herself into that pulsing sphere of heat until she had shrunk down to infant size. She knew she could shrink further—dwindle down to *tomte* proportions and even smaller, shrink until she was atomic. Then she'd step into that flame and be cradled there inside the acorn like a seed that could sprout again in a better world.

IT WAS 7:00 A.M. by the car clock. To drive home would mean defeat, so instead Greta cruised the city Inner Loop twice around, cranking awful classic rock to keep herself awake. Sometimes she pushed twenty miles over the posted speed limits, but the cops running traffic did nothing more than wave when she passed. She eyeballed every other driver on the road because some whacked-out fantasy had her believing that Luc's abductor was out prowling this highway himself, and that Greta would somehow recognize him by instinct. She veered into lanes and got horn blasts for doing it. She saw dark figures on the roadside that weren't. When she finally chose an exit, the destination had been brewing in her unconscious ever since she'd slammed herself into the car.

It was a townhouse condo complex, a spanking new east-side place, where Sandy and Max had bought a unit soon after their engagement. Greta drove the horseshoe row of identical townhouses with a small park in its center, a yuppie enclave built to resemble some quaint French village. Rock gardens in the courtyards, sculpted shrubbery now brittle with ice.

Greta spotted the place she knew was Sandy's and saw the first-floor lights were on, a single shadow moving behind closed venetian blinds. She watched for five minutes priming up her courage, but the longer she stalled the more twisted and fever-hot concepts spewed up from her subconscious like volcanic bursts. Like a night fifteen years ago when a young girl cop off duty was stuffing clothes and toiletries into trash bags, then rushing to her daughter's room to pack clothes and toys. With her baggage the girl cop fled a sprawling dream suburban house and spent her first night estranged from her husband in a Super Eight using cash to pay for the room. She'd brought Sandy with her, a kid barely ten years old but sharp enough to comprehend what was happening, crying over her McDonald's chicken nuggets eaten on a motel bed, begging to go home.

Why Greta left her husband that night, the precise trigger—it was too long ago now to remember. Even a clear head can forget. There'd been bitter arguments, but no cheating, and not even the slightest threat of violence. Greta kept a loaded gun nearby that first sleepless night in the hotel room, not because she feared her husband but because she feared the world. Overnight that click, click, click of her soul inside her chest was winding down and she was terrified it would just stop completely.

So the catalyst was violence after all: what she lived in her cop world had bled into her, a black stain poisoning her heart. She'd lost the will to feel for anyone, even her own child—and that was the ugly secret she'd never even told herself. But here she was now at her daughter's home, a place she'd never been before, and it was no more than a ten-minute drive from her own apartment. Ten minutes was all she'd ever had to travel to reach her daughter.

Sandy answered the door in plaid pajamas. She said, "Mom?" and shivered as the winter morning struck her. She tried to grin to disguise her bafflement, and she shot repeated glances over Greta's shoulder like she was wary of hidden cameras.

"Hey, kiddo, how are you?" Greta said. Her voice crackled and lost syllables.

Sandy's grin sagged, but not much. She gave her mother a delicate hug and said, "I'm happy to see you—though I'm shocked as hell. What's the occasion?"

"Epiphany?" Greta suggested.

"Must've been a rough one because, no offense, but you don't look so good."

"I'm getting over a flu," Greta said.

"You better not get me sick on the eve of my wedding."

"It's not catching anymore."

"Come on in, Ma. I'm cooking eggs and bacon. Did you eat?"

"Not yet," Greta said. The doorway led directly into Sandy's kitchen. It was decked out with pale wood cupboards, and behind the sink was an open counter overlooking the living room, a basic prefab setup just like Greta's own place, only newer. Max was on the couch watching morning news that featured a female anchor from a local affiliate using her gravest inflection to explain Luc Moberg's abduction, and over her shoulder loomed the still shot of the pregnant blonde at Shop-Mor, the latest entry in the Channel 10 CrimeStop series. The crawling text on the bottom of the screen gave the number to call if you had any information.

When Max saw Greta, he punched another channel on the remote and shot upright like he'd just been caught leering at pornography. He said, "Greta—is everything all right?"

"Fine, Max," she said. "I'm just visiting."

"Oh," he said, looking to Sandy for assurance. "It's good to see you."

Sandy drank tea and prodded her scrambled eggs with a spatula. The bacon sizzled on the next burner over, wafting a greasy stench that ignited Greta's nausea anew.

"Looks good," Greta said. "Thanks for letting me crash in unannounced."

"You're my mom," Sandy said, like it was the indisputable fact it was supposed to be. She warmed a cup of blackberry tea in the microwave and gave it to Greta after adding some honey and cream. They headed toward the upstairs bedrooms, and Greta sipped the hot tea down low enough so she wouldn't spill it as she walked.

In the bedroom was a new king-size bed and a familiar old vanity with oval mirror that Sandy'd had since childhood. There were stacked boxes probably full of wedding gifts mailed by invitees who couldn't make the ceremony. Greta took a seat on the edge of the bed, and the down comforter was so much like a nest of warm snow that she wanted nothing else but to lie back and sleep for hours. She set her tea mug on the nightstand so it would block her view of a desktop photo displaying her ex-husband and his second wife, Corrine the paralegal, the permed Italian princess. Greta had never been quite spiteful enough to spill the intelligence she'd gleaned about beloved Corrine's arrest back in 1975 for public indecency and disorderly conduct. She figured it was old news, and there was no denying that the stepmom had been as good a mother for Sandy as anyone could hope.

Sandy said, "Your thing has been all over the news this morning, on every local channel. You know her pretty well, right? Lucia Moberg?"

"Yeah." Greta felt her throat clench, listening to her daughter speak that name. She raised a hand to hide her face, but she knew Sandy had already caught sight of her wet eyes, her puckered chin. Greta shoved her knuckles against her lips but she couldn't stop the crying.

"Mom?" Sandy said. She batted aside a pillow and sat down next to Greta, slid her hand over her mother's. "It'll be all right, Mom. I'm sorry."

"It's hardly ever all right. I don't think I can handle this stuff anymore."

"Your job?" Sandy asked, fiercely attentive, like some trained grief counselor. It was shameful to Greta that her estranged daughter should have to be the one to dole out support—and so much more willingly than Greta could've ever managed herself. But despite the shame Greta still wished she could lie down and camp inside this moment forever.

Greta said, "I don't know what I'm doing anymore."

"You're thinking of retiring?" Sandy asked. "You've been at it twenty years."

"I feel like I'm just waking up inside my skin. I've been asleep." She pressed her wrists into her eye sockets and wiped the moisture away. "I'm sorry I'm dumping this shit on you right now. I just wanted to see you, not hit you with some crazy therapy session. You have more important things to worry about—"

"It's fine," Sandy assured her. "I'm glad—not that you're dealing with all this—but that you came here to talk with me. Look, I want to tell you something, Mom. I want to tell you that you don't have to come to the wedding tomorrow, all right?"

"Sandy—" Greta protested.

"No, I'm serious. I can see what you're dealing with is torturous, and there's nothing I can do about that—but what I can do is help your stress a little bit. It's more important to me that you don't have a nervous breakdown than if you're stuck in a reception hall with a bunch of people who all hold grudges against you. We'll get together after the honeymoon and I'll tell you all—" She stopped, sprang off the bedside, and said, "Crap—just a sec. I need to make sure our breakfast doesn't burn." She was halfway down the stairs before her sentence was through.

Greta pulled a tissue from a Kleenex box and rubbed her eyes dry. Years ago, her husband had made their separation easy, letting her go with small protests, but Sandy had fought the change with every cruel weapon a child could wield, until Greta finally relented. She packed her daughter's belongings and waited in the motel lobby for Sandy's father to come fetch her. That moment of giving up her child she couldn't forget because it ran endless loops in her mind. She had been too weak, too bitter, too guilt sodden, and she hadn't even been able to face her own daughter's pain.

Greta's pager chirped, so she folded back her jacket lapel and saw that the readout listed Moe Arslan's number back at Public Safety. She rushed into Sandy's bathroom to kneel down at the toilet bowl and dry-heave her empty stomach until her nausea faded off. Afterward she soaped her face and splashed cold water and gargled some mint mouthwash she found in the medicine cabinet. To dry her face she used a purple hand towel folded over the rack. The towel was part of the set that Greta herself had bought for Sandy's wedding present, the gift she'd sent by mail like some kind of peace offering.

Back in the bedroom she used Sandy's nightstand telephone to call Moe back, and he answered on the first ring. Greta said, "So let me guess—Wendt spilled his beans for you."

"Not even one bean," Moe told her. "But we've got a guy out in Wayne County, a citizen, a newsstand owner—that is to say a porn shop owner—named Alfredo Cuomo. He saw the news feed early this morning and he's absolutely convinced he had a run-in with our anonymous mother-to-be last week in a bank parking lot. She literally hit his car with her own."

"Please tell me they exchanged insurance information."

"She gave a false name and number, and Alfredo was foolish enough to trust her."

"License plate?" Greta pled. The nausea was already resurfacing.

"Afraid not. He figured someone as pregnant as this young lady ought to be trustworthy, so he didn't bother to jot down a plate number. You'd think a man in his line of business would be more sensitive at recognizing fellow crooks."

"Moe, I'm dying here. Tell me what we have that we didn't have ten minutes ago."

"We might have a tremendous lot. See, this woman hit Alfredo Cuomo's car as she was pulling into the parking lot to go into the bank and do some business. Chances are that business was at the front counter—"

"And at the very least Cuomo knows what time this was?" Greta guessed.

"He even has the deposit receipt that gives his transaction time as 10:33 A.M. last Friday the third of December. What I've done is I've called the bank, which just opened for limited Saturday business a few minutes ago. They have the security footage from this date and time, which we can use to identify our female suspect. The time code on the security footage will match precisely with the bank's log of transactions. If we get her face, we can match it to her name, and then we're off."

Greta couldn't breathe to speak. While Moe had explained his magic, she'd noticed a Polaroid snapshot tucked into the frame of Sandy's vanity mirror, a picture of Sandy as a baby, her toothless smile covered in green Gerber slop. It recalled for Greta some dream she'd had recently, though the details had already faded from her mind.

TANYA ATE FROOT LOOPS with milk that she had kept cold in a cooler packed with snow. After breakfast she pulled on winter boots and a heavy wool jacket wide enough for her belly and followed Mason as he headed back outside with an old hatchet in his hand. The morning was clear and so sharply cold that it stung her cheeks. Ten yards west of the house the truck-hitched trailer was locked, quiet, still. Mason trudged a trail through the snow, and Tanya walked behind him past the trailer, wishing the girl in there would knock just once to show she was alive.

"Over here," Mason said as he pointed the hatchet toward a cluster of young fir trees just on the forest edge. "Buck told me we could pick one to cut for inside."

"We don't have any ornaments," Tanya said. "And there's no electricity for lights."

"We'll get ornaments in town maybe. And you don't need any damn light strings, Tan. Just pick one. Whatever one you want—your choice. Get a nice one, though, because, who knows, probably the baby'll be here in time to see it. We still got a couple weeks." He palmed the back of her head and planted a surprise kiss on her mouth that for a second quieted her doubt. They stood in the tree nursery among the stunted pines like two giants in their wilderness domain.

"Mason?" Tanya said. "Should we give her some food or something?"

He glanced over his shoulder, red cheeked and grinning steam through his teeth. "Don't worry about her right now. Let me handle it. You just worry about picking a tree."

Tanya made a show of choosing while she wandered through the tree cluster, brushing her fingers over the needles, but really she didn't give a crap what tree they picked out of all these that looked the same. She stalled for five frigid minutes before she pointed and said, "There."

Mason said, "Kind of squat, ain't it?"

"It's got no bald spots."

"All right, then." Mason dropped to his knees and bent aside some lower branches to find a good stretch of trunk for his hacking. He swung fast and the blade did its work: sliced a thick gouge into the bark. He shimmied out the hatchet and inside that deep cut the meat was so naked white that Tanya winced in pain for it.

"Mason, I'm getting crazy," she blurted. "I need you to tell what happened last night."

He stopped midswing, hatchet poised. "I already said don't worry about it."

"I know, but it's not that easy when there's this girl—"

"Her name's Lucia. She's the professor's daughter." He chopped some more wedges of tree trunk and after ten blows the tree eased backward, almost severed. He took one more swing and the trunk snapped clean off its stump. Mason said, "I'm using her for collateral. For ransom. That mother is playing this bullshit brain damage game so hard that I almost bought it. I came this close to killing that woman last night, Tanya, but all I kept thinking was how bad we need this money to get our life started. I had to think quick and I decided to take the girl as insurance so the mother will pay up what I ask. You satisfied? You feel enlightened now?"

"But what if the girl dies, Mason? How are you gonna get the money?"

"She ain't gonna die. She's fine—and let me figure out the money part. What I'm gonna do right now is I'm gonna get this fucking tree inside, then I'm gonna warm up some water and make myself a cup of coffee. How 'bout that?"

Tanya didn't bother pressing further. She said, "I'll make you your coffee."

Mason grabbed their fresh-cut Christmas tree by its lopped end and set himself to dragging it back across the yard. The pine sap scent was on the air and it reminded Tanya of better holidays in warmer places. But maybe Mason was right: if the baby came by Christmas then they'd have something real to celebrate. Even now she felt it stirring inside her, full of life.

BY LATE AFTERNOON on Saturday, December eleventh, Investigators Greta Hurd and Moe Arslan had become confident that the name of the man who had abducted Lucia Moberg was Mason Ronald Renault. They'd followed the lead supplied by Wayne County businessman Alfredo Cuomo, driving a half hour out to the Ontario Community Bank to check more security footage. They played the tape in the bank manager's office, fast-forwarding a few minutes beyond 10:33 A.M. This video was sharper than the Shop-Mor one, and in color. There'd been four open counters that morning, and the footage continually cut, every five seconds, to an overhead shot of the customer at each of those counters.

It was like working a slot machine, waiting for the jackpot image to appear, but the investigators had only reviewed three minutes of tape before the camera eye caught their pregnant female slinking forward like she expected an ambush. She had just slid a weighty stack of cash from her purse when the camera cut away from her, oblivious to the importance of this particular human being in comparison to the others in line.

"I'll wager that cash is five thousand dollars," Moe said, jotting the time code in his notebook. The bank manager recorded the transaction time and within a minute his computer produced a record of the receipt, which indeed listed a deposit of five thousand dollars, and also gave the customer's name as Tanya Yasbeck, and a home address on Rochester's west side. Greta and Moe refused to let themselves get excited about the address because there were at least five Ontario Community Bank branches between their current location and Rochester. The more likely scenario had this Tanya Yasbeck woman living at an unknown Wayne County address, probably at one of the ubiquitous trailer parks that cluttered the woods around Ginna Nuclear Power Plant. Nonetheless, on the way out they radioed the dispatcher to order backup units for their visit to the west-side location listed on the receipt.

In the Taurus, Greta said, "This Yasbeck woman deposited that money the day before Oscar Moberg's murder. Lucia Moberg claims she saw that hidden cash days afterward."

"So it's two payoffs—one before, one after," Moe concluded.

They stopped for a refill at a county line convenience store—gas for the car, Pringles and soda for them. Into the store stumbled two back-country gals sporting insulated flannel shirts and sweatpants. They staggered to the cooler for a case of Bud Light, and it took both of them to haul it up to the cash register, giggling like cheerleaders all the way. Moe and Greta watched the drunkards fumble for loose change and bills. One gal's cigarettes spilled all over the countertop lottery placemat.

Back outside Greta spotted their idling pickup truck blasting country rock.

"They sure as hell shouldn't be sold more booze," Greta said.

Moe glanced back at the femme rednecks still inside amassing funds at the pay counter. He popped open the pickup's driver's door, pulled the key from the ignition, and tossed it under the driver's seat. He said, "By the time they find it, they'll be sober."

An hour later the investigators were both wearing Kevlar vests and standing in the dingy hallway of a west-side tenement building with eight Emergency Task Force cops decked out in riot gear. They were pounding on the door of Tanya Yasbeck's last known address and were not at all surprised when a haggard hippie couple answered smelling heavily of pot. The hippies blinked at the arsenal of guns and explained that they'd been living at this address for almost a year and knew zilch about Tanya Yasbeck except her name, which they'd learned only because they'd been returning her bills to senders at a rate of almost one per day.

"Any mail come in under anybody else's name?" Greta asked.

"Nope, just hers," the guy hippie said. He scratched his hairy shirtless chest and yawned.

Greta found the landlady's apartment number and Moe knocked. She was at home with her cats and delighted to have company, but she offered scant info about her former tenant, except to say that Tanya had lived with her boyfriend and vacated unannounced, rent in arrears, fourteen months ago. The landlady knew of no forwarding address, though she recognized Tanya from the Shop-Mor picture that Moe displayed for her. She'd not been watching the news closely enough to know this same picture had been disbursed all over the airwaves. If she had, she said, she would've certainly called.

"You don't happen to remember the name of Tanya Yasbeck's boyfriend, do you?"

"Oh, sure," the old woman said. "It was Mason, though I never knew his last name."

The investigators drove back to Public Safety and logged another two hours on databases, Greta high on lukewarm tea and her flu fever, Moe chugging Mountain Dew. Searching through first names was typically needle-in-a-haystack work, but the blessing in this case was a screwy first name like Mason, which after an hour of modem processing yielded only seven hits on the statewide arrest records. Moe accessed them one at a time and printed the data for each convict on a dot matrix printer that screeched like a flock of scavenger fowl.

The first guy was listed as black, but they didn't discount him because race was often a matter of opinion. The second guy was sixty-seven years old and also black, arrested for public drunkenness and lewd conduct twice in Niagara Falls. They yanked him from the running and Moe tore off a third print sheet that displayed the stats of a white male in his

twenties, collared five years back and way downstate for DUI and narcotics possession. Such a slight record and the great distance probably
meant a long shot, but Moe slapped him in the maybe pile.

Greta paced the row of computer terminals, mulling the new developments that swirled like vertigo through her thoughts. Meanwhile the
printer spat out two more convicts, both white, though one had already
been age forty at the time of his arrest three years prior. The other was
twenty-six and from Dansville, a couple hours south. With over a dozen
assault charges, he was a strong candidate.

The wait was maddening, and by the time the seven reports had run,
only the Mason who was black and sixty could be instantly disqualified.
Deeper research ditched two more: Dansville Mason had graduated to
corpse status one year back via heroin overdose, and another was serving a rape sentence in Attica. These two exceptions left the investigators
with Masons Kopecny, Renault, McDouglass, and Stanton. Moe made
phone calls, and Greta waited for the database to produce some arrest
photos.

Mason Stanton was first and he was unmistakably black. Kopecny
was old and obese. McDouglass was the man with just the one DUI,
posing horrified in his business suit. When the last mugshot came
through Moe took a glance and passed it on to Greta, telling her, "This
is the guy." Mason Renault, twenty-three years old. Arrested in Buffalo
two years prior for possession of cocaine with intent to sell, though a
wider search net had snagged this more recent glamour shot from his
hometown of Detroit. In the picture, Renault was handsome, like a
low-rent Elvis in his early years. The haircut was mostly what made
him look like a fifties greaser refugee—that and the undershirt with the
rolled-up sleeves. Six months back he'd been charged with assault
while visiting his Detroit family home for the weekend. A domestic dis-
pute with Mom and Older Sister, and Renault had punched his sib-
ling's face hard enough to make her spit teeth. Sis pressed charges that
she later dropped.

"We need this in a six-pack to see if Blair Moberg can ID him as her
attacker," Moe said.

"Fine, but I'm not doing it. I don't think I could stand to see that woman again," Greta said. "And I'm getting this guy's name and picture up on the wanted board pronto. You've got no idea how pissed I am that we're jumping through these hoops while Mitch Wendt lounges in his jail cell, laughing at us, basking in every last shred of information we need to nail these people."

"Go ahead and gloat if you need to," Moe said.

Greta said, "Believe me, I'd forfeit my badge if it could make Wendt squeal for you."

They headed on foot down the block away from the Public Safety Building, out to get hamburgers and fries for late afternoon lunch. Greta was appalled at herself for giving into food, stuffing greasy junk into her face while Luc Moberg was still missing, possibly starving and freezing somewhere. All this self-sustaining bullshit that Greta had to force herself through—showers, coffee, even stopping for a piss break.

Moe said, "I'm skeptical about how far we're going to get with this Mason Renault name. It'll show up on the news tomorrow if we leak it, but we can't expect to catch another lucky break like Alfredo Cuomo. Not to mention we don't have the time."

They were crossing over the Bausch Street bridge with the Rochester War Memorial on their left and the icy Genesee River flowing sluggish thirty feet beneath them. Woozy, Greta skimmed her hand along the rail to brace herself. She announced, "We need to get at Wendt."

"You said yourself he's looking like a dead end," Moe said.

"He knows, and we need to figure out how we're going to make him talk."

"What do you suggest—we beat him until he spills his guts?"

Greta stopped and wrapped both her hands on the railing. Upstream, the aqueducts spat dark river water in steady driving currents—all of them except the single dry duct on the far right that had an entire tree lodged inside its gate, spindly roots and all. The frigid wind draped her hair across her face when she said, "Moe, I need this girl to be safe. If that doesn't happen, it's over for me. I'm not going to be able to do this police work anymore. Look—I know how to get at Wendt, but it's way under the radar, and it involves releasing him ASAP."

Moe squeezed her shoulder and she turned to face him. He said, "Listen, I want you to go home and get at least five hours' sleep, all right? You do that, and in the meantime I'll see to it that Mitch Wendt gets released with surveillance. If nothing comes of it by tonight, I'm willing to do whatever you think will get this over with the fastest."

"Cut the condescending tone," Greta said.

Moe told her, "Only if you'll do what I say."

LUC WOKE UP to the sound of rattling metal, and a sudden burst of daylight splashed on the trailer's back wall and burned her eyes shut again. She groaned in defiance of the wind gust that shoved her from behind, and she refused to turn herself toward the open door and that man who was recognizable by the long jagged shadow he stamped against the wall. She'd been dreaming of sounds—boots crunching through snow, a key stabbed into a lock, a latch snapping open—sounds that weren't dreams after all.

"Hey," the abductor barked. "Hey, kid." He leaned inside and his extra weight tilted the trailer almost level. He grabbed her shoulder, jostled her. When she didn't move, didn't even breathe, he shook her harder, clawing his fingers into the blanket wrapped around her body. He said, "Look, I got you some water here, all right?"

Luc was too desperate with thirst to resist. She turned, but without her glasses the man looked like nothing more than a wavering shape. She reached, both hands bound together as if in prayer, and she took his offering. It was a plastic Sprite bottle without a cap, refilled with water. Her swollen hands shook and water spilled onto her knuckles, pinpricks of warmth. She took an urgent gulp that made her choke and cough in a violent spray.

He pulled something out of his jacket and tapped it against his mouth—a cigarette—then he burned it with a lighter until the tip glowed orange. Luc didn't want to be this close to him, but if she crawled any farther back she wouldn't be able to see him well enough to read his intentions. This man who had ruined her life and was now hoarding whatever scraps of it were left for her to salvage.

He said, "Thought you were really dead there for a second. Nice acting."

Luc drank spoonfuls at a time. The moisture stung her hard chapped lips.

"Look, I know things got fucked-up, all right? I'm aware of that. But right now you need to understand that I just need to finish up this situation with your mom and then all this shit will be over with. You got no reason to trust me, I know. But let me tell you this—whatever happens from here on, none of this was the way I wanted. It was your mother that messed it up. She can blame herself if anything goes wrong. It's all on her."

"She's dead," Luc told him. Her voice was full of grit.

"She ain't dead. I made sure of that."

"My dad . . ." Luc said.

His long sigh pushed white steam into the air. Luc wished she could see his face more sharply, but when she looked it was contorted into nightmare configurations. She wished she had the strength to pounce, to wrap her bound wrists around his neck and twist until the bands choked him dead.

Finally he said, "I ain't gonna talk about your dad. I know it sucks you had to be there to see him get hit, but the guy who did it—he told me he thought your dad was in that car alone. The way I hear it your dad was sitting in that bookstore by himself, and when he comes out into the parking lot, it looks like he was alone, you know? Then the guy who did it, he didn't spot you in the backseat of that car. If he'd of seen you maybe things wouldn't of happened like that."

Luc said, "You did it. You killed him," but then she bit her lower lip to stop herself from throwing any more accusations that could get her killed.

"Whatever you want to think, I don't really care either way," he said.

"But I want to tell you this other part first. By now it don't matter whether you know or not because your mother fucked us over big time. What I want to say is that she paid for that hit. Five thousand bucks up front, and another five thousand when it was finished. That's the truth. There it is, take it or leave it, the whole story. Except the part where she never passes along that second five grand she owes us, and now because of her being so stupid, all this other shit has to go down."

"Why?" Luc said.

"I can't answer that because I don't know. Alls I needed to know was how and when it was gonna happen, and how to collect the rest of the money afterward. And don't give me any shit about it's gone or missing or she can't remember where it is. When your mom gets out of the hospital she's gonna find money fast. Savings, insurance—I don't give a fuck. And I'm gonna shoot for triple interest, owning to circumstances. Like fifteen thousand, maybe more. What we need to do right now is make sure that happens."

He stabbed his cigarette toward her like a potential weapon. He deepened his voice when he said, "Look. I don't know how stupid you are, but I got an idea. I for one ain't falling for that amnesia bullshit. I ain't playing that game. She had that cash in hand the day before she dumped herself off that pier, and then all a sudden she doesn't have it anymore. Nobody but you and her knew where it was, so she's got to have it someplace. Either that or you got it stashed somewhere. Is that how it is?"

He flicked away his cigarette and fished around the inside pocket of his jacket. What he produced was the size of a nail file, but then he folded it open twice as long. A pocketknife. Luc gasped and lunged herself toward the far wall, thrashed her feet to keep him at a distance.

"Hey! Hey!" he yelled. He grabbed both of Luc's ankles and squeezed the bindings so hard that her nerves burst with blinding pain. She was too weak now to stop him from pressing her legs immobile on the trailer floor. He held them there and sawed between her boots with his knife until the pressure of the snap-cuffs slacked. When he was finished slicing away the binds he grunted the rest of his way into the compartment beside her. Luc lay sprawled on her stomach and cried though she despised herself for showing her tears to him. The water bottle was spilled almost empty on her blanket.

"Shut up for a second and give me your hands," he said.

"Don't—" Luc said.

"Just give me your fucking hands! Come on!"

Luc shoved her two arms toward him and he tugged at the bands while he slashed at them with his knife. Each swipe dragged the plastic into the open wounds on her wrists with such searing pain that there was little relief when the bands finally fell away. The ghosts of their presence still sizzled through her lacerated skin.

He folded the knife and made it disappear, then he leaned against the trailer wall with his arms crossed over his knees, like they were just two kids chilling out in a tree house. Luc thought of Gina and Kit and especially Quinn. She wondered if they knew yet what had happened, if they thought she was dead. She wished she could make them hear her desperation somehow.

The man said, "You hungry? Want me to bring you something from inside?"

"I'm not hungry," she lied.

"Hey, look," he said, and he nudged her boot with his own. He ran his palm against the upward slope of his bangs to ensure that his pompadour was still intact. His blurry face bulged and shrank like it was breathing. "This ain't exactly pleasant for me, neither. I got you here, I got this situation with your mother, it ain't easy." He set his hand on her ankle just above her bootlaces. It seemed at first that he was just examining the wounds, but then his fingers slid along her shin and up toward her knee, tracing the fishnet patterns. His lungs worked faster now. Luc twisted her leg out of his grip and dragged it away, but he reached again, more forceful.

She bent her knee up against her chest to escape his touch, and for an instant her boot was poised midair, reared back, trained toward his face. She let loose the rage that had been swelling all night and kicked him full force. It seemed unreal, an inborn action separate from her

shattered will. Her boot sole jammed between his chin and his collarbone and punched the fleshiest part of his neck. He gagged as the back
of his head smacked the metal siding like a gong.

Luc threw off her blanket and lunged toward the open doorway and
sent herself tumbling into empty space. She hit soft bottom and sank
into the fresh snow there. A sudden bright fire in her mind compelled
her to push herself upward again, and then she ran cockeyed and dazed
toward somewhere she didn't know.

Just ahead was white ground—trees with dark bare trunks—needled
branches bursting on the tall pines—a long, boxy car heaped with snow.
Nothing but aerobic breaths throbbed from her mouth. Every muscle
sore but alive. Close behind her the attacker's loping boot steps bashed
through the snow as he charged with a low growl rattling in his throat.
The daylight reflecting off the snow made her squint almost blind. Too
far ahead, a faint light appeared soft and dancing like candle glow. This
glow was hovering out where the road must've been—not a single flame
but four dim points of light circling around each other. Luc recognized
the omen she was seeing up there beyond her reach, and she knew that
she was meant to lunge toward it.

FROM THE KITCHEN window Tanya watched with her hands gripped
on the sink ledge. Outside, the girl stumbled over a snowdrift that
reared almost to her knees and she sprawled down into the frozen white
wave. Mason pounced and grabbed hold of the girl's jacket collar and
yanked her upward again. The girl gasped like she'd been rescued from
drowning, and her scream ripped through the trees with enough noise
to send birds fluttering from their roosts.

Tanya turned away from the window, dizzy with disgust for what
she'd seen, ashamed at herself for watching. Both of their desperate,
manic faces—Mason's and Lucia's—were now printed like sunspots on
her eyes. She rushed back down the hall to the bedroom stall where Mason had left her, thinking she was sleeping. There were no windows in
this room to watch from, so she lay back down on the queen-sized bed

that almost filled the whole stall. It was the only big bed in the cabin, though there were close to ten other cots scattered among the stalls.

She kept alert, even though her eyes were shut in bogus sleep while she counted off the seconds in her head. She was trying to figure how much time Mason needed to load that girl back into the trailer. Any extra time and she had some reason to worry. At the three-minute mark she leaned over the bedside and opened her suitcase and took out the Smith & Wesson handgun—but then she shoved it right back under a folded pile of pants. Five minutes dragged by and finally Mason trudged inside alone, slamming doors, grunting off his boots and tossing them against the woodpile. She could hear his plodding from far down the hall as he came into the stall on his sock feet with his belt buckle open and clinking. Tanya had heard enough. She shoved her face into a dusty pillow.

"Little bitch tried to escape," he said. "I had to lock her back up again."

Tanya mashed the pillow in her hand and wrenched it at Mason. It struck him harmless in his chest and flopped onto the floor. No question she could see his dick pressed hard against his pants, his belt unstrapped and his fly unzipped.

"What the hell's up with you, Tanya?"

She said, "What did you do to her?"

"Nothing," he said. "What do you think?"

She slid to the edge of the bed and traced her fingers against the inseam of his pants.

Mason said, "That's for you, Momma."

She tugged his pants halfway down his thighs and pulled his dick out with both hands and kneaded it like clay. He gave off a salty stench after four days of no bathing, but thank God there were no other scents or tastes that didn't belong to him. He nudged the back of her head with his fingers, leading her onward. Tanya closed her eyes and opened her mouth. She gagged on the taste but it was hers alone and nobody else's. With her free hand she pressed down through the stretch band on her pants and sought the moist itch that was bothering her there. Rubbed herself less than ten seconds before her nerves all sang relief in one rowdy burst.

GRETA DROVE WHILE Moe rode shotgun—the first time in months she'd taken the wheel from him. There were heavy snowfalls and black ice and cars skidding into ditches on the roadside. At 10:00 P.M. she parked at the 7-11 opposite the Submarine Bar and Grill, the same familiar spot where they'd arrested Mitch Wendt. But no cruisers appeared for backup this time—just Greta and Moe watching the lot loaded with bikes, watching until snow dusted their windshield white.

She'd finished her five-hour penance at home, but she'd spent only two of those hours sleeping. Each time she dozed, a bodily jolt woke her again—electric, like touching a nine-volt battery to her tongue. It was evident now, nearly undeniable, that Blair Moberg had been somehow involved in her husband's murder, and the implications had been writhing in Greta's mind, roping themselves around her own buried guilt and dragging it upward out of the dark. Greta refused to empathize with a murderess—but there were parallels to be drawn between two women so desperate to free themselves from their families. Greta could almost hear the echoed mantra: I don't deserve this life I hate this life I don't want to bear this life. There was a time fifteen years ago when Greta lived that panic, but she hadn't resorted to killing her husband.

Because she was stronger—that's all. She was stubborn enough and cold enough to bear the daily remorse. But now years later Greta was just sick and exhausted and she knew what it meant to feel weak, to stand above that churning water staring down, because she'd done it that morning on the Bridge Street bridge with the Genesee River below her and those jutting rocks just under the surface. She'd felt no urge to jump, but still the moment had helped Greta see—she could track the mental pathway that led Blair Moberg to conclude that the best way to forget is to dash your brains on the rocks and let the currents wash guilt away.

It was one means of saving yourself, but there were others.

In the car with Moe she sipped a French vanilla coffee in a Styrofoam cup and hoped her stomach was settled enough to chance such a beverage. She was stalling because old business was still clouding her head. Over the last few hours Moe had kept busy—first by arranging a surveillance tail and wiretap warrant for Mitch Wendt, then by overseeing Wendt's proverbial Monopoly release card. Preliminary reports said that Wendt had been collected by a young female in a Ford Mustang registered in Wendt's name, then driven to the West End Motor Lodge, where he rented a room and settled in for the evening. The surveillance cop had set up business in a room directly across the parking lot, but so far there'd been no action except a Little Caesar's pizza delivery. The wiretap was still awaiting court approval.

Moe had also prepared another photo array, this one including Mason Renault and five look-alikes, which he then couriered to Genesee Community Hospital, where Blair Moberg had been transferred and readmitted under the care of Dr. Fred Mahoney. The security officer stationed at the hospital reported to Moe no unusual phone calls, no suspicious activity. Blair's mother Norma Crowley was back from gambling, now undertaking a vigil at her daughter's bedside. Norma had also been back to the Moberg house recently enough to verify that nobody from the Skeleton Crew had yet made contact, to demand ransom or otherwise, and wiretap recordings confirmed this claim. As for the photo array, Blair recognized Mason Renault as her attacker with absolute certainty and the utmost dread.

While they watched the front entrance of the Submarine Bar and Grill, Greta said, "We need to make a decision on Blair Moberg. Ultimately it's going to be the DA's determination, but he'll want our opinions and he'll need our evidence."

Moe said, "Part of the reason I went out to the hospital this afternoon was I needed to be more convinced that this Moberg woman was legitimately brain damaged. I don't purport to be an expert, but after seeing her today I have little doubt that she's badly mentally handicapped."

"If we'd caught her just before she jumped, I think she'd have confessed."

"The fact is, the woman is a mess no matter how you cut it, and she's not calculated enough to arrange such an elaborate hoax. Dr. Mahoney believes that the recent assault won't affect her current condition, which remains rather poor anyhow. And speaking to Mrs. Moberg herself is like speaking to a five-year-old."

Greta had kept her fingers hooked under the door latch for over a minute now. She was like a child awed by an elaborate domino stack, itching to tap the first one down and watch the whole thing topple. She set her coffee on the dash, turned the engine off, and said, "You ready?"

Tonight the stereo in the bar played the blues, a singer crooning with sand in her throat. It was a slow night, most booths empty, yet still no vacant barstools. Along the counter was a redneck lineup of black leather and denim, among them at least a dozen bearded men tracking Greta and Moe and shoulder-nudging comrades who were too drunk to notice the arrival of the cops. Liquid blue lights shimmered in the bar mirror, and the nautical décor cast them all like they were pirates pounding rum below deck. It was cornball enough to make you grin, unless you knew that their scars, their stench, and their black hearts were all perfectly authentic.

Greta let Moe take the lead that he was gunning for. Meanwhile she scanned the twenty-odd patrons for familiar faces, maybe a glimpse of that Skeleton Crew death's-head logo. For his confrontation, Moe chose a trio of obstinate bikers who refused to break their stare-down with him. He showed them the shield on his belt and said, "Rochester Police Department, Physical Crimes Unit." Their faces washed in such blue light made them look dead and drowned.

One of the three sneered and asked, mock-polite, "What can we do you for, Constable?" He looked about fifty, an old-time grizzly bear disguised as a parody of himself. He faced Moe with his elbows behind him on the bar, gray beard puffing from his neck like a third-world tumor. His grossly protruding gut stretched his bald eagle T-shirt. He wore a black leather fedora bearing a miniature silver animal skull.

"We're looking for a guy named Mason Renault," Moe said.

Grizzly Man scraped a yellowed canine with a toothpick. He eyed

Greta like she was lunch meat and said, "Can't place that name, but that's because I'm from out of town, man."

Moe said, "You're quite outgoing for a stranger."

Grizzly Man nodded at Greta, then asked Moe, "Did you bring your date with you?"

Greta unclipped her badge and waved it like it was an ace from up her sleeve.

"Equal opportunity—the RPD—chicks and A-rabs," Grizzly Man said.

There were chuckles from several other patrons close enough to hear Grizzly Man's remark. Greta let them laugh. She held her tongue because all this extra slack was just going to make her noose knot stronger, better to hang them come reckoning time. Moe's hand curled into a fist against his thigh, but he still talked smooth: "Is there anybody around here who's more of a regular than you?"

The grizzly leaned backward and his belly bulged against his belt like rising dough. He howled down the lineup, "Hey, Gordo, come over here a sec, will you?"

At least three patrons used this lull as their cue to split, and Greta studied their sulky departing faces for later reference. She also watched them to be sure they all made their proper exits. Sure as hell she didn't need them circling around and sneaking up behind her, sniffing and nipping like dogs in heat.

Meanwhile a Latino moseyed over to answer the bear's call. He was shorter than Greta, and not a trace of body fat to justify his nickname. His mustache was like an inverted U, and two missing fingers made his left hand look like one of those arcade claws that grab at plush toys. He wore a plain black T-shirt hugging weight-trained shoulders and pecs— a figure you could only cut from full-time lifting, which usually meant a prison spell.

"These cops wanted to talk to a regular," the grizzly explained to Gordo.

"A regular asshole," somebody muttered. Wheezy laughter all around.

"We're looking for a guy named Mason Renault," Moe said. "We've received notice that he frequents this establishment."

"Mason Raw Not?" Gordo said, butchering the name, scowling like he'd sniffed a fart.

Greta exhibited for them Mason Renault's mug shot. She raised it high so Gordo, Grizzly Man, and vicinity could all catch an eyeful. "This is an old picture, but that's him," Greta said.

"Don't know him," Gordo said with his chin hiked to give himself another inch of height. "Somebody told you this guy hangs here? Whoever told you that is a liar, man."

Moe explained: "We're working on a case, and we're anxious to speak with Mr. Renault. An individual we have recently interviewed has indicated that Mr. Renault would be a useful resource for our investigation, and that we could possibly find him here. So here we are."

A glance between Gordo and Grizzly Man. Gordo said, "Your informant is bunk."

"Huh—that's a shame," Moe said. His mock chagrin was somewhat overplayed, but Gordo was probably oblivious to subtleties by this stage of the conversation.

"Who told you this Mason dude was a regular here?" Gordo asked.

"Someone with a lot to lose by lying to us, I'll tell you that," Moe said.

No telling how close to the Skeleton Crew these scumbags ran, but they were all part of that network, that intricate swirl of dominoes waiting to be toppled. Greta was confident that she and Moe had just indicted, convicted, and sentenced Mitch Wendt before a jury of his peers. She'd framed Wendt for an act of treason. She'd flicked that first chip and already the stack was clattering down, an inevitable trail climbing up planks, through tunnels, stretching beyond her reach—and it rushed headlong toward its target waiting idle at the finish line, waiting to get knocked down flat.

INSIDE HER TRAILER PRISON, Luc was lost in dream realm, locked inside a casket buried in some timeless zone between her own short life and the vast white hall her dead father now haunted. In her dream she was hovering barefoot over snowy ground in woods lit by a heavy moon.

Another light shone amid the trees but it seemed miles off—a soft candle glow in four distinct specks. She was sailing toward it somehow, invoking it, and the pines with their green bristles drifted through the undisturbed snow like a flotilla of tall-mast ships.

The light was the glow of her patron saint Lucia standing in the clearing ahead, ten feet tall with her head blazing in a halo of painless fire. The saint smiled like a mother fawning over her infant child, like a goddess whose orbit reached far above human agony. Her head itself was the source of the light she emitted. It streamed from her nostrils and her tear ducts, her ear canals and her hair follicles. She held a wooden bowl low enough that Luc could see inside the basin.

What Luc saw floating in the bloody soup were eyeballs glassy and perfect like marbles, glimmering, not the yolky globs she might've expected. These were Saint Lucia's own eyes, at least six pairs of them, all plucked by her own hand from their sockets, only to grow back again by some magic. Saint Lucia who was burned at the stake for her miracle— her own living pyre.

The saint dipped two fingers into the bowl and her fingertips came up dripping red. She leaned down and all her dozen bobbing eyes turned toward Luc and gazed at her from inside the bowl like a chorus of witnesses. Luc closed her own eyes, not because she was afraid but because she knew that the saint would lay her fingertips over her eyelids and brush them with the warm blood that would soak into her pores. When Luc opened her eyes again, she was not surprised that her vision was sharp—more perfect even than it had been with her glasses. She could see every needle on every pine branch. Bright rays of distant stars. Patterns on snowflakes that fell past her face.

SUNDAY AT NOON Mason let Tanya take the Cadillac down to the mini-mart in the village. They'd run out of booze and meat and other essentials, like fresh batteries for the portable radio. Mason didn't like her going alone, but there was no chance he'd go anywhere to risk his face getting out there for people to see. Without the portable radio working, without clear reception from the car antenna, he couldn't find out what the rest of New York knew about him. He'd been itching to flee five states away before nightfall, if only Buck Hanson would contact him and approve such a plan. But then the girl in the trailer—Mason didn't want to dump her and forfeit that money, not just yet. He told Tanya that there still had to be some way to finagle it.

On the way down the four miles of steep rugged hill, Tanya drove slow to keep from slipping, taking the sharp curves at under five miles per hour. She passed cabins boarded up for winter, and then the long thin lake appeared, sprawled out in glimpses through the trees, the lake with the Indian name she couldn't remember—frozen white on the edges, dark bluish slush in the center. Even the village looked abandoned, just a mile drag with a few diners, churches, tourist shops. Tanya parked at the mini-mart, where there were just three other cars. Across the street was a bowling alley called The Fast Lane with a lit OPEN sign in its window. Behind the mini-mart a hillside reared up, blooming with pines and so steep that a surprise avalanche would probably bury half the town.

Tanya waited in her car a few minutes, scared to get out or even shift into park. She kept her hands on the steering wheel and her foot on the brake because just then the world seemed so vast and so loaded with prospects that it might crush her. She could do whatever she wanted and that allowance was horrible.

What she did was turn off the car, then she headed into the store and snagged a small pushcart from a train of them and pushed it toward the beer aisle. She checked the grocery list Mason wrote on the inside of an empty cigarette pack. She threw a case of Molson into the cart. Next she went for the sausages and whole chickens, a carton of eggs, a large package of bologna. Following this easy list was all that kept her from screaming—that, and her baby taking its long warm bath inside her womb.

The cart was almost full when she pushed it up to the checkout, where a grubby cashier lady stood reading a tabloid and munching on a Three Musketeers. Tanya passed groceries onto the stalled conveyor belt, but stopped with a tub of peanut butter cup ice cream still in her hand. She'd spotted a stack of day-old *Rochester Democrat and Chronicle* newspapers in a rack by her hip. Her own black-and-white picture was smack on the front cover under a headline: HUNT FOR ABDUCTED TEEN GAINS MOMENTUM. Next to it was a picture of the girl Lucia in a yearbook shot, Lucia looking artsy with her glasses and black hair and not really smiling.

She turned away and almost butted heads with a white-haired man in a grocer's apron asking her if she needed help with the heavy items. It sounded like a threat to Tanya, but she didn't know why, except that he seemed to be some kind of manager. She said no and hurried so fast now that she almost smashed the eggs. The cashier was scanning, slack jawed and ignorant.

Outside Tanya opened the back trunk so she could pile in the grocery bags and the beer case, but she stopped and stood gazing into the empty trunk while the wind tried to nudge her cart away. She was thinking about Lucia, who'd been locked inside this same trunk, the Abducted Teen. For a second Tanya considered going back inside and buying a newspaper, studying the picture of herself so she could figure out where and when it had been shot—where she had been watched. But then she worried that manager would think she was a shoplifter, that he'd stop her and ask more questions and recognize her from the picture.

Back in the driver's seat she peeled open a one-pound bag of circus peanuts she'd found in the candy aisle. She shoved a fat orange one into her mouth and closed her eyes. Fresh and melting gooey while she chewed, her first one in years. Her mother used to buy them, and Tanya had asked her once at a bowling tournament why they called them peanuts if they were banana flavor, and why they were orange when both peanuts and bananas weren't orange. "You think too hard, baby," her mom said, and they both had a crazy laugh over it.

Tanya had exactly three quarters' change in her pocket and she knew the phone number for information. It would be so simple to get the

Mobergs' home number. Probably it was even still listed under the dead man's name, easy to call and leave a message to let them know that Lucia was alive and safe so far. Maybe she could even call the cops and tell them about Buck Hanson's camp in the woods, and then as soon as she hung up she could start driving. Only five dollars left in her pocket, but she could speed miles away before the gas ran out. These possibilities swarmed like hornets, and she knew any one of them could sting her.

Suddenly she left her car again and headed on foot toward the bowling alley across the street. Nobody on the sidewalks or passing in cars, but Tanya held her keys so that they jutted between her closed fingers like claws—because she didn't trust this village quiet and because surprises were always disastrous. Nothing happened on her way through the front doors except that familiar thunderclap of a ball rolling down a lane and crashing into upright pins. It was just four lanes and it stank of stale beer, cigarettes, and the grease they used to slick the floor. A teenaged boy was shooting a fake gun at an arcade screen. A couple of potbellied old men in polyester shirts were bowling in lane one, but the other lanes were open.

"Size five," she told the attendant. She slid her five-dollar bill onto the counter.

"Just you?" he said, but Tanya didn't answer him. Except for the better graphics on the video games, this alley could've been from 1980, and that fact alone was already cooling her nerves. Even the drink machine in the corner dispensed old glass-bottle sodas for fifty cents each. The front countertop was carpeted, just like Tanya remembered from her mom's favorite alley in Cleveland, where Tanya used to have to stand on her tiptoes to see the shoe racks behind the counter. She was a kid again, blameless of anything that would get her face printed on the front cover of a newspaper. Nobody here would recognize her.

The attendant gave her lane number four and handed over her rental shoes, a paper scorecard, and a squat little pencil. He kept glancing at her stomach, maybe wondering why a full-term pregnant lady was bowling by herself on an off-season Friday afternoon. But she wasn't worried about his suspicions or anyone else's—not in here. She bought an Orange

Crush from the vending machine and twisted the cap off with the bottle opener built into the side of the machine. Then she chose a standard black ball from the rack of house balls because it was an easy six-pounder and her fingers fit into the holes. That was all she needed.

She went to her lane and laid the scorecard down on the table and slipped the pencil behind her ear like her mom used to do. When she slid her fingers into the holes was exactly when her hands stopped shaking. She raised the ball up to her chin so that she could peer over its curve and it seemed like she was an astronaut floating in orbit over a miniature black Earth.

Down the lane the pins stood waiting for her attack. Tanya didn't have the technique her mother had—how the ball used to skirt along the gutter edge like a parlor trick just before it curved back to the center and smashed the pins. She didn't have the arm brace or the headband or the T-shirt that said she was the women's-league champ. But still Tanya's ball shot straight and fast and toppled every pin but two, split on either side, wobbling like drunks in their places.

She bowled for twenty minutes and got a few spares, no strikes. She didn't keep score because she didn't know how and besides the numbers hardly mattered. What mattered was that thunder and that clash, how it rumbled in her belly where even the baby could hear. And how the mechanical arm brushed away the pins after every frame: no matter how many stood or lay cluttered on the lane, all her mistakes were wiped clean and the pins restored perfect every time as if nothing bad ever lasted in this world.

She pulled her rental shoes off and slid her feet into her own tennis shoes. She had one quarter left in her pocket, probably enough, but then again she probably didn't even need money to call the police. The bowling had flatlined her feelings and all she wondered now was if Mason would incite a showdown when the police came to get him, if he'd get himself killed or just yield quiet with his empty hands raised. She figured there'd be no bail, more years of prison than he could live. She could be rid of him and raise her baby girl, who he would've disowned anyhow, and Tanya didn't need to feel anything but righteous about it.

She returned her shoes and watched the attendant spray disinfectant into them.

"Is there a payphone here?" she asked.

"Near the bathroom but it's out of order," he said.

So Tanya hurried through the exit almost strutting. She dug into her pocket for that last quarter and even the cold air kicking her hair across her face didn't faze her. She stepped off the curb and kept her eyes on the phone across the street by the mini-mart entrance, so intent that she didn't hear or notice the person on the sidewalk until he grabbed her by the elbow and yanked her back onto the sidewalk. Startled, reeling, she swung at him with her car-key knuckles and missed his face by at least ten inches.

"Relax," he hissed. He was wearing sunglasses and a gray hooded sweatshirt with the hood slung over his head, and black gloves and a padded vinyl jacket full of slices and holes with loose stuffing aflutter. He smelled like smoke and sweat and you wouldn't know him from anybody else on an inner-city street. But here in this village he was like an ink smudge on a pretty postcard. He was a friend of Mason's that she'd seen a few times at bars and parties, a Skeleton Crew hangaround whose handle Tanya couldn't remember just now.

"What do you want?" she asked. Her quarter slipped between her fingers and burrowed into a curbside pile of sludge. A car puttered by, and the driver was a wrinkled old woman watching the two of them instead of the street ahead of her.

"I saw you go into the bowling alley there and I waited for you. I need to see Brick."

"Don't you know where he is?" Tanya asked.

"Brick told me the town but not the exact place," he said. "I know it was crazy coming all the way down here not knowing where to find him, but I needed to see him. There's stuff he should know—and you, too. You shouldn't be out here in public. Take me back to where you're staying, all right?"

"Did Buck send you? He's been waiting to hear from Buck," Tanya asked.

"No, Buck don't know I'm out here." He was jerky, scraping his feet on the crusty ice like he had to piss something fierce. "Otherwise I'd know where, right? This is bigger than Buck Hanson and he don't need to know. Brick would agree if I could talk to him, I know it."

"I forgot what they call you," Tanya admitted.

"Red," he told her. "You remember me, Tanya, right? You've seen me around."

"Yeah. Red. I remember but Mason said don't talk to nobody. Just get the groceries."

"He didn't know I'd be here, right? Just call him up and tell him I'm here."

"There's no phone," Tanya said. Her head was clouding up again and she couldn't think fast enough to know what choice would turn out right. It all seemed so treacherous now that Red was here like a bomb set to blast. She said, "How did you know you'd find me?"

"I didn't. I came down hoping one of you'd need to show up somewhere in town—and if not then fuck it, I'd just start combing the backroads for your Caddy. I'd end up finding it."

"I don't want to know anything about what's going on," Tanya said. She sidestepped over a snowbank and hurried across the street before Red could say anything else. If she could just get to her car she could drive herself to the nearest cop station. But Red followed right behind her, saying, "Listen, Tanya—I need at least to know what's going on with the girl."

"She's locked in a trailer with no heat or food," Tanya said.

"She's still alive? He kept her alive?"

Tanya stopped at her driver's door while Red circled around the car to the passenger side. He tried the latch and the unlocked door popped open, but he didn't get inside. He waited, watching across the rooftop, eyes hidden behind the black lenses of his sunglasses. When Tanya didn't say anything, he slid down into the passenger seat. Tanya looked around once more to see who might be watching, but there was no one. She glanced again at the payphone and wondered if she'd ever be able to rally that resolve again.

On the way back Tanya drove ten miles under the speed limit while her passenger tore off his gloves and rubbed his bare hands in the heater blast. He flipped back his hood and his scalp was shaved raw, littered with razor cuts so bad it looked like he'd done it in the dark without a mirror. Tanya had excuses ready if Mason tried to blame her for this—Red jumping out from nowhere, begging and shouting and forcing his way into her car. Not exactly true but at least it was some kind of explanation she could give.

Red munched on a circus peanut while he said, "Man, this whole thing has gone to hell."

Tanya saw something glint off a side mirror. She shot her eyes toward the cockeyed rearview. She adjusted it down to her eyeline and right off saw the flashing blue state trooper lights tailgating behind her. Her anguish was full and instant. She pressed the brake and veered toward the road shoulder without even willing herself to do it. Red caught on and whipped his head around to get a look behind them. "Oh—fuck this!" he said. "Keep driving, go, go!"

The shoulder was sunken and loaded with dirty snow thrown off the road.

"No! Keep driving!" Red demanded, screaming in her ear. She was already stopped, hand on the gearshift to rack it into park. The cruiser whisked by at a fifty-mile-per-hour clip. It drove on past the road leading up toward the camp and headed around a curve until it disappeared past the town limits. The Caddy's muffler rumbled. Every few seconds the whole jalopy shuddered. "That was close," Red said with both hands pressed to his face.

THE ONE SMALL MIRACLE was that by Sunday afternoon Greta's flu had mostly cleared. No more medication to keep her groggy, and just a trace of that pink tissue rash under her nostrils. Even a skeptic might be nudged by such fortune, especially while sitting in church. She was wearing a lilac-colored gown that she'd bought at JC Penney. The string of pearls on her neck belonged to her mom—pearls Greta had worn only once, at her mother's funeral five years back. This morning she'd spent a full hour on makeup to conceal the marks of no sleep around her eyes.

Twelve hours since she and Moe had visited the biker bar and sentenced a bad man to possible death. She'd used her badge and breached every known conduct code, and still Mitch Wendt was breathing easy in his motel room, still Luc was lost. Her efforts had not been enough, not nearly enough, but today these failures would be suppressed. She was at the United Methodist church watching her daughter get married. She'd known she would attend since the moment Sandy gave her leave to avoid it. That much mercy couldn't go ignored—or heeded.

Greta sat in the first pew before the altar on the same length of plush cushion as her ex-husband, his second wife, his parents. Every cough echoed in the vaulted ceiling, every camera click. There were four bridesmaids in matching sheer purple dresses and Greta didn't know any of these girls, except the maid of honor, who'd been Sandy's friend for ages. Greta recognized a scant few seated behind her on the bride's side, just a few of the dozens of friends her daughter had amassed. Greta supposed her own funeral, when it came, wouldn't draw a fraction of this crowd if not for the obligated cops. But still she sat in her place of honor, part of the family. She sat trying to usher that elusive esteem that felt appropriate, trying not to let her head stray back toward Luc's disappearance.

The pastor was British, Greta's age, and she recited vows that Max repeated to Sandy. Greta eyed the faces behind her and saw women dabbing tears with tissues. She wanted that much heart herself, just for a few seconds, but such breakdowns take years of buildup and there is no life lived backward. Try to erase your failure, your bad memories, and you get what Blair Moberg got: permanent trauma, like stripping down ugly wallpaper and then facing nothing but empty black space behind it.

The reception came immediately after. It was at the downtown Rochester Sheraton in a fifth-floor ballroom overlooking a skyline that only seemed majestic when viewed between velvet curtains, under the light of a crystal chandelier and the influence of one champagne flute. Greta stood by the window with her drink and watched the light Sunday traffic glide below, the thousand lights burning in the distant high-rises. She wondered how many cars and how many rooms sheltered monsters who were even now sharpening their teeth.

They never ceased, these thoughts of Luc and where she might be. Greta decided that if she should bear witness to Luc's empty corpse, then her own breath and blood would surely also drain away. Greta was desperate enough to toss herself through that glass and soar out over the city like a hawk in flight, and to believe it was possible.

But then she turned and watched her daughter mingle with the guests all decked out in their suit coats and pearls, neckties and panty-hose. Sandy was glimmering in her gown, her bright hair in spirals, earrings flashing like beacons. From across the room Greta willed herself toward this banquet of life because it was partly hers, some extension of herself that she could only reach with sharp focus in a clear and concentrated moment.

Even then the veiled chaos outside that ballroom window was clutching toward her. She turned away from it deliberately and walked toward her daughter and her ex-husband in his gray suit and gray trimmed beard, his second wife in her pink shoulder-padded blouse and frosted tips, his elderly parents who had once years ago told Greta they loved her—if only because she'd given birth to their first and so far only grandchild.

"Mom, you look beautiful," Sandy told her, and they were hugging like some hard-earned victory had been won. Even her ex-husband grinned and raised his glass to salute her. You actually managed to make it, his smile told her.

Greta thought she heard Luc's voice screaming from somewhere distant and unreachable, but she didn't turn to look. Instead, she sipped her champagne empty and swiped a bacon-wrapped scallop from a silver tray on the buffet line and bit it off of the toothpick. A couple in their seventies came to her and reintroduced themselves, but Greta had no memory of ever meeting them before. She smiled with her mouth closed, chewing, and shook their bony hands.

FIVE MINUTES UP the hillside Tanya inched around a curve but somehow still fishtailed the back left tire into a deep snowy rut that grabbed and wouldn't let go no matter how rough she gunned the engine. She cried quietly while Red was out of the car giving it a shove. Soon enough they were loose again, but Tanya couldn't keep herself from blubbering. She found an old tissue in her jacket and wiped her eyes with it while Red got back into the car. Even in this cold his bald head was glistening with sweat.

"You all right?" he asked. He put his hand on her elbow but she flinched it away. He said, "It's okay—we're out, we're out. Just keep on driving. I know he's not gonna like my showing up here at first, but I'll talk him down. Don't worry."

"Please don't tell him I was bowling. I was only supposed to get groceries."

"Look, Tanya, I'm nobody to judge you."

They moved along at a good clip the rest of the way, and when she turned into the driveway she gunned it and came up hard against the bank of the area that Mason had shoveled for her. Red lurched forward like a crash-test dummy and planted his hands on the dash. Tanya waited while the car still idled. She watched the cabin door and wondered why Mason wasn't rushing out onto the stoop. No way to tell if he was spying out a window, waiting for what, she didn't know.

"What's the matter?" Red asked.

"Nothing," said Tan. Over on the far side of the property the trailer was shut tight, and it didn't look like Mason had gone anywhere close to it while she was gone. Tanya realized now how cruel she would've been if she'd abandoned that girl to these frozen woods and the monsters that lurked in them. In some ways it felt like a victory being back here to watch over the girl like a surrogate mother, keeping her safe.

"Is that where he's got her—in that trailer?" Red asked.

Tanya nodded. She turned off the engine.

They were both out of the car when Tanya popped open the trunk. She lifted one of the bags and Red hoisted up a couple more, one in each arm, and followed her up the trail of hard-packed snow that Mason had made for her. She hated the silence that was coming from the cabin. It made her knees want to buckle. She took careful steps on the icy cinderblocks and then shoved her shoulder into the door to open it.

Mason was there, just inside the doorway by the woodstove. He was standing flush against the wall, shirtless and stiff as an upright corpse. He glared at her unblinking. He snapped his head once to the left, telling her without words—keep moving, keep quiet. Tanya held her breath and stepped forward into the dark void. It felt like free-falling out of an airplane. She moved the grocery bag down against her belly to protect it. She saw that Mason had taken Buck Hanson's pee-wee hockey stick down from the wall and was clutching it in one hand.

"Is he—" Red started, but Mason checked him against the door and gripped the hockey stick crosswise in both hands and rammed it up underneath Red's chin, into his throat. Red gagged bug-eyed and when he fumbled the grocery bags a plastic milk gallon slipped loose. It struck the concrete floor with a fatty shudder, unbroken.

"What are you doing here?" Mason growled.

Red hacked up drool and stuck out his gagging tongue.

Mason said, "Tell me what the fuck is going on, Tanya," not looking at her.

She said, "I went down to get groceries—like you said—and he was there, in the town on the street. He told me to bring him back—because you said what town—I couldn't stop him—"

Mason crammed his face an inch from Red's. His jaw pulsed and his nostrils exhaled short angry breaths. Red's face had tinted almost purple before Mason finally eased off enough to let Red stumble free. The grocery bags slid down his legs and settled safe on the floor. Red held his neck like he was choking himself and said, "Brick—you told me—this town—I thought I could come—try to find you—"

Mason said, "You led the police up here, didn't you?"

"No!"

"Bullshit!" Mason's voice was like razor blades. Red's was like meat pushed through a grinder. Tanya still held her grocery bag against her stomach, shielding it with cereal boxes and raw steak packages. She stood watching them as if they were not part of her world, something to gawk at on TV but not to accept as real. She didn't move until Mason barked at her, "What'd you bring him up here for, Tan?"

"He said it'd be all right, that he needed to talk to you."

"Only I say what's right!" Mason screamed. "He don't know shit—you got it? Stupid bitch—you want to have your baby in jail because of this fuckup? He ain't even a member."

She muttered, "No," like it was a question that needed answering.

"Brick, nobody's following me, man, I'm positive," Red told him.

Mason said, "Man, you've fucked everything up from the start."

"I was trying to help you get your member patch, man."

"What you're gonna get me is a lethal injection. I should fucking kill you! I should take you outside and blast your brains out all over the snow. I been trapped up here expecting SWAT teams and Feds in helicopters because of you. I'm sitting here waiting for my son to come out and there's nowhere else I can go. What kind of shit is that for a kid to be born into?"

"I didn't—" Red started to say, but Mason stopped him. A few seconds of bleached-out violence and it was done. At first Red was sitting on the floor rubbing his throat and coughing, but then Mason knocked him over with a swift-booted kick across the forehead. Smeared mud on skin and a torn-open gash just over Red's eyebrow. Mason straddled him, shoving a fist into his face again and again. Red squirmed onto his side and kicked his frantic legs. Nobody screamed: they just grunted like rapt varsity wrestlers, both of them. Finally Mason stood up and gave Red one last football punt to the back. The hollow impact of that kick blasted through Red's lungs and fired out of his mouth like a gunshot. Tanya was sitting on the couch now with the hockey stick in her hand, and she couldn't remember how all of this had happened.

Mason said, "You could've been dead right there, fucker. You don't listen."

Red moaned and scraped his boot toes on the floor.

"You didn't tell me you thought the police were coming," Tanya said.

"I figured it was implied," Mason said. He wiped blood off his knuckles with the untucked tail of his flannel shirt.

"If you think—shouldn't we leave, then?" Tanya wondered.

"And go where?"

"I don't know. California. Back to Detroit maybe."

"Are you as thick as this asshole here? We can't go anywhere, Tan."

"You shouldn't of kidnapped that girl. Because now we're trapped here."

"Don't tell me—" He yanked the hockey stick from her hands easy as a wind gust. Tanya cringed and raised a forearm between his aim and her face. He said, "Wake up, Tanya—I ain't gonna hit you. What do you think? I'm just saying we need the money—we need that girl for the money that's owed us, you understand?"

Red was up on his hands and knees now spitting quarter-sized starbursts of blood onto the floor. Mason turned toward him again—but this time he held out his hand. Red glared with the eye that wasn't swollen shut, and by doing nothing he refused that offered hand. Mason advised him, "Just admit you deserved it and then relax. Now, you want a beer or what?"

GRETA LEFT THE WEDDING reception after cake and drove west toward Hammersport. On her passenger seat was a portfolio full of Mason Renault mugshot copies, and she intended to use them to query the Mobergs' neighbors about whether they'd ever seen him before. In a hotel restroom she'd changed into jeans, sweatshirt, and gunbelt. Her fancy gown now hung by a clothes hanger in the backseat, covered in plastic. At an intersection she waited and squeezed the steering wheel and failed at convincing herself that these last few hours of celebration were justified, that she would not forever regret them if Luc Moberg turned up dead.

But even now, all she knew were basic truths that couldn't help Luc or alter the danger that she faced if she was still alive. Blair Moberg had hired Mason Renault to kill her husband for insurance or spite or some other motive that meant nothing except a prosecution strategy and a news headline. And Greta, for her own sake, had failed to reach that victorious high that often came with nailing a case. There was no thrill in pondering the arrest of a bludgeoned child-woman who couldn't remember or even comprehend her own crime. No closure without Lucia.

It was still daylight when she passed the Hammersport Shop-Mor coming into the village, but the gloom was dark enough to make the outside lights shine. The M on the neon sign was blown, evoking one-half of an imperative choice: Shop- or. The glut of cars in the floodlit parking lot seemed to indicate that the locals were content to shop, regardless.

She turned right on red into the village proper, where the commercial sprawl gave way to narrowed streets and leafless branches encroaching overhead. Another right and she was on the Mobergs' street, pulling alongside the curb near their house. The kitchen light was glowing, but Greta knew it was a ruse. In little more than a week that house had emptied itself of its occupants, one by one—to death, to pain, to oblivion.

She grabbed the folder of photo arrays and headed toward the Cutler home, the most logical start point for a neighborhood tour. The cold wind ripped at her like ice knives, but trudging through this relentless night was Greta's way to keep herself moving, a way to subject herself to whatever parallel hell Luc might also be enduring. Crossing the front walkway, she noted the open garage door at the end of the drive and the Harley Sportster propped inside. She hadn't tagged Quinn Cutler as a bike enthusiast, and the oversight made her gut clench tight. At its rotten core the Skeleton Crew was a motorcycle gang. That factoid was just as significant as all the other fruitless case evidence.

Lydia Cutler took her sweet time answering the doorbell. She squinted through the chain-bolted opening, dressed in the same rugged poncho she had worn almost two days earlier, reeking so pungent of cigarettes that for an instant Greta's own devotion to the habit faltered.

"Ms. Cutler? I'm Investigator Hurd. We spoke early yesterday morning?"

Recognition failed to dawn on Ms. Cutler's face, but she unbolted the chain anyhow.

"Ms. Cutler, is your son Quinn at home?"

"No," she said, dragging out the word like it was a sentence. Her attention drifted toward a corner of the interior that Greta couldn't see from where she stood bone cold on the porch.

"Is someone else in there with you, ma'am?" Greta asked.

"No, it's just a movie I'm watching." Lydia opened the door wide enough to demonstrate her television in the corner of the living room. On-screen was a children's cartoon featuring a redheaded mermaid and a singing lobster. The TV was a thirty-inch in ultramodern black, the newest fixture in the room by a decade at least. In her early-morning stupor Greta hadn't noticed this television, nor had she noticed the gleaming new VCR underneath it.

"May I come in?" she asked. "It's rather cold."

"Yeah," Lydia said. She shuffled a few steps toward her TV and then added, "Sure."

Greta closed the door behind her. Inside was an instant sixty-degree temperature spike, but the cartoon music blared loud enough to make her wince. Lucky for her, Lydia had left the remote control on the foyer side table, so Greta swiped it and thumbed the volume down. Lydia had already eased herself back down onto the edge of the couch, gawking at the screen with her hands pressed together between her knees. She didn't seem to notice the fading noise.

"Do you know where your son is, Ms. Cutler?"

"He went out. For a little while."

"How long ago was that?"

"Maybe like just before lunch. About noon."

"That was almost eight hours ago," Greta said.

"He's okay. I'm not worried," she said, never once glancing away from the TV.

"I'd like to know where he is so I can speak to him," Greta said. She moved around the coffee table, which was cluttered with magazines and boxes of Avon orders that appeared to be meant for distribution. Only after Greta shimmied between Lydia and the television did the woman's dull eyes finally rise to meet hers. Greta repeated her desire to know Quinn Cutler's whereabouts.

"He didn't say where he was going."

"Can you find out?" Greta insisted. "Can you call anyone? This is important."

"I don't know who—"

Greta blurted out, "May I have permission to take a look in your son's bedroom?"

"He's not there. I know he didn't come back yet."

"But I'd like to see his room anyway. I know that Lucia Moberg was in there just before her kidnapping, so I'm hoping that she might have left behind some clues that would point me in the right direction." The logic of her request was zilch, but Greta banked on Lydia's low capacity for doubt.

"I guess it's okay," Lydia said. "It's upstairs on the left. He keeps it a mess, though."

Ten seconds, Greta was upstairs entering Quinn's cramped room where the ceiling sloped down against her head. Girly posters, biker mags, crumpled bedsheets, dirty clothes sprawled on the floor and wafting up rank hormonal stench. She kicked aside a few pairs of shirts and jeans to give herself a clear place to stand, then she regarded the room laid out like an exhibit before her.

She unbuttoned a badge-sized leather compartment on her belt and scooped out its contents—a tight package that unfolded into two rubber gloves. She pulled them over her hands. The bed lying before her was unmade, blanket balled in a corner and fitted sheet peeling away from the mattress. Greta touched a gloved hand against the surface of the bed, remembering that Luc had been here just before her kidnapping, that some force of fear had caused her to abandon this suffocating room and rush toward an even greater disaster.

Greta took her hand away. Whether or not she hoped to divine some lingering charge from that moment, some glimpse of Luc's inner self, nothing came to her. Instead, she moved toward a shelf of boxed compact disks, noting that many of them were still sealed in their shrink-wrapped packages. She almost decided they'd been stolen, but then she found the cash receipt folded between two of the boxes. It was from Wonderland Music and Video, dated on Friday, two days prior, and amounting to over six hundred dollars in merchandise, including several VHS tapes, *The Little Mermaid* among them. Greta suspected that Lydia's TV and VCR were also recent purchases.

She opened desk drawers and found them loaded with more biker magazines featuring bikini-clad bimbos on their covers. Digging down farther, she found two manuals on motorcycle maintenance and a Mead fifty-page, spiral-bound notebook with a black cover. She flipped through pages and found nothing but erratic pencil sketches, scribbled flurries that coalesced into images of dragons and knights with blood-slicked broadswords and monstrous phalluses vomiting black liquid. A naked female zombie whose flesh was rotting away, except where her cleanly rendered tits loomed as two ample globes against her exposed ribcage. Wolves and demons, skeletons and vampires—a bestiary of medieval fetishism that Greta guessed might serve as an amateur tattooist's portfolio. On the final page, Quinn Cutler had sketched a crude, but starkly recognizable, rendition of the death's-head miner that served as the Skelton Crew's rocker.

Greta braced herself against the desk, but her mind burned too strong now to be fazed by shock. She let her heart slam while she worked out the truth. Judging from her short parlay with Quinn Cutler, she knew he was too green for full membership in an outlaw gang, chiefly when such gangs were often known to require their prospects to commit murder as part of the club entrance agreement. He wasn't a member, yet there was no doubt about his complicity. Whether he was a wannabe hangaround or an actual prospect, he was party to Luc's kidnapping, and he'd lied boldfaced as he sat smoking cigarettes and bemoaning her disappearance. Greta resisted the shame of having swallowed his lies because no time remained now for pointless self-loathing. And because deep in her ticking pendulum of a soul, she'd recognized his guilt. Only half-conscious of her motives, she'd come back to this house tonight because she'd known.

On the inside back cover of the sketchbook were deep grooves from pencil marks. Greta shifted the cover against the light from the desk lamp and recognized the outline of another miner skull, this one more carefully and precisely drawn. This sketch was gone, but the last page had been torn away, leaving behind thin tattered strips where it was ripped from the spirals. At some point Quinn had taken the sketch with him, most likely to have it made into a tattoo. If Quinn Cutler had gotten that tattoo, and if he'd marched off to flaunt his spanking-new body art, then Greta knew he ought to be praying for deliverance. An outlaw gang like this one would never permit a prospect or a hangaround or anyone outside of the club to wear their insignia. They considered it copyright infringement, and bikers were not known to sue for damages.

Greta bolted back out of the room. In the hallway she saw the bathroom where Quinn claimed Luc had pretended to hide. She pushed the door open and turned on the light with some crazed idea that Luc would be there, still hiding, unharmed. She'd allowed herself to think for an instant that Luc was an accomplice to these crimes—boyfriend, Wonderland Music, convenient disappearance—but such a thesis was too sickening to uphold. What she found instead of Luc was a sink basin covered with strands and clumps of long black hair that she knew belonged to Cutler. In the sink were also a pair of barber's scissors, several Bic disposable razors with black stubble clogging the double blades.

The breakthrough adrenaline thrill was leaking through her again. Downstairs she veered toward the kitchen, where Lydia Cutler was pouring vodka into a glass of grape juice. Greta hated the sight of that woman so brainless and utterly ignorant of her own culpability, and she wished she could cast just a smidgen of her own parental guilt at the bitch.

"Are you positive you don't know where your son is?" Greta barked.

Lydia flinched, splashing vodka on the countertop. "Oh," she said, "I didn't hear you come down. I wish I knew where he was for you. I would try to help."

"Did he look different in any way when he left?"

"Yes, he shaved his head bald. It was strange." She grabbed her drink, ignoring the spill.

"Not strange enough to tell me about?" Greta asked.

"I'm sorry. Is there something wrong?" She took a loud sip of her vodka and grape juice.

"You could say. The people who live next door. How'd they get along with Quinn?"

"He was an angry teenager," she admitted. "He calmed down so much, so I forgive her."

"Her? Who's her?" Greta demanded.

"The mother. She was always calling the police on him. For stupid things, I think."

"Like she had something against him personally?" Greta said. She was blocking the doorway to keep Lydia from getting back into the living room with her Disney cartoon.

"Yes, exactly," Lydia said. "She used to watch him from her windows. Weird. But he calmed down and now he keeps to himself good. Even last month I bad-mouthed her by accident and Quinn, he scolded me for talking about her like that. I felt pretty ashamed for it. That's how he's changed. He even made a casserole for them when the husband— he brought it over himself."

"Has he done other nice things lately, like buy you that VCR and TV in there?"

Lydia grinned like a bobby-soxer with a valentine. "Yeah," she gushed.

"Did you ask him where he got the money for it?"

The smile dropped away. She put her drink back on the counter. "I didn't want to pry."

Greta wanted to inform Lydia Cutler that her philanthropist son was accessory to kidnapping and probably murder, that maybe Mommy better just wipe her bastard brood from her memory because no matter what he was fucked forever, and that the worst choice Lydia ever made was prolife. Instead, she asked, "Can you get me the home phone number for Hammersport High School's principal?"

THE KEY IN THE LOCK again. An instant panic triggered Luc's pulse and her breath, and she crawled away from the trailer door where she'd been huddled, now pressing herself against the back wall with both palms against the cold metal while the bolt cranked open and the door was raised. In the burning light her visitor appeared as a shadow. "Go away!" she screamed, and her voice slapped the metal walls and stung back against her eardrums.

"You're coming inside for some food," he said.

"Fuck you," Luc told him.

He sucked on a cigarette—orange blip of fire jutting from his face. He said, "Don't say I didn't try to be nice, bitch. Now get your ass out of there unless you want me to crawl in and kick some dents into your skull for you."

Luc pressed her bare knees into the grit and crawled, wary of weapons or a sudden open hand that might grab her and push her down and tear at her clothes. Now she was close enough to see that he did in fact have a gun aimed at her. She found her footing in the snow this time, but her knees wouldn't hold still.

"Come on," he said, his voice flat and pissed. He hooked his free hand under her armpit and raised her up. She teetered with her legs shaking like a newborn fawn's.

Tall pines, the car, the cabin, the soft mounds of snow—all of it washed in sunlit watercolor. As she walked, strange fragments of clarity flitted in her peripheral sight. Each lone needle on a pine branch, every distinct blade like a dagger made of velvet. The crystallite deer tracks pressed into the snow. A knuckle on her abductor's left hand that was scabby and swollen from some recent wound. She couldn't comprehend what these selective visions were meant to convey, what promises they made.

Luc trudged through snow that swallowed her boots to the tallest eyelets, and she hardly found enough strength to lift them out again. They passed a rusty tractor that looked like it hadn't moved for decades. Up ahead, the cabin screen door opened and someone else was leaning out of the doorway, someone with an explosion of bright bleached hair. If her abductor shot her now, Luc wondered, would she even sense the impact before it splashed the harsh white ground with her blood, or would she die before she realized she was dying?

Luc tripped over the two cinderblock porch steps, but her abductor still clutched her arm, and his leverage stopped her from smashing her head on the concrete. He yanked her back onto her feet and squeezed her above the elbow hard enough to make her fingers prickle with blood loss. He told her to stand up and march. The woman on the porch stepped aside and kept the door open. She was wearing an extra large T-shirt that came to her knees and bowed outward from her pregnancy— a massive orb that stretched and distorted the monster truck decal printed on the shirt. She wore thick wool socks bunched around her ankles, and she grinned as Luc passed. For a second she was in such focus that Luc could see the sheen of lip gloss around her mouth and the sleek oily shine on her skin. "Hello," the woman said, smiling with her big teeth, like she was greeting a guest for dinner.

The heat inside was noxious. It attacked Luc's lungs, suffocating. Her skin came back to life and it was screaming. The sudden air change hit strong enough that it seemed to make her bones crack and split just like the wood popping inside that stove. The abductor led her into a kitchen, and now he pulled a chair out from the table, pushing her down into the seat. Luc obeyed. She felt the gouges in the table even through her numb and swollen fingertips.

Her abductor slipped his gun into a brown-leather holster attached to his belt. He told her, "Give me your wrists," but he didn't wait for her offering. He grabbed her nearest wrist and twisted her arm backward, pulled it through two vertical dowels in the chair back. Someone inside the cabin was muttering names and numbers. Only gradually did Luc understand it was a radio tuned to a Rochester Amerks hockey game. So familiar, and yet Luc was an untraceable distance from anyone who could help her, lost in a strange world parallel to the one she'd left. Her flesh throbbed but she didn't listen, not even when she felt new plastic snap-cuffs burning into her old wrist wounds, doubling the ache in her sprained wrist.

"Do you really need to do that?" someone else asked, a second man's voice.

"Shut your mouth," the abductor said. A minute later he'd bound her shins to the chair legs up past the horizontal dowels so she couldn't slide the bands down toward the floor. The second man in the kitchen was a blur, but Luc could see his dark outline seated at the opposite end of the table. He was scarfing down a plate of what looked like raw bloody animal entrails, but Luc couldn't focus enough to be sure.

She felt like she was still half inside that dream of the saint dabbing miracle sight into her eyes. She'd already seen hints of this magic vision at work while marching up here from her prison, but what she wanted most was a sight turned inward so that she could focus on the mess of sensations churning through her heart. The pregnant woman stood over by the woodstove, too far away for Luc to discern anything but the pulsing mass of her body. Everyone looked shapeless in this world. Everything pumped and breathed as Luc's eyes tried and failed to see.

"You're gonna eat," the abductor told her. He grabbed a saucepan and slapped it down on the table in front of her. A wooden spoon was propped inside the pan against the rim, and inside was instant chicken noodle soup with pasta in the shape of tiny stars and little cubes of chicken, broth steaming. He said to someone else, "Get over here and help her out."

The man across the table didn't move, but the woman skittered over. Close enough for Luc to see, a kerosene range still burned blue flame under a pan sizzling with what smelled like breakfast sausages. The abductor pulled back a chair and the pregnant woman took it, still grinning—grimacing maybe. She grabbed the wooden spoon from the bowl and brought it up to Luc's mouth. Luc sipped the broth, the slippery noodles that singed her tongue. She didn't want to let them feed her, but there was no willpower left for resisting.

"You gonna eat these sausage links?" the abductor asked.

"In a minute," said the woman. "I'm not hungry right this second."

"Don't screw around. You need lots of protein, so eat these eggs, too. I'm cooking them up now. My boy needs protein."

"Fine," she said, then she asked Luc, "Is it too hot?"

Luc didn't answer, didn't even gesture. Broth dribbled down her chin and over her neck and her shirt collar. In this warmth her nostrils were finally awake, and above the smell of broth and sausage and wood smoke she caught the sour scent of the piss-stained blanket she'd been forced to wrap herself inside.

Luc also noticed a tattoo on the underside of Tanya's forearm. It was the size of a poker card and it looked in that brief flash like a wolf standing upright on its back legs with a long snout and sharp teeth and a barrel chest. Its red eyes were two bright pricks like infected needle marks.

"This is good practice, you know," said the woman. "Spoon-feeding."

The abductor snorted. He'd turned his back to them and now he was cracking eggs into the fry pan. Luc thought of all those fairy tales she'd heard—the ones where children came upon cottages deep in the woods and inside those cottages the stoves were always burning, always hot and ready for their arrival. Carrots and potatoes and broth boiling, waiting for the meat to be added.

The second man across the table sat silent and hazy, eating his gory food.

The woman leaned toward Luc and said, "I'm going to have a baby."

"She can see that. She ain't as stupid as you are," the abductor said.

Luc said, "I can't see anything."

"Your glasses—" someone said, a voice that was crushingly familiar.

"Yeah, those were some serious Coke-bottle lenses," the abductor interrupted. "You probably can't see for shit right now. It's good you can't see how banged up your boyfriend is."

For an instant the man across the table came into perfect focus—the sharp curves of his cheekbones, one eye bruised shut and a bandage on his head. He was biting at shreds of dead chapped skin on his lower lip. His head was shaved bald, and he looked like he'd just escaped from some quarantine camp, but it was impossible not to recognize the boy she'd almost loved.

GRETA PARKED IN the Hammersport public school compound—kindergarten to graduate school all in one square mile. The high school bordered the college campus and was hardly different from those other brick, Depression-era public works buildings. On a Sunday, hers were the only tire tracks to mar the thin layer of slush that the steady snowfall had left on the blacktop of the faculty/staff parking lot. She jumped out of her Taurus and hurried to a nearby walkway sheltered by an awning from the wet snow. The full force of the wind burned against her cheeks and curled her fingers into claws as she gripped the public phone receiver. Even the plastic stung her ear with its cold, but she huddled against the wall and slipped her quarter in.

Three rings passed before Moe answered and Greta blurted her tale of what had happened with Lydia Cutler, what she'd found in Quinn's bedroom. Moe kept silent through her account. He was brooding, as she knew he would brood for days, on his own failure to mark Quinn Cutler as a suspect, especially now that the facts were printed in boldface.

When she was finished Moe said, "You have the notebook?"

"It's bagged," Greta said. "And as soon as I hang up with you I'm calling Hammersport PD to have them set a watch on the house in case Cutler decides to show his face back at home."

"All right," Moe said. "I can accept that Cutler is capable of stealing the five thousand, but then the motive for this Mason Renault home invasion is void. He shows up to collect his money, but Cutler has already been spending it for days. These scumbags could be trying to take advantage of a deeply confused woman, squeezing another five thousand from her, unless—"

Even over the phone line Greta could hear the gears grinding in Moe's head.

"—unless," he repeated, "nobody knows Cutler has the money, right? Not even the Skeleton Crew. You figure Cutler isn't even a member, so they don't know he has the money, and he isn't going to admit it. It's certainly not his to spend on music and television sets. So he's complicit in the assault and kidnapping like nothing's amiss. He's thinking he's free and clear."

"If that's true, Cutler is one seriously idiotic thief," Greta said, bellowing against the wind to be heard. "Stealing from an outlaw gang is one sure way to get yourself killed."

"Maybe he's gone on the run from them, disguising himself by shaving his head."

Greta pressed herself against the brick facade to keep warm. She spoke through gritted teeth. "I'm trying to figure out how Cutler knew where to find the money. I mean, who'd know to look under a dryer? I'm thinking either Luc foolishly told him about it, or Blair Moberg gave it to him herself."

"As in Cutler was the original go-between for the payoff?" Moe asked.

"All he needs to do is pretend the transfer never happened. Amnesia handles the rest, and Luc Moberg gets kidnapped for no reason. She thought this asshole was her boyfriend, Moe."

"Would a legitimate reason make it any less ugly?" Moe asked.

Next, Greta called Hammersport PD and requested the watch on the Cutler house. While she was settling arrangements, a gray minivan pulled into the slot designated for the school principal. Greta hung up and met the principal on the walkway. She was a woman Greta's own age decked with pearls, perfume, and a hundred-dollar hairdo, the sort of getup one wears when she has something better to do with a Sunday night. The dusky cold made her grin like a maniac.

"Thank you for coming out, Dr. Torelli," Greta said, badge in hand.

"You're lucky you caught me at home," the principal snapped. "I was on my way out."

Greta waited for Torelli to unlock doors, switch on lights, and then call the RPD from her office telephone to verify Greta's authority. By the end of these ordeals, Greta was wringing her hands, trailing the principal down endless hallways and up a flight of stairs to finally arrive at Quinn Cutler's locker. It had a combination dial, but Torelli had already accessed the proper code in a reference book. She spun the code right-left-right and popped open the locker door. Since school lockers were public property, no warrant was required.

They found a few textbooks and loose papers stacked on the locker floor, a pair of jeans and some compact discs on the middle shelf. Nothing taped on the door except one of those frosted mirrors kids win at carnivals, this one with the word METALLICA in sharp 3-D lettering. Two items on the topmost shelf: a Camel hard pack containing three cigarettes and a black five-and-a-quarter-inch floppy disk without a sticker label.

"Is there a computer here I can use?" Greta asked, floppy disk in her hand.

Torelli sighed and checked her watch, but Greta offered no apologies.

LUC WANTED TO SCREAM and thrash at Quinn Cutler like any rabid primate would. She wanted him flayed alive in retribution for the hell he'd led her through, but she felt also this strange urge toward him, a hope that he was here to save her from this awful place. Solid black hate punctured by so many beams of hope that it was like a night sky loaded with stars.

"Fuck you, Quinn Cutler," she muttered. "Fuck you for everything."

"Luc—come on—I didn't want any of this to happen," Quinn said.

The abductor scoffed. He said, "That's what you get for being a motherfucker, Red."

"What are you going to do to me?" Luc asked, but the pregnant woman choked off her question with another spoonful of soup. The woman's forearm tattoo came into focus again, but now instead of a wolf it looked more like a female human, naked and bisected down the middle so that she was black on one half, white on the other. Inked flames roiled around her figure, and those same red pinprick eyes were peering from her two-toned head.

"Never mind what I'm doing," the abductor said. "Collecting my money is what."

"It'll be all right, I know it. Don't worry," the woman told Luc.

"Shut up, Tanya," said the abductor. He prodded the hissing sausages with the patula.

"I'm just—she's afraid," the woman said, the woman who had just been called Tanya. Luc tried to will that name out of her memory. She didn't want to know because knowing was deadly, but already the word had burned itself into her brain forever.

"How are you gonna get the money now, Brick?" Quinn pushed.

Brick couldn't have been his real name, but now Luc knew yet another password to hell.

The man called Brick wielded his metal spatula like it was a flyswatter. He turned on Quinn and barked, "Why don't you tell me, asshole? She's your whore, so why don't you give me a clue? Why don't you go ahead and tell your little girlfriend there what you been up to this last year, you sick bastard?" He twisted his voice cartoonish and mocking and added, "I didn't mean to do it, really I didn't."

Quinn said, "The woman is brain damaged, man. What're we supposed to do?"

"That's bullshit," Brick said. He aimed the spatula at Luc and told her, "Let me explain something to you, kid. Your mom ain't good for shit, after what she did. You don't even know."

Tanya said, "You don't need to go back there. That woman isn't any kind of mother for you. What kind of mother is she?"

"Just shut up and eat these sausages," Brick said. He slapped the pan on the table.

"Do you want one?" Tanya asked Luc.

"Hey," Brick said. "Those are for my boy, understand? You take even a bite of that sausage and I'll slit your throat right here at my breakfast table. I'll let you bleed to death right here and fuck your mother's money, too."

Even while this man called Brick threatened violent death, his girlfriend pushed another spoonful of soup against Luc's closed mouth.

The woman seemed oblivious to Brick's fury, as if it rode on sound waves that she couldn't receive. Her tattoo had transformed again, this time into a giant serpent that coiled in upon itself, scaly and black with red eyes on fire.

"All I'm saying is you should probably forget about the money," Quinn persisted.

Brick slipped the handgun out from where he'd holstered it. It was a silver blur, but Luc didn't need perfect vision to know what object he was aiming. Her arms went taut enough to scrape the plastic binds into her scabby wrists.

Brick lunged at Quinn and cracked the gun butt against his face, one fast jab like pulling a lawn mower cord. And Quinn let it happen—barely lifted his hands to protect himself. He went slack on impact, leaned over in his seat, then crumpled to the floor with both hands pressed up to his nose. Tanya threw the wooden spoon back into the saucepan and covered both her ears with her open palms, but there was hardly any noise for her to evade. Just Quinn, knocked down and huffing into his hands like he was breathing through scuba gear.

"Shoot him," Luc said. Her vision focused on silvery nicks in the gun muzzle.

Brick faked a laugh and said, "Maybe I should let you do it, kid. Seems like you want the honors pretty bad. You hear that, Quinn? She wants to blow your brains out herself."

Quinn's groan was wet and gargled.

Brick said, "You know, if you'd of asked me a year ago—even a couple months ago—I'd of counted this asshole among my few friends in this world. Or at least a workable—what do you call? Protégé. But I'm here to tell you, he's got no fucking aptitude for who he thinks he is. It was him, you know. He's the one who got all this shit started with your parents, and then got me fucked up with it. Now here we all are, a bunch of stupid assholes. And, frankly, Quinn, I think this young lady here deserves to take one good shot at you."

Brick reached over the top of Tanya's head. The gun he offered toward Luc was turned backward in his grip, aimed directly at his own heart. Luc wanted to believe that she could grab the gun and that this sporadic miracle vision would help her now—her sight would focus just long enough that she could shoot these two men dead. She could do it without hesitation, but of course it was all just fantasy. Her hands were still bound to the chair.

"Psych," Brick joked, and then he tucked the gun away again.

GRETA WAS IN PRINCIPAL Torelli's office hunched over the desk while the computer booted. When the operator screen appeared, she slid Cutler's anonymous disk into the drive and latched it in place, double-clicked the folder. A single file appeared. A:\\Blair. Greta opened it and read:

dear q,
i hate writing but we never get time to talk. even when we do i cant make clear whats jumbled in my brain. i know im crazy and i doubt writing will make it any better but i need to spill my guts u know? im at work and youre at school so why do we have to keep playing this stupid game? why not just disappear people do? i'm at the shopmor by myself on my lunch break. i wonder what youre doing? if i ever get the guts to let u read this please just remember the important parts and chuck the rest it doesnt matter. u already know whats most important is that we keep this secret for everybodys sake. i told u before i dont want to hurt oscar whos a weak man for all his supposed brains. i dont want to hurt him b/c hes mostly good but deluded he still loves me after all this time i think. he tells me and i believe him even though i dont understand that emotion anymore. love is chemicals and eventually it ends and whats left is the guilt u feel for losing it and the guilt feels like love it pretends to be. never tell me u love me.

dear q,
does it seem like u and i have any kind of life together? we can't even show our faces its like were sentenced to this PRISON life only allowed

inside my house and only during certain times. im afraid youre going to fail school b/c of me. im sick of this place and these bitching customers all day. i was supposed to have a college degree by now but of course i set it aside for him and somehow i got stuck in this life. i dont mean to be so negative its just this MOOD i cant seem to get out of where i start feeling guilty and regretting everything. i know this might hurt u but its the truth. sometimes i think thats why we got together was guilt. do u remember how i hated u how i treated u like shit b/c i was afraid of u and thought i was righteous i thought i was ABOVE u but today i figured out who i am isnt any part of who i really am.

dear q,
sometimes i think if i told him about us hed say he already knew a long time ago and was just keeping his mouth shut b/c he didnt want anything to change. he depends on everything around him staying just the same or he says he cant think. thats all he cares about. theres something i never told u about the day when u came into the shopmor and i caught u stealing that stupid pair of sunglasses? u thought it was all by accident like your dumb luck but really i was following u around since u came into the store. but not b/c i wanted to turn u in or anything but b/c it was a thrill. whats wrong with me to be thrilled by that? by the time u came to my house to apologize it was already too late for me. but the apology was bullshit we both know it. the apology was sex. do u ever think about going back to erase the things u regret?

dear q,
when i try to tell him that i want to leave him he doesnt understand or else he cries. i cant help wanting to love him back so im never going to leave him this will just stew inside me until it drives me NUTS. bad enough to think of oscars feelings but my shame is worse. id rather he was gone from my life than have him find out. i want to stop this with u its plain boring lust so why can't we? please lets stop. i keep wondering why u? because youre so close u have been there forever it seems when i cant sleep at night i lay in bed thinking youre sleeping

only yards away or maybe my feelings are haywire i cant tell the difference btw love and hate anymore. i wish there was a pill to make me stop
feeling everything. we dont love people we love serendipity hypocrisy
destiny tragedy irony thats all.

For five silent minutes Greta was lost inside Blair Moberg's jumbled,
frantic head—fragments of another woman's life hurtling at her like
stones pitched by an angry crowd. The letters were themselves undated,
and the "last modified" date was September 12, 1980, a calendar glitch
that misdated the file by more than a decade. Nothing indicated how or
when Quinn Cutler had received the disk—or if, improbably, he had
forged the letters himself. But Greta knew the letters weren't contrived.
They flooded her with too much understanding, too much truth. She
could see that Blair's motive was nothing as coldly calculated as an insurance payout. Guilt and fear had pushed her into becoming a killer-
by-proxy, and she'd been too deranged to realize that Oscar's death
would do nothing more than feed that gluttonous angst. She'd moved on
to other curatives—like refusing to make the second payoff, like attempted suicide.

"Investigator Hurd?" It was the school principal voicing her impa-
tience again.

"One minute," Greta said. She was adrift inside these letters, and
Torelli's voice struck her as so flat and distant that she could barely understand it. What she heard most clearly was the phantom clatter of
Blair Moberg's fingers typing furiously at her keyboard—racing to save
her soul with these frantic words, and failing to save anything. It was
mental hell, delving this deeply into somebody else's life, even when it
meant resolution.

DULL PANGS HAD been hounding Tanya's gut at least since the strain
of her bowling game. She knew her womb by now, so she didn't fret, not
until a deep and relentless cramp left her gasping at the kitchen sink
where she was washing the lunch dishes in water she'd boiled for

cleaning. It was the worst pain yet. She pressed her damp sudsy hands against her belly and it felt like holding an iron wrecking ball. For thirty seconds it crushed her, and then it was gone.

She was alone in the cabin, fending for herself. Mason was still outside gathering more timber for the fire. Red and Lucia were locked away in the trailer, both of them. They'd gone at gunpoint after lunch, hands on their heads like soldiers in a prison camp show, but they were both just kids. Red belonged to that world Tanya didn't believe was real, so she'd never guessed why he slummed around. They'd met him at some cornfield shindig, maybe three years ago, and he'd sidled alongside Mason—Brother Brick, with his chopper and his badass attitude. Red wanted to be a crew hangaround, but he was too soft-hide suburban. He'd badgered for it, and now he had nothing to show for that hope but a stint in that freezer cell.

Since lunch Tanya wished she never let that stupid-ass boy ride along with her, but she feared more for herself now, afraid the stomach pain would punch at her again soon. She watched through the kitchen window for a sign of her boyfriend. Instead, she saw Buck Hanson's Dodge Ram truck pushing up the road with its plow attachment. It slowed down and turned toward the cabin, angling a curled mound of hard-packed snow onto the private drive. The Caddy blocked the route, so the truck carved a clean path around it. Framed by the windshield were Buck in the driver's seat, his wife, Brenda, riding along with the Doberman in her lap. The wipers pushed aside the hard-driving snow.

Then came more movement farther off—first one, then two snowmobiles leaped out from the woods downhill and glided toward the cabin. The two helmeted riders buzzed up to meet the truck where it stopped. Both snowmobiles were splashed with bright glittery colors like toys for children. One rider was that dyke Paula, nicknamed Dread for the dreadlocked hair that sprouted out from her helmet like a bundle of sticks. The other she guessed was the Mexican Gordo, familiar by his brute size filling up the cushioned seat of his snowmobile.

Buck Hanson was sliding down from the truck's cab through the open driver's door. He wore his black-leather fedora with the silver cow skull dead centered on the brow. Watching him, Tanya tried to read some meaning into his scowl, but she had no skill for such guesses. She knew only that this group was the Skeleton Crew inner circle, raiding in from the living world where her own face was printed on every newspaper and probably broadcast on every television show. She was branded like cattle with no mind to predict whether it was headed for milk or for meat.

She turned away from the window so she could light the grill for more hot water, but she was back again in seconds squinting through a hole in the torn window plastic. Mason was with them now, leaning against the trunk hood, nodding at Buck's point-blank lecture. It was all mute to Tanya—nothing but fast lips and arms jabbing upward. Mason faked calm, but Tanya knew how all morning he'd flipped from gloom to fretting and back again to gloom. He'd listened to the radio and downed black coffee, flinching at the sudden jolts that fired only in his mind. Since he'd installed the radio batteries, he'd also learned that Tanya's face was out in public. He hadn't made any comment on the news, and his silence worried Tanya most of all.

Dread paraded inside and smirked while she unzipped her jacket and tossed it on the couch armrest. Underneath she wore nothing but a white tanktop, nipples peeking hard against the fabric. She came toward Tanya chewing a thick wad of gum and play-feinting with padded winter gloves. She said, "Hey, bitch," and gave Tanya a fast stinging punch on her shoulder. She laughed through her nose while she peeled off the gloves. Tanya muttered, "Hello" and tried not to look at Dread—those dark nipples, that vicious throat scar, her left eye blue and her right eye yellow.

"So how're you liking it up here in the boonies?" Dread asked.

"It's fine," Tanya said.

Dread poked around the shelves until she found an unopened bag of Cool Ranch Doritos that Tanya had bought earlier. She tore open the bag and mouthed a whole chip, right along with her gum. She chewed slow like she was daring Tanya to fuss about it. But Tanya learned a long while back that nothing belonged to her and nothing ever did.

"I hear you have some little chickadee locked up around here," Dread mumbled with a mouth full of corn chips. "What's she look like, huh? She hot?"

"I don't know—she's—a kid. How did you know about her?"

"She's all over the news this morning. So are you, Tanya. You should fucking see it."

"I saw the newspaper—" Tanya said.

"Hey, can I have your autograph?" Dread asked her, snorting out a laugh.

A new round of pain clamped on Tanya's gut like a bear trap. She grit her teeth and wrapped her forearms across the underside of her belly, staggering toward the den couch. The cushions were damp and pellety and mildewed, but they were as near to heaven as Tanya could reach. Fake pains, she told herself, false alarms—just like all the other craziness piling onto her.

"Hey, you all right?" Dread asked. She came into the den with the chip bag and two streaked orange handprints across the chest of her shirt that she'd used for a napkin. Sitting on the couch near Tanya's feet, she showed her concern by pulling her Game Boy out of a thigh pocket on her cargo pants and firing up a game of *Tetris*. Her left thumbnail was dull purple from getting bashed someplace.

Mason came in cradling a load of wood he'd lugged from the pile outside. Behind him Buck grunted, "Happy holidays," like it was the punch line to a filthy joke. Buck hung his fedora on a set of deer antlers mounted by the door, then rolled Mason's woodpile into his own arms and dropped it onto the floor beside the stove. Furnace the dog trotted in circles while his chain leash dragged behind him. He pushed his nose along the concrete floor until he sniffed out Tanya on the couch and nuzzled up against her hand like they'd been pals all along, like maybe he could smell her pain and was trying to calm it. She scratched him behind one ear. When she stopped he nudged her with his muzzle to get her to do it again.

"We're hitting him tonight," Buck ranted. "I made up my mind that Ox will settle it."

Mason said, "I thought Blisters was locked up."

"Naw, he's out and hiding at some fuck pad with his skank jailbait girlfriend. Fucker's cowering in a corner. I always knew that fairy boy wouldn't be able to hack it, but the bitch and A-rab city cop duo had to come into the Sub Bar and flaunt it that they turned him over. Now they're gonna see what happens when they run their mouths."

Brenda Hanson came in lugging three grocery bags of steaks and beer and other staples. She was panting from the strain it caused her, but nobody offered help until Tanya lifted herself off the couch. The cramps had passed again, simmering enough that she could manage her way back into the kitchen, where Brenda sat pressing her fingers against her forehead. She bitched about her headache and chain-smoked cigarettes while Tanya brewed her some coffee: poured boiling water over some grinds cupped inside a cheesecloth.

Buck said, "We're sending you off tonight, Brick. You and Tan are dumping that girl and you're getting the fuck out of New York State. Slit her throat and bury her in the woods for all I care." He tore open one cardboard case of Pabst and tossed Mason a can.

"Where exactly am I supposed to be going?" Mason said.

"We'll figure it out," Buck answered.

They threw logs in the fire and made merry like it was Christmas morning—even tuned the radio to holiday music and pounded their beers and passed around a vodka bottle, drinking to the season. They'd brought three boxes of bulb ornaments for the fir tree that Mason had cut. Gordo and Dread worked together to decorate the tree, which was leaning against the wall without a base and getting dry from lack of water. They hooked the red globes onto the branches and made ugly faces at their fish-eyed reflections in the mirrored glass.

Buck was in the recliner saying, "I tell you, it don't surprise me in the least how they got to Blisters. What did they have on him? Some road violations? Some failures to appear? This is the kind of fucked-up system we have that if the authorities suspect you, they can hold you and strip your rights on the basis of some totally unrelated charges. These fuckers get their way because they buy their asses into office and then use their blue goons to push martial law. I've been telling you this shit for years, man." While he talked he used his pee-wee hockey stick as a wise man staff.

"You sound like some militia nut, man," said Gordo, the squat Chicano built like reinforced concrete, tough enough to break flabby Buck in six places. Gordo was the only club guy with the chops to sport a dandy handlebar mustache and a hairdo like an underwear model. He was the only one who shot shit at Buck and skirted the holy hell that anyone else would get.

"Shut up, spic," Buck said, then he raised a leg and farted one quick blast.

In the kitchen Brenda drank her coffee and talked low enough so only Tanya could hear. She said, "All this shit is giving me a nervous breakdown." It was maybe fifty degrees, even with the stove and the warm bodies, but still Brenda was leaking sweat on her clammy forehead and in the fatty pockets underneath her eyes. For the first time in her life Tanya could peer right into another person's soul and know it was dying. Tanya recognized the symptoms.

The next contraction hit and she leaned against the counter, worked at deep breathing, but still that clamping hurt bore down deep inside her gut. With her eyes winced shut the earth seemed to sway like the deck of a ship lost in a storm surge. The whole round earth was breaking apart.

"You okay?" Brenda asked.

"I'm getting these cramps. False labor. They'll pass."

"From here it looks a hell of a lot worse than false labor."

"How do you know?" Tanya snapped. "You never had a baby."

The den was five feet off, but it was another universe. Buck was in there saying, "You laugh, but why you think we put this club together? To have some fucking brotherhood against these fascist goons and their cop lackeys, that's why. And I'll tell you something, especially you, Brick. I don't regret for a minute what any one of you's done, except that fucking rat Blisters. You've all shown balls—even you, Dread."

Dread told him, "Yeah, they're hanging from my rearview mirror."

"Nobody's ever viewed a pair of balls hanging from your rear," Buck said. He smoothed out his beard and pressed a marijuana pipe against his lip. Tilted his lighter into the bowl and sucked the flame down into the weed to make it glow orange. Held it in his lungs before he let it come out through his nose. Passed the pipe on to Dread and kept talking: "But I mean even this fucking college professor business. Any of you dropouts know the first thing old Adolf did after he invaded Poland?"

"Gassed kikes?" Gordo said, taking the pipe with his three-fingered hand.

Buck said, "No—even before the Jews, man. He rounded up the intellectuals—all the college professors and newspaper writers—shot them, mass executions in Warsaw's town square. He knew the real danger and he wiped it out. So Brick here is just upholding the tradition, and I for one applaud him for it. Them college pansies are all imperial show ponies, them and those Hollywood Hebrews with their propaganda flicks."

When the cramp was over, Tanya wandered through the den with her palms cupped on her belly. She passed by Mason, who was too rapt on Buck Hanson's sermon to notice her pain. She rushed faster down the hallway and barely reached the toilet bowl before she puked up her lunch.

IN THE DARKNESS Luc heard Quinn breathe. His nostrils were stuffed with snapped cartilage and clotted blood. She and that bastard were locked too close together inside the confines of the cold trailer cell while Quinn rattled the door and whimpered like a caged ape, desperate for a way to spring the lock from inside. There was no way, Luc knew. She had inched herself up against the back wall with her dog piss blanket that she would refuse to share even if Quinn's flesh went dead from frostbite. Let him try to steal it from her. She'd find a way to tear him open and plunge her icy hands into his organs to warm her frigid fingers.

"I came here to help you," he said. "You should know that."

"Fuck you," Luc said. "I don't want your help."

"Look, it's all right. I'll talk some sense into Brick as soon as he calms down."

Luc shivered and pressed her hands together to keep them warm. She thought of death. At one time, at the controls of a motorcycle, Quinn had driven death away for almost ten full minutes. She wanted that strength to return again, to feed her from some new source. She wanted back the hope that Quinn himself had crushed.

He told her, "You know what I risked coming here? My life, Luc."

"You don't have any life," she said.

"You're right about that." He grunted, and something he'd tried caused a metal clutter that loosened nothing. Then he thumbed two quick scratches on his lighter flint to make it strike an orange flame. It was like a molecular sun with Quinn's battered face caught entranced by its orbit. Within seconds the lighter went out and he didn't strike it again.

Luc said, "You're Humphrey Reid. You're nothing but a ghost."

"I don't know what you're saying. Who's Humphrey Reid?"

Luc saw much now with her inner eye, so she couldn't stop herself from envisioning how her faithless mother had submitted herself to Quinn, the utter weakness and depravity required to let him violate her—just as Luc had almost done. It was a crime against truth, because Oscar Moberg was so much greater, larger, mightier, eclipsing Quinn like a planet darkens a moon. Dad with his big hands and voice, deep weathered creases in his face—like a god he'd been, teetering from the burden of his own might, and he'd toppled because his heart had made him blind.

Luc burned in her breast like she was a goddess herself, and every moment she was growing away from here, her aura throwing ever-wider ripples. She walked barefoot across jutting pebbles, lost in a mist while leaves skittered against her ankles. Strewn boulders looked like they might be breathing. An anemic sun was drowned by the smog overhead. A bridge of gray stone that crumbled like stale bread when she stepped onto it, and her weight sent dust and rock raining down into the chasm that burned miles below with a dull red hellfire. Across the bridge stood a throne of bleached human skulls where sat the guardian of Hel, whose name itself was Hel, a queen naked and hairless and littered with sores, her eyes two gaping wounds, her body split down its axis, half-black and half-white like ash and charcoal, like she was a painted corpse whose last threads of blood were dripping from her eyes like tears. She was the daughter of Loki the rebel god, the Nordic devil. All human souls, both pure and evil, came to her in death for their suffering. Luc begged this devil's daughter to release her father Oscar Moberg from her cursed land, but Hel would sit silent in her throne, mouth wide and spewing black moths. On her knees Luc pleaded while the sharp rocks pierced her kneecaps. The guardian's eyes bled, moths flittered out, and this was Luc's only answer.

Quinn said, "I want to tell you I got that money—most of it. Not here, but safe. Brick don't know your mother gave it to me the night before she jumped. She didn't want to see me but I convinced her. I said the whole thing would be finished if she gave up the money. That's all. I said they'd leave her alone and there wouldn't be any more threats. She didn't care about herself anymore, if she died or not, but she worried about you enough that she gave over the money. She didn't want to do it because to her paying meant—I don't know—it meant she wasn't sorry for what happened with your dad."

"She wasn't sorry. What did she care?"

"That's what I'm saying," Quinn told her. "She wouldn't see me or even talk to me. She wanted to pretend nothing ever happened with us, but I knew she couldn't fool herself about that. She hated what happened, but there was no way anymore for her to fix it. Brick already did what he did. We both felt so fucking guilty, you know, we couldn't think."

"Your guilt is phony. You stole her money."

"I thought she was dead from that fall. When I found out, it was too late. He'd kill me if he knew I lied and had the money."

"Instead, you let him go after us—"

"Luc, when we get out of here I'm gonna send you half of that money I have left. I'll send it in the mail from wherever I'm going. See, I'm telling you this because I need you to trust me now so we can get out of here safe."

She swiped her arms at him, nothing but her numb fists for weapons. She missed with a left swing and the momentum kicked her sideways against a squirming mass that she realized was Quinn. She kicked and punched what moved and a screech lifted from her throat like a siren. His bone pressed under her boot heels, his skull against her knuckles— it lasted maybe a second and his hands out of nowhere shoved her backward. She was knocked down again and stinging from the impact. She panted feral and she didn't give a shit what it sounded like. All her vigor was drained in that split-second fury.

"My dad," she cried.

"I'm sorry about your dad," Quinn said. "I'm really sorry."

"You didn't kill him, you know. He was invincible."

GRETA DROVE TO THE West End Motor Lodge. It was on Linux Avenue, a city strip of used auto dealerships and greasy fast food stops, porno warehouses bigger than some supermarkets. A few places were decked with festive lights, and the car radio was already playing holiday music—Elvis crooning "Blue Christmas." Greta sopped up that blue like she was two-ply paper towel.

Snow fell wet and thick onto her windshield, raining hypnotic in the sodium-vapor lamps. She was coming straight from Hammersport High School, no stopover at Public Safety, no call to Moe Arslan's pager to brief him on developments. What she had learned was still too raw to turn into words that could explain. And there was no time, not while Luc was still lost in the void.

The motel was a horseshoe building with a center parking lot, like a slumlord's version of Sandy's yuppie complex. It was two stories with exterior stairwells no sturdier than fire escapes. Fifty units total, maybe a third of them lit from within—blue Christmases, every one. It was the sort of place folks stayed for either an hour or else months at a time, and tonight it was the only place left where Greta could keep herself sane.

She parked at the Qwik-Fill across the street and jogged over to the surveillance room. She framed her face in the peephole and raised her fist to knock, but the officer inside opened the door first. Larry Sheppard: thirtyish, unshaved, grimy cowlicks under a baseball cap, a few dozen pounds too hefty in his gut—a guise not so out of character for this dingy motel. He was holding half of a meatball sub, chewing a bite he'd torn from it. He plucked one earphone bud out of his ear and said, "Saw you coming." Then he closed the door behind her, drew the bolt lock, returned to his canvas collapsible window chair.

Even with her nostrils stuffed, Greta could smell the stale sweat and old food. The room was dark but she could discern one bed with no headboard, a nightstand with drawers, a bunny-eared TV missing its channel dial. It was hot enough in there to make her woozy, so she unbuttoned her jacket and spread it down on the comforter where she'd be sitting.

Sheppard peered through the window with a pair of binoculars, watching straight across the lot to Unit 43. This was the motel room to which Mitch Wendt had retreated upon his release from jail, the room that he had occupied nonstop now for over twenty-four hours. Sheppard's earphones were clipped to a receiver on his belt, and on the nightstand was a phone recorder box with a cassette on deck, ready for voice-activated recording. The earphones and recorder were both getting transmissions from a telephone test set that was tapped into Mitch Wendt's phone line somewhere outside his room.

"I see the warrant came through," Greta said.

"Yep," Sheppard said. "And let me tell you, either this guy's dull or he's acting the part. I've had a whopping three phone calls since we installed the test set around, say, ten hours ago. A pizza order, and two nonsense phone calls that his girlfriend made to female friends. Her name is Slinky, or that's her handle, at least. She's been in there with him since the start." He scratched at a bare strip of belly that emerged below the hem of his T-shirt, then he took another bite of meatball sub, flushed it down with some Coke. He said, "In all likelihood, Wendt made most of his important phone calls before the wiretap was installed. That's red tape for you."

"Did we get a location for the girlfriend's outgoing phone call?"

"Sure thing," Sheppard said. "It was the Submarine Bar and Grill, both times."

"That's where we first picked him up, the same place I met this girlfriend—Slinky? Assuming she's the same girl."

"Big assumption," he said. "Some of these guys get themselves a harem of old ladies, plus they make trades, like baseball cards. A lot of their girls work tricks on the side. You know—dual-income families, pretty progressive. Sit here a couple hours and you'll see quite a bit of the oldest profession practiced right here at ye olde motor lodge. I should tell you: when Slinky was on the phone the last time I heard Wendt tell her to cut it short 'cause the cops were probably listening. These biker club guys are pretty paranoid to begin with, even when they aren't high-profile. I'd say he's not likely to incriminate himself, so I wouldn't bank on him too much."

"Keep at it anyway," Greta said, flatly. She stepped into the bathroom and kept it dark while she splashed cold tap water on her face. Her flu was almost kicked, but she knew if she loitered much longer in this stuffy rat hole her fever would surely spike again.

When she came back out into the bedroom, Sheppard said, "I usually don't get any company when I'm out on these safaris." He was flippant, like a kid playing at cops and robbers. Greta repressed a strong urge to tell him to shut up and get serious. She was still reeling from the letters she'd read at the high school, and she was pissed at her own blind hope that Wendt would lead her straight to Luc, as if he were some short-leashed bloodhound. Instead, he'd likely spend his night ass-picking, boozing, zoning on the one available TV channel.

"How do you do it?" she asked Sheppard. "Just wait around like this?"

"It's a Zen thing."

"I'll die if I sit here too long," she said.

TANYA GROANED UNDER blankets on the queen-sized bed in the stall she'd been sharing with Mason. She held the Smith & Wesson automatic in her right hand, stuffed underneath her pillow. She sweat and shivered and gasped between labors that punched her awake every ten minutes, maybe less. In a fitful dream she found Buck Hanson standing by her bed, shadowed in the shaft of pale light that lurked through the hallway. He leaned over her, grunting hard and wheezy, with one hand planted on the wall and the other kneading the crotch of his jeans.

"Where's Mason?" Tanya asked in this dream that seemed so true.

"They're all outside having a snowball fight. He told me about that kid you brought up here, that Indian boy you got locked in the trailer with that girl. You know you're a stupid bitch for doing that, don't you? And your boyfriend's a dumbass for letting you get away with it."

Tanya squeezed her fist. The gun was still there, even in her dream.

"I think you could do me a little favor to make up for it, girly."

"Mason said I don't need to do favors for nobody no more."

"I cut Brick some slack. I'm cutting you slack, too. You should fucking appreciate it."

"Buck, I got these bad cramps in my stomach."

"It ain't like you never did favors before, right? It's like your job, is all. Come on, Tanya. Where's your Christmas spirit?" He took his hand off his crotch and started tugging at his beard, wringing his own drool out of it. His breathing was getting faster.

"You know I'm pregnant. And I'm having these horrible cramps, Buck. Please."

"It ain't like I'm asking to poke your baby. You're big enough to know there's other ways to get the job done. Take your pick, and while you're at it maybe you should think of all the nice fucking things I've been doing for you and Mason lately. Think on that."

Tanya couldn't have guessed her own dream mind until after she'd already pushed the covers off and stretched her arm out straight. She aimed the automatic square on Buck's darkened face, close enough for a bull's-eye, not so near that he could swipe the gun from her hand.

Both his hands went up beside his shoulders in surrender. He chuckled like this was all just typical foreplay. "Man, Tanya, you do got some spunk in you," he said. "Good for you."

"Get the fuck out of my bedroom," she said.

Buck took a step backward. He said, "Actually, it's my bedroom. My whole fucking cabin. But I ain't gonna mince words because I'm just loving your balls right now, Tanya. Here to tell you, though—anybody else besides you and I'd of fucking twisted that gun out of your hand and used it to knock out every one of your skank yellow teeth. Anybody but you, Tanya. Just remember that the next time you wave guns around, all right?"

"All right," she said, and she kept the gun aimed for a full minute after he left.

OUTSIDE THE WIND rushed against the trailer walls, pushing for hours like it would never cease. Too dark for sight, but Luc heard Quinn hurtling five sidesteps toward the trailer door, smashing himself against it, sliding back down to his knees with a whimper when it wouldn't break. The trailer jumped like it was startled by his sneak attack, but it refused to set them free. He'd been bashing for hours it seemed—or maybe just a few slow-motion minutes.

He stomped backward from the door and rushed again, yowling barbaric this time. The impact burst Luc's every sore nerve into full blooms of pain. She clamped her eyes shut, pressed her knuckles against her forehead, only dimly aware of the light that had invaded her cell. She squinted into a blinding gray that could've been her saint coming back for her. But the trailer was empty. The gray was winter daylight cast through a mess of bent and hanging slider partitions broken apart from their hinges. Quinn had smashed through the door into the known world from which Luc had been stolen, or maybe even farther through, deep into some other existence.

Luc crawled toward the aperture, where the light particles were coalescing like fireflies. She looked down into a world as if from cloud height—a wide stretch of bay dotted with lush evergreen islands—islands colonized by cedar huts, smoke streaming from chimneys. The sea was pale slush lapping against rocky shorelines and a coasting longship—the *Ringhorn*—with Baldr's impossible corpse interred on the fiery deck. Flames leaped from the wood and grasped toward heaven and lighted the water bright as dawn. The hull glowed red like a flashlight shined through thin human flesh, and the snake-tail ornaments blackened and curled inward.

Far off, a man's voice chided, "Hey, Mason, your birdie just broke the coop."

The snow drove downward hard as rain. The trailer door swayed creaking on its broken tracks. Luc's eyes refocused on the cold truth of Quinn Cutler sprawled on his back in the snow outside, thrashing like a possum in its roadkill throes. His nose was purple and swollen and dribbling fresh blood from each nostril. One eye black and the other fused shut. Luc saw it crystal clear with the vision the saint had bestowed on her.

Luc faltered at the tailgate. She was afraid to run because there were new noises on the wind—angry dog barks, and somebody laughing, sickly like a smoker's cough. Four, maybe five figures were tromping toward her through the snow, and they looked not like men but like the shadows of men raised upright off the ground. And a black dog snarled as it bounded chest deep in snow. It tugged a taut chain leash so the links ground together. The man holding the leash yanked it like a fishing line. It was this man who was laughing, the one with the dog. She could see him as clearly now as a binoculars dial adjusted into focus. He was built with a beanbag gut, ruddy face sprouting a white beard spilling halfway down his chest like he was a nightmare Santa eager to steal her spirit away.

TANYA WAS STILL ARMED with her S&W handgun as she crept down the hallway. The stalls flitted past her like slides in a slideshow—there seemed to be hundreds now. Her stomach burned. There was no blood yet, and she knew because she'd just been to the toilet to check herself. She'd been locked in the bathroom when they all came raiding back into the house with their boots and their savagery.

This screaming, this hallway—it was like those haunted houses she braved back when her mom brought her to the carnivals in the K-Mart lot. Walking through cheapo pop-up attractions on trailer hitches with hands reaching out and grabbing you from nowhere, those sudden startling bursts of smoky air.

The room where she found them was empty of furniture. Nothing on the floor but rat droppings and a roiling carpet of dust, most of it kicked to the corners by their stomping and by the boy named Red, who was lying fetal and pleading while Dread cracked him in the spine with a shovelhead, while Furnace shredded the shirt off his body with his jaw. And this awful romp was floodlit courtesy of a rechargeable workman light that Buck held overhead.

When Mason spotted Tanya watching, he rushed to block the doorway. Like a madman he bit into his lower lip and flared his nostrils. A blood vessel had burst in his right eye and left a deep red blotch floating in the white, as big as a dilated pupil. He said, "You don't need to see."

"I'm having contractions—" Tanya muttered.

Behind Mason, Dread yelled, "Buck, what the fuck is this? You see this?"

Mason spun around to face the torture scene again. Red was shirtless and bloody. Dread and Buck loomed over him. Furnace paced along the back wall, primed for his next command. Buck squatted down and grabbed the boy's arm to keep it from squirming, then he shined the light on a naked shoulder.

Buck said, "Looks like a fucking Crew tat."

"Man, oh, man," Dread laughed. "You are one stupid fuckhead, boy."

"I didn't mean to get it yet—" the kid groaned. "I was drunk."

"Shut up," Dread told him, and she clocked him in the head once more with the shovel. His eyes went white but he kept his swooning head raised three inches above the ground like some small victory. Tanya turned away to keep herself from crying.

"Red, you shit-for-brains," Mason said. "Look what you did now." It was said with true regret, like a father casting shame down onto his son. Like a final judgment.

LUC KNEW THAT SHE was back inside the cabin again, lying on the floor with her left arm twisted underneath her. She'd been thrown there by rough hands, tossed into some room no bigger than a horse stall, between two metal cots draped with dusty blankets. She pressed her face against the chill concrete and willed herself to stay alive. Everything tilted and spun. Her captor was nothing but a silhouette filling the doorway, but Luc saw with perfect clarity that his hand was just a thumb and two fingers, two pink scarred stumps where fingers should've been. His bare arm was a mess of scars and smudged tattoos, like he'd once been attacked with a razor and an ink gun.

She'd seen them all in bursts of light, these phantom shades in human shape. The wicked Santa's red-pocked nose and his steel-wool beard. His snarling dog with coals for eyes and black smoke chugging from its nostrils. She'd seen a woman with electric cables for hair, with a gaping purple mouth ripping across her throat. They were all shadows now smashing down the hallway, where doors slammed and wood crackled and where a voice she recognized was ringing out. Quinn Cutler, screaming for his life, and the hell hound was snarling back at him. Someone yelled, "Furnace, off!" The dog ceased with such immediate silence that Luc thought she'd gone deaf. But there was still noise: her own panicked breath, the wind roaring against the cabin, a whimpering that could've been either human or animal.

TANYA WATCHED BRENDA Hanson drag herself down the hallway by sliding along the wall like a slug. She was drunk or stoned or both, a zombie blinking at the dark with one flabby arm outstretched. She was still wearing those impossible black stilettos that shuddered under her weight and were bound to snap an ankle if she ever lost her footing.

"What the hell—what's going on in here?" Brenda wondered aloud.

Tanya ignored her. She pressed forward through the funhouse tunnel. She didn't want to see any more, didn't want to think about how she could've escaped this. Not enough spirit left to agonize—not with her baby demanding so much, and now that orphan girl Lucia who'd been dropped into her custody from out of nowhere.

LUC FOUND ENOUGH strength to drag herself onto a cot and sit there with her boots on the floor. Both her wrists were a mess of purple bruises and red lacerations. Her fishnet stockings were shredded and bunched at her ankles, rust wedged underneath her fingernails.

Those screaming voices pounded in her ears. She was alone now and caught in a world full of werewolves and living corpses, demons whose mouths gnashed in their throats. The saint had abandoned her—the saint who gave her eyes that could see this awful hell-place unmasked. Luc couldn't even remember the saint's name anymore to invoke it. It was Lucy. Or maybe Greta.

"You gonna watch her for me?" someone said—the man with the claw hand.

When Luc glimpsed again the claw man was gone, and in his place that woman Tanya stood full-bellied and armed with a gun. The woman eased herself down onto the cot opposite Luc—so close that even Luc's naked vision could read her face. It was dull and wasted, but there was a pleading glint caught inside her irises and in the hesitant upturn of her mouth.

"Are they going to kill me?" Luc asked.

"No," Tanya blurted—but it was just a word, just one possible answer. The woman grit her teeth and pressed one hand against her belly and breathed hard air through her nostrils. She leaned herself against the wall and kept pounding her armed fist into the soft mattress. Her finger was on the trigger, flirting with a misfire. Luc shifted to keep out of her aim. She crouched against the mattress until the pounding stopped.

Luc said, "You're having labor."

"Yeah," Tanya grunted. "Small ones. Not big ones like the baby's coming. Not yet."

A notion kept nagging Luc's mind: if she ran, Tanya wouldn't shoot her. In seconds Luc could rush from this room and through the den and out into the yard. But there was no telling how many monsters were prowling out there, hungry and desperate to tear her apart. The urge to run fired through her legs like spark plugs that wouldn't conduct. Instead, she kept talking with a strange calm in her voice that was rising up from someplace primal. She said, "What are you going to name him?" like she and Tanya were two gals chatting at a sidewalk café on a warm summer afternoon. As if there were no dogs and demons barking down the hall.

"We don't even know if it's a boy yet. Mason thinks it is."

"I don't want to go home," Luc heard herself saying. Her voice was an otherworldly chant, bleeding into Tanya's song and dredging up its secrets. Like the abductor's real name for instance.

"I hope it'll be a girl—like you and me—"

"I don't want to see my mother again," Luc said. "She makes me sick."

Tanya took Luc's hand and squeezed it—warmth like a rush of faucet water. She said, "I know Mason will let you stay with us. I told you that already. I know it'll be all right." But even as she vowed she dropped her eyes, nodding at her own bulging lap. Tanya knew that all her promises were empty. Her promises were no more certain than this crazed recurring vision she'd been having of Mason cruising the Cadillac Deville into downtown Hollywood with Tanya herself in the passenger seat wearing sunglasses and pink Capri pants, with Lucia and the baby napping in the backseat while "Hotel California" played on the radio. In this dream Lucia wasn't exactly like a daughter—more like Mason's second girl, because she'd be old enough soon, too pretty for Mason to resist. Tanya could learn to understand. She could learn because the dream felt proper, at least better than those rotted old family virtues that she'd never trusted anyhow.

"Did he touch you?" Tanya asked. She gestured shyly at her own swollen outcome.

Luc uttered, "Yes." A blatant lie, but the monster called Brick had been so close in that trailer that he'd made her answer seem like the only true one.

There was a commotion in the hall. Tanya slid the gun along the mattress and aimed it toward the floor at her feet. Luc watched that gun and thought about the lie she'd just concocted. She wondered how far those words could drive a woman like Tanya.

Somebody rushed against the doorway. He was panting like he'd just come in from a jog. He stepped forward into the stall, close enough to Luc that his image solidified into the man Tanya had called Mason. Here was his true face staring down at her, and if Luc survived she'd never lose her memory of the creases in his dried lips, that caterpillar hair strip on his chin, the whitehead pimples on his nose. When she tried to look away he yanked her chin back upward. His eyeballs twitched as he read her face. Luc needed something now that would save her life, and it had to be the truth. So into his scrutinizing face she told him, "Quinn stole your money. He took it from my mother and kept it for himself."

"How the hell do you know that?" he asked. His breath smelled like raw ground beef.

"He told me in the trailer. He said he came to rescue me, but I don't want to go back."

Mason's larynx cocked in this throat.

Behind him, Tanya complained, "My cramps are getting worse. They're killing me."

"Sit tight, Tan," Mason said. "It ain't time yet." Like a spring-loaded trap he grabbed Luc's wrist and yanked her upright. The hurt was enough to make a corpse cry out. She tumbled over Tanya's legs and braced herself against a cot frame, but Mason was still dragging her along. She righted herself and let him take her.

Behind them Tanya pleaded, "What are you doing? What's going on?"

YOU CAN LIGHT the fuse, but you can never know for sure when it will blast.

"Motorcycle," Sheppard muttered from his window perch. Greta had been dozing on the motel bed that was stripped of everything but the fitted sheets. Those dreams of a baby in a crib. But now she shot upright, legs thrown over the bedside, eyes on the clock that said 11:00 P.M.

She crouched beside Sheppard and watched through the break in the curtains. The rough weather had passed, but there was still an inch of snow laid over the parking lot and the vacant cars. Through that snow tire marks had crossed over each other like tracks at a train station. While she watched, a motorcycle entered the lot with one rider hunched over handlebars behind a windshield, his head covered by a helmet and visor. He was dressed from neck to toe in sleek leather that shone like oil in the street lamp light. He made of himself a curiosity, if only because road snow and near-negative temps were crap conditions for a late-night joyride.

Sheppard held binoculars up to his eyes and fingered the focus wheel. The bike had driven past their sightline, but Sheppard was aiming his sights toward Mitch Wendt's doorway. Lights had flicked on over there, and a shadow tall enough to be human was poised behind the window curtains. Two feet left of the window, the motel room door jerked open and expelled yellow light and Mitch Wendt himself. He hunched against the doorframe and watched in the direction the motorcycle had gone. Wendt was in a white tanktop and jeans, barefoot, his hair a tangled mess.

"Is that a handgun tucked into Wendt's jeans?" Greta asked Sheppard.

"Looks like it," he said. "Call it in—you want to?"

"Give it a second. I don't want any false alarms."

Wendt took another step out onto the walkway. His bare feet pressed into the snow, but he didn't seem concerned. He laid one hand on his gun handle and gripped the doorframe like it was a barrier that could protect him. Behind Wendt another figure moved across the bedroom. The girlfriend, whose name was Slinky, whose turn-ons were home-delivery pizza, Native American jewelry, and scumbag thugs.

"Get back inside, dipshit," Greta whispered. She didn't need Wendt out in the open and setting a scenario in which bystanders could get clipped if bullets started buzzing. She knew this was it: a mercenary revving into town on motorized horseback, here to execute Mitch Wendt on the grounds of betrayal. It never mattered that Wendt was mostly innocent—first time in his life, most likely. There were probably worse crimes that needed reckoning, and Greta mustered no remorse for the crooked cop trick she'd played on his associates.

"Go back inside, Mitch," she repeated. Wendt seemed to mind her as he slid back into his room and slapped the door shut. Greta couldn't see the biker anymore, but somehow, wherever he was, he'd evaded Wendt's rapt attention—probably by jumping off his bike and disap-pearing into some nearby stairwell, a simple ruse.

"What do you think?" Sheppard said. He knew squat about Greta's setup against Wendt, but he was keen enough to realize she wasn't hanging around with him for his thoughtful banter.

"Wendt's satisfied, but I'm not," Greta said. Just two minutes had been clocked but already she loathed the waiting. She hunched with her hands propped on her bent knees, watching through the curtain, and the result was an awful throbbing in her back.

Then something moved at the left of their windowpane, shockingly close. Greta bolted upright. Sheppard tore the binoculars away from his face. The shadow materialized into a pair of shoulders and the perfect curved dome of a helmet. It was the biker, creeping down the walkway, obstructing their sightline, near enough to feel their breath if there'd been no window. For ten hastening heartbeats the two cops froze like mannequins in a department store window.

Greta back-stepped until her calves touched the bed. In his seat,

Sheppard leaned backward as he propped his shoe heels against the radiator. He groped for his holstered gun on the floor, grunting as he reached. He was unarmed, an easy target at point-blank range. But the biker wasn't moving, wasn't shooting, wasn't even facing them at all. He was facing clear across the lot toward Wendt's motel room.

Sheppard's vaulted shoulders slacked, but still he lifted his harness by the strap—his holstered gun dangling like a fish on a line. He slung the harness over his head and positioned the gun under his armpit.

The only move Greta made was to sit back down on the bed. Too much action could attract the biker's notice, and so far he seemed unaware that two cops were sequestered inches behind him. He raised both hands, lifted off his helmet, and a cascade of nappy hair burst out, more like a mane than a hairdo. He gripped the helmet in the crook of his arm and dug into his pocket with his free hand. Greta held her breath, waiting for a gun to be drawn, but instead he produced a cigarette and a flip-top lighter. He thumbed the flint and the flame bred a rosy aura around his skull and lit up for an instant his jungle of hair. Then it was gone.

Sheppard glanced back at Greta. She raised her index finger against her lips. The lone biker sipped a few tugs of nicotine and then flicked the cigarette against a support beam. The cherry burst its orange ashes before it stabbed into a snowbank.

Then the biker stepped down off the curb and began stalking between two parked cars with the helmet still headlocked under his arm. He reached into his jacket, elbow upraised, and drew out what Greta knew this time would surely be a handgun—and it was.

Sheppard said, "I'm calling it in. We need units out here."

"Right," Greta said. She put her hand on the doorknob and turned. The door creaked open but the wind was louder. She hunched outside and crouched with one hand on the cold pavement while the sudden negative Fahrenheit shocked her. She pulled her Beretta from its holster and the gun was heavy in her hand, resisting her draw like it didn't want this fight. Across town Sandy and Max were probably sipping wine in their honeymoon suite at the Ramada, making love maybe, or getting a good night's sleep to prep for their early-morning flight to Paris. Somewhere else Luc Moberg was facing violent death—or already gone.

THE BEARDED MAN carried a chainsaw in one meaty hand. It had a rubber handle and a foot-long blade, and the only sign of wear was sawdust pulp caught in its teeth. Luc saw this lucid snapshot from ten feet away, and she could count with her hawk's eyes each steel notch on the chain. She knelt in the snow where Mason had shoved her, staring into the maw of her own potential death. Her mind refused to dwell longer than one panicked instant at a time, but it was the pain that scared her. The impending pain loomed so much larger than the nothingness beyond.

The driving snowfall battered slantwise at Luc and at Quinn where he crouched like a bag of trash dumped under a tall pine. The tree was stripped bare of branches almost ten feet up the trunk, and Quinn's hands were pressed into its rough naked bark. He was oblivious to the snow clumps slapping down onto his shirtless back from the high branches above. He did not seem to hear the miner skull branded on his left shoulder as it chanted an incantation. Luc heard, but she did not understand.

Nearby, the tubes in the demon bitch's hair chattered like wind chimes. She stood in formation with Claw-hand and Brick like they were three points on a pagan cross. The leader stepped forward and tugged the chainsaw starter cord. It came to life in one pull, and a dozen birds burst from the endless trees surrounding them.

Luc slammed her eyes shut. She pressed her hands over her ears. She screamed loud enough to drown out the roar of that terrible grinding searing metal, but it would not be silenced. The chainsaw revved twice like a motorcycle waiting at a stoplight, then it growled low and quiet again. Luc feared they were coming at her, but she needed to witness her own fate. When she opened her eyes to look, her vision was perfect.

She saw Quinn slumped against the pine tree with the snow around him drenched red, like saucepans of blood had been tossed there. His tattooed arm had been sliced away at the shoulder, and that wide pulpy gap was raining bloody threads. His face had gone ashen gray, the cast and pall of death already. His arm itself had vanished, and that seemed strangest of all.

The bearded man paced around Quinn with the chainsaw like he was a painter plotting his next brushstroke. He said, "That's how we do it, Tonto. That's how we take our dues." His gray beard was speckled dark crimson now. Quinn didn't answer his chide. Quinn breathed, and his wide unblinking eyes refused to forgive.

Nearby, Mason said to Luc, "You wanted to see him die, but then you closed your eyes."

THE RADIO BATTERIES were dead now. No Christmas music left to drown out the noise that Tanya didn't want to hear. But she heard the chainsaw snarl, she heard the screaming. She tried not to think what was happening, what would happen. Instead, she carried around a black trash bag picking empty and half-drunk beer cans off the floor, off chairs and tables, dropping them all into the bag with a weak wet clatter. As long as she kept moving, her pain lessened, and the false contractions seemed less like they were real.

Brenda Hanson pushed herself up from where she sat at the kitchen table and struggled to get her winter jacket up over her shoulders. Her eyelids were wet and red like rust leaking down from a bathtub spigot. She said, "I'm getting the hell out of here. I'm leaving. I've had enough. You're welcome to come with me, Tanya. I can take you to a hospital, where you belong."

But there was venom in her voice, like she didn't really mean it. Furnace was pacing around the room with his chain dragging, whining at the outdoor ugliness that he also did not want to hear. When Brenda called him he perked his head and set his docked ears erect. She hunched down on one knee—made a fat grunting freak show just to grab the leash.

"Where are you gonna go?" Tanya begged.

"I'll figure that out when I get there." She was slurring words, still drunk. She teetered and Furnace gave her a wide berth, cowering sideways with the fear that she'd come crashing down on him. "But you better get the hell out of here, too, that's all I'm saying."

"You have the truck keys?" Tanya asked.

"I know how to wire the goddamn thing. Furnace, come."

Tanya followed her out as far as the front porch but stopped there on the slab with the tied bag of recyclables still in her grip. She watched Brenda slog down the path toward the truck with her arms raised up like a high-wire act, those ridiculous heels wobbling in the snow. The dog bounded ahead, urging her onward with his tongue lolling out. From this distance Tanya could watch Brenda Hanson without much heart.

The commotion behind the cabin was quiet now. Tanya had never seen a person killed, never heard it until this moment, and the thought of it left her naked inside, as if her soul had been stolen from between her ribs and then hanged someplace like a lynched outlaw. If you cut a soul down from that much trauma, even if you can save it, it's bound to leave you torn and broken and near enough to dead yourself.

The labor pain threw its battery charge into Tanya's head. It was almost like a power that helped her guess at certain things before they happened: like how Brenda would reach the truck, pull open the door, like how she'd worm herself inside and the dog would follow. How she'd sit there wasting minutes and second-guessing herself, and when finally she got the motor sparked it would be too late. Tanya knew. Sure enough Buck appeared from around the side of the cabin, splashed in blood like a rampaging grizzly. He ripped open the driver's door that Brenda hadn't even locked behind her. He was grabbing her, shaking, clawing—roaring curses that the woods swallowed up, just like Tanya expected. Furnace barked in the passenger seat, vexed as hell, not knowing which of his masters to serve.

GRETA LET THE BIKER CROSS halfway over the parking lot until he reached the farthest point from potential cover. She hunched forward between cars, ducked below the window frames, used an Escort for shielding, laid her arms across the snowy trunk, aimed her Beretta with both hands.

"Police!" she bellowed, deep enough to affect a man's voice. "Hands up!"

Sheppard wheezed behind her, trampling outside on awkward feet to back her up.

The biker dropped the helmet from under his arm. It smacked slushy blacktop and rolled like a head fresh off the guillotine. He had one free arm now and he swiveled the gun to shoulder height, then higher, aiming cloudward with all the appearances of a textbook surrender. The green pinprick glow of Greta's Trijicon night sight clocked him square on the heart.

"Lower the gun to the ground!" Greta said. Sheppard was at her fringe, standing upright with his arms draped over the Escort's hood and his belly mashed against the driver's-side window, dumping snow in clumps off the glass.

The biker's pistol was still aimed upward, unreleased, while his right hand lingered by his waist, as if it was poised to grab what might've been hidden there. Greta filled her lungs with air enough to blast her command again, but then Wendt's motel room door swung back open.

New light cut over the lot and doused the biker and flashed his shadow across the ground. Wendt wasn't there in the open yet, but the biker aimed his gun toward the vacant doorway.

"Son of a bitch!" somebody yelled through the blast of a gunshot. Three guns drawn, maybe four, and in the chaos there was no telling which had fired, except that it hadn't been Greta's. The biker sprang toward a car parked mere paces from Wendt's doorway. He took cover too fast for Greta to keep her aim on him. She cursed at this sudden reconfiguration. Now it was more like war than an arrest.

"Backup's coming," Sheppard said, squatting down and panting.

Greta said, "Did you fire?"

"No. I think it was Wendt."

More lamps were coming on, renters on both levels waking from the noise. Any second now they'd come wandering to their windows, open-ing doors, stepping out onto ledges—fearless and stupid and exposed. They'd all be junkies, johns, and whores, but Greta still couldn't let them get shot. Hidden in their rooms, they were still at risk to bullets coming through the paste-and-cardboard walls built so flimsy that even the cops' Federal Nyclad rounds could penetrate.

Greta yelled, "Mitch Wendt—police! Close your door! Do not fire again!"

She waited. Sheppard wheezed. Wendt's door stayed wide open.

She crouched low and peered under the car at ankle level. She spot-ted the biker prone beside a slush-caked wheel well, maybe thirty feet off. Five minutes from now the squad cars would arrive, but Greta didn't know what would happen then. They'd race into the middle of this showdown, sirens screaming, wreaking havoc.

"Screw this," Sheppard said. He bolted past Greta into the open and stomped hard across the lot, beelining toward Wendt's door with his squat shoes gouging tracks through the snow.

The concealed biker perked upright like a cobra on alert.

Somebody yelled, "The fuck is going on?" Some bitch on the second-floor balcony.

Sheppard pivoted at the last instant and slapped his backside against the brick facade near Wendt's open doorway, gun gripped in both hands. He yelled, "Wendt! Drop your weapon and put your hands on the floor!" In this position Sheppard was exposed to the biker hidden behind the car. No choice for Greta but to lean back over the trunk and train her gun on that biker's wild hair sprouting from its hiding place.

Slinky appeared in the motel room window, standing in the break she'd made between the curtains. She squinted out into the dark. Dead stupid, Greta thought, even before the biker raised his firearm and pulled one shot that echoed through the courtyard. A penny-sized hole punched through the window glass. Slinky flinched and fell backward out of sight. If she was bullet-struck or not, Greta couldn't tell, but the wound in the glass went milky white and the curtains closed by themselves.

The biker burst from his position, and Greta ran in pursuit. He was sprinting back toward his motorcycle, parked on the lot's far side. He had at least a fifty-foot lead on her, even when she pumped her stride as broad as it would stretch. By rotten luck she kicked the biker's helmet and it spun wild and she almost tumbled onto the black-iced pavement.

The biker mounted and kicked the starter. His motorcycle growled and revved. Greta was still too far behind, so she stopped, heaving breaths. The only way out was past her. And sure enough the biker raced toward her with his headlamp bright and his muffler crackling like a dragon spitting fire. She raised her gun, but she couldn't shoot wild for fear of hitting vitals. This killer was her only thread left back to Luc. Kill him and she could break the line forever.

So she aimed low and set the green night sight on the biker's left leg. She pressed her double-action trigger and the gun kicked hard. Her ears rang. The bullet sparked off a V-twin engine. The biker grit his teeth and veered directly at her. Greta leaped sideways and rolled onto the hood of a car, plowing the collected snow with her body. She bashed her elbows against the windshield and then she bashed her skull. A sudden pressure in her ears was like plunging underwater. The bike smashed lengthwise into the front bumper. Greta didn't see it happening exactly, but she knew. For a second she looked through the swipe she'd cleared on the car's windshield and saw silver coins on the dashboard, a coffee mug shoved between the seats.

Her gun was still in her hand, but trapped between the car hood and her stomach. She rolled herself again to get it loose. She aimed but didn't fire. The biker kicked the car hood with his wounded leg, now spilling blood. His bike was still pushing forward as it cut away from the car and gained speed. Greta'd seen his face. It was pale with the shock of a gunshot, wooly bearded and yellowed toothed like something from out of the woods. It was hardly human.

Greta slid off the hood and chased again, this time certain she could catch him on foot. Except the bike was gaining speed. And her brain swam in her skull. And a dull pain throbbed in her neck. And a bitter taste was on her tongue.

The biker was already jumping the street curb into the cold white light cast from the Qwik-Fill flood lamps across the street, gliding so fast he could've lifted off and taken flight. An eastbound pickup was motoring forward—aqua paint, psychedelic decals on the sideboard. Countless light points reflected like bright stars in the pickup's windshield. The biker raised one arm in defense against the ton of truck rushing toward him, and the impact was like the clatter of trashcans hurled from rooftops. In that instant, the pickup swallowed the motorcycle into its undercarriage. The bike's single taillight went dead black. Metal folded up flat and threw off a barrage of sparks. The pickup squealed and swerved and came to a full stop forty feet past the collision point.

The stripped metal on the road looked like pencil shavings scattered among the streaks of oil or blood that trailed off toward the wreck. Laid over a curb was a tattered rubber tire casing. Up ahead two cruisers rushed westbound with blue lights flashing and their faint sirens getting louder. An elderly black man in a wool cap and flannel jacket was walking up the sidewalk toward Greta and the crash site. He walked with his hands in his pockets, considering the debris on the road. He seemed resigned to it, like anyone so long on this earth should be. Only when he saw Greta approach with her gun did he ease back with his hands drawn up and a grin on his face.

The pickup driver opened his cab door and slid his snow boots down onto the street. He was flabby, in his forties, with a big winter parka and hair like a koala's. He stumbled along the length of his truck while sliding one gloved hand against the sideboard. He was delirious—and from more than just shock. It was nobody's lucky night.

"I think I hit a deer," he told Greta, slurring, beer on his breath.

"Shut up, asshole." She shouldered him against his truck as if landing a hockey check, then she unclipped a flashlight from her belt and knelt to peer under the tailgate. What she expected to find was a mangled biker with dead eyes staring back at her like a hex. What her beam caught instead was the broken hull of the motorcycle without its rider. She stood again, and found the ejected biker where he'd landed— sprawled on his back in the truck bed, one leg propped over a cinderblock, one arm reaching skyward and shuddering, his shaggy head at rest on a bag of road salt. She hadn't seen his landing, but the aftermath told her that it hadn't been smooth.

The biker winced and kicked his heel at the plastic bed liner, arching his spine in pain. Greta aimed her Beretta and told him not to move. The drunk driver was saying, "Hey, lady—hey—calm down, lady," but it sounded like dead recorded talk on a radio, not meant for her.

four

RAGNAROK

The woods stood so hushed it could've been that the earth had slipped back to that age before man—except that this land was blighted by a leaning clapboard cabin, a tractor, a trailer-hitched truck, a rusted Cadillac parked askew on a driveway that was buried in snow. Deep swerving muddy trails were cut out of the snow where other vehicles had recently been, though now gone. In the yard behind the cabin, the fresh snow was trampled by boot tracks circling around a pit of carnage that soaked the ground like a pig slaughter—some patches seeped black, others had tinted the snow a pale rose color. Quinn Cutler's body was gone now, but any bird's-eye witness could mark the earth where it had been cocooned in garbage bags and dragged around front to a Cadillac. Exhaust fume puttered from under the trunk where his corpse was stowed.

Inside, dusk shadows filled the cabin like a black flood draining in through the wall cracks. Tanya found a box of matches on a shelf and lit one. She used it to light the kerosene lamps—one on the kitchen counter, one dangling from a hook over the table, another hung in the den like a rustic chandelier. The Christmas tree was slumped in the corner with its sad scattering of ornaments. With the lamps lit, the cabin glowed in orange warmth that swelled and shrunk as if it were illuminated breath.

The Skeleton Crew had vanished as fast as they'd arrived, and there was no way now of knowing how Brenda Hanson would be punished for her stupid flight plan. All Tanya knew was the heifer had been still alive—unconscious, but breathing—when Buck drove the Ram truck away with his wife slumped in the passenger seat. That was all Tanya cared to know because more important was Red's corpse and Luc Moberg lying silent on the couch.

The girl looked twice her age, a mouth like a straight razor cut. Her wrists were dark with purple-spotted bruises. She didn't seem fazed that Mason was slouched in the recliner five feet away knocking Buck's hockey stick against his cheek and aiming his Colt .45 limply at her head—like he was sick of this game and wishing the girl would just cry uncle. The Indian boy's spattered blood was drying on his pants legs.

"You got your gun?" Mason asked Tanya.

She put the matchbox in her pocket and took her S&W out from where she'd hidden it on a shelf behind soup cans. The safety was off and the clip was loaded, bullet chambered.

"You remember how to use it, right?" Mason said. "Because I need you to watch her for a while until I get back. I got to get rid of him somewhere far from Buck's property."

"You mean Red?" Tanya asked.

"Shit, Tan. Don't say his name. He's dead—he don't need a name no more. It's just a body that's gonna rot in that car trunk if I don't take care of it. I'm gonna be gone two hours tops, hopefully less. All you need to do is watch the girl and shoot her dead if she tries to move. You got that?"

Luc was balled sideways with her knees up to her chest—bare and raw knees that were naked now that the fishnets had tattered away. She laid the side of her face against the back cushion like it was a pillow, but she kept her eyes alert and drawn to the stove where the wood burned with a red heat that was mottled black in spots.

"The cramps are getting worse," Tanya said. Even now she could feel her womb hardening down to the size of a football, and her knees shook so bad she wanted to crumple.

Mason said, "It's just that fucking false labor. You wouldn't be standing if it wasn't."

"What if something happens?" Tanya begged.

"If she even tries to leave this couch, you kill her—that's what. And I mean aim for her head. Don't worry about the mess because everything's getting cleaned out of here so nothing gets traced back to Buck. Then we're leaving as soon as it's done."

Luc didn't blink, not even while they talked through the options of her death.

Tanya said, "I mean what if something happens with the baby?"

"Nothing—Tan, I told you—I'll be two hours, no more."

"I can't have my baby here in this cabin."

"I'm not talking about this shit now. Kill her if she moves. I mean it." He stormed back down the hall, already too rushed to bother hearing Tanya's answer. What she said didn't matter anyway. She was fastened to this weight no matter how far under it dragged her. Tanya had hoped, for Luc's sake—but the girl was like a broken thing now, only four years younger than Tanya and shattered even worse than she'd been at that age. Tanya knew that hurt, how bad it was. It would be almost like mercy if she had to use her gun.

"Come over to the kitchen," Tanya told Luc. She pointed the gun at Luc's chest, dead-aim on the Nine Inch Nails logo printed on her T-shirt. Luc obeyed but she walked like she was wading through sludge, feeling blindly along the couch with her fingers. Tanya pressed the gun between Luc's shoulders to get her moving faster, but the girl had her own pace, which was almost stillness.

"In the chair," Tanya said. Luc pulled back a kitchen chair and lowered herself down. Tanya came around the table and took her own chair facing the girl. The hardwood chair dug into her aching muscles and calmed them some while she leveled the gun at Luc and rested her arm on the tabletop. She pulled back her elbow a little so the girl couldn't reach if she tried to grab for it. It was still in close-enough range that Tanya wouldn't miss if she fired.

Then Mason came back carrying a spade with a handle splintered jagged at the top and a halogen flashlight big as a truck's high beam. He was panting from more than just hurrying. It had to be those hormones pumping in him—the ones that fired up your panic and your rage. "What the fuck already?" he said, riled almost purple. "I thought I said she doesn't move?"

"I moved her," Tanya said. "I can't sit in there. Isn't the ground frozen outside?"

Mason considered the spade he carried. "I'll find someplace, so don't worry about it. All you need to worry about is that kid right there. If you let her go I'll kill you, too. And I fucking mean it. You got that?"

"Yes," Tanya said, then she added, "hurry up," but he was already headed out with the spade head scraping across the floor behind him. Outside, his footsteps crunched icy snow. In a minute, the Caddy rumbled when he revved the gas. Something about that sound made the girl across the table bow her head like she was praying, and her tangled oily bangs came down over her eyes. Through the kitchen window Tanya saw the headlights shine, fading backward down the driveway until Mason turned the car and his taillights shuttered through the trees and then were gone.

LUC WAS DREDGING courage from the last live currents in her blood. She was boosted by hate for Mason Renault, Quinn Cutler, even for this shadow mother aiming a loaded gun at her. She could hear the fragile new life sloshing inside that woman's belly. And she let herself look slack and defeated so that she could rest and maybe feed some strength off the dim light and the fire in the stove. Quinn's ugly death was still fresh in her head, but Luc didn't wince when it flashed vivid through the dark of her memories.

The three lanterns weren't enough to illuminate Luc's vision, so she set her eyes on her tortured wrists piled in her lap, at the dusty tabletop and the length of steel that she knew to be a loaded handgun, at Tanya's blurred shape like a figure seen through tears. Luc waited out the time—twenty minutes or more if she had a clock to track it, and Tanya barely moved except to press her free hand into her gut every few minutes. Tanya was trying to keep her pain secret, but it wafted from her like poisonous gas. Luc waited slow minutes until Tanya's agony flared the worst shade of red, then she blurted, "When he comes back he's gonna kill me."

"Not if you do what he says," Tanya answered, labored but hiding it.

"The money's gone. There's no reason to keep me alive anymore."

Tanya didn't answer. She was holding her breath against a wringing cramp.

"I saw them kill Quinn—and I know everything about what happened."

"You'd be dead by now, already, if he wanted you to be dead."

Luc swallowed, and her throat was so dry that it almost sealed shut. Her words needed strategy, but her mind was muddled like her sight. She said, "Can I have a cup of water?"

"No tricks," Tanya said. "I'm not stupid. I can shoot you. I killed people before, so I ain't afraid to again—even you."

"What did I do to make you want me dead?"

"Nothing, yet. But if you give me bullshit I will." Tanya waved the gun as a threat, and it moved in spectral streams through the air.

Every new second Luc imagined the bullet firing and cutting through her heart, but still she couldn't guess how it might feel. She said, as flatly as she could, "He wants to rape me again. That's the only reason why I'm still alive."

"That's not why," Tanya said. The words came clenched through her teeth.

"I need water, please," Luc said.

"Shut up, girl."

"Is the baby coming?" Luc asked. She squinted to catch sight of how her question had struck, but it was no better than talking in the dark.

These strange questions were flashing in her mind a second before she asked them. Time was running thin, time and space falling away until only the cabin stayed, only Luc and Tanya lost in a universe of blank after blank after blank.

"It's not time yet," Tanya said.

"It looks like time to me," said Luc.

"It ain't a boy, no matter what Mason says. He don't have this kid inside him, so he don't know. I know it's a girl, and there's nothing he can do about it when she comes."

"He could hurt her," Luc said. "Like he hurts you sometimes."

"Shut up, bitch!" Tanya screamed. She groaned and slumped against the table, so lost with pain that Luc guessed she could snatch the gun away if she tried. But Luc had to keep talking because only talk kept the dark from smothering this last lighted patch of the earth.

"Sorry," Luc said. "I don't know your life. I just thought with the baby coming—"

"You're right—that you don't know my life."

"I know how you can get out."

Tanya scoffed. "That's long gone."

"We can help each other get out," Luc said.

"What I can do is shoot your face if you don't shut up. Please."

"We can leave before he gets back. You don't have to have your baby here."

"Are you stupid? We're miles from anywhere. We'd get lost in the woods."

"That truck out there—" Luc started. "The one the trailer's attached to—"

"—ain't moved for twenty years. Just give it up."

"It's my life," Luc said. She was pressing her hands against the table and pushing back the seat. She kept her eyes on the gun. "I'm not dying because you're a coward. You want to have your baby here with him?"

"What the fuck are you doing, girl? It's too late. Just don't move, and sit down."

Luc hadn't quite realized she was standing. Even her body was tied

to its own intentions that were apart from hers now. She said, "Please—
if we go now he won't be able to find us."

TANYA KEPT HER AUTOMATIC leveled on the table. She was reeling, more scared than she'd ever been because she didn't want this task
anymore, didn't want to be aiming a gun while her baby was born. She
hated Mason for being gone. She hated Luc for messing her up with
tricky words and forced decisions. She wanted out of all this dizzy
thinking.

Tanya didn't aim when she fired the gun, but she pulled the trigger
because she was Mason's girl and he had saved her so often and always
kept her safe, because this little bitch was trying to pick all that sense
apart. Roaring loud above all the other garbage in her brain was Mason's voice telling her in simple words what to do. He always made it
easier.

MITCH WENDT LOOKED drugged—lolling his head, eyes drifting in
their sockets. His uncuffed hands were set on the interview table one
foot apart. Raw wounds on all eight knuckles made it look like he'd
been punching at a brick wall. Greta watched him taste one skinned
knuckle with his tongue.

"We saved your life," Greta said. "You understand that, don't you,
Mitch?"

Moe Arslan sat with them, still groggy and unshaven from his early
muster. He hadn't even taken off his jacket yet. Elbows on his knees, tie
hanging down between his legs like the chain of some shackle he'd broken himself free from. Greta, on the other hand, was more awake than
she'd been in years.

"I get that, yeah," Wendt said.

Greta said, "And you understand that you need our help now?"

Wendt lowered his eyes and said, "Yeah, I get it." He had to be aware what a pure fluke it was that he hadn't gotten killed, murdered by one of his own crew—a fluke that his girlfriend, Slinky, was only grazed in the shoulder by the bullet that hit her through the motel window.

"They were going to kill you for ratting on the Skeleton Crew," Greta told him.

"I didn't rat nobody." He pinched his lower lip and squeezed it until the pink turned white. He stared at the tabletop like it was a TV screen broadcasting Technicolor video loops of the evening's events.

"Sure—but they turned against you anyway—just like nothing," Greta said. "I'm sure you know the guy who came to kill you tonight, right?"

Wendt said, "Somebody fucking set me up. Probably you cops."

Moe piped in, "Cut it out, Mitch. You know we've played fair with you."

"Guy's name's Jesse Potts," Wendt said. "But his club name is Ox."

Jesse "Ox" Potts was currently nursing wounds at Genesee Community Hospital, guarded by a handful of RPD. He'd been less than lucid during the arrest, suffering from the effects of diving headfirst at fifteen miles an hour into the bed of a pickup truck, but Greta knew they wouldn't have convinced Potts to sing no matter how they coaxed him. From the start Greta had scheduled this gig so that Mitch Wendt would be the star attraction.

"Tell me where they're keeping the girl," Greta said. "Where's Renault?"

"I don't know, man. You know damn well I been out of it for days."

"Mitch, who's in charge of the Skeleton Crew?" Greta asked.

Wendt made a fist against the side of his face and then slammed that fist on the table. He snorted phlegm and took a glance at the floor like he was thinking about spitting on it. "You people—" he said, shaking his head. "Renault's a fucking moron. Fucking prospect should've been dumped a year ago, before any of this happened."

"Come on, Mitch. You already gave us one name," Greta said.

"Yeah, because that motherfucker tried to kill me."

"Should we wait for the next ambush, then? See if you survive round two?"

Wendt gave a meek nod, and then he opened his mouth to talk.

THE GUN REPORT rattled empty mason jars in the doorless cupboards. A hole the size of a beer cap burst in Luc's left thigh, halfway between knee and hip, a raised crater that erupted just before she slapped both her hands over it. She crumpled left with one bloody hand reaching for the table and missing. She crashed on the floor and rolled onto her back, wincing at the lantern light above.

Tanya sat at the table panting. She was still in that rut between contractions, but the gun blast had forced her into a new kind of panic. She couldn't see Luc on the floor from where she sat, but she listened hard for an end to the girl's short panicked breaths. Finally Tanya got up teetering and went to the sink, where there was a damp white dishrag hung over the faucet.

Luc was on her back, still gazing openmouthed at the lantern. Dark blood seeped through her fingers where they were pressed against her wound. Her good leg was bent at the knee and shivering, her boot heel grinding across the floor. The gunshot leg jutted out straight like something that wasn't part of her body.

Tanya hated to see the girl in such agony, and she couldn't bear to move much closer to that writhing pain she'd caused. She tossed the dishrag, and it billowed once in the air before it landed on Luc's hip. Luc pet the rag with bloody fingers several times before she understood what it was for, then she took it in her fist and pressed it against her leg. The gun was hot in Tanya's grip, its blast still swelling her eardrums. The trigger had pulled so slight, so sudden, that she couldn't now remember why it happened. What she knew for certain had crumbled down to one small truth: no newfangled family was going to bloom between them like a rose out of dog shit. She'd doomed this girl for some sick dream, and there was no turning backward from here no matter how much Tanya wanted to dream it all again without blood or bullets or anger.

Tanya could barely see through her own tears when the next contraction seized her and threw her back into her seat, groaning. She
set the gun on the table and squeezed both of the wooden handrails until they creaked. She arched her back and kicked the floor, desperate to
tear that hurtful thing out of her body. She screamed inside of her shut
mouth.

LUC DRAGGED HERSELF a few inches across the floor, hoping she'd
stay conscious. If she had to die she wanted to die awake, not in some
senseless dream. What her eyes showed her was bleached out and negative, but she reached upward for the handle on the sink cabinet and
grabbed for it. The cabinet creaked open an inch, shut, opened, shut, and
Luc pulled herself almost seated. She didn't want to die on the cold concrete ground. The pain in her leg kept biting biting biting like an animal
that wouldn't quit. Tanya was still behind her with that gun she could fire
again, but Luc thought nothing more could hurt worse, not even a hundred other bullet holes. She was almost standing now, elbows on the sink
ledge, hoisting herself up and her one good leg pushing to give her leverage.

She looked into the sink basin at the few coffee cups, plates, beer
cans, and utensils waiting to be washed there. There was no curtain on
the window that showed Luc the brownish dark outside. On the sill between the sink and the window stood a *tomte* in his animal rags, holding
a tiny shovel, raising his lit acorn lamp like before. He smiled his
bearded rodent face at Luc, and then he leaned toward the sink like he
meant to leap inside it. Instead, he pointed down into the basin with his
shovel. There among the other dirty dishes was a dull silver carving knife
with a wooden handle and grease smeared on its blade. Luc was teetering one handed on the countertop, and she took the knife by the hilt.
Like nothing, it was hers.

A warm rush burst between Tanya's legs, dampening the thighs of
her stretch jeans. She moaned, "No—" and lurched backward. She
pulled at her waistband and raised her ass off the seat until the jeans
were down to her knees and the fluids from her womb splashed the

chair and dribbled on the floor. Her water was breaking, the baby coming for sure, and she couldn't fret over anything else. Mason had left her
to give birth in the woods like any other animal.

The girl had struggled herself back around. In her pain and bliss,
Tanya ignored shame. She let the girl watch the waters spilling down.
"My water," Tanya said. Luc lurched toward her, clutching out like she
wanted that fluid for herself. They shared something like an embrace,
then Luc stumbled backward just as fast and hit the sink cabinet with
her shoulder blades. She slipped down, seated herself on the floor.

Tanya said, "What—," but couldn't find the breath for any more talking. One of her lungs was screaming and shriveled, popped like a balloon. Something hard was poking against her ribs, stuck there just
under her heavy breast and above her tight cramping belly. She pressed
her fingers down on this strange jutting rod. It was rigid to her touch,
pushing deeper every instant. It was underneath the skin, pressing between her ribs and stabbing through organs she didn't know the names
for. It was a knife, six inches or more, thrust inside her where the girl
had stabbed it so fast and sudden that it seemed almost like trick magic.

Tanya gasped but couldn't breathe. So weak already she couldn't
close her hand enough to pull out the knife. She gagged and stared
down at this awful weapon that was killing her in some way that she
couldn't understand. Blood blossomed where the knife pressed her
T-shirt against her chest. She coughed, and she tasted the blood in her
mouth. Luc was watching her die, and Luc had fingerprints of blood on
her cheeks like war paint. The dishrag on her leg was soaked red. Her
hands were on the floor and turned upright and bloodstained like the
nailed palms of a statue in a church.

Luc dreamed she was burning in the core of an endless red fire. She
dreamed of her father bashing down mountains with his sledgehammer
in a wild crusade to reach her, but Luc was trapped in the jaws of a serpent dragging her deeper under. Then the fingers touched her eyelids,
and she could see again. The lanterns were still lighted, still dim. Her
pain snapped awake and it was sharper now, burrowing up through her
leg and her body, into her brain.

What Luc saw was Tanya in her chair, bent sideward with one arm sprawled across the table and her head lowered down into the crook of her elbow. Clear again, as if Luc were wearing her glasses. She wiped the chill sweat off her eyes with her thumbs but her sight was still perfect enough to see that Tanya's eyes were shut softly in sleep. Blood streams leaked from Tanya's mouth and cut across her cheek. Her pants were at her knees. Her right arm was curled so that her hand, now bearing that loaded gun again, was laid across her naked crotch. The knife still deep in her ribs, sealing the wound almost bloodless. Belly still ripe with that child inside her.

Only slowly, over endless seconds, did Luc remember that she had done this—she'd murdered this mother and child together. She didn't mean it, didn't want it, but after she saw that knife something primal had overtaken her. Even if she wanted, she wouldn't have been able to stop what happened after that *tomte* with his lantern showed her what to do.

Luc hunched forward, and the agony in her leg fired like another gunshot. But she dragged herself forward, reached for the tabletop, grabbed one of Tanya's cold wet knees. She lifted the dead hand with its weapon and saw Tanya's forearm tattoo for the first time clearly. It wasn't some Norse etching of wolves or serpents or devils. It was just a bad cartoonish sketch of three bowling pins getting smacked by a red-inked bowling ball.

Luc dropped the limp arm aside and then pressed her open palm against the pregnancy. She waited for a sign of quickening but she couldn't feel anything. She cried there in Tanya's lap, and while she cried she bashed Tanya's naked thigh with her fist and screamed at this dead waste of a woman who'd crippled her with a bullet.

Tanya opened her eyes and raised the gun. Her breaths were short and shallow, like airbursts from an infant aspirator. Her hand shuddered, but when she pressed the gun against Luc's ear it held there still and certain. Luc stiffened and said, "Don't."

They considered each other while Luc was prone at Tanya's knees like a beggar. Luc wrapped her fingers over Tanya's weak hand and guided it away from her face. Then she slipped the gun out of Tanya's grasp and was holding it now for the first time herself. Tanya's arm dropped again, but she was still alive enough to utter some low throaty groan that Luc couldn't interpret. Luc wanted to believe that Tanya was telling her to escape.

When the lantern overhead went dark without warning, Luc pushed herself away from the dying woman. There were still two lanterns burning, and now a new light was stretching across the open cupboards on the back wall. Luc marveled at her own crisp eyesight—how in an instant she could read the words on every box and food can that this light reached—but the lights had arrived with the noise of a car engine. They were the headlights from Mason's returning car.

Luc had never held a gun before. She couldn't even remember how many bullets Tanya had fired, didn't know how many were left. She could pull a trigger, yes, but she knew nothing about aim or angle. And if she waited in hiding for Mason to come inside, if she tried to shoot him by surprise, she'd surely miss, and then he'd kill her, maybe worse. She was certain of that.

She used the table edge to raise herself up, careful not to be seen through the kitchen window. She took a cautious step with her healthy leg, and it was good, until her wounded leg bent for a step and the ache twisted into her like screws driven through bone. She lurched and caught a countertop hard with her elbows. Outside, car tires spun in snow, and Luc had moved mere inches, wanting nothing else but to collapse and rest for hours before trying another step.

The den was ahead with its chairs and couch laid out like an obstacle course. Everything she could grasp looked so far out of reach, though it was all still a gift for her steady eyes to see. That stunted peewee hockey stick Mason had been toying with earlier—now it was lying across the recliner seat, wrapped with grimy tape and looking old and battered.

It was half a room away, and outside the Caddy engine died. She lowered herself back down onto the floor and hissed at the cold, crawled with one dead leg to hinder her, slapped her arms hard on the

concrete to wrench her body forward, cursed at the clunky boots weigh-
ing her down, cursed the gun that she couldn't let go. She wanted silence, but a moan wouldn't quit pushing from her throat. Even now the
car door slammed outside, and that hockey stick on the recliner was still
miles away from her reach.

Luc had to stand no matter the torture. She used her one empty
palm and her knees and tried to imagine her nerves were all dead to any
sense. She limped one hesitant step full-weight on that leg, and the
harsh red pain sent her fumbling like a toddler freed from a mother's
grasp. She crashed into the recliner. White nausea flashed in her head,
but she staved off the shock. She took the pee-wee hockey stick and
planted it upside down against the floor, raising herself so the crook of
her elbow pressed down over the wooden blade. Lifting the wounded
leg was torment, though it paid her far less hell than walking two legged.
She hobbled, but she was convinced she could keep walking like this if
there was any time to spare. She hunched onward down the hallway
filled with empty stalls and ugly memories, pointing the gun at each
passing room as if someone hidden might spring out.

The lantern light dwindled before she'd moved even halfway down
the hall, but Luc kept on through the dark because she remembered a
back door was straight ahead—and because by now she was managing
blindness better than sight. After a few more lurching steps, she saw the
door faintly ahead, closer than she expected, and that surprise spurred
her onward faster. Back in the main room the screen door screeched
and the doorknob rattled. The clatter of Mason's arrival hailed from
everywhere like a hurricane wind.

Luc had no time now to reach her exit, so she slammed herself
against a wall and held her breath. Mason was out of her sightline, but
his boot clomp and the scrape of his burial spade were unmistakable.
Luc prayed that the shadow where she hid was dark enough.

"Tanya? Tan?" Mason said. He came into view—pausing in the open
where he could look either toward the kitchen or down this hallway.
From where he stood, he'd see Luc if she moved. He was silhouetted:
hunched and weary, leaning on the broken spade. He carried the oversized

flashlight, still beaming, and even if Luc didn't move he could still aim that light and catch her. Instead, he flicked off the lamp and set it on the ground. He was looking toward the kitchen.

He pleaded, "Tanya, wake up," and then he moved toward her—not rushing, because anyone could see that haste wouldn't fix what Luc had ruined. Mason was screaming when Luc pressed forward again. Two more painful limps and she was at the door worrying at a bolt lock with her shuddering fingers. The gun—she had a gun—but it was no consolation.

"God damn it! Oh, fuck—you stupid whore! I told you!" Mason roared. The outburst made Luc glance back, and she saw him lifting his spade, swinging it full-fury against the second lantern, still aglow on the counter. On impact, an airborne wreckage of metal and glass and oil splashed against a wall that was nothing but exposed stud beams and tufts of insulation. The oil ignited and fired across the wet tendrils it had soaked into the fiberglass.

Still in his throes, he spun himself away from the sudden fire and lobbed his spade like a javelin. Luc couldn't see where it went, but she heard the fierce metallic clatter.

"Stupid whore—what did you do?" he howled.

Luc's escape hatch opened outward, and a wind gust urged it wider. There were no steps, just a cracked cinderblock propped too far below her reach. The drop was two feet, maybe less, but it looked fatal to Luc. She let her breath free because the wind and the swinging door were already noise enough to betray her. So Luc jumped, and midair she thrust the hockey stick out in front of her with some mad hope that it would break her fall.

She tumbled down a slope of mixed fresh and crusted snow. The hockey stick was gone, buried somewhere she couldn't find even as she searched with one clawed hand over every twig and mound within reach. The pratfall had left her facing again the door she'd jumped through, and it was filled with the yellow light of the fire spreading down in the kitchen.

Luc was lying close to the reddened ground where Quinn died, and

a few steps farther were the woods that could hide her. On the edge of
those woods, her father walked blithely, like he was out for a quiet night
stroll. In his life he'd never worn formal clothes, but tonight he was
wearing a stark white suit that seemed to hoard moonlight into its fabric. His hair was unruly, his face covered in a wild beard that would've
taken him months to grow when he was alive. He did not look at her, but
instead out toward the woods. He put his hands in his pockets and
turned his back to Luc as he stepped in among the trees. She thought
she could hear him whistling a tune, but it faded when he passed out of
sight beyond a wide knotted tree trunk.

She stood once again without her crutch and the pain was no less vicious. She walked the uneven ground like a dead and mindless corpse
rising from its grave, walked into the snow-powdered pines and the leafless elm and maple and oak. There was a thrum in her brain that kept
her alive, and it carried her footsteps faster, until she was almost trotting
lame legged, snapping twigs and crunching ice underfoot. Once the
trees were in reach, she used them for balance and for propelling herself
on toward the next trunk. She could hear them whispering, those trees,
goading her onward.

A few strides farther and the earth began to slope down, as if molding itself for Luc's progress. But the snow was slick and it skated her too
quickly down the hillside while she grabbed for branches to keep herself
upright. A whiteout was beating softly down on her, piling like confetti
on her shoulders and in her hair—but the heavy snowfall also formed a
bleak wall between Luc and the woods ahead. Even her miracle eyes
couldn't pierce that thickness. She let the earth slide her where it
would, and she watched behind for a trace of Mason's halogen beam.

It was there—too soon, too close. It flashed above her at the crest of
the slope, back at the edge of the wood where she'd seen her father. It
skimmed the high branches, as if Mason were searching for her high in
the trees. In the beam light the snowfall seemed to hang inert, and Luc
cried out at this strife that wouldn't quit.

Mason had to know she was carrying Tanya's gun. He had to know
she was hurt from all the blood she'd left behind. The falling snow was

trying to conceal her, but he'd followed too soon for her tracks to be buried. If he ran now he could overtake her in a minute or less.

The downward slope leveled into a narrow valley, where a frozen stream lay banked with reeds trampled over by wind and ice. No telling in the dark how sharply inclined the stream banks were, or how deep the ravine, but Luc saw that just past this obstacle was where the earth turned against her by climbing upward another ten feet before leveling again.

Mason's voice rang through the forest: "Where the fuck are you, bitch!" His flashlight wiped across the ground and painted her shadow in a thin crooked strip that shivered toward the stream and the hill beyond it. She saw, in that brief shine, a rusted metal grate serving as a bridge across the stream. And it was only a few feet away from her, as if she'd followed the trail toward it by instinct. The bridge had metal beams laid parallel, wide enough apart to jam a foot down through if you weren't careful. Luc's stride was too awkward to manage, so she dropped and crawled. The beams stung with their bitter chill as she willed herself across.

Behind her a gun blast barked. It was answered by its own voice repeating across the wooded mountainside, then the padded thumps of Mason's descent into the valley. He whimpered like a wounded beast, spitting faint curses that the wind carried to Luc's ears. She managed one last lunge to reach the far end of that footbridge that was no longer than Luc herself, and the butt of the gun caught against a beam. The gun twisted out of her grip and slipped through the gap and fell down into the dark ravine, clattered on the ice below. Luc thrust her arm through the bars to grab for it, but the bottom was beneath her grasp.

She left the gun behind, terrified that Mason was near enough to catch her now. She covered the slanted, treeless ground by tromping like an ape on four limbs and grabbing at patches of dead weeds for leverage. The weeds held fast like the open hands of strangers pulling her onward. She crested the hill and there beheld a flat, treeless patch of land bordered by more limp reeds. It was a pond so perfectly round it must've been man-made, and its water was iced over white by winter freeze. Just a pond nestled in the woods, serene as a nature painting.

"You bitch! You murdered him, you cunt! You killed my son!" Another gunshot, and a chunk of icy snow leaped from the ground just right of Luc's shoulder. Mason's boots bashed over the metal footbridge. Luc rushed through the reeds and sprang out onto that ice surface. With each panicked step she twisted her torso to keep her lame leg from failing. Her lungs burned and her hot breath shot white steam into the night. She raised her face to the moon that was dulled and blurred behind the clouds, and she screamed until her throat surrendered.

Luc was ten steps across the pond when her boot slid askew and she dropped onto the ice. The slick surface ushered her limp body along another few yards. The cabin was far behind her now, half-concealed by trees, and Luc saw that it burned from the inside with a pale orange fire that pulsed in all the windows like jack-o'-lantern eyes.

Much closer, Mason leaped over the reeds with his arms raised—gun in one hand and the flashlight beaming skyward in the other. He was so frenzied he didn't seem to know what he'd jumped into. His landing was solid, but his balancing stride broke through the ice surface like a knife stabbed into cellophane. A sudden trapdoor swallowed him down into thick watery mud that splashed up, black and vulgar, onto the ice around it. The ice cracks thrummed with a deep-soaked beat that ran through the mud below the surface. For a second he was submerged, and Luc saw nothing but the splattered mud and the halogen lamplight underwater, still glaring, spreading under the translucent crust like a subterranean sun.

First the flashlight went dead, then Mason burst gasping from his water grave, and he slapped at the solid ice with empty hands. He was doused in mud, faceless except for his wide howling maw. He looked monstrous as a demon birth. "Come back here, bitch!" he roared, with such demand that he seemed convinced Luc would listen.

Instead, she crawled to the far shore and climbed through the dry matted brush until she was free of that ice pond and its howling prisoner. In the backdrop, the cabin was engulfed in surging red flame spears. It flung embers and burning debris, and it collapsed on itself like a funeral pyre, like the ghost of Baldr's longship set to sea and consumed in its last brutal light. Ahead, the snowstorm still raged, and the deeper woods were poised for Luc to get lost inside. There was a buck standing not far off, and he raised his antlered head when she approached. He watched her for a moment, curious and fearless, then he reared sideward and bounded off into the dark. Luc followed him.

THE SECOND HAND on the clock had sped up to twice its normal speed. Greta was barreling down Public Safety Building hallways like some goddess enraged and scheming flood fire famine for all humankind. The trace on Jesse Potts's mangled bike plate had arrived: a dealer plate from Buck Hanson's Bike Emporium in downtown Rochester. By the time Greta read the report, a hard copy shuddering between her two clenched fists, the name Buck Hanson was old news to her. She'd heard it from Mitch Wendt's own mouth. Not to mention she recognized Hanson's mug shots when she accessed them. He was on file for old arrests in trafficking and assault, attempted murder, and he was also the grizzly bear she'd met in the Submarine Bar and Grill.

His bike dealership was on Linux Avenue just a mile east of the West End Motor Lodge, close enough that you would've heard the overnight gunshots if you'd been standing in his sales lot. Almost laughable, the proximity, and how long she'd been waiting to make the link. Funny in a way that made Greta want to crack herself in the forehead with the claw end of a hammer.

LUC CAME UPON the white ash tree after ten more minutes of agonizing progress, grasping and stumbling, watching behind her back for signs that Mason had survived the muck and was after her again. She'd lost sight of the deer almost as soon as she'd spotted him, but he'd already done just like those other talismans. He'd shown her the way.

The white ash dwarfed all the other foliage around it—taller than Luc could mark, wide enough for three grown men to lock hands around. Its bark was rugged with ridges and furrows crashing into each other.

While the other trees were bare from autumn, the ash retained its tear-shaped leaves in clusters running green and yellow and orange and red and purple, as if it commanded all the colors of nature at once and even in the dark—because the leaves seemed to emit their own pale light. Luc wasn't in such a stupor that she couldn't recognize this Nordic tree transplanted into these woods from some watercolor in her father's storybooks.

She leaned against the bark and wasn't surprised that it felt warm like human skin. There was a split in the trunk base like a dark wound, and it ran down into the snow, where the roots pushed deep. Luc dug at the snow there with her numb hands. She flattened a fresh snowball in her palm and pressed it against her gunshot wound. The cold stung, but it worked the nerves there into a lull. She scooped more snow away from the trunk and uncovered proof that the split grew wider below the surface. It was a hole torn by some trauma ages back, and it had hollowed out the base with such depth that the ash should've long since died a leafless husk.

Luc clawed back the snow until her hands were too stiff and frostbitten to dig anymore. By the time she'd excavated a burrow, the snowfall had powdered her shoulders and hair. When she was ready, she lay on her stomach and slid toward the unburied lair. She searched with hesitant jabs to see what might be sleeping in there. Soft warm sawdust on the cavity floor, walls like the caverns of bones without marrow, but nothing living to disturb. Luc eased herself inward headfirst through the thin split, worried that she'd be trapped inside forever, that she'd die in there. But other voices spoke louder than her conscience, and Luc willed herself to listen to them.

Once inside, Luc saw that the warm hollow was wide enough to house her sitting upright with her knees bent. She could watch a stretch of forest through the gash, and she could crawl back out if she wanted. The snow was piled around the entrance near enough that she could hoard much of it back toward the split to cover her entry. She labored at this until she had only a thin slit left to see through, and she trusted that the storm would soon bury all signs of the tracks she'd made there.

There was no explanation for her efforts. She could've kept going, could've found another cabin, maybe people. But a dread persisted—a sense that her abductor was still coming, and maybe those other monsters would be back to hunt her, too. Instinct guided her now, a forgotten understanding that was prodding her decisions. Or she was following a thread of plot from one of those fairy tales. She had a sense that she'd been here before in her dreaming.

Luc decided: if she died in this place, then it was fated by larger motives than her own. Maybe she deserved death for the murder she'd done. She'd killed Quinn with her spite, then two more with one furious knife thrust.

This hideaway was warm but it stank like animal dung, and Luc couldn't find a way to twist her leg to keep it from flaring such torment. She shifted, and the crusted wall jabbed at her back. Sawdust flittered down from where her head scraped the upper limits of the cavity. She had almost decided to leave this burrow when she heard a cough. She heard twigs snapping. She watched through her sliver hole and saw him trudge under the canopy of her tree and linger there like he was also engrossed by this impossible leafy giant. His hair was matted and mud-caked, his face swiped only partially clean, eyes swollen and raw and wet. He gawked at the tree and reached out to touch its bark. Two strides closer and he stepped out of view. Luc pressed her face against her shoulder and squinted her eyes shut. This close, he smelled like rancid pond muck. His breath was loud and desperate. Maybe he had been drowned dead and was now coming to haunt her.

TWENTY MINUTES BURNED away. Now Greta was with Moe in Winslow, a suburb on the east side, driving in the dark though it was supposed to be morning. Nothing but starry twilight and the fire tails of comets pounding through the atmosphere. They crept in first gear through a quiet subdivision, past houses strung with Christmas lights flashing like distress calls from an abandoned colony. Trailing behind them was a police van loaded with surveillance equipment and the cops who were running it. Greta hated the sight of that van and its two head-lights glaring in the rearview because there was no more time for spying, no more watching and waiting.

Moe steered around the center of a cul-de-sac circle where plowed snow had been piled tall enough to bury a car. Buck Hanson owned the third driveway counterclockwise, where empty, unshoveled asphalt rose up to a Cape Cod with dark shaded windows. Christmas lights were strung on the sharp-sloping roof, but they were shut off. More than one pair of fresh tire tracks stretched down the driveway through the snow.

The slow two-vehicle convoy kept driving, circling now back down the street like a funeral procession for nobody. Moe said, "We'll have to set up the van on this side street a block down from the house."

"There's no point," Greta said. "They've fled because they found out what happened to Potts." She felt herself strapped, hostage to her own seatbelt. She wanted to burst through the car roof and soar like a Valkyrie over the rooftops fast enough to overtake those coward child snatchers in their retreating cars. She wanted claws to tear them apart with.

"Listen—" Moe said.

On the police radio, a grainy voice repeated a call: "Dispatch to 362."

Greta grabbed her portable and answered, "Three-sixty-two, over."

The dispatcher spoke the message like it was prophecy. The subjects being sought by Car 362 had just been observed by the second surveil-lance unit deployed to Buck Hanson's Bike Emporium downtown.

GRETA'S THOUGHTS WERE all funneled down through one narrow chamber, set to blast. They raced across the interstate toward the city's west end, and the sun finally spilled out its pale blue morning, dimming out the stars. They'd left the surveillance crew back at the Hanson resi-dence, hunkered in the van one block down the street, just as planned. Those fortunate men would spend a dull dreary Monday waiting for nothing.

Four blocks up from the Linux Avenue exit, they sighted the dealer-ship lot full of gray crumbling pavement kept intact by winter ice. It was neighbored on the east by a diner called Friendly Family, on the west by a patch of snowy weeds marked with a fading realtor sign. Across the street was a defunct Chinese buffet with a big red gateway like the sign of pi.

In the Friendly Family lot was another white van parked among the cars of early-bird diners, five feet from the orange cyclone fence that bordered Hanson's commercial property. Moe pulled alongside it while Greta unrolled her window. The cop in the van's driver's seat was named Kozlowski—a straitlaced Aryan that other cops called Android behind his back. He was wearing sunglasses at dawn and subtly chewing gum on one side of his mouth. Without taking his eyes off the motorcycle shop he told Greta, "Five subjects from two vehicles entered the establishment twenty minutes ago."

The dealership was a flat-roofed building with a single wall of glass in the front to show off the display bikes to passing traffic. Rainbow-colored writing on the window said, WINTER BLOWOUT SALE! The two vehicles parked outside were a flashy red Dodge Ram pickup with a plow attachment and a boxy old Lincoln Continental colored fecal brown.

Kozlowski said, "They moved quickly, yet furtively. At least one subject appeared restrained by the arms. She was being forcibly escorted into the building. A female, heavyset by appearance. The low-light conditions made our visibility poor, but we were able to obtain positive ID on one Buck Hanson, also a Hispanic male, another male or possibly female. There was also a dog—looked like a Doberman pinscher."

Greta said, "Could the hostage have been heavily clothed, padded down?"

"It's possible," Kozlowski said.

Greta said, "This could be Luc. We need to get in there."

"I can radio two backup units," Kozlowski said. "I've got dispatch ready on the radio."

"Not fast enough," Greta said.

"Calm down, Greta," Moe said. "We need to wait on this."

"I'm not waiting any longer," Greta said.

Behind the building the sky was pale blue and cloudless, full of sun and telephone lines. The bright sun made the icy ground seem like end-less glass, and across it whirled small tornadoes of snow dust. Greta's breath was held and her heart thrummed like a war drum underneath the Kevlar bulletproof vest she wore.

THE SIREN'S WAIL, and the ticktock of the universe pumping so fast now that the gears all spiraled into chaos. It could've been possible, in such bewilderment, that the asphalt suddenly burst and spewed a geyser of fire and ash and blood. Greta wouldn't have been surprised.

There was a hopeful minute when Greta's actions made sense, rush-ing the building with nothing but a wild hope that she'd catch them by surprise, and that Moe, Kozlowski, and the other two cops in the van were galloping up behind to reinforce her. She could hear the ETF backup cars squealing into the lot behind her, but she'd rushed it all thirty seconds early, gun drawn and heart molten. Blood roared through the capillaries in her head. She bashed headlong into the unlocked glass double entrance doors and catapulted inside.

Then came the moments of darkness punctuated by snapshots from hell and the voices of the dead still wailing with their terrible, desperate siren noises.

"Down, down, down, down!" someone screamed. "Get out of here!"

Three cops tackled a steroid-pumped Mexican first because he was lingering just inside the entrance, drawing a Colt Python, eight-inch barrel. They'd hit him with enough surprise that the Colt didn't aim any higher than the floor before the tackle. In the melee, Greta noted that she knew him. The one called Gordo, Submarine Bar and Grill, the one who swore he'd never heard of Mason Renault. All the lines that Greta had tossed this past month, all were reeling taut now, and she felt like she'd get torn apart by their tugging. She wanted to fire her Beretta into Gordo's perjuring mouth, but he was facedown with Moe astride him clamping down handcuffs. The Mexican screamed his *No-halbo-inglés* bullshit while his tight-cuffed, three-fingered hand snapped like a lob-ster claw.

Cops spread out, and their raiding shadows swarmed along with them. Shouts like the howl of primates. The sales room was the size of a basketball court, floors covered in rubber matting that pressed like soft-tilled earth where you stepped. Shelves were stocked with shining silver bike parts, lubricants, riding gear, jackets on hooks, helmets, scale-model motorcycles in plastic packages. The heat ducts rattled light fixtures in the ceiling high above. The whole place smelled of leather and oil and treated wood.

A woman sprang out from underneath the cash counter. Her long clumped hair swirled around her scalp that was shaved at the temples and tattooed. Her black shotgun swung down straight at her hip, too fast for comprehension before the gun roared and bucked and a hole punched through the front window. Glass came down like an avalanche of ice pebbles.

Greta kept her eye on the dreadlocked bitch as she pumped her spent shell and leveled the shotgun again. The outside wind and traffic noise sucked in like a deep space vacuum. Greta caught a glimpse of something rushing her, leaping. Sleek black-and-tan coat, slender snout, lips curled back over its teeth, and a hot red fire in its eyes. She batted her forearm against it, but the animal came snapping down, digging fangs into her left arm below the elbow. The dog knocked her backward two steps and she hit a display motorcycle and flipped over it. The dog clamped its jaw. Its twisting, twitching body pulled, teeth shredding skin and muscle, and Greta flailed because the pain was a black hole sucking out consciousness. All around her, guns blasted and she didn't know which of these swift bullets would take her life.

"Drop it!" Moe's voice, and then another shotgun blast.

This dog on her chest was killing her. She aimed the gun but the dog kept twisting itself away from her aim until Greta pressed the barrel deep into the rock muscle in its neck where the pelt was already damp with her blood. She fired a shot that made her eardrums blast. The dog's blood peppered her face, warm, and she felt its teeth pull away. Not even a yelp and it became a dead heap on the ground.

Greta's arm was ugly gore she couldn't look at or she'd lose her mind.

She rolled off the overturned bike, pressed her ravaged arm against her ribs. There were cops scurrying through the white fog—but Moe she couldn't see, couldn't find in the pandemonium gale. Instead, she saw Buck Hanson as he dived from the vortex with a weapon crackling like a line of fireworks. It was a nine-millimeter mini Uzi held one-handed at a tilt while he sprayed his ammunition in a wide sweep. He wore a white tanktop and his beard bulged against his neck, arm-flab trembling with the automatic kick.

Bullets pierced white wounds in the display windows, rounds pinging off bike frames. On the shelves a row of plastic oil bottles popped and spurted their black liquids. The machine gun rattled, glass broke, the gates into hell burst wide. The sea caught fire, mountains crumbled, the stars plummeted from heaven. It was the last battle. It was the twilight of everything on earth.

The shotgun bitch leaned against the back wall and gnashed her teeth, screaming words so fast Greta couldn't catch any but the curses. The bitch was wielding her shotgun in wide arcs, aiming nowhere. In the air loomed white dust, but Greta aimed through it anyway. She thought about telling the girl to freeze, some warning to get her attention, but instead she just fired. The bullet struck just above the bitch's left eyebrow. A red dot the size of a dime. She squeezed one last shell from her shotgun, blew a hole in the ceiling. Light fixtures buzzed and threw sparks. The dead bitch slid out of sight behind the counter. On the wall behind her was a wet red streak running slantwise like some pageant ribbon that she never would've won.

"Motherfucker!" Hanson said, like it was the only word left to utter. He dislodged a spent clip and let it drop like an empty cigarette pack, then slipped in a fresh one picked from his back pocket. Greta was crawling through pools of oil and her own blood, packages of gaskets and plugs. Price tags fluttering. Ravaged arm pressed against her body and drumming up more scorched pain. She knew if she fainted she'd die.

There was Moe hunkered down beside the counter, five feet south of Hanson. And time was coming to its end—unreeling faster and faster like a film winding out of its spool. With time so awry, Greta couldn't know if what she saw had happened twice before or was bound to happen soon. Moe sprang, swiveling with his arms outstretched, gun seeking its mark. Buck Hanson reeled, but Moe's bullet caught him first, dragging a divot through one jugular. Buck slapped his neck to staunch the blood, but it was spewing through his knuckles. Moe fired again, and Buck twitched like he'd been surged with an electric shock. He leaned against a doorframe—the entrance to the back room he'd sprung from. He placed one hand on his heart, where the second bullet had entered. Moe waited, gun trained, but he didn't need to fire again. Buck coughed once, dribbled blood, stumbled backward through the door, out of Greta's sight.

Something like calm hit her now, a pocket of silence hidden beneath the sirens and yelling. Greta dragged like a sleepwalker toward the firefight debris. She was just behind Moe now, dazed and weaponless. Moe advanced on the doorway to the back room. From inside the office came a faint feminine whimper, almost drowned out by siren wail.

"Luc—" said Greta.

It was a crowded room with Greta and Moe and also Buck, who was seated on the floor against the desk with the shotgun laid across his lap. Both his hands were on the floor. Blood bubbled out of his neck and ran currents down his left arm like a map of his veins and pooled on the waxed tile floor. He blinked at them but made no sound.

On the desk were scattered sales forms, a jumbo place mat calendar, and two fresh Uzi clips, unused. Several duffel bags were filled with more weapons than Greta could fathom in one glance—enough for a militia. There were clipped stacks of money and loose fifties scattered about the desktop. It was clear they'd stopped here for supplies and cash on the way out of town.

The Uzi itself was on the floor by Greta's feet. She stepped on it and dragged it toward her reach.

Greta bent down and said, "Tell me where Luc Moberg is."

"Fuck off, pig," Hanson said, baring bloody teeth. His thick beard shivered and his breaths were shallow.

Moe had maneuvered behind the desk, wheeled aside Hanson's leather office chair.

Greta asked Hanson, "Is she alive or dead?"

Hanson: "Fuck—off—"

Greta's own blood was dripping on the floor. A sudden whiteout hit her head, and she swooned backward against the wood-paneled wall. The impact of her body knocked a picture off a hook hung there. It fell on the floor: a photo inside a cheap metal frame, an aerial shot of a cabin in the woods somewhere.

"Greta?" Moe said.

From under the desk, a beastly woman shuffled out like a walrus rippling across dry land. Mangy graying hair tangled over her bare shoulders, limp pendulous breasts sinking almost to the floor. She was stark naked. Hands tied with duct tape behind her back. Her face was splotchy red and wet and snotty from crying. More duct tape was pressed across her mouth.

Greta gagged, pressed the back of her hand against her mouth.

Old tattoos on the woman's arm were faded green and blurry. She spotted Hanson on the floor and loosed an awful guttural groan that made her mouth tape bulge. She collapsed, mashed her breast against the tiles. She was like a huge turkey plucked and prepped for baking. Moe grabbed a tuft of her hair, raised her head with it. In one fast swipe he stripped away the mouth tape. With her mouth now free, she gasped low ugly animal sounds.

"Who are you?" Moe said.

Nothing but whimpers.

"I said who are you?"

"I'm—that—I'm his wife. That fucker there. I'm Brenda Hanson."

"What is this? What's going on?" Moe said.

"He was—him and that spic—he was gonna kill me because I wanted to leave."

"Do you know where Luc Moberg is?" Greta asked.

"I said it was enough—and he—he killed me—I was leaving him—"

"Where is Luc Moberg?" Greta demanded. "Where is the girl you took?" She didn't know whom she was asking anymore—Hanson, his wife, God—but Hanson wasn't breathing and God was silent as ever.

The woman said, "The cabin. She's at the cabin."

She nodded her head at the framed aerial snapshot that Greta had knocked to the floor. Greta lifted it and, in doing so, left a thumbprint in someone's blood on the dusty glass. She knew by the wretched gaze in Brenda Hanson's eyes that this was the place she meant. Greta said, "Tell me where."

IT WAS A CLOUDLESS dawn no less frigid for its bright sun. The snow piled under the white ash stirred and then crumbled into clumps nudged away by cautious hands. Luc emerged from that snow like a malformed hatchling, groping on her stomach. She was speckled with sawdust and leaves, dirt, broken twigs. She squinted at the harsh morning light and heaved great white gusts of breath as she groaned at all the hurt waking again inside her. Her frozen hands wouldn't clench, so she pressed them against her stomach under her shirt, gasping at the cold that bore down deep into her fingers, and warmed them until she could make fists again.

Mason's ghost hadn't found her overnight, though it had paused at that tree for what seemed like hours, trampling so near to her hideout, throwing curses from his throat like he knew she was there to hear them. Eventually he'd wandered on deeper into the woods. How many hours had lapsed since then, Luc didn't know. It was luring enough to believe that it had been another dream, since any tracks he'd left were long snowed over, and Luc's delusions were firing stronger than ever. She barely trusted the morning itself as the truth.

Standing was an agonizing ritual, but she managed. Her wound was clotted and her thigh was inflamed and purple as crushed grapes. A new and grinding pain was ripping out from the overnight numb. She wanted to scream, but there were ears in these woods that were listening.

Luc hobbled just a few steps before an awful ache brought her down again. She sat ten minutes or longer but afterward she toiled again.

She'd managed to cross a clearing into another stand of trees when she dropped and leaned against a fallen log. The forest encircled her, endless, and she watched the wooded horizons for a beacon that wouldn't come. Every direction looked impossible. Even the white ash was lost somewhere back beyond sight of Luc's morning tracks.

The ground where she rested was littered with dead branches and logs, and one stick jutting from the snow within her reach was rigid enough to work as a makeshift cane. She rubbed the ice from it and plucked away dead bark and twigs. This was another gift offered up by the gods. They were with her again this morning after all. Luc realized—oblivious until now—that her eyes were still sharp and clear, better than they'd been with any pair of glasses she'd ever owned. There was no rationale for this magic, but here it was enchanting her, giving reason enough to keep moving.

She disturbed nothing but the flat soft snow and a few crows cawing in the trees. Moving hoarded all of her attention. Mason could've strolled up behind and she wouldn't have known until his hands were on her neck. Only when she rested could she watch for him, her eyes darting at every falling twig, every windblown leaf. When the sun was a full globe perched on the eastern slope, she entered a clearing and saw what was inside it. She collapsed out of sudden overwhelming grief and slapped her hands over her face, then she bashed her walking stick against the ground until something cracked.

What she'd seen in the clearing was the same iced-over pond she'd crossed the night before. She had blindly retraced her own path, headed back toward whatever remained of that blazing cabin she'd escaped. Sprawled on the pond bank, she despaired with such psychic force that she expected to die from it. She eyed that jagged wound in the ice—frozen over, snow dusted, but still a recognizable divot lined with jigsaw ice shards and splattered black sludge. She guessed Mason's gun and halogen flashlight were sunken under there somewhere—those things, but probably not his corpse.

When her senses settled, Luc admitted to herself that this detour wasn't fully accidental. Some unconscious impulse had driven her back here. Because: no telling where Mason was, maybe still prowling those woods or hours away in his car by now. The only road Luc knew stood in this direction. If she'd taken some other route, she might've wandered until she died hunting for her way out of the woods.

She strived at turtle pace around the solid ground bordering the pond and finally reached the slope curving down to the stream. In this daylight the stream was just a dry ravine hardly three feet deep. Down the gentle incline—sidesteps led with her unhurt limb. The ache bashed inside her brain like a heavyweight slugger working to knock her out.

This morning the footbridge that she'd crawled across was softened with fresh forgetful snow. But Luc's memory returned lucid, and what she remembered most was the gun. It had seemed lost forever last night when she dropped it between the bars, but now an impulse had brought her back to find it.

Luc crouched and eased herself down the shallow ravine. She brushed aside the reeds impeding her, and her boots unsettled the pebbles on the barren streambed. The gun lay under the footbridge where she expected it to be, stenciled with two white slats where the snow had fed between the bars overhead. She strained to grab the gun, then brushed away the snow when she had it in her grasp. She wondered if the tumble or the chill had busted it. She checked that the safety was still unengaged—but she didn't know which position was safe, and she didn't dare fire it to see. She didn't want to have to touch it at all, though her heart still raced at the sensation of its protective load in her grip.

The hardest acre to cross was the last, the abrupt slant running uphill toward the cabin. The only sight visible over the crest was the smoke lingering like a low storm cloud, trailing up from the wreckage Luc couldn't see just yet. She wanted to walk these last few yards, but her slack right leg refused to climb even when she stabbed her walking stick against the ground for leverage. So she whipped the stick away and proceeded on all fours, grabbing for rocks stuck solid in the frozen ground. Some came loose and clattered down behind her. She stumbled, with only one free hand to manage, and her progress was mere inches per minute. The angle of the rise seemed to tilt more sharply. Luc needed both hands, so she opened her mouth and bit the gun between her teeth, aimed leftward so she couldn't blow her own jaw to shreds.

She heard the ruins sizzle and crackle. Then, crawling over the rise, she saw the cabin and its stables razed by fire, all except a few enduring beams charred black and scalloped but still thrusting skyward like grave markers. The bonfire was dead, though a few meager flames coughed from a collapsed wall here and a blasted stovepipe there, never lasting. Smoke billowed dingy and cottony from the crumpled mass where embers still glowed orange like watchful eyes. Burned things were almost discernible—a couch frame, cans, a sink basin, metal bunk-bed rails, mattress springs—but nothing was there to salvage except the wood-stove still abiding.

The ground snow was thawed in a lopsided ring spanning yards around the wreckage, and the earth there was stripped, black and wet like oil. There was the hockey stick, lying muddy and boldfaced in the grunge. Gray ash floated dreamlike on a breeze that carried to Luc the heady reek of scorched wood. The derelict tractor was blackened with soot, nearby trees were scorched where they faced inward, limbs cooked down to stumps. Far enough away, Luc's prison trailer stood untouched by either flame or cinder.

Luc closed her eyes against that ugly stinging smoke and pressed her face into the snow around her. Again her mind conjured the *Ringhorn*, Baldr's ship, and she wondered whether the pyre flames had finally sunk that vessel or if it floated onward forever with its flotsam charred black and craggy and petrified like rock.

When she looked at the rubble again, Mason was there. He sat stark naked on the Cadillac hood. The car was now parked closer than it must've been when the fire was raging. He hunched like an ape, mud slicked and soot grimed. On his chest, his arms, his legs, he'd dragged his fingers through the black film, leaving crude marks like cave drawings. His proud pompadour had buckled flat and sticky onto his forehead. Arms rinsed clean up to the elbows, but then soiled again with blood matted into the black fur on his forearms and staining his hands, as if he'd staged the work of a surgeon or a shaman. His face was a black gorilla mask. His eyes bulged and darted behind that mask as if they were trapped there and desperate to be freed.

More than a dozen rocks were scattered on the car hood beside him, some as large as baseballs. He lifted one and he bellowed and he pitched it at the burned husk of the cabin. The rock smacked against an upright beam and spun, lost in the coals. Mason's bare feet were hiked up onto the bumper, and below them in the snow lay Tanya's corpse, stripped from the waist down. She was curled embryonic with her back and her rear aimed toward the woods where Luc was hiding. Tanya's flesh was as bloodless and papery as peeled skin. Her hair was burned away from her scalp, though a few curled strands were still attached and wind-tossed.

Luc continued her military crawl several more yards before Mason stood up and stepped over Tanya's body. Luc froze. She'd never seen a man nude before, not even her father, but it was a vulgarity that meant nothing to her now. His stomach and groin were mostly clean, though he'd dabbed himself around the navel with bloody fingerprints. The muscles in his abdomen were raw and distinct like skinned chicken. His dick hung limp from a thicket of fuzz that concealed all but the strawberry-shaped head of it.

There was a rifle slung behind his back, held there by a strap that slanted across his chest. He stepped barefoot over the scorched ground until he was almost standing in the live embers of his pyre. Then he took his dick in both hands and pissed down onto the coals that hissed and steamed when the urine hit.

Luc was crouched by the tree where Quinn had died, where heat had melted the stained snow away. She was exposed enough that Mason could easily spot her, but she braced herself against the tree and stood up shivering, damp and muddied where snow had wetted her clothes. She stepped toward Mason and raised her gun in both hands, gripped it so hard that her finger bones ached. She aimed everywhere in the space that his body occupied.

And he did seem to notice her then—the way a cautious deer watches the hunter yet stands firm. He made no move for his rifle, even as he pissed over the remnants of his ugly life. He raised his chin up toward the rising sun, then he lifted his bloody hands and put them in the air. Cleared his throat but said nothing. He was still pissing.

Luc fired a shot and the gun bucked but she didn't lose hold of it. Mason flinched and planted one bare heel backward to keep his balance. His urine stream halted abruptly, but he hadn't been hit. Wherever the bullet went, its impact was silent.

They were twenty feet apart and Luc stepped closer. She crooked one elbow against her hip, shut one eye, peered past the sight pin, and raised it toward Mason's head. While she aimed, he grabbed for the rifle strap and ducked away.

Luc pulled another round. Clear across the yard the jalopy pickup's driver's window burst in a rain of glass. She'd missed again and now anguish sapped Luc's strength like an electrical short. She ground her teeth and held her breath.

Mason was crouched, feinting right, both hands raising the rifle overhead like soldiers hoist their guns when marching through swamps. But the strap caught under his neck. His eyes bulged with a sudden show of fear, and Luc drank that nectar up. She'd closed the gap between them another five feet and couldn't miss this time. She pulled the trigger.

Mason grimaced and stooped like he'd been punched in the gut. Luc couldn't see where she'd hit, but blood was streaming down over his thigh, fanning across to the opposite leg. It was speckled on his abdomen. He tore his rifle free one-handed and it sank too heavy in his grasp and fired a round at the snow. Then Luc saw where her bullet had struck: the pink tip of his cock had burst in a sprout of gore. He gripped his wound in one tight fist and the creases between his fingers filled red like knife slits. His face wrenched with a silent agony that was almost slapstick.

Luc shot again but missed because Mason was already teetering. The haphazard rifle crossed between his shins and he faltered over it. He plunged into the outermost scattering of coals and a cloud of ash ruptured around him. He kicked and screamed and arched himself backward out of the pit that had already sizzled bubbles and sores into his flesh. He was out in seconds, but specks of black debris were cooking deeper into his chest and his face. The smell was instant and noxious. He was on his knees, disarmed, batting at his burns while the red void between his legs dribbled out blood like a spigot.

Luc limped forward and aimed Tanya's gun at Mason's flailing head. The first bullet punched through his teeth and opened a second screaming mouth in the opposite cheek. He was dumbfounded—that vain hair smudge under his lip was quivering. Luc's last round pushed her father's killer's left eye deep into his head and rendered the socket empty and black. He shut up fast. His arms dropped and his head slumped back into sudden sleep. A strange postmortem sway kept him up on his knees for a full five seconds, then his body laid itself down in a tangled heap.

Luc cried until her eyes blurred up. It was a guttural sobbing that inflamed her throat. At that instant, somehow, she remembered a stuffed monkey she'd owned because it had slept on her pillow in this same twisted pose that Mason assumed now. On her fifteenth birthday she'd finally relented to Gina's teasing and packed it away in a closet with other teddies and dolls. That was just one year ago. Now, on the morning of her sixteenth birthday, Lucia kept that gun marked on Mason's head in case it made the slightest twitch. She'd shoot until all those fucking bullets were gone if he moved.

Another minute passed before she hobbled past both corpses and approached the dying bonfire. She wanted to burrow down into its hottest core. It seemed like the only way she could ever be warm again. And she might've stepped into those orange coals if not for the black smoke that sought down into her throat like fingers to gag her. Coughing, wincing, she lurched instead toward the Cadillac parked a few feet away. Her vision of the car was blurred and shifting. She mashed her knuckles into one eye and rubbed, blinked, but the gift of perfect sight had been carried away forever by the smoke.

She slid along the Caddy's driver's side and pulled the door latch, expecting it would be locked. But the door popped open and Luc slumped down into the seat. She kept her legs thrust outside while she strangled her injured thigh in both hands and hissed. Nothing left to confront but pain, and it attacked her with nausea and brutal shivers and an electrical shriek deep in her ears. She coughed up the smoke coating her lungs, bashed her fist on the steering wheel. The horn quacked once.

She pivoted, brought one leg inside the car. Laid the pistol on the passenger seat and then prodded her fingers around the ignition to find that there were no keys. Bit her bottom lip until her eyes flooded up again. Swiped her hands over the seats and up along the dash, nudged something wooden that she lifted and held just a foot away from her face to see it clearly. It was the carving knife she'd used to kill Tanya, wiped clean except where the blood had soaked into the handle.

She tossed the knife out the open driver's door, then she searched the dash again, yanked open the glove box, and rummaged, finding nothing but napkins, papers folded inside a Baggie, and a tube of breath mints. She scooped them all onto the seat until the glove box was empty, and then she slammed it shut.

No keys anywhere. Even if she found the keys, she'd never driven a car and her eyes were shit. Chances were she'd back the car into a snowbank or slam it against a tree, kill herself after surviving all these others. No strength left to go hunting for keys, and nowhere else to look. Mason was naked, and Luc guessed that whatever mania coerced him into stripping his clothes off had also caused him to burn them. Maybe he'd planned to kill himself, and for that sort of plan a ring of keys was useless.

Luc sat with both hands on the steering wheel as if the illusion of driving could stand for the truth. Her breath was fogging the windows white. She wanted only to sleep, and if death came in her dreams then she was prepared. She shut her eyes and held her breath. In the near utter silence Luc heard somebody else breathing in the car. Quick helium breaths, serene. Too distinct for an illusion.

Luc flailed, grabbed for the gun that she'd tossed on the passenger side but it was buried in the clutter she'd unloaded from the glove box. She found it, propelled herself sideward out the door, and backed away two steps. She teetered, but kept herself upright and pointed the gun at the car while blotches of white burst in her vision and made her want to faint. Her first absurd guess was that Quinn Cutler was in there, un-buried and still faintly alive—but she'd seen the outcome of his butchering and she knew better.

Luc tested the back door latch with her gun poised like she'd seen on cop shows. The door popped open and she eased it wider. Nothing sprang out at her, nothing even moved, and her eyes were worthless for spotting anything but shadows in the Caddy's backseat. She gripped the roof and leaned herself in. There was a quilt bunched there on the seat like a pile of laundry. There were brown moose and pine tree patterns repeated diagonally across stitched diamonds, a motif so familiar that it was almost comforting. The mood of calm was so potent that Luc set the gun on the back window ledge and reached out for the quilt. It was dry and clean and Luc was fearless of what she'd find inside it.

She shifted closer and craned her head. Now she saw that the new-born's face wasn't covered. Only its body was quilt wrapped and swad-dled tight like it'd never left the womb. It was lying on its back facing her, green eyes wide and searching beneath the faint fuzz of its eye-brows. If it saw Luc, it regarded her with no more interest than all the other new curiosities.

There was space on the edge of the backseat for Luc to lie down be-side the infant. She made a pillow out of her arm and laid her head just inches from the baby's. Its face was still streaked with blood and white powdery mucus, and its tiny head was hardly bigger than a softball. The skin tone was strong, the lips pink, the black fetal hair sprouted downy in the areas on its scalp that had dried. Luc touched its cheek and it turned toward her, mouth wide and head bobbing for something to nurse. Luc smiled against a tightening in her throat, but she didn't know whether relief or anguish was forcing her tears.

Sleep dragged her down. In her last conscious moments she realized the doors were still open admitting frigid air and smoke, but she couldn't lift her body again, not even her head. She remembered the last time she'd lain prone like this across a backseat, back in those final sec-onds before her father was murdered. And here she was again like a story retold. Here she nestled with Mason's child poised on the brink of life and maybe death. Listening to each of her own heartbeats thrum louder and faster until it seem to fill the sky with noise and its shadow grew overhead and gusting god breath cast away all smoke.

THE THUMPING WAS deeper now. Luc's eyes broke wide and she blinked at such stark brightness and the blurred silhouettes of two helmeted figures haunting above her, glowing merciful orange. She was lying flat on her back and straining her arms to reach them, but both her arms were strapped down to this bedding that wouldn't stop rumbling. Luc understood she was airborne in a compartment full of clanking apparatus, spiral cords leaning weightless as the helicopter banked midair. One of the two ghosts was just clear enough that Luc could see he was black. He pressed a soft hand against her forehead to keep her from thrashing her neck. A plastic mask was fitted over Luc's face and it leaked cool air into her nostrils. She gasped at first, but she found her rhythm after a few panicked breaths.

LUC WASN'T LUCID again until after dark. Mostly she wandered through the dream worlds that were being built for her by pills from a paper cup—dreams of throbbing color and white noise. Her room was like any other hospital room, with dull tiled floors and pastel green walls and the same medicinal scents. There was a television mounted on a stand but no remote to start it. Luc thought she'd seen one, but it was gone now, and her naked eyes were too weak to be certain of anything they caught.

Both her hands were bandaged and they throbbed and they itched under the dressings, but Luc was too tired to fret about it. A nurse wearing a thin cotton shirt with teddy bears patterned on it, a nurse whose odor was stale cigarettes and lemon, whose hands were brittle—she fed Luc with ice water that Luc drank through a long plastic straw. She didn't want any more water but it kept coming.

"I have to pee," Luc said.

"Just pee. You're all set up."

"But—" A helicopter blade was thrumming louder, bearing down on her. Her body seized into a sudden bout of shivering that Luc couldn't stop, so strong that it rattled the bolts in her cot. She asked for more blankets from a blurred shape in the corner of the room.

"You can stay with us," Tanya said. She stood naked and pale with pendulous breasts and nothing but a pulpy red hole where her womb should've been. Tanya raised her arms as if for an embrace and her fingers were broken and twisted. She exhaled a swarm of gray chalky moths from her mouth.

WHEN SHE WOKE again to the sound of hushed funeral voices, her eyes saw the world as it was supposed to be. Gramma Norma was seated in a chair beside the bed looking haggard and red eyed, her mouth slack. Luc wanted to touch her grandmother to see if the woman was real, but then Luc remembered that her hands were mummified in bandages to help heal the frostbite. The sky behind the curtains was black.

"Gramma?" Luc said, and her voice sounded ancient to her own ears.

Norma's mouth shut with a clack, and she shuddered as if someone had just snapped her out of hypnosis. Norma said, "Lucia. We were letting you sleep."

Luc touched her bandaged hand to her temple and felt her glasses frames there.

"We had those fixed for you," Norma said. "Your mother did."

Luc's neck was stiff and sore for a dozen possible reasons, but she rotated it far enough to see that Blair Moberg was there in the room and rolling her wheelchair cautiously closer. Her busted leg was encased again, and her face was bruised and blotched—one eye taped over with a circular bandage, her lower lip twice as large and scabbed on one side. Despite this battering, Blair's smile was so large and oblivious that it looked maniacal.

Luc felt a violent cramp inside her gut. She didn't want to see this woman so soon while her impressions were still tangled—didn't want to see her mother coming at her like an ambush. Blair steered alongside the bed and grabbed for Luc's bare arm like she was a child snatching at a Christmas gift.

Luc didn't even let her mother speak before she hunched toward her and spat the phlegm that was in her mouth. It sprang out amoeba shaped and struck in a drooling thread on Blair's cheek just below her unharmed eye. Her smile sank, and that instant disillusionment gave Luc a dark thrill. Her mother didn't even reach to clean the spit away. She sat dumbstruck and sad with it dribbling down her cheek.

"Lucia," Norma gasped.

Blair finally dabbed at the phlegm. Her one exposed eye was fixed on Luc, her baffled pupil that filled the iris with its black. She studied her wetted fingers like she had expected to find something worse than spit, something like blood or venom.

Norma hurried around the bedside while digging into her pocket for a tissue she could use to wipe Blair's face. She was muttering, "You're confused, honey, that's all," but Luc didn't know which of them Norma was talking to. Norma pulled the wheelchair handlebars to slide Blair away from any further sneak attacks. Luc couldn't watch this drama unfold anymore, especially her mother's vacant, one-eyed alarm. The spitting hadn't appeased Luc in the least, and what she felt now was almost akin to sorry.

"Sorry," Blair announced suddenly, like an echo of Luc's thoughts. "Sorry, sorry."

"For what?" Luc said. "You don't know why you should be sorry."

"Because they took you and hurt you. I couldn't stop them," Blair said.

"You're allowed to forget," Luc told her. "I have to remember what I'm sorry for."

Norma knew well enough to turn her daughter away and lead the chair out into the hallway. Only seconds after they'd left Luc was already wondering if they'd been just a dream like everything else. There were shadows darkening the walls and there were low, but awful, noises hailing from just inside the thin rippling door between this world and the next. Luc was alone again with her monsters.

LATER SHE WAS screaming, drenched in sweat. The hallway light shaped the figures of the two nurses who'd rushed to attend her, hush her, stroke her hair with their hands.

"Where's the baby?" Luc asked. She didn't know what she was saying.

"He's fine. He's down the hall," they said.

"I want to see him. Please—"

They wheeled the cart into her room a few minutes later. With the dim bedside lamp glowing, Luc could see that the cart was topped with a clear plastic tub, blanket-lined, and underneath it was a shelved collection of towels and diapers and aspirators. A blue index card said, "My name is," but on the line below it was written only "baby boy" with Magic Marker.

The nurse lifted the swaddled sleeping baby out of the tub, one hand propped behind his head, and Luc sat upright and accepted him across her lap. His eyes were closed and his head was snug in a knitted cap, lips smacking in his sleep. There were capillary blotches on his cheeks and eyelids, tiny white pimples around his nose. Luc held him and her heartbeat calmed and she imagined that strangers passing by this hospital room might guess the baby was hers, that she'd just given birth to him. But Luc was just sixteen—and powerless. She was nobody's mother.

"What's going to happen to him?" Luc said.

"He'll be fine," the nurse said. "They'll take good care of him."

"Who? Foster homes?" Luc said.

"Or he could be adopted. I'll bet he's adopted right away. Look at him."

Luc did look, and wondered again how she could ever let herself release him.

THE COUNTY HOSPITAL was just off a rural route that serviced vineyards in the summer and ski slopes in the winter. It was a single-story deal with a parking lot no bigger than the ones at fast food joints, and to-day it was overcrowded with news vans and brutish cameramen with their equipment loaded on their shoulders like weaponry. The street re-porters milled about, tethered to microphone cords. In her career, Greta had seen enough of this circus to remain unfazed. Pulling into the lot, she was more attuned to the ski resort laid out on the mountainside just behind the hospital, where skiers floated through the snow serene and oblivious to the ruckus just downslope from them.

Greta wasn't even out of the car with the wrapped gift in her hand before the news crews crowded her with their microphones and their jackhammering questions. One local celebrity anchor was viciously shouldering her way toward Greta through the rest of the throng. She said, "Investigator Hurd, you're here to see Lucia Moberg, is that correct?"

Greta said, "I really can't make any comments now."

From the left: "How do you characterize yesterday morning's events?"

From the right: "How are you holding up today?"

Greta knew how to decode these questions, though she still wasn't going to answer. The first was a shorthand way of asking how a simple arrest at Buck Hanson's Bike Emporium had deteriorated into a five-minute war that would take months to sift apart—and how exactly Greta was to blame. They wanted her to make pithy sense out of some-thing that the oncoming months' inquisitions would not successfully untangle. The second question was simpler—they wanted Greta to ex-press the pain that seared inside the stitched-up dog bite on her ban-daged arm. Her answer wouldn't have been appropriate for television.

Greta found Luc in a sunroom that overlooked the ski slopes outside. Potted plants galore, on hooks and covering tables, so green that one could be convinced it was summer if not for the view. Luc had guests already—two girls her own age costumed in all black like nightclubbers. The one wearing a dog collar was bald, and the other's hair was bleached, but they had identical faces. Gina and Catherine—Greta supposed—Luc's twin friends. The girls were seated on one of the three available couches, and the bleached one was playing with the kid's game found in every waiting room, the twisted metal rods along which you guided colored wooden balls. Luc was in a wheelchair with a blanket on her lap, facing her friends. It looked to Greta like she'd interrupted absolutely nothing.

Luc didn't quite smile at Greta, but the scowl on her face straightened out.

"I know it's not exactly a happy birthday, and I'm one day late, but—" Greta said. She passed the wrapped box to Luc, who pawed it with two bandage-wrapped hands. They were both looking at Luc's hands, at Greta's arm, and it seemed that these injuries made them even more identical than the two girls on the couch nearby.

"I knew you'd show up," Luc said. "But you didn't have to—"

"It's a Walkman for CDs," Greta said, nodding at the gift.

"I guess I don't have to open it now."

"I'm not huge on surprises," Greta said. "They usually suck."

"This is Gina and Kit," Luc said.

"Girls," Greta said in her stern cop voice. They seemed wary of her and she was willing enough to let that feeling persist. The bald one stood up and muttered something about getting a drink from the vending machine. She grabbed her twin's hand and the two of them skittered away, chains clanking.

"I don't have any discs with me," Luc said.

"There's three in the box there with the Walkman," Greta explained. "I remembered some band posters from your room—I was in there, you know, after you went missing—so I only bought stuff that I knew you'd like. Probably you have these CDs already, but I figured you'd like some entertainment while you're holed up in this place."

"Thank you. You didn't need to—but it's good because they don't let me watch TV. All those reporters—I guess there's a lot about me on the news."

"They don't want you to start getting a big head from it all. On TV they're calling us a couple of women warriors, that kind of stuff. You don't want to hear that."

Luc flashed a gratified smirk that was gone by the time Greta took a seat where the twins had been. She set the child's toy back on the ground with the plastic trucks and limbless action figures that were scattered there.

"It was you, right—the one who found out where I was?" Luc asked.

"Only after you rescued yourself."

"But I was stranded up there. I would've died—and the baby."

Luc was assuming that Greta had already been briefed about what happened up at that cabin—and she had heard the reports, though only scraps of the story were coherent. There was ample time now to get the chronology straight.

"The twins told me what happened with you," Luc said. "They heard it on the news. Those awful people that you fought with—the ones—I saw them up at the cabin—and they were all monsters. Oh, my mom came to see me yesterday. I spit in her face."

Greta knew this was coded language just like the reporters outside had used with their questions. It meant Luc had somehow learned the truth up in those woods and now she was testing Greta to see what she'd uncovered. Neither one of them was going to say out loud that Blair Moberg was guilty of conspiring to murder her husband. To speak it aloud was to leave them with only one option.

"She came back this morning—and my grandmother, too," Luc said. "We sat for a while but we didn't talk. I guess yesterday they checked into a motel around the corner so they could be close by. They gave me the phone number to call if I want."

"Will you?" Greta said.

"I hoped you could tell me what to do."

"It's not my place, Luc. This is family stuff. I'm no good at family."

"But some stuff's bigger than family."

Greta leaned forward and took Luc by her arm. She said, "Look at me," and Luc did. Greta told her, "My business is this murder investigation. The man who shot your father is dead, the kid who arranged it is dead, and everyone else in that group is in the morgue, in jail, or far away from here by now. There's very little else to report and I'm finished with this thing, Luc, unless there's anything more that you want me to dig through. That's your call."

They were hunched together. Luc's expression was desperate, but Greta refused to answer it with anything more than the explanation she'd provided. Even though it pained her to leave the girl adrift like this, Greta wouldn't make a choice that belonged to Luc alone. During this silent interval the twins passed by in the hall outside, though they didn't come back into the sunroom.

Luc said, "She was devastated when I spit on her. In her eyes I saw— she had no idea why I did it. She's just this, this kid inside her head. She can't understand anything. I guess I'm saying—children are innocent, right? That's what I think."

"I think so, too," Greta admitted. "Like that baby you saved."

"Not me—" Luc amended, briefly distant, as if a chronic memory had called to her again. "But—have you seen him yourself? He's here at this hospital, just down the hall. Do you want to go see him?" Luc wheeled her chair toward the door. With that offer, they both shook off some of the dense aura that had settled over their talk.

Greta allowed Luc to take her to see the baby. It was a game they'd need to play—pretending they were not going to be forever shrouded by the trauma and the secrets they shared. Greta pushed Luc's chair down a hospital wing and through the swinging door that read, MATERNITY. She realized their whole acquaintance was based on tragedy, that they'd only been together a handful of times, yet they'd managed to bash out a rapport that was almost familial. Greta didn't understand it, but it felt real enough. Like gravity letting her loose, like some clock winding inside of her that she couldn't give a name to unless she dared to call it a soul.

AFTER

Martin drove the Dodge Neon along the Rochester downtown Inner Loop with Luc Moberg riding in the shotgun seat. They were low on gas because they'd forgotten to check it when they left Hammersport, so Luc had her fingers crossed that they wouldn't putter out—especially since the car really belonged to Gina, and Luc had only borrowed it without Gina's knowing. It was barely eight in the morning on a Wednesday, and Luc figured they'd have the car back before either Gina or Kit was even awake.

"This exit," Luc said. She had her fingers crossed for more than just the car.

"Sure, sure," Martin said, and he veered the car into the exit lane. He was wearing his corny European sunglasses with the mirrored lenses that reflected the road backward twice. It was late September of Luc's freshman year at SUNY Hammersport, and it was still humid summer weather that called for rolled-down windows and concert T-shirts, at least for Luc. Martin had on his Czech soccer jersey, and the flowing air did nothing to displace his hair that was gelled into stiff little spikes.

Luc hated driving, especially in cities, and even though she had a valid international driver's license she always pawned the job onto whomever was willing to chauffer, this time her boyfriend, Martin. He hadn't even been out to visit Rochester in the month he'd lived in the United States, but this traffic had to be a breeze for him after having learned how to drive around Prague and Warsaw and Budapest. He'd lived all over Eastern Europe with his Polish mother and his Ukrainian father, and now kids at college said his accent made him sound like Dracula. Martin objected: Transylvania was in Romania, and he'd never even been there.

As a kid, Martin had been sent to Prague to live with his grandparents after his mom and dad died together in a carbon monoxide incident. Luc knew only the sketchiest details of his history. After all, she'd only met him in late August, a month ago, and she'd been dating him now for just two weeks. They knew almost nothing about each other, and they both seemed fine with preserving the mysteries. For instance, all she'd told him about this trip was that she meant to visit an old friend she hadn't seen in almost three years.

The brief city skyline was above them now: aging stone buildings, glass skyscrapers, and road ramps curving over one another. Luc bit her nails until they stung and bled because she was anxious—a perpetual state that had dogged her for weeks now, ever since she'd flown back into the country after a two-year detour in Sweden. She'd come back to Hammersport as a foreign admit, which was a tough distinction to explain to professors and fellow students who learned she was actually born and raised right there in Hammersport.

"I'm from everywhere," Luc would explain. The same thing Martin said, one of the parallels that drew them together. Another—the fact that they were both orphans—was only half-true. Dorm and class acquaintances, even Martin himself, had been led to believe that both Luc's parents were dead, and there was no need to embellish. Some truth was unavoidable: many professors had known her father and what happened, and they treated Luc with too much delicacy because of it. Others had lived there long enough to remember, or had heard rumor, but so far most people had been merciful or afraid enough to leave Luc alone about it.

But this state of being was all new, barely a month underway. She'd not yet visited the English department in the former Brocton Hall, where her father had taught, though it'd been renamed Moberg Hall during a convocation ceremony the year after his death. At a backyard party once—the second Saturday of college, in fact—a soused hippie had asked her why she wasn't an English major, you know, because of her father. Luc was baffled that this strange kid knew her, knew of her father, and knew that Luc took criminal justice classes instead of re-tracing her dad's literature career. She'd felt that everyone there was covertly dissecting her, so she'd left the party after only half an hour and locked herself in her dorm for the rest of the weekend. Only her old friend Gina could coax her out of the room, and only after Luc reminded herself—after refusing food for a full day, after pouring hot candle wax on her bare legs, after pricking a sterile sewing needle into her fingertips—that she'd come back to Hammersport specifically to confront these black emotions and to live again in the shelter of her father's memory.

Gina and Kit were both juniors rooming together in an off-campus apartment, even though their mom still lived in their childhood home three blocks away. They were the only friends who knew that in truth Blair Moberg was alive and staying in a Binghamton assisted living facility just a few miles from her parents' house. They'd all lived together for a year after the incidents—Luc and Blair and the Crowleys—but Blair's condition was constantly volatile, sometimes lucid but increasingly withdrawn and infantile. After a spell when Blair lost control of her bowels for two unnerving days, they'd moved her to the facility permanently. Doctors were almost certain that she'd never regain her lost memory or her full mental faculties.

Nobody else knew Luc well enough to uncover these sordid bits of her former life. No one needed to know that Luc called her mother once or twice a week for fleeting conversations. Their talks had been traumatic at first, but time forced Luc to accept her mother's child mind—and these chitchats with a mental five-year-old concerning the nice nurses and the salty food no longer caused Luc too much distress. The notion that Blair had ever been an articulate adult, a mother, a wife, a murderer—it was almost wiped from Luc's mind. That woman was dead.

Luc believed that someday she might want to visit Blair in person, but she hadn't found the courage yet. Hadn't, in fact, seen her mother since the summer after Luc graduated high school in Binghamton. Soon after graduation Luc had been in contact with Oscar's relatives—aunts, uncles, cousins, siblings from his dead father's earlier marriage—and they'd invited her to Stockholm that summer, a visit that eventually lasted two years.

She'd chased ghosts and lost gods all over that magic country, and she sometimes caught glimpses of them: in the ancient underground cafés of Gamla Stan, on the university walkways of Upsalla, where once there stood a pagan temple dedicated to Odin (to whom human sacrifices had been hanged from the surrounding trees), along the wooded lakes and the maypoles in Dalarna, inside a Lapland hotel formed of pure ice that never melted under an endless arctic night.

There'd been a brief suicidal urge in the first year of her exile. Luc had been standing on the edge of an icy fjord where she'd come to release the last of her father's ashes—and the sea was crashing a hundred feet below her, and in those waves she'd sighted the serpent twining itself like a black river, waiting for her to join her father in the afterworld. She'd stepped back, she'd saved herself, and now she didn't expect that the urge to die would strike her again.

Coming back to Hammersport was just the next in a series of trials Luc had staged for herself, her own brand of therapy. Whether a doctor would approve she didn't know. The last time she'd seen a psychologist was in Binghamton two months after her sixteenth birthday. She'd stopped making appointments after the last mandatory session.

Now Martin drove past the Rochester War Memorial ice rink while Luc searched for metered parking, but all the spaces were taken. The Public Safety Building was just ahead. Luc had come here this morning on a whim, though she'd been contemplating this reunion since she'd moved back. It would be another test of her strength, like those mythic challenges that the Norse gods endured in the old poems. Luc didn't even know if Greta Hurd would be working this early on a Wednesday, or if she'd retired or moved to somewhere halfway across the country. She didn't know if Greta could help her find what she was looking for. Luc hoped, because hope was something she still managed to do on occasion.

By dumb luck they found a parking space directly across the street from the Public Safety Building. Luc kissed Martin on the cheek. In return he lifted her hand and kissed her on the knuckles. These were the best intimacies they could muster, and Luc doubted she could offer more. Soon he'd want more, probably, as the weeks and months progressed, and Luc guessed they'd break up within half a year. Eventually he'd ask her if she loved him or trusted him and Luc would have to tell him that she was locked away from trust, body and mind. People asked her sometimes, "Why don't I ever see you smile?" and Luc would tell them, "Because I'm never happy." Talking like this scared people off because nobody understood how she could live with this secret pain. For a while Luc herself had wondered, but the answer had struck her in Sweden, on the edge of the fjord—so plain, so unromantic. She lived because her heart was what she'd paid to save her life. Most of the time now it seemed a minor sacrifice.

"A half hour or less," Luc said.

"No problem," Martin said, and he turned up the music they were playing, one of the CDs that Greta had given Luc for her sixteenth birthday. Luc got out and stuffed two quarters in the meter, then she climbed the stone staircase leading toward the entrance. The bullet wound had caused a permanent limp that slowed her ascent a little, but once she reached level ground it was almost imperceptible in her stride. The kids at college asked her why she limped, and she told them pokerfaced that a woman had shot her in the thigh. They begged to hear more, but Luc never yielded. This kind of cryptic talk was a small, perverse pleasure that Luc indulged, a glint of happiness after all.

In the lobby she approached the cop attending the welcome desk and asked to speak with Investigator Greta Hurd. For a second he scowled at her like the name meant nothing, then he said, "What's your name?"

"Lucia Moberg."

"She expecting you?"

"No, she's not, but she knows me."

The cop nodded and got on the telephone. He shifted to the far edge of the welcome desk ten feet away so Luc couldn't hear what he said. When he was done talking he put down the phone, folded some papers, and told Luc indifferently that Greta would be down in a minute. Luc waited, standing on a giant mural of the Rochester Police insignia etched into the floor tiles. Her blood was flushing fast in her ears, because now she realized that this supposedly spontaneous visit meant more for her spirit than she'd wanted to admit. In fact it meant everything.

In less time than projected, Greta came through a set of double doors. She approached as if Luc were some apparition. Luc knew it was natural enough to be wary when a ghost came to call after several years of silence. If Greta looked at all changed since Luc last saw her, she looked younger. Rested eyes and the gray hair vanished—Clairol, Luc guessed, unless pigment could actually restore itself.

"Luc—my goodness," Greta said. They hugged and Greta stood back again to study Luc. She lifted a strand of her bright blond hair and said, "So this is the natural color, huh?"

"Yeah," Luc said, coy to this scrutiny. She'd long since abandoned the black dyes, the polishes, the fishnets, the jacket with a thousand safety pins. She was two years older than most of her fellow freshmen, Martin included, and decades older in her soul. Unlike them, she had no interest in making fashion statements anymore. Her hair was flat, shoulder-length. She wore jeans and tennis sneakers and faded rock band T-shirts most days, nothing more than lip gloss for makeup. Her only chic item was her glasses: the same old black rectangular frames that made her look hip as a coffeehouse loafer.

"It's good to see you," Greta said. "Do you have time? We can go upstairs to my desk. It's not too private, but it's better than the front lobby." Greta used a key card to open the double doors again, and then once more to work the elevator. They rode up to the fourth floor and headed to Greta's tiny cubicle in a room full of twenty other identical stalls. Greta's own personal touches consisted of a wall calendar from a Chinese restaurant, a plastic barrel full of Bavarian pretzels, and a framed studio photograph of Greta with a blond woman in a cable-knit sweater and a curly-haired toddler in a black tuxedo. Luc guessed the blonde was Greta's daughter and the toddler her grandson.

"How's your family?" Luc said.

Greta rolled a stray office chair over for Luc to sit in. She said, "Sandra and Max are doing great. They've got a son who just turned one. We had his birthday party last weekend."

While they both sat, Luc glanced again at the grandson in the studio photo with Greta and Sandra. He sported a head of curly brown hair and a full set of teeth, and he was strapping enough that he looked at least two years old.

Greta cleared her throat and said, "Your mom?"

"I don't see her much," Luc admitted. "She's in assisted living, which is fine with me. I mean—the way she is now is hard to deal with, but I'm probably the only daughter in the world who prays against her mother's full recovery."

"That makes perfect sense to me," Greta said while she hunted through a stack of papers on her desk. She'd nudged a tissue box so that it now hid the desktop picture of her family.

"Greta," Luc said. "I wanted to ask you for your help."

"Anything," Greta said.

"I need to find out what happened to the boy," Luc said.

Greta inhaled a tortured breath, as if she'd already known the question, and most likely she had. She said nothing while she scrutinized Luc, reading through skin and bone for false intentions. But Luc was sincere, almost desperate. She'd been coping with nightmares about that boy for over a year, imagining herself as his mother, screaming for him in a barren wasteland full of fog, and in those dreams she never found him. Luc had always mixed her own remedies for pain, and she knew now that finding the boy, just checking up on him, would be all she needed to keep her from considering that mortal leap once again.

Luc said, "I know it's all confidential, but I thought a police detective could—"

"You wouldn't want to upset anyone," Greta warned.

"I won't intrude. The foster family or the adoptive parents. I don't want to meet them or anything. I just want to know that he's doing all right. That's all. If I could just find out if he's doing okay."

"I knew you'd come looking sooner or later. I kept thinking later."

"I can't get my head straight without knowing."

"Under normal circumstances, I couldn't do a thing to help you."

"Normal circumstances?" Luc asked.

Greta coughed out an ironic laugh. "You and I never dealt with those, did we?"

"I'd understand if nothing could be done," Luc said. She'd had enough of fruitless evasive talk, even with this woman who'd saved her life. Everything in Luc's world had become so urgent that she doubted it would ever slow down.

"Look—all right," Greta said abruptly. "Come back downstairs with me, will you?"

Luc followed her without question into the hallway, and Greta ran her key card across a sensor to open the elevator door. They got in, turned back toward the doors sliding closed together. Greta pushed the button for the ground floor and they started to descend. As they were descending, Greta cleared her throat again and said, "Typically an infant in that situation would be given over to the deceased mother's next of kin, but in this case her mother had been dead for years and her father refused custody. He was terminally ill with cancer anyhow. Same situation when they tried to contact the father's relatives. Briefly, the father's older sister expressed interest in caring for the child, but she was a drug addict and unfit. So, long story short, he was adopted. His name is Oscar."

"Oscar? My dad's name?" Luc said. She felt unhinged, unsure whether it was the settling elevator or her own mental vertigo. She gripped the handrails that bordered the elevator car and she said, "You know where he is? Why didn't you tell me?"

Greta said, "You told me not to, remember? You said to make sure he's safe but don't let you know. Remember when you took me to see him in the hospital? You had such concern for his well-being and you begged me to do what I could to make sure he was taken good care of. But you also said you didn't want to know, and I listened. So that's why I didn't say."

"Hey, I can't keep my mind straight on anything."

"Are you sure you want to know now?"

"Absolutely," Luc said. The doors opened to the ground floor hallway. Luc thought they'd be heading back to the lobby, maybe over to the courthouse next-door to examine documents, but instead Greta pointed left and walked her deeper into the building, past the Vice Office and some empty conference rooms.

Luc said, "So you've been keeping track of him?"

"Yes, I have," Greta said. She gestured toward the wall, which had become a plate glass window running the length of the hallway. Through the window was a gymnasium with a padded floor that seemed to be a child care center loaded with toy bins and changing tables and plastic slides and children from infant age to preschool. When they reached the doorway into this space Greta ran her key card once more and said, "In here."

The door opened with an electronic bleep, and the noise made a dozen kids turn their attention away from a teenaged day care worker seated in the center of their uneven circle, reading to them from a picture book. One of the children broke away from the rest of the pack, a kid about four with a tangle of curled brown hair. He was wearing a Power Rangers T-shirt and matching untied sneakers. Greta crouched like a catcher at home plate, and the boy barreled into her with his arms wide, howling, "Mommy!" into her ear. Luc recognized the boy from the picture on Greta's desk, and now she understood that he wasn't Greta's one-year-old grandchild. He was her own adopted son.

"Oscar," Greta said, "I want you to meet somebody."

She turned the boy toward Lucia and held him in place with her hand spread open on his belly. He glanced at Luc bashfully, then tucked his chin down against his chest. Luc knelt down beside them both.

"This is my friend Lucia," Greta told Oscar. "You probably don't remember her, but she was actually the first person you ever met in your whole life. Your birthday is the same day, too. She brought you and me together."

Oscar forced himself to regard Luc once again, curious now about this strange girl he surely didn't remember. He said, "Hi," and extended one chubby hand to be shaken.

Luc shook the boy's hand and said, "Hi, Oscar. That's my father's name, too."

"Me, too," Oscar said. He indulged them for two more seconds before he lost interest and sprinted off toward the other kids huddled around the storyteller, a girl who was a probably a volunteer college student, an education major, pampered cheerleader type. She read to the children as if recounting a brilliant dream that she desperately wanted to be real. Oscar kneeled down with his friends and would've been instantly charmed by the storyteller's spell if she hadn't stopped and glanced down at him.

"Uh-oh, Oscar," she told him. "I just read the best part, and you missed it. What are we supposed to do now?"

"One more time?" Oscar pleaded, bouncing his butt off the heels of his shoes.

The girl leafed backward a few pages in the oversized picture book, and then she winked at Greta and Luc as if they were all part of some delightful conspiracy. Luc couldn't stop herself from smiling for once, especially when the storyteller began to read the best part all over again.